LOSING WENDY

THE LOST GIRL SERIES

BOOK ONE

T.A. LAWRENCE

For Wilson,
We shall see if this one is dark enough for you

CHAPTER 1

*S*ometimes the shadows whisper.

Sometimes I whisper back.

They writhe on the white oak windowsill, splaying like hand-prints clinging to the wood lest they slip and fall two stories onto the cobbled street below, slain by the dingy glow of the faerie dust street lamps.

"I could end your pain, Wendy Darling," they promise.

My hands tremble, causing the light radiating from my lantern to falter.

"I'm a happy person," I say, though the way my voice hikes in pitch is hardly convincing.

The shadows lick at the edge of the windowsill, crawling down the wooden slats before spreading outward across the ivory chaise upon which I'm perched.

"Of course you are," the shadows say, but they're only placating me.

The shadows slink like spilled ink, staining the plush chaise pillow. They linger at the hem of my silk nightgown. If they were to spread just a hair more, they'd seep into the baby blue fabric.

But the shadows don't have to close the gap for me to feel their

1

touch. A chill chases my dread, my skin tingling just underneath my skirts where the shadows come close to engulfing my knee.

"*I could end your pain,*" the shadows promise again, as they always do.

"I have no reason to be in pain," I insist. As I always do.

It's a tired game the shadows and I play.

So why do I never grow weary of it?

"*Of course you don't.*"

We perch together, the shadows and I, in silence for a moment.

"*You could come with me tonight, you know. It's foolish of you to put off the inevitable.*"

Blood thuds against my ears, my chest, the forefinger I have stretched out against the windowsill, chilled by the evening breeze that creeps in through the slat where I've left the window cracked.

"I don't want to come with you."

The shadows laugh, and it's somehow pleasant and terrifying—the way the sound reverberates through my bones. "*What pretty lies you speak.*"

I clench my fist, shuddering at the way my perfectly rounded fingernails scrape against the cracks in the wood. "Haven't you heard? I'm going to free myself of you."

The shadows tremble. I get a sneaking suspicion it's not at all similar to the tremble of dread that inhabits my bones, but rather the echoes of morose laughter.

"*If you don't wish to come with me, Wendy Darling, pray tell why you cast the glow from that lantern against the windowsill every night.*"

My throat constricts, but I keep my chin level. "If I'm going to be stalked by a monster, I'd rather keep my eyes on it."

The shadows swirl, spilling onto the floor, weaving warped paths around my feet and skirts, until I'm surrounded by glittering darkness. A dreadful flicker fans at the edges of my fingertips, prickling at the bottoms of my bare feet. The sensation reminds me of standing on the precipice of the clock tower that serves as the centerpiece of my parents' estate.

"*You're miserable here, you know.*"

Anger, hot and bubbling, roils through me. I jump to my feet, careful not to let my toes dip into the swarming shadows. They shift with my sudden movement, splaying out around me in a flurry of smoky tendrils.

Still so careful not to touch my bare skin.

"I'm miserable here because of you. Every second of my life that could have been joyful has been soiled by the knowledge it was all fleeting."

To my surprise, the shadows actually deflate, separating the two of us—flesh and darkness—with a wide berth. When the shadows speak, their usual silkiness is absent, replaced by cool indifference. *"If that's the case, you might as well let me have you."*

I stand my ground, even as the estate clock tower tolls midnight. "One more day. One more day before you can have me."

"Oh, Wendy Darling. Have you forgotten?" The shadows circumvent me in a playful dance, resuming their taunting demeanor. *"You're already mine."*

I fight not to close my eyes as the shadows deepen around me, their wisps concentrating into a black as thick as sludge. When I was a child, I made a habit of slamming my eyes shut when the shadows visited me.

Closing my eyes never did much to drown out the darkness. So now I watch, keeping a close eye on them at all times, tracing their approach lest they come for me.

They never do. They can't touch me. That part of the curse I learned the night I burst into my parents' bedroom screaming.

My mother meant well when she told me they weren't allowed to touch me. Yet.

As the midnight bells toll, "yet" is a dwindling wick, a dry twig readying to snap.

I watch the shadows take form at my feet, spreading across the rug in a pool of tar. As they pile atop themselves, they grow, until directly in front of me floats a whirl of darkness. Beads of black spread out behind the swirling form, the silhouette of wings slicing across my petal-patterned wallpaper.

When the wings beat, I shudder, a chill too direct to be slipping in through the cracked window caressing my face.

"*Come on, Wendy Darling,*" whisper the shadows, and for the first time, it's not a slippery taunt I hear. This time, the shadows offer a sincere invitation. "*What have you got to lose?*"

From the shadowy mass appears a tendril that soon snakes into the shape of a hand. Extending. Offering.

My chest heaves. And not for the first time, I reach out—not to touch—at least, I tell myself I won't. Just to revel in the space between its outstretched hand and my trembling fingertips.

Only a flicker of light from my lamp separates us now—flesh from shadow.

We're so close, it would only take a mildly violent tremor, and I will have initiated contact.

Just one more day.

There's nothing about the offer that should tempt me. I should be taking advantage of my last day in the light of this world. Should be plotting and scheming just like my parents to break my curse. Their bargain.

But part of me wonders if the curse has already been fulfilled. If I've been living it since the moment my mother pulled her sweat-soaked daughter into her lap and told me of the fate that awaited me upon my twentieth birthday.

A tutor once told me that humans receive more pleasure from anticipating an event than from the event itself. I can't help but wonder if anticipation and terror share this phenomenon. Perhaps I welcome the moment the shadows engulf me, taking me for their own, drowning me in darkness. At least then there will be nothing to fear.

One cannot fear what one knows, after all.

"*Come on. It won't be so bad,*" whisper the shadows. "*I promise.*"

I made a vow to myself years ago I wouldn't close my eyes, but tonight I make an exception.

And reach.

"Wendy?"

My eyes shoot open as light floods my bedroom.

When I turn to meet my brother's concerned gaze, the shadows have already retreated, leaving me to wallow in my last hours of freedom.

"You were talking to it again."

My brother's silhouette is framed in the doorway, backlit by the faerie lanterns that line the hallway of our parents' manor.

"Talking to what?" I ask, schooling an ever-practiced smile onto my face.

John frowns, letting his shoulders sag. He's only eleven months younger than me, so it's no surprise that the spindly frame I'm used to has filled out with lean muscle over the last few months. Still, the weight he's put on, coupled with the set of round spectacles he switched to last week, gives him the air of a man rather than a child.

It makes my heart ache a bit, and I can't place why.

"You don't have to do that, you know," he says, stepping into my room and closing the door gently behind him.

The light from the hallway extinguishes with the clicking of the door handle, but John's lantern glows more brightly than mine, the glass pristine enough to ward off the shadows.

For now, at least.

Sometimes I wonder if it's the light that truly keeps them away, or if the shadows simply allow me to believe as much as a courtesy.

"I don't have to do what?"

"Smile like everything is okay. Like your life isn't ending one way or another in"—he pulls out his glass pocket watch—"twenty-three hours and forty-eight minutes."

It must be habit now, because I actually have to coax the muscles at the edges of my lips down from my smile. Mother keeps a yogini on staff and is always urging me to join them in their morning ritu-als. I stopped going long ago, when I realized my body was never going to obey my commands to relax, and that the well-meaning woman would never understand why.

"If Mother and Father have it their way, my life as I know it will end a few hours before then. They don't want us cutting it that close."

John lets out a noncommittal noise before padding over to my bed. In the laziest motion I've ever seen, he unlatches his satchel, dumping a pile of dust-ridden books on my silver-etched sheets.

"I'm not entirely certain of the terms, but I don't know that the Prince of Never will permit me bringing along reading material," I say.

John raises a brow over his thin-rimmed golden spectacles. Mother makes him cut his bangs obscenely short. Perhaps she thinks this will prevent him from growing up. "You're not even considering the fact that you might succeed in breaking the curse."

I let out what's supposed to be a laugh, but it ends up sounding more like a sigh as I plop down on my soft mattress next to the pile of leather-bound books.

"If it were up to my will or your determination or Ma and Pa's optimism, I'd be certain of victory." I bite my lip, allowing my fingers to caress my neck, where just below my chin, a rivulet of my skin glows the faintest of gold, swirling in delicate lines up my jaw, framing my left eye at my cheek and forehead in freckles of shimmering light. "But we both know breaking the curse has been left in the hands of men. I imagine the Sister knew what she was doing when she left my fate up to them."

John grunts in dejected agreement, then drops a rather hefty volume onto my lap. "Well, the way I see it, we have twenty-three hours and forty-five minutes to figure out a way to make it up to us."

CHAPTER 2

When John and I were young, we sometimes stole down to the base of the manor's clock tower—our excursions scheduled around when our nanny snuck out to spend time with her suitor, of course. We'd pick the lock on the door with my hairpins, then make wagers on which of us could climb to the highest rung of the rusty ladder. As children do, we adored the danger—the thrill it offered in exchange for letting it hold our safety in its precarious fingertips.

Looking back, it's strange to think that John and I rebelled in such a way. Neither of our temperaments leans toward disobedience. But by the time we found the clock tower, we were already aware of my curse. Perhaps we felt as if the world had already betrayed us, and this was the last bit of recklessness the two of us could manage before reality swept in and stole it away.

When our youngest brother, Michael, came along and showed a preference for running and climbing, we brought him into our game. At random times in the day, one of us would shout, "Last one to the top is dead meat," which would send us into a frenzied dash for the clock tower, the three of us shoving and clawing at each other the entire way.

Once upon a time, that clock tower was my haven. Now it clangs with a reminder of what's to come, screaming at me with every hour that slips from my fingertips, along with the pocket watch Father gifted me on my nineteenth birthday.

I'm fairly certain he gave it to me intending for it to hasten my search for a husband. An ever-present, ever-ticking reminder that my time in the light is running out. I'm also fairly certain he realized how inconsiderate of a gift it had been because he gifted John a matching one on his birthday.

I'm making my father sound worse than he is.

It's ironic really. My father is rather progressive. The last man one would expect to make his entire life's mission to catch his daughter a husband, but the Fates had other schemes.

My father doesn't really have a choice.

In the end, John and I find nothing substantial to help free me of my fate that's to take place in, say, eighteen hours now.

"Don't worry," he says. "I have something else I'm working on."

There's little confidence in his voice to inspire any in me.

John leaves my room at first light, rubbing at his eyes and sending his glasses askew. It makes him look boyish again, and I sketch a portrait in my mind, silently promising never to forget my brother's innocent sort of determination.

It's a good thing he leaves when he does, because my mother comes barreling into my room not a minute later, almost tripping over my rug as she does.

My mother isn't the barreling and tripping sort, but today isn't exactly a normal day, either.

"Wendy." She says my name with such feigned optimism, it snaps my ribs one at a time.

Mary Darling is a woman built of poise, the by-product of countless generations of aristocratic mothers passing along their grace and tact until it all became concentrated in my mother. My smile—the one I don so that others won't have to feel the rattle of my lungs as I drown in the twilight tide of my future—I got from her.

She beams down at me with such love and adoration, it almost hides the way her stomach must be twisting on the inside. Almost. She's a professional at hiding agony, my mother. She has the look perfected, even down to the wrinkles at the edges of her eyes upholding her smile.

But if you look closely, you can see the way her jaw bulges ever so slightly. Like she's keeping that smile not buoyed but bolstered, feet planted in the sand as she holds her breath and hoists the edges of her barely wrinkled lips above the crashing waves.

"Mother," I respond with equal affection.

"I suppose we should be getting you ready."

She makes it sound as if it's not a death sentence.

If my Mark weren't raised, simple ivory paint would probably do to cover it up completely. The golden tint has a tendency to shimmer in the light, but the color itself is faint enough to be easily obscured.

At least, it is with two coats.

My maids twist my chestnut hair into a plait at the crown of my head. I prefer to wear my hair down, but Mother says if my pretty features are going to be buried underneath a mask, we'd better let the men see as much of my face as possible.

I'm just thankful the gown she's chosen for me better covers my bosom this time. As desperate as my mother is to marry me off and break this dreadful curse, I suspect the modest gown is meant to be an apology of sorts for a betrayal neither of us dare speak aloud.

When the maids finish preparing me for a night full of charming men twice my age, they step aside, clearing the path for my mother to look at me.

For me to look at her.

In so many ways, I'm her mirror image. In her eyes, I find the same deep blue that dwells in mine. She keeps her chestnut hair pinned back, but if she ever let it down from its ornate combs, it would fall in the same cascading waves as mine. Her pinkish face has a heart shape to it, one that makes her full cheeks stand out.

My mother is lovely, but she's aging faster than she should.

I suppose that's mostly to do with me.

"You look stunning, Wendy," she says, her words a muffled whisper as she covers her mouth, probably to give her lips a break from her feigned smile. "It's amazing, the young woman you've—"

The facade of my mother's impenetrable face fissures—a cracking line that snakes up her slender neck, tensing the muscles in her throat as she fights back a sob. And just like that, she's weeping, her hands still dutifully clamped to her mouth like she owes me the memory of a smile, rather than whatever warped and twisted thing her mouth is currently doing.

"Mama." I take my weeping mother into my arms, settling her tear-soaked face into my chest as she cries. Rivulets of salty tears trail down my silk dressing gown. The maids were foresighted enough to know better than to fully dress me yet.

Indeed, I peer over my mother's pearl-crested comb as my maids slip into the corner of the room, making themselves unobtrusive.

"It's all my fault," my mother—my strong, sanguine mother—wails into my chest. She clutches the fabric at my back, the silk protecting my skin from her fingernails digging in. It's as if she's convinced herself that if she only clings tightly enough, she might get to keep me. "It's all my fault. I should have never spoken to that wretched creature. Should have known the evil I was inviting into this house."

"You didn't know," I say, wrapping my hand at the back of my mother's neck, allowing my thumb to scrape the chain of the three-pronged pendant she wears for me, John, and Michael. "You thought —" I stop myself, correcting myself mid-sentence. "You did save me. I would have died from the plague if it wasn't for the bargain you and Papa struck."

"I condemned you, my sweet little girl."

My heart aches, and when I shake my head in disagreement, my mother's tears wipe against my cheek. "You bought me time. And time—isn't that the most valuable thing we have?"

My mother pulls away from me, and now that her hands are

removed from her face, occupied with holding me like she intends to force the shadows to wrench me from her arms themselves, her smile has returned.

It's not the happy sort, but it's there. Clinging for purchase on my mother's jaw.

"I'm so sorry, Wendy."

I open my mouth to protest, but Ma shushes me.

"No. Sweetheart. I thought I was bargaining for your life. But all I gifted you were years of dread. Years of anticipating your nightmares being fulfilled. I fear—" She sweeps her gaze over me, taking me in, and she curls her finger above her quivering lip. "I fear I've sold you from one miserable Fate to another, always bargaining for more time, never considering it would be you who paid the higher price."

I stare at my mother, unable to blink back nonexistent tears.

It's not that I don't hurt, don't ache. It's not that her words don't reflect a wound I've refused to speak aloud my entire life.

It's that as long as she's here, weeping over me, I cannot bring myself to feel it. When she's gone, leaving me alone with my thoughts—that's when I'll absorb her words. That's when the truth of them will sting. If I know myself at all, I'll probably find myself bitter toward her for voicing those words on my behalf, for finding them before I could. For daring to hurt alongside me when this is my pain, my torment.

But for now, it's as if my mother's grief takes up the whole room, overshadowing mine, drowning me in the numbness of analyzing my own pain like it's a modern painting hanging in an exhibit. If I were to reach out, I wouldn't feel the colors, just the texture of the swirls and divots.

Her words fold over my ears in waves of crimped parchment. One miserable fate to another.

It's not fair for me to blame my mother for my curse. As much as she indicts herself, if it weren't for her, oblivion would have claimed me long ago.

I was five years of age when the plague swept through the

coastal city of Jolpa, where we live. No one knows for sure where the plague came from. Most think it crept in under the cover of the salty mist that so often obscures the harbors, leaching into the lungs of the hardened sailors, who then carried it over the soaked piers. Onto the cobblestone streets. Passed it onto the lips of their wives with the press of a homecoming kiss.

Others say it crawled up from the sewers on the backs of rats who made their nests in the rafters of the fisheries, chewed holes in the gill nets, and poisoned the fish with their grimy teeth. Still others, those skeptical of magic, say it came from the faerie dust imported from the West, poisoning our lungs as we burned it to light our street lamps.

Regardless of its origins, Mama and I both fell ill. Papa sent John away to the summer home in Kelton with a nurse, lest he catch the illness too.

Mama recovered with time.

I did not.

From the way my mother tells the story, I was so close to Death, I told her I felt him planting a kiss on my forehead, though there was no one else in the room with us.

I was so far gone, the physicians recommended I be given an opiate that would alleviate the pain of the cysts forming in my lungs.

My mother was distraught. Torn between yearning for her child to be free of agony and knowing the opium would certainly kill me.

But that night, as she held the vial of opium in her hand, a voice whispered to her from the shadows.

"I could save her," it said. *"I could take away her pain."*

My mother had been warned by her mother and all mothers before her not to speak to the shadows, especially not those who lurked close to children or the stench of death. But my mother was addled with grief and forgot the warnings, just as all mothers before her would have done had their child's chest been rattling with the Reaper's bell toll.

"Anything," she'd said.

"*Anything?*" the shadows had whispered back. "*I doubt that very much. A tender lady like you—I doubt you've ever allowed your skin to be kissed by the sun, your feet to develop calluses from frolicking bare in the earth. Anything seems quite far-fetched.*"

"Please," my mother had begged. "Anything to save her."

And anything it had been. The way Mama tells it, the shadows had pounced from the wall like a cat, then melded into the shape of a woman.

The woman had bent over me, pinching her hands against my nose, covering my mouth until shadows filled my lungs, causing my chest to rise, my eyes to cloud over with darkness.

And then I had taken a breath.

But not before Mama had made a bargain.

One she'd thought would be simple to keep.

"My Prince of Never, my Shadow Keeper, needs companion-ship," the shadowed woman had said. "I fear what he might become if allowed to continue on as he is. If I heal her, you may keep her until her twentieth birthday. But from the moment this child begins her third decade, she will belong to him."

My mother had hesitated then, knowing well the atrocities of which mortal men were capable. Who knew what an immortal such as the Shadow Keeper might do to her daughter once she was of age? She had heard of the Prince of Never, the shattered remnant of an ancient fae who kidnapped children from their beds at night, stealing them away with promises of adventure. It was a modern folktale, meant to keep children from sneaking out of their beds and bothering their parents in the middle of the night, but as with all folktales, it was seeded in truth.

"What if she were to marry before then?" my mother had asked. "Surely you wouldn't take a woman away from her husband."

The shadow woman had laughed, amused that my mother assumed she would care about such frivolous human concerns as matrimony. My mother had known it was unlikely to succeed, knew she was grasping at the wind, but to her surprise, the shadow woman had conceded.

"Very well, then. Find the girl a husband before the turn of her third decade, and the vow tying her to my Shadow Keeper will become void."

My mother hadn't hesitated before grasping at the shadow's hand and forming the bargain, the stains of which stretch the length of her forearm to this day.

I had been healed, and the sun seemed to shine down on me for a while. John was brought back to the manor. My parents were aristocrats, so though my mother fretted over finding me a husband, she acknowledged there was no genuine need for concern.

Who wouldn't want their daughter for a wife?

When I reached maturity at twelve, the Mark appeared, a smattering of golden freckles like glistening dewdrops collecting on my upper left cheekbone, falling at its cusp and tracing my jawbone, where they slowly trailed away at the curve of my neck in a smudge of liquid gold.

That's when my parents knew they'd been tricked, for what man would marry a girl Mated to another man? Sure, it was common knowledge that the chances of a Mated individual ever crossing paths with their match were slim, but jealousy is not a rational advisor.

"We'll beat the curse tonight, Mama," I say, regardless of whether I believe the words. "You, Papa, me, John—we've all thought this through. Planned for every possible outcome."

My mother actually raises her delicately trimmed fingers to her mouth and begins biting on them. "Of course. Of course we will."

Of course you do.

The memory of the shadow's voice is so clear, it's almost palpable.

And as the maids place the finishing touch upon my bridal attire —a pearl mask designed to obscure the golden freckles snaking over my cheek—I wonder if, from the shadows, I truly can hear a rumbling laugh.

CHAPTER 3

This is not my first ball. Such is the life of a girl who's attempting to avoid the shackles of a curse through the bonds of matrimony—balls with their bloated guest lists tend to be efficient. But it is my first masquerade.

"Well. The Darling line has officially given up on any sense of propriety and honor," John says, adjusting his tight collar next to me like it's irritating him. His metallic half-mask hardly covers the upper half of his face, but it's not *his* mask he's referring to.

His russet eyes linger on my pearl mask in disapproval as we wait on the dark side of the door to my parents' buzzing ballroom.

"I thought you wanted this to work," I say. "And look at you— scolding me for making my best attempt."

I nudge John on the shoulder lightly, but he's too tense tonight to notice.

After a moment of silence, I escalate to poking him. "I truly am sorry, John. I know when news of our deception gets out, I'll either be married or..." I pause when he gives me an irritated glance. "Well, either way, it will be your name and your prospects that will suffer."

"You think I care anything about my name?" he asks, incredulous. "Wendy, have you ever considered what a pompous aristocrat —a possessive aristocrat—might do to you once he finds out what that mask is hiding?"

A shiver curls around my forearms, but I straighten my spine and shrug my shoulders. "That's tomorrow's problem."

John glances at the grandfather clock on the wall. Even in the faint lantern light, I catch his pallor tinge green. He opens his mouth to say something else, but it's no use. My father's voice rumbles from the inside of the ballroom, no doubt introducing me to a room full of unsuspecting suitors. In a moment's notice, the doors fling open, and I step into my fate.

At least, what I hope will be my fate.

As if they can hear me, the shadows chuckle.

My appearance must work as Mother intended, because the crowd of eligible bachelors goes quiet as I step onto the raised platform at the forefront of the room. I'm dressed from head to toe in gleaming ivory, the color of coastal trade coins and the full moon, long said to bestow good fortune.

More importantly, it's also the color of wedding garb.

Mama thought dressing me in a wedding gown would prepare the suitors' minds for the idea of marriage. When I had countered that my generous dowry would doubtless prepare their minds for marriage more than any color ever could, my mother had sighed knowingly.

Still, it appears she was correct.

Except for the few brutes who holler and whistle as John escorts me onto the platform, the crowd of men goes silent. Some of their mouths hang ajar.

I shuffle, trying and failing to wriggle my toes in my stiff heels.

I would have thought I'd recognize the ballroom that has hosted so many events like this one, but as this is our last hope for my freedom, my parents have gone all out. Faerie dust not only lights the tips of the crystal chandeliers hanging from the ceiling, but someone has taken its liquid form to the indigo velvet wallpaper. It's as if someone handed my youngest brother, Michael, a paintbrush and a jar of faerie dust paint, and encouraged him to flick it across the walls, the pillars, the silk tablecloths.

Everything glistens, even the guests, in the gentle glow of the faerie dust.

I can't imagine what my parents must have spent to fetch paint dabbled with faerie dust. The city of Jolpa paid a steep price to use the rare substance in the streets' lamps, but deemed it worth the tariff given faerie light is a sustainable source of light, one that doesn't have to be replenished like gas or oil.

But to have it mixed with paint...I'm starting to wonder between the decorations and my dowry what my parents will have left. What my brothers will have left.

My father's voice interrupts my thoughts. "May I introduce to you Wendy Darling, heiress of the firstborn's portion, the next lady of Darling Manor, my lovely and precious daughter." My father's voice breaks on that last bit, and I have to swallow the lump that forms in my throat. He never wanted it to come to this either. He wanted a nice flock of lords' sons to court me when I was sixteen, for me to fall in love over the span of several years, then marry the man my heart truly desired.

My Mark ruined that dream of his before I was old enough to let it become mine.

Unable to meet the hungry gazes of the roomful of suitors, I search the ballroom for Michael. The flanks of the room are where I check first. Since the wallpaper is velvet, John and I used to drive the staff mad, writing messages to one another in the soft hairs of the fabric. Of course, Michael continues to drive them mad, being only seven years of age and a free spirit even beyond what is typical for those his age. Though he prefers to trace out the alphabet rather than messages.

I find him at the edge of the stage, standing on his tiptoes as he's apt to do, tying a complex knot in a shoestring he carries with him everywhere, blissfully unconcerned with the large crowd gathered in the ballroom. He's wearing a suit like John's, except Ma had the tailor design his without a collar.

I'll have to see if I can get him to draw me any pictures on the velvet walls before I leave.

I stop that train of thought, not wanting to consider which way I'll be leaving this manor—in the carriage of a stranger intent on taking me to his bed this very night, or in a whirl of shadows intent on stealing my very soul.

When John elbows me in the side, I curtsy toward the crowd of men, and a few of them whistle and holler. My grip tightens around John's arm for support. I try not to look at him, lest I have to witness him gritting his teeth in rage.

The ballroom itself is dimly lit tonight, other than the gentle glow of the faerie dust. The theme is "An Eve in the Stars," but that's mostly a back-up plan in case my mask were to slip. At least if it's dark in here, there's less chance anyone will spy the scar-like tissue of my Mark.

"As you all are well aware, given your invitations, tonight my daughter, Wendy, will choose from among you a husband of her liking. Win the affections of my firstborn, and you'll find yourself wed to the heiress of Darling Manor, as well as a man whose pockets bulge considerably with the weight of the finest dowry in all of Estelle."

The whistles and hollers are slightly less pronounced this time. I can't decide how I feel about the men deeming the money the less exciting of the two prizes.

"Idiots," John grinds out through clamped teeth.

"At least I'll know which ones to avoid," I whisper placatingly under my breath. I say it in jest, but I've already marked an oily-looking male wearing heeled boots to make him appear taller in the corner.

My father dismisses me to make my rounds about the room, and John escorts me down the platform's stairs.

My heels click against the floor, the sound cueing my racing heart in on the fact that everyone's attention is directed at me.

Although, this whole ball being about marrying me off probably should have done that already.

Thankfully, the string quartet launches the event off with a festive tune that soon masks the clacking of my lone set of heels.

There were other women invited, of course. It wouldn't do to have all the men in the room waiting around awkwardly as I danced with each partner.

At least, I'd convinced my parents it wouldn't do.

I think if it were up to them, they would have made sure the men were forced to stare at me all night long. Until the clock strikes twelve.

As the music fills the hall, several men pair off to dance with the select women Mother invited. They're all a bit homely-looking, and something pricks at my heart—how obvious it is that my gentle mother chose them for that particular quality.

I suppose I can't fault her for what she does to protect me, though.

Servants pass out faerie wine, the tangy scent filling me with longing. Father pulled me aside earlier to apologize for the presence of faerie wine at the ball. Said he'd commanded the servants not to offer me any, even if I asked.

That's likely for the best.

I follow John through the swarm of men, all of whom are strangers to the kingdom of Estelle. That's rather intentional. Over the years, the Darlings have approached just about every available bachelor in the kingdom, and even if there were any left, they'd have at least heard of the Marked Girl by now.

The Lost Girl. That's how the papers refer to me. They have no idea about my true curse, the one that promises me to the Shadow Keeper. But the fact that I'm Marked is enough to make me lost in their eyes.

The last few months have been spent inking invitations. My parents, John, and I each took a stack. We soon cast them upon the waters, cajoling any aristocrat we could track down from the continent, hoping the Shifting Sea would provide enough of a barrier between the gossip surrounding me and their ears.

We shall see if our hopes prove effective.

So far, the men seem intrigued by me, if not leering.

My stomach whirls, and I clench my fingernails into my palm through my silk gloves to remind myself I need this.

I want this.

"There's another one on the left. Leaning against the doorframe like he owns the place. I'd steer clear of that one too," says John, still irritated, though mocking the suitors has returned the levity to his voice.

Eager to continue his game, this proffered respite from my imagination carrying me into scenes of how my next few hours will unfold, I search for the man John is referring to.

When I find him, the marble floor shifts underneath my feet.

He's the type of beautiful that cuts, every detail sharp. The intense greenish glow of his eyes, rimmed with jet black lashes. His ink black hair, cut short to frame his forehead in jagged but somehow neat lines. The set of his jaw, even down to the slight stubble rimming it. The crisp line where his forearm bulges over the tanned arm folded beneath it. Everything about this man screams that touching him could draw blood.

And why has my mind wandered to what it would be like to touch him?

I let out a breathy chuckle, meaning to affirm John's commentary on this stranger, but I'm silenced when the man unfolds his arms and tugs at the golden buttons of his sleeves.

Perhaps it's the panic of my limited choices: find a husband tonight or be condemned to the shadows. Perhaps it's the silly girl who, despite her mother's warnings, spent her adolescence dreaming of the man to whom her Mark belonged. But for whatever reason, my gaze snaps to his hand. The way his crimson coat sleeves go taut as he adjusts them.

There's a faint trace of gold etched around his wrist, up his hand.

A gold that matches mine.

CHAPTER 4

"*E*xcuse me." I slip out of John's arms and toward the stranger.

Faintly, like my ears are clogged with water, I hear him calling out after me, but I hardly pay him attention.

My heart is racing. In panic or wild, desperate exhilaration, I can't be sure, but it's off-beat with the clicking of my heels against the marble floor.

It's then that it hits me what exactly I'm doing.

I'm not one who by nature or temperament would typically be comfortable approaching a man like...well, like him. John was supposed to be my buffer. Was supposed to introduce me to the suitors, steer me away from awkward silences, ensure my evening avoided wastes of time I can no longer afford.

But I've never seen another Mark before. Well, besides the ones in the dreams I learned to stifle years ago.

Still. I've always held out hope. Just a glimmer. Just a morsel. That one day, he'd come for me. But now, several paces away, I'm second-guessing myself.

He's leaning against the cedar frame of the balcony doors, so that at least provides me with a bit of privacy as I sneak behind a pillar and toward him.

With the subtlety of a predator marking its next meal, the man tilts his head. His sleek black mask only emphasizes his daunting presence. Metallic ears, fashioned to razor-sharp points, jut from the side of the mask, a nod to the legendary fae that once ruled our realm before the curse that dwindled their numbers. Curiosity flares in those ivy green eyes of his as he detects me approaching him.

Oh no. He's seen me now. Meaning there's no turning back. No throwing myself behind the nearest pillar to get away from his assessing gaze.

The stranger lifts a haughty black brow over the curve of his mask.

"Hello," I say, because that's the only word of the millions in the Estellian language to come to my head at the moment.

"Hello," the man drawls, flicking his gaze down my body and back up again, though there's nothing really to examine given the modesty of my silk wedding garb.

My face flushes as I realize how forward this must seem. I'm not typically this nervous around men. The same way a market vendor isn't shy around her customers, I assume. All my life, I've been in the business of selling myself. Practice has made me competent, if not comfortable, with engaging potential suitors in conversation, even if I have to shed my natural reticence to do so.

I'm unsure whether it's this man's Mark or his demeanor that's tying my tongue like a knot on Michael's shoestring.

I can't think of what to say, so I blurt the first thing that pops into my mind. "Would you like to dance?"

The man says nothing, just stares at me in that brutally assessing way, so I add hastily, "With me, I mean."

"I assumed as much," he says, and not kindly. There's a jeering in his tone, one that catches me off guard. Perhaps in his home kingdom, it's offensive for a woman to ask a man to dance.

"I'm so sorry, I didn't mean—"

"What are you apologizing for?"

I'd say my words are getting hung in my throat, but that would require me having an answer to begin with. Finally, I gather my swarming thoughts. "I didn't—I didn't know if perhaps I had offended you by being the first to ask you to dance."

As to whether I offended him, he doesn't say, but he shifts on his feet, sounding utterly weary as he says, "Why would I be interested in dancing with a spoiled heiress who looks as if she's hardly been weaned?"

Heat flares at my neck, shock stunning my lips for a moment. I blink. Now that I'm close enough to get a better look at him, the difference in our ages is rather evident. Though I can't spot the telling folds at the corners of his eyes due to his mask, he has that rugged appearance that sometimes inhabits men as their faces shift with age. Leaner at the cheeks, firmer at the jaw. He must be at least fifteen years my senior, if not more. "I thought—" My eyes betray me, searching for a glimpse of the Mating Mark I'd thought I'd spied on his hand. Surely it hadn't simply been a trick of the light.

It's the briefest of glances, but the stranger must catch it, because understanding dawns on his face. He tilts his chin up ever so slightly, crossing his arms at his chest and gesturing to his hand, his Mark shimmering in the low light. "Ah. Let me guess. You have one of these too, don't you? I suppose it's not a piggish disposition your parents are trying to hide underneath that mask, after all."

My jaw drops.

A cruel grin plays on his lips. "Come now, Wendy Darling. You can't blame a man for wondering."

Tears sting at my eyes, each of his condescending words plucking at the corset strings I used to tie myself together tonight.

"Forgive me," I seethe, "for assuming predisposed interest in a man attending a ball—the very function of which is to name the inheritor of my dowry."

The stranger lets out a wry laugh, pushing himself from the wall in a fluid, graceful sweep. "I assure you, there are reasons for attending these functions that far exceed procuring a child bride."

A child bride.

Images of a little girl, dancing barefoot with the shadows, careful not to let her skin touch, assault my mind.

"Now, if you'll excuse me," the stranger says, shoving past me on his way toward the center of the ballroom. "I'll be looking for someone with slightly more wit to engage my attention."

CHAPTER 5

I scamper off, intent on fleeing the crowd before anyone notices the tears creeping out from underneath my mask, smearing my paint. Unfortunately, the stranger had been occupying the only remote alcove in the ballroom, and though he's escaped into the crowd I can't quite bring myself to turn around.

The shining double doors of the hall stretch out on the other side of the ballroom, but there is a battalion of coin-mongering aristocrats between me and there.

In my moment of hesitation, a hand clamps on my shoulder, forcing me to spin around.

"Might you grace me with a dance, my lady?" If the boorish stranger considered me an infant, this man surely should. Tufts of wiry gray hair form a wreath around the shine of his pale bald head, a monocle magnifying one of his watery blue eyes to twice its size. His voice is just as damp as his eyes, as if whatever he last ate is still dawdling in his throat.

Normally, I would not despise a man for the unfortunate ailments common to advanced age, but given the way his gaze focuses in on my bosom like a robin to a wriggling worm, I seem to have lost my knack for sympathy.

"I—" I don't get the opportunity to object before the aristocrat slips his large wrinkled hand over my waist and pulls me into him, his dank breath wetting my hairline just below where his quivering lips linger.

"Such a little prize, aren't you?" he says, wetting his pale lips with his tongue.

My stomach turns over, my tears forgotten as panic kindles inside my chest.

"My lord, I'm afraid we've yet to make introductions," I say, fighting to keep my voice from shaking underneath the weight of his firm hand at my waist. My vision threatens to tunnel, to sweep me away to the parlor and the feel of velvet and the smell of incense and the touch of... But no. I slam those memories away and scramble for a polite but efficient way out of this situation, but my mind is still reeling from my mortifying encounter with the handsome stranger.

I like to think myself intelligent, despite what that horrid man might think about me, but my wit is the quiet sort. The kind that flourishes in solitude, in the shy pockets of the day. It spews from my pen rather than my mouth, and I often find my tongue clumsy where my script might have been elegant.

My mind slows in a crowd, and the effect worsens with stress.

"Lord Credence." He says his name as though I should recognize it. When I don't, he frowns. "You wrote to me by your own hand, Miss Darling."

"Oh."

"I must say, you're much more eloquent in ink than you are with that tongue of yours."

The words sting, though I shouldn't let them. Fire spouts within me, and I long for a clever retort. I'm confident one will come to me as soon as I deliver myself from this man's clutches.

"But no matter," he continues. "In Estelle, the men might be weak-minded enough to allow their daughters to choose their husbands, but we know better in Kruschi. When I make you my bride, that your lips are heavy will be of little importance."

"And why…" I say, slowly, to emphasize my point, "do you assume I would pick you to be my husband, Lord Credence?"

"Because, my dear," he says, pulling my body closer to his as he leans in, his damp lips grazing my forehead and issuing a cringe through my bones as he does, "I'm the only one in this room who would dare take a claimed bride."

My limbs freeze underneath the weight of his words, and he practically has to drag me through the next few steps of the dance.

"I'm not sure what you mean," I say.

"Now, Miss Darling. Don't pretend me dull. It wouldn't be fair. I've not determined as much of you, despite your sluggishness in expressing yourself. Your family might play this masquerade off as fun and games, a show of extravagance and a display of extreme wealth, but no Estellian puts his daughter's body into the wandering hands of strange men without reason."

The foul man takes his thumb and begins pressing circles into my belly.

Disgust flares within me, but Lord Credence isn't finished with his accusations. "We're all thinking it, Miss Darling. Your father can flash your substantial dowry all he wants, but what good is all that money if it will go to an illegitimate son, bartered off upon an unsuspecting husband? Was that the plan, miss? To declare what a lucky and fertile woman you were for becoming with child so swiftly after the wedding night? Passing off your babe for one of noble birth?"

"Lord Credence, I assure you, no such thing has occurred."

The foul man laughs. "Then explain to me the importance of your being married off with such urgency."

The freckles of my Mark sting underneath my mask.

It's not so far from the truth—the story this lord has concocted in his mind. No male has ever wanted me after realizing I'm Marked to another man, one I likely will never meet. As rare as it is for a Mark to appear, it's even rarer to find one's match.

Unfortunately, the rarity of it does nothing to assuage the paranoia and possessiveness of the male mind. Sure, perhaps the men invited to this masquerade have no inkling of my Mating Mark, but Lord Credence can't be the only male here suspicious of my family's motivations in marrying me off so quickly.

If the noblemen attending this ball think I'm with child, there's little chance of them desiring me, no matter how large a dowry my father attaches to me.

Shadows swirl in my vision, but I'm fairly sure they're conjurings of my own morbid imagination.

You're mine, they whisper.

Because I always have been.

"If you're not to be dissuaded, my lord, then why not leave me abandoned on the dance floor?"

Lord Credence chuckles, his breath foul as he flashes me a straight set of teeth which I imagine did not originally belong to him. "Because, Miss Darling, I shall tell you a secret. Though it's about as much a secret in my homelands as your dalliances are to the men in this ballroom. I've outlasted five wives, none of which ever succeeded in bearing me an heir. Not even an heiress. Now, though, I'll claim 'til the day they rest my body in the grave that it was my wives' assets that were to blame, I'm no fool. I'm aware it's likely I who am unable to produce offspring. While your condition might prove a hindrance in the lives of other men, it would solve a great tragedy in mine."

"You wouldn't care that the heir would not belong to you?" I ask, so caught off guard by this man's way of thinking that I find myself momentarily apprehended in this preposterous lie.

"I have suffered shame long enough. No one would know the child was not mine. At least, no one could prove as much, even if they suspected. I told no one of the urgency of this ball when I left, and Kruschi is too remote for news to travel back."

Indeed. That is the very reason we sent an invitation to Lord Credence to begin with.

"You're offering a sham of a marriage, so that I might bear an heir in your name?" I ask, biting the inside of my cheek. The idea of being wed to this man makes me long to squirm out of his arms, but if he has no intention of coming near me...

"Oh, sham is not the word I would use," he says, his trembling voice going gravelly. "A man is not without his needs, after all. Though several of my senses have been dulled with time, I am sure a beauty such as yourself..." He traces my hipbone with his fingertips, allowing his hand to slip down and cup my backside. I flinch, which only provokes him more. "I assure you, Miss Darling, you will fill my last few years of life with pleasure. Though I'm confident you'll be grateful to fulfill my needs, considering what I'm offering you."

My limbs seem to have frozen underneath his hungry, weathered touch. I long for nothing more than to free myself of his vulgar advances, but no matter how vehemently my mind screams at me to shove him away, my limbs don't appear to be listening.

I remember my biology tutor telling me that prey often utilize one of two effective responses to being stalked. Fight or flee.

Then there are the unfortunate fools whose bodies are not meant for survival.

I can't breathe, can't move. Even Lord Credence has stopped dancing. I should cry out against him for his impropriety, but it's as if I'm in a dream in which I'm trying to flee my pursuer, but I'm trapped within my own worthless body, unable to command my limbs.

"What do you say, Miss Darling? Grant an old man a little enjoyment in his last few years to live? Secure a fortune for yourself and your child?"

Ink creeps into the corners of my vision.

It occurs to me that this awful man might be my only hope to escape the shadows.

But could the shadows be worse than this?

"Forgive me," says a voice that strikes me out of my stupor like a match to sandpaper. "But given the fact that Miss Darling must be married off by the midpoint of the night, it only seems efficient that a single suitor not hog her ever-dwindling time."

Lord Credence's hands immediately find a more appropriate

place to sit on my waist, and though his grip on me still churns my stomach, relief sinks into my chest.

"Of course, Sir...erm..." Lord Credence scans the foul stranger with the Mating Mark painting his hand.

"Captain, actually. Captain Nolan Astor," he says, but not to Credence. To me. His glowing green eyes set upon me with a fierceness that might have my cheeks flushing, if they weren't already drained from my encounter with Credence.

"Dance with me," says the captain, though his voice remains steady, balancing between a question and a command.

"Of course," I say, only to get myself out of the hands of Credence.

Credence delays in relaxing his grip, at which point Captain Astor says, "In my homeland, three do not dance at a time."

The elderly lord grumbles something under his breath. For all his confidence earlier, he's clearly bewildered by the captain, who towers over him by a head. And Credence is no small man.

When the lord lets go of me, a noticeable weight lifts off my body. It's as if the shackles binding my limbs have released, and now that I'm free to move, immense frustration irks me for not having run. Not having fought.

As the string quartet transitions to a more graceful tune, the captain leads me to the ballroom floor. I can't help but notice the tension in his fingertips as he keeps them firmly but gently planted at my waist. Never faltering. Never roaming.

It would likely be proper to thank the captain for rescuing me out of the eely hands of Lord Credence, but I'm too mortified that I needed rescuing at all to say as much. Especially to a man as coarse as Captain Astor.

"I was under the impression you weren't interested in a child bride," I say, forcing my gaze to meet that of the captain. It's easier now than it was several minutes ago. Captain Astor is still intimidating, his presence just as imposing. But compared to my dread of Lord Credence, my fear of the captain tastes more like the respect one gives a challenger.

"I'm not," he responds, his green eyes flashing.

"Then why, pray tell, are you wasting your time dancing with me?"

The captain actually averts his eyes. I watch, tantalized, as his throat bobs underneath his dark stubble. "It seems your evening is destined to take a turn for the worse. No need to add to your suffering."

Something about his open admission, the acknowledgment of the terrors I'll likely be subjected to this very evening, digs at the raw spot in my chest. "Perhaps dancing with you is the very definition of suffering."

He makes no effort to counter. Just returns his attention to me and drawls, "Perhaps," with an unshakeable look of boredom on his face.

As we dance, the cadence of the tune picks up, and the captain adjusts accordingly, guiding us through the steps with more grace than I would have expected from someone so hardened. My parents had initially hoped to marry me off to a nobleman, but as my prospects dwindled and the shadows of my fate crept closer, they thought it best to stretch our nets to those of self-made wealth. A captain would be among those, though I don't recall signing a letter to a Captain Astor when we posted the invitations. Though considering how many males are here tonight, I suppose I shouldn't expect to remember each one of them, especially with my parents and John having helped me write the letters.

I'm about to tell the captain he's a skilled dancer, and expect for him to say something about life on the waters giving him steady feet, when his jaw opens, then works.

"Yes?" I ask.

"Nothing."

"You seemed about to say something."

Captain Astor sighs, annoyed. "You shouldn't have let him touch you like that."

I reel back, but the captain is prepared for it, adjusting his hand on my waist accordingly.

"What would you have had me do?"

Captain Astor doesn't frown. Perhaps I'd find him less perplexing if he would. "Anything other than the nothing you did."

My throat stings, his words lodging there. I'm used to being insulted by haughty suitors. Never have the insults echoed my own recriminations so precisely.

"It's not so simple for me as it might be for you," I whisper.

The tune changes, but rather than end our dance, the captain pulls me closer, transitioning with ease into the slower piece.

"Tell me why that is." The surety with which he gives the command startles me. Though it shouldn't. He's used to captaining a ship after all. "And don't hide behind a difference in strength between the sexes. The lord is one hip-snap away from teetering into the grave."

"He had a generous offer," I say, because I can't bear to admit the truth—that my dulled instincts had me freezing underneath the lord's predatory touch. "One I would have been foolish not to consider."

Maybe it's because I'm so used to conversing with noblemen that I'm not at all prepared for his response. "You're not a talented liar, are you?"

I grit my teeth, averting my gaze from the captain's taunting stare. "Are you blaming me for a cruel man's unwanted advances when I myself am in a...precarious position?"

I shouldn't have let the truth tucked between those vague words slip, but if Credence is right, the captain is too cunning not to errantly suspect an unwanted pregnancy.

The captain snorts. "We all hold dreams of a utopian sort of world where those in power refuse to oppress those with less of it. But Darling, that is not the realm in which you and I reside. Forgive me if I'm not one to placate the mentality that just because this world is a cruel and unjust place, we should take it lying down while we wait for others to change."

"There's no shame in meekness, Captain."

His piercing green eyes linger on my mask for a moment. "None at all. But to possess cowardice and call it meekness is a different sort of deception entirely."

I let out an exasperated sigh. "You despise me so thoroughly, yet we've only just met."

He doesn't blink, doesn't give me the dignity of averting his eyes when he responds, "That's because I despise weak things. Especially those for whom it is within their power to be strong. You, Darling, are the type of girl who allows life to happen to you. That's why we're here, isn't it? Why you're gambling your future away on a night of frivolity in the hopes of finding a husband. Surely you recognize what a frail reprieve that would be from the fate you so wish to escape."

My words hang in my throat. How does he know...?

"Tell me, have you ever considered a life outside of the little shadow box in which you've been content to wither away?"

"Everything I've ever done has been in service of preserving my future."

"And what a life you've squandered in the meantime."

He watches me, his gaze so sharp I feel as though it might penetrate my mask. Spiced scents of teakwood and pipe smoke waft off of him, permeating my senses until I'm dizzy. I search my chest for rattling anger, but find none.

I should be incensed; I know this. And yet I'm familiar enough with myself to know that if I were to be given another night in this realm, I would retire to bed numb, calm. Then, as I replayed the events of the evening, the harsh words this man dared to speak to me would kindle my anger, boiling over until sleep fled me. Until rage consumed me.

But I won't get another night, so I suppose I'll never taste the hatred I should feel toward this man.

So we dance, and I say nothing. Because what's the point of conversation when one's dance partner sees through them?

The music continues lazily, and I glance toward his left hand, his fingers interlocked with mine. Beautiful golden tendrils curl around his fingertips, tracing his knuckles and swarming the back of his hand before converging around his wrist. His crimson sleeves have slipped just enough that I can follow their path, except there's no more path to follow. Where a normal Mating Mark might curtail into a natural end, there are dreadful, inky gashes on his wrists that slice his golden tendrils in half.

Below the gashes, the Mark has grayed like a day-old corpse that's long lost its warmth.

"Oh." The word escapes my lips before I can reel it in.

"Oh, indeed," he responds, following my gaze.

"Did you find her before..." My words trail off as my eyes trace the severed mark, like flesh dangling from a three-day-old wound.

"Which answer do you find more tragically romantic?" he asks, his voice calcifying.

I snap my attention back to him, his hard lines and sharp edges suddenly softening in my perception, despite the way his jaw is set. As I return my consideration to his hand, I notice the gentle circlet of paler skin, untouched by the sun, curving around his ring finger —a wedding ring he must still wear and have taken off for the ball.

Mating Marks might be rare, but the legends of them are told around the hearth of every home in Estelle. I suppose we have a tendency to find them romantic—at least, people who aren't born with them do.

Of course, the stories always end the same way. With one of the Mates meeting a terrible end, leaving the Mating Mark of the other severed in a gruesome display of grief. An interwoven life picked apart like meat from the bone amongst a horde of scavenging birds.

"You're lucky to have found her," I find myself saying. It's insensitive, the sort of thing I'd never typically say. But something about the captain tells me he's the type to appreciate someone who speaks their mind rather than wrapping their opinion in lies to make it more palatable.

The captain laughs, but it's the wry sort with no smile to lift its edges. "Luck? Is that what you'd call it? Do you think it's luck to have one's soul ripped in half, like a sail down the seam?"

"Better to lose love than die searching for it," I say, though more to myself than to the strange captain holding me in his sturdy arms.

"Best of all to find love and be strong enough to protect it," he responds, his hand tensing at my waist.

"But that's not the realm we live in, now is it?"

It's not a smile that grazes the captain's full lips, but there's a softening there. Perhaps seasoned with a hint of surprise.

"I think—Darling—" the captain says, spinning me around with a flourish before catching me at his firm chest, "that you and I might very well be the most pitiful creatures in this room."

"Then it's a good thing we found one another," I respond, trying not to let my mind linger on the smokiness of the teakwood scent wafting off of him, the way his chest ebbs and flows against my cheek, pressing the edge of my mask into my face. It will leave a mark against my sensitive skin later, but I can't bring myself to readjust. "Imagine the number of people we might have infected with our misery had we been paired off with anyone else."

"Well, perhaps that old lordling will catch the fever and die before you can accept his proposal."

My heart stutters. Anticipation wells in my chest as the familiar song on the strings hurries through its bridge, racing much too swiftly to a close.

The captain and I have already danced two songs tonight and other suitors are beginning to crowd. No one is foolish enough to stare. They mostly inch toward us, their feet pointed in my direction, though their conversation is elsewhere, ready to pounce at the last second.

"You think I would accept?" I ask, hating how obvious my silent question is by the way my pitch heightens.

"As I said," the captain says, bringing us to a stop as the song comes to a close, "I think you're the type of girl who lets life happen to you."

My stomach drops, any flicker of connection I felt for this man clearly absent on his end.

Stupid. Stupid to dance with him. Stupid to get my hopes up, if only for the exchange of a few beautiful words.

My throat is closing up with embarrassment, my cheeks heating with mortification, so I step backward, but the captain's hand lingers in mine, and in a swift motion he pulls me back into him.

And then his hand is on my neck, the rough ridges of his fingerprints staining my memory with his touch. He tucks his fingers into the underside of my braid, slipping his thumb against the crook of my neck, where my pulse is frantically giving me away.

My anger I might not feel until later tonight—but this stranger's touch? It drowns out the present, lighting me on fire.

"Your paint," he says, stroking the ridge of my Mating Mark underneath my jaw. "You missed a spot. Had better clean that up if you're hoping for a proposal from a less aged suitor this eve."

And then, quick as he pulled me into him, the captain slips away.

I lose sight of him in the crowd, and can't help but notice the way my fingers trace the ridge that marks where he last touched me.

CHAPTER 6

*T*he next hour is spent in a whirl as I'm passed from the arms of suitor to suitor.

I'm sure some of them are adept at conversation, but my mind is elsewhere, so I make a rather poor conversational partner.

Focus, Wendy, I tell myself, but focus has never been my strong suit. At least not when I have something else rattling in my head, competing for my attention. Like searching over the shoulders of my dance partners for an elusive captain who seems to have disappeared from the ball completely.

Questions I should have asked the captain berate my mind. I could stomp my foot for not thinking to ask them in the moment.

What sort of ship are you captain of?

Where do you sail out?

For which company do you sail?

If not to compete for my hand in marriage, why accept our invitation?

I have a sneaking suspicion the answer to that last question has to do with networking amongst a gathering of nobles. I'm not sure what all goes into being the captain of a ship, but I'm sure brokering deals comes with the territory. It's clever, really, to attend a ball such as this one under the pretense of finding a wife, when really the captain is likely hunting for his next business venture.

On the other hand, one would think a dowry substantial enough to purchase five pristine ships would be the most lucrative use of his time.

"Miss Darling?"

The hesitant voice of the suitor I'm currently dancing with breaks me out of my trance. He appears to be about my age, with dark brown skin and kind eyes that glisten through his silver mask. He seemed to have barely summoned up the courage to shuffle over to me when he asked me to dance, and I feel a bit of a prick in my soul for not paying better attention to him.

"Are you quite well?" he asks, scanning my face for any signs of illness, I suppose, to explain my lack of attention.

"No. I mean, yes. I do apologize, Lord..." I hesitate, wracking my memory for his name.

"Evans," he provides, quite graciously, with a full, knowing smile playing at his lips.

"Of course, Lord Evans. I truly am sorry. I'm not sure what's come over me this evening."

"Could it possibly have to do with the gentleman who you graced with not one, but two dances?" he asks.

Where I expect annoyance, I find only teasing.

I open my mouth to deny it, but given the way Lord Evans is looking at me, I figure there's no use.

"Am I so obvious? How mortifying."

Evans shrugs, his lean shoulders carrying my hand with them as he does. "It is your marriage ball, after all. One would hope you'd be able to find someone to your liking by its conclusion."

"You're being extraordinarily polite for someone I've practically spurned," I say.

"Well, you seem like the type of lady who deserves someone to be kind to her tonight." The smile on my partner's face lingers, but there's something more restrained to it now. My stomach turns with unease.

Does everyone at this ball pity me over the false assumption that I'm with child? Or do I simply give off the air of a woman who's spent her entire life shackled to the whims of her dismal future? I'm about to toss aside decorum and ask Evans which it is, when over his shoulder I glimpse him.

My breath catches in my throat as I take in Captain Astor. My heart races. I'd convinced myself that he'd already left. There's a part of me that wishes he'd look my way, but that part of me is a fool.

He's mid-conversation with another suitor, this one clad in glittering cuffs of rubies. Just as I suspected, the captain is making rounds, buttering up the rich noblemen, probably convincing them to let him haul their cargo or man their vessels.

But then the captain does something strange. He glances over his companion's shoulder at a suitor leaning casually on one of the ivory pillars, then flicks his head to the side, almost like it's a tick.

That's not the strange part; it's what he does with his hand. The way he claps his fingers together.

Immediately, the suitor leaning against the pillar, a bulky pale-skinned man with a shaved head, pushes himself off his resting place and follows the path where the captain just gestured.

I follow the direction of the captain's signal and find...

No, that can't be right. My years of talking to shadows must have driven me mad, taught me to perceive mystery where there is none.

Because the captain can't have been pointing to my brother Michael, who, as expected, is tracing squares (his favorite shape) into the velvet wallpaper.

"So, whose idea was it to throw a masquerade rather than a regular ball?" asks Evans, politely still even as I've been ignoring him.

"My father's," I clip, then realizing how disinterested I sound, add, "He's always been drawn to the excessive."

The bald man is making his way over to Michael, who doesn't seem to notice him approaching, though surely there's something behind the pillar I can't see. Or perhaps I've made up this entire interaction in my head.

"Let me guess—you're drawn to the simpler things in life?" Evans twirls me around, a bit too early for this particular tune. Perhaps he isn't familiar with it.

When I'm back to facing him again, he's pivoted, out of step with the dance again, so that I no longer have a good view of Michael. I bite my lip, aware of how my fingers are now shaking. Then, conspiratorially, I whisper, "I believe the turn isn't until the second round."

Evans just smiles. "Surely you break the rules on occasion, Miss Darling."

A bead of sweat forms at Evans's temple.

I can't help myself. I glance over my shoulder, praying desperately that my anxieties are just that—the paranoid machinations of a woman who's spent her entire life in dread. But the bald man has reached Michael, and he's on a knee next to him, talking to him. Michael's paying him no mind, of course. He rarely acknowledges the existence of strangers. But then the man pulls something out of his trouser pocket and offers it to Michael, who takes it without looking at the man. When the man grabs Michael's hand, my brother swats him away, but with little effort.

Panic seizes my gut.

"Excuse me, but I really must—" I turn back to Evans, but the smile has been wiped clean off his face.

"But we aren't finished with our dance."

My heart feels as though it's in my throat. "I do apologize, but I'm feeling quite ill."

I step back to excuse myself from the dance, but Evans's grip around me tightens.

"I truly am sorry, Miss Darling," he whispers through his teeth, his brown eyes wide with apology. "You really do seem like a nice girl."

Panic sets in, and for the second time tonight, I freeze. It's only a moment, only a fleeting second before the urge to protect my youngest brother overtakes my spirit and ushers me to fight back.

I'm a moment too late.

Evans tugs on me hard, yanking me into his chest and spinning me around, pressing my back to his front while, in a single fluid motion, he brandishes a glistening dagger to my throat.

Gasps overtake the crowd, but are quickly cut off as what must be two dozen suitors slit the throats of the noblemen and women conversing next to them.

Their sparkling wine glasses hit the floor first, fracturing in chinks. The bodies follow soon after, landing in the shattered glass of their own drinks.

All the while, my eyes are on Michael.

In the moment Evans overcame me, the bald man threw my youngest brother over his shoulder. He's thrashing at the man, but he's so slight, so spindly, nothing he does is much use.

"Michael," I cry, but my brother is too overwhelmed to notice. I watch in panic as he digs his teeth into the bald man's shoulder and the man lets out a growl.

The bald man carries my brother through the nearest door and slips away.

My mother screams.

Or perhaps it's me; we've always sounded so similar.

I thrash in Evans's arms, but despite his narrower frame, he's strong, and the knife he holds to my throat proves effective.

"Please, my brother. He's done nothing wrong," I beg, thinking surely this kind-eyed man will care something for the life of a child.

"Come with me," says Evans. "Don't make this more difficult than it has to be."

"No!" My cry isn't as shrill as I want it to be. It comes out choked. Weak. Stuck in my throat. But I slam my heel on Evans's foot all the same. He lets out a grunt. The moment his grip falters, I duck beneath the knife and break into a run.

Bodies scatter the floor of the ballroom as I race toward the door where Michael just disappeared. Where is John? Where are my parents? I wonder, but there's no time to search for them in the crowd. I don't want to search for them in the crowd. Not when half of the crowd is on the floor, the other half's hands are dripping blood.

I make it several paces across the throng of bodies before someone dares to step in my way.

Him.

The captain's green eyes flash with warning, but I don't heed it. I scramble to the side, but I'm not fast enough, and he snatches me into his grasp, hauling me toward him.

"I'm truly sorry, love," he says, his body practically motionless against my struggle. I flail against him, but his grip on my wrists doesn't budge. "Wendy," he says, like I'm an animal or a child to be placated, an infant to be hushed.

"Please. Please, just let them go. Please, my brothers are innocent."

"Are you not?" The captain cranes his head to the side. He's maskless now, though I don't know whether he removed it or someone else did in the struggle. He's even more beautiful than I would have guessed, and it enrages me.

I scream, making to slam my fists against his chest, but his grip is too tight. As I stare into his face, gnashing my teeth, something catches my eye. A glint underneath a tuft of raven black hair. A single golden ring shines, but the position of it is disorienting—too high and far back to be an earring. But then as the captain shifts, his hair does too, and the realization dawns on me with the revelation of the pointed tip of his ear.

All sharp lines—that's what I'd thought when I'd first laid eyes on the captain.

The mask wasn't a nod to the past, but a means to hide his nature.

"You're fae," I whisper, dread crawling through me as I realize just how hopeless it is to fight. Why the captain seems so unfazed by my attempts to escape.

"Astute," he says, but before I can respond he whirls me around, tucking me into his chest as he presses a serrated blade to my throat.

My mind reels. The fae are supposed to be extinct. Or if not extinct, close enough. In the ancient days, the fae overcame our world, enslaving humans with their incomparable strength and agility. But when the fae were cursed with mortal lifespans, everything changed. Fae don't procreate as easily as humans, and without centuries to spend producing offspring, they quickly began to die out. The captain is a rarity, a fae come out of hiding.

"George and Mary Darling. Do come out, won't you?" he calls to the crowded ballroom.

The still-living guests tremble at the hands of the captain's men, several of them holding their dance and conversational partners at knifepoint.

"There's no use hiding," says the captain, his deep voice rumbling through the hall. "We will find you anyway. Might as well offer your daughter the gift of remembering you as the noble parents who gave your lives in exchange for hers."

"No," I cry, but it comes out as more of a whisper. I search the crowd for my parents, for John, but I find no sign of them.

"Come out, and I won't tell her what you did," calls Captain Astor.

No. I beg my parents inwardly not to reveal themselves. I'll be handed over to the shadows come the end of the night anyway. There's no reason for them to sacrifice themselves, not when they need to find Michael, need to get him and John to safety.

Footsteps clatter on the floor. Two pairs of them as my parents appear out from underneath the trapdoor in the stage where they've been hiding.

Between them, they've clasped their trembling hands. A united front as they meet my captor in the center of the ballroom.

"Why are you doing this?" I beg.

"Count it as a mercy that I'm choosing to keep that information to myself, Darling."

The knife is cold against my throat, the tip of it exactly where my parents' gazes are fixed.

"Please, they took Michael," I tell them.

My father tenses, my mother searching the room for my youngest brother in panic, but I hate myself instantly for telling them. There's nothing they can do. They're going to die in the center of this ballroom, and now I've plagued them with the horror of what might happen to Michael.

I search the crowd again, desperate to find John, but relieved when I don't. Perhaps he heard me. Perhaps he'll go after Michael while the crowd is distracted.

Perhaps he's not one of the bodies that litter the tile floor.

"What do you want?" my father asks, his bowtie bobbing as he attempts to swallow and fails. "Money, I assume. We've got it. Anything you want. Just return our children to us unharmed."

"All of them?" The captain's voice is a taunt.

My mother's face drains of color.

"And what if I made you choose? What if you could only have two of them back? Which two would you pick? Which would you save?"

"No," I cough, miserable at the hapless looks on my parents' faces, when the choice is so obvious. "John and Michael. They choose John and Michael," I say, because it's the logical thing to do. Because it's the only thing to do.

"There you go again, just letting life happen to you," says the captain, his breath tickling my ear, sending shivers down my body. "Do you even know who I am?" he asks as my parents tremble.

Of course they don't, but my father and mother exchange knowing looks, and my stomach falters.

"Please. Just don't hurt her," says my father, holding his palms up.

The laugh that escapes from the captain's mouth is crackling ice on a frozen lake. "Do you know how many times I've woken in the middle of the night, begging the same of you?"

Something in my mind stops. Homes in on that tiny sentence.

"What is he talking about?" I ask my parents, my jaw nudging the knife still pressed against my throat.

"Please," my mother says, clapping her hand to her mouth, like she always does when her expression threatens to betray her.

"Please, it wasn't her fault. She's not the one who should be punished."

"You mistake my intention." I can feel the captain's cruel smile break out, his lips grazing my ear. "Any harm that befalls her is meant to punish you."

CHAPTER 7

"Y ou'd punish a child for the sins of her parents?" my
father asks, jutting his cleft chin out, though his legs
are trembling.

"Please," says the captain, drawing the knife away from my
throat just long enough to gesture toward both my parents. "Do go
on with your ethics lecture."

"Not until you release our daughter," says my father.

The captain laughs, the sound more bristly than the stubble of
his jaw scraping against my temple. "So entitled to your loved ones.
Tell me—what makes her so much more significant than everyone
else's?"

"Ma. Pa." I scan my parents' forlorn faces. "Please. What is he
talking about?"

My father won't look at me, but my mother will. Pools well in
her lower lids. "I'm so sorry, Wendy. I only wanted to protect you."
She turns her face to the captain. "Please. Take me instead. Kill me.
Punish me. Whatever revenge you've been plotting, take it out on
me. The blame is mine and mine alone."

"Oh, how I would prefer it if that were enough," says the captain.
"But I'm afraid I wish you to hurt as I do. Thankfully," he says, "I,

unlike you, have a meager set of ethics by which I abide. I won't kill your daughter simply for revenge, no matter how much I'd love to watch that lovely smile slip from your face as I bled her lifeblood."

My mother breathes a sigh of relief.

"Your son, however."

The captain snaps his fingers, and my heart caves in as a man appears from an adjacent room.

Michael. No. But it's not Michael fighting against the bulky man's grip. It's John.

"Let go of my sister," he screams, but it's no use. I'm not the one whose blood they intend to spill.

"Please. Just take me instead," I whisper, awed at the way the trembling in my voice stills, the sobs go quiet. All around me, the world goes numb. I don't feel it at all. Don't feel this wretched man's hands around me, the touch that set me aflame only half an hour ago. Don't feel the pounding of my heart against my chest or the agony in my parents' eyes or the dread of what will happen to John.

I'll feel it all later. It will cascade around me in a torrent of grief, shoving my face underneath the water and drowning me, over and over, until the shadows take me into their blissful oblivion. That is, if I weren't about to die.

But for now, I feel nothing. "Please, Nolan. I'm begging you."

The captain's breath falters; the blade against my throat stills. "Very well."

He removes his blade from my throat, tossing it at the feet of my parents. It clatters when it hits the marble floor. His stubble scratches my cheek as he gestures toward it with his head.

"Slit your own throats, and I'll spare the boys," he says.

"No!" John cries, fighting against the henchman. But my brother, though he's gained muscle mass over the last few months, is still slender-framed compared to the man holding him. In the end, his fighting proves little use.

"No." I'm not struggling against the captain anymore. Not when my mother meets my gaze and smiles, the edges of her lips quavering.

"Spare her too," says my mother, but the captain shakes his head.

"The boys will go free. It's that, or all your children meet unfortunate ends."

My mother and I make eye contact, and in that single look we exchange a silent acknowledgment. It's okay, I tell her. Because this is the end we've been preparing for my entire life. It was a fool's dream, thinking we could escape the shadows. Clearly the captain intends to steal me away as bounty, but he doesn't know to whom my soul and body belong. He doesn't know that at the hour's end, the shadows will come to claim me, dissolving me from his reach.

If we can just save John and Michael, I can welcome the shadows in peace.

My mother nods in understanding, tears streaming down her face. She kneels and plucks the blade from the ground, her fingers as delicate with the hilt as they might be with the handle of a steaming teacup. My father lurches forward to stop her, his hands shaking as they close around the blade.

For a moment, they wrestle for the hilt, but my father's desperation shows through at the widening of his eyes as he pleads with my mother. "Forgive me, Mary Darling. But we both know you've always been the stronger of the two of us. I can't bear to watch you go."

My mother smiles gently and lets go of the hilt.

"I'm so sorry, children," says my father.

In a motion swifter than I would have thought possible, my father brings the blade to his throat. There's the sickening slicing of flesh, then blood pours from the wound, and the room goes silent as my ears flood with a deafening roar. Faintly, I think I can sense my brother screaming, but I can't actually hear it.

My father crumples to the floor, still clutching his throat. I watch as my mother picks up the blood-soaked blade and brings it to her own.

It takes longer for her to die than my father. I'm not sure if she simply missed an artery that would have hastened the process, or if she fights longer to stay in the same realm as her children.

When she goes down, there's no smile on her face. Except for the bloodied sliver of crimson curving against her throat.

I'm not sure how long I stare at my parents' bodies, crumpled on the floor. My mother pale in her gown of blush silk. My father's cravat crooked.

I'm not sure how long it takes for the noise of the ballroom to come crashing to my ears again, but when it does, it's because the clanging of metal brings me back to the present. Bells. Signaling the third quarter of the hour. Just how my parents set the clock tower for the night so I could keep up with the time.

A quarter hour until the shadows take me.

A quarter hour until the captain with a vendetta against my parents realizes he's been duped.

"Captain," I say, fighting the blackness threatening to steal my vision. I need to stay alert. Find a way to get John and Michael out of here before the shadows come for me. "I believe you said my brothers could go free."

The captain hesitates, his grip still firm on my shoulders, but he mutters something to Evans, who must have appeared next to us while my vision was tunneling. Evans disappears through the door through which Michael disappeared with the bald man.

"Go get your brother," the captain says to John, whose glasses are askew, balancing precariously on the bridge of his nose as he stares blankly at my parents' corpses. The henchman holding John releases him, and John blinks rapidly, stumbling forward. He takes two steps toward our parents before righting himself and swerving to follow Evans, but he stops in front of me and the captain.

"What are you going to do to her?" John's voice is analytical, technical, though I know from years of studying him the tells of sorrow in his logical features. The way his brown eyes glisten, the slight way he scrapes his teeth together.

"I'm not sure you want to know," responds Captain Astor, meeting my brother's stare.

John blinks. Like he's wiping fog from his glasses.

"Will you wait? To do whatever it is you're planning? Until my brother and I are gone, I mean."

Captain Astor sneers. "What a courageous brother you have. Sure you don't want to revise your previous request to take his place?"

John's throat bobs. His gaze flits to the floor, but I know my brother. He's no coward. He wants to know if the shadows will take me before the captain can lay his hands on me.

"Rest assured we don't have time to dally," says the captain, which, though it doesn't appear to reassure John, at least convinces him he can leave.

He turns to go, but before he's made it two paces, he spins back around. A few of the captain's henchmen make to stop him, but Captain Astor holds up a hand as John runs up to me and places something cold and metallic into my palm. "Something to remember us by."

The matching glass pocket watch to mine. I fight the urge to give it back. This pocket watch isn't something that reminds me of good times. John thinks of them as gifts from our father. I only think of them as my father's well-meaning but pushy method to get me to find a husband.

"John, I—" I go to hand it back to my brother, but instead of accepting it, he pulls the crown from the body of the watch and twists.

That's when the pocket watch explodes.

It happens so quickly, just as the second hand hits midnight—ten minutes early. Dust and cinders and lightning spark from the watch, causing a rattling boom to echo across the hall.

All around, the pirates keel over, covering their sensitive pointed ears in agony as the pocket watch squeals. Light soars from within it, ballooning out across the room, though it doesn't burn me to the touch.

A bomb made of faerie dust.

John meant to banish the shadows when they came for me. As

the room lights up in a flash of blinding white, I wonder if perhaps his plan would have worked on the shadows after all.

"Wendy, come on!"

A hand grabs mine. Free now from the grasp of the stunned captain, my brother and I take off into a sprint. I can't see anything. Nothing but the burning white light that envelops the ballroom.

We trip and stumble over bodies on the way, but John and I have spent years of our childhoods running around the manor in the dark. We don't need our vision to make our way to the exit, so long as we don't get caught up in the limbs of a corpse.

Eventually John stops in front of me, and I can hear him scrambling for the latch on the door. There's a click, and then a welcome shadow pours through the crack in the wall, cutting through the pixie light.

We push our way through, and suddenly everything goes dark. Like spending the noontime hours strolling in the sun, then entering a dimly lit home. My eyes refuse to adjust, but still, John and I run, hand in hand.

"They took Michael," I cry. "They took him this way."

"I know," says John. "I know."

We race through the halls, and slowly my eyesight corrects itself, bringing the walnut-paneled corridors of my familiar home into focus. My mind races for where they might have taken my brother. The manor itself is huge, but there's a staircase at the end of the hall that leads...

"Toward the stables," I tell John. "That way, they could make a quick escape if they needed to. Take him hostage if they needed a way to get me to cooperate."

"A back-up plan." John nods.

We throw ourselves into the tiny winding staircase, our haste accentuated by our panicked breaths and the pads of our footsteps.

It's only when we reach the bottom of the staircase, toward the stables, that we hear him. Inside, my sweet little brother is whimpering. "It's okay, Michael. Mommy's got you. Don't be scared. Mommy's got you, Michael."

John and I exchange quiet glances. The accuracy with which Michael has captured our mother's voice chills the space between us.

"Something wrong with you, ain't there, boy?" says a low voice from the other side of the door. "Something not quite right."

On any normal occasion, hearing anyone insult Michael would incite rage within me. At the moment, I'm too preoccupied with coming up with a plan to get Michael out of the stables and to safety to dwell on it.

I jerk my head to the side. Toward the stall whose adjoining wall has a hole in it that John and I used to crawl through as children. It was too small for a horse to get through, so my father never bothered fixing it.

John blinks at me from behind his glasses. His eyes go wide as I step out from behind the barrels, my hands raised above my head.

"I'm here," I say, my voice shaking. "Please, surely you don't need my brother. Just let him go and I'll come with you."

The bald man's eyes sweep over my figure, hay needles already sticking into the fabric of my ball gown.

"Captain didn't expect you to put up a fight. Surprised you made it this far," he says.

I swallow, my eyes trained on Michael. He's plucked the button off his non-collar and is twirling it in his fingers as the bald man keeps his hands firm on his shoulders.

"Just let him go. Captain Astor doesn't want him anyway."

The bald man's eyes go to slits. "Pardon me, but were you there when the captain told me to take this one away?"

I shudder at what the cruel captain might have planned for my innocent little brother. How deep he's allowed revenge to leak into his heart.

Just then, a steel horseshoe comes flying. It smacks the bald man's head, his eyes rolling back into his skull as he slumps backward. Michael yelps, then skitters out from underneath his grip and toward me.

"It's okay, Michael. Mommy's got you," he says, threading his hand through mine.

John appears from the shadow of the stall behind the bald man, staring down at his unmoving body.

He's wondering if he killed him or not.

"We don't have time to check," I say, remembering Evans wandered down this way at some point.

John nods, then we're off.

We make it up the stairs and down the hall when we hear the yell. A glance through the window reveals the captain and his men, their figures warped in the glass of the windows from the section of manor across from us. From the looks of it, Evans has met back up with his crew. There's only a bridged walkway between us and them.

John and I both reach for Michael, and we sprint through the hallway and down another set of stairs. As soon as we reach the door at the bottom of the steps, we hear angry voices on the other side.

There's nowhere else to go.

We're surrounded.

We're in a viewing room. One that looks out into the courtyard. If it were daylight, there would be speckles of colored light painting the floors and benches.

I don't let myself think before I rush to the window opposite the door and shove my elbow into the stained glass. Pain lances my arm, shards of glass peppering my skin. I bite back a scream, then pick away what's left of the window before climbing through.

My feet hit the grass, damp from the downpour of rain. Thunder rolls overhead, but I ignore it as John passes Michael through the window to me.

As soon as John has wriggled through the window and into the courtyard, we sprint across the lawn. I open the door to the base of the clock tower, and nod for John to climb.

CHAPTER 8

*J*ohn jumps onto the ladder first, scaling quickly and efficiently. I put Michael on the ladder next and pray to whatever higher being might be listening that my brother won't fall.

"You have to climb, buddy," I say.

"Last one to the top is dead meat."

"Yes," I say, unable to help my grim smile as I lean my forehead against a cold metallic rung. "Last one to the top is dead meat."

Michael climbs a few rungs, singing as he goes, but the further he climbs, the higher pitched his song becomes, until he sounds like an opera singer blaring the final note of the performance.

"John, he's not going to make it to the top like this," I say, careful to keep my voice to a whisper, though it can't be doing any good with how Michael is yelling.

John, halfway up the rungs, turns his face back down, his glasses hanging precariously at the tip of his nose. He starts to come back down, but I shake my head. "No, you keep going. I'll get him up."

Already, Michael is climbing back down, his little song becoming ever quieter the closer he gets to the ground. I quickly search the cramped little space for anywhere the two of us could hide, but we'll be discovered eventually. I've no doubt of it.

It's up, or wait to be found.

It's probably a fruitless endeavor either way, but a desperate plan is forming in my mind, and it won't work if the pirates get a hold of the boys.

"All right, Michael," I say, gripping my brother tight. "Let's play koala, okay?"

Instantly, my brother links his arms around my neck and crawls onto my back, wrapping his legs around my waist.

"Wendy, you can't—"

Before John can convince me out of this, voices from the courtyard reach my ears, questioning which direction we could have gone. It's only moments now until they turn the corner and find the door to the clock tower.

So I put my hands on the rungs of the ladder and ascend.

A FEW TIMES on the way up, I fight the urge to tell Michael, "Don't let go." Michael has a tendency to home in on every word in a sentence but the negative ones.

"Hold tight," I whisper instead. "Hold tight to sissy."

"Hold tight," he says back, squeezing his legs around me with increased vigor each time he says it.

Even with adrenaline coursing through my veins, the climb is arduous with Michael on my back. He's rather small for his age, but that doesn't make this easy. Halfway up the ladder, the sweat beading on my palms begins to present problems.

Three-quarters of the way, my limbs are quaking.

"We all fall down," Michael starts chanting, which doesn't at all help. Neither does craning my neck to look down. My stomach drops, the height of the clock tower gaping beneath me.

"Wendy. Come on. Just a few more rungs," says John, infusing his voice with a calmness I know he can't be experiencing. "Just a little further."

The next rung is effortful. The one after that—I have to bite back a scream of exertion.

"Push with your legs," says John, his finger tapping anxiously along the edge of the platform.

When I almost slip and let out a gasp, John yelps.

No. No, I will not fall. Not with Michael on my back. I've climbed this ladder a thousand times. Climbed more treacherous surfaces, just to escape having to think about my fate. I can do this.

I steel myself, bracing myself with my breath, then scale the next rung. Apparently Michael feels more confident seventy feet off the ground than he did eight rungs up, because he scrambles off my back, climbing up the last few rungs until John practically yanks him from the ladder and catapults him backward onto the platform. Michael's foot finds the crown of my head on the way, and I have to fight to keep my fingers fastened around the slick metal.

Once Michael's weight is off my shoulders, I find it easier to climb. By the time I get to the top, John has his hands underneath my armpits, hauling me up.

"You should have let me do that. Should have let me carry Michael." Though there's scolding in his voice, my brave younger brother is shaking with the trepidation of having watched us from the top. "Pretty impressive, though," he admits with a shrug.

I extend my finger vertically over my mouth. John places a hand over Michael's just in time for a crash to come resounding from the bottom of the tower.

The three of us huddle together on the platform, trying to keep out of sight from below, but the entrance to the platform itself is angled such that if one of the pirates backs up enough to get a good angle...

"Up there," one of them says. "Stupid children fled up there."

Do I resent being called a child by a man who attended my betrothal ball? Hard to tell when my siblings and I are fighting not to breathe.

"Well then," drawls the captain's menacing voice. "You'd best go and bring them back down."

The ladder rattles as someone weighty grabs onto it from the bottom. John's eyes go wide, and since he's the one holding Michael, he gestures toward the screws holding the ladder in place. I nod, panicking a bit until I remember all the pins hidden in my now-drenched hair. I remove one, ready to detach the ladder and allow the climbing man to enjoy the fall, when something happens that causes the entire platform to shake.

The shadow of the minute hand clicks into place.

Up above us, from within the cogs and cobwebs, a bell sounds.

No.

Part of me expects the shadows to have the decency to wait until the twelfth bell chimes, but the Shadow Keeper has been waiting for me for almost fifteen years now, and he'll be made to wait no longer.

I feel him before I see him. Strange when I'm talking about a shadow, but his very being crawls up my spine, icy fingertips playing over the ivory keys of my vertebrae. His substance fills me from within, thickening the cloying air.

I wonder then if I have morphed into shadow just to meet him.

But no. I glance down at my hand, still fully flesh as I abandon my task of disconnecting the ladder.

Then I turn to face him.

The Shadow Keeper cocks his head.

AT FIRST, the shadows take the form of a cloud, but as the bells continue to chime, the shadows assemble, morphing into the form of a man whose great wings are outstretched from end to end of the clock behind him. He's perched on the ledge, his limbs catlike as he examines me. Moonlight filters through the glass, backlighting the Shadow Keeper in a violet glow.

"Are you ready, Wendy Darling, for me to take away your pain?" It's not the voice I'm accustomed to, but the one he used for just a moment last night, when he promised coming with him wouldn't be so bad.

If only I'd agreed, the masquerade would not have occurred, and both my parents would still be breathing. My brothers would not be orphans.

I swallow that thought and face my fate.

"I'm ready," I say, though the way my voice shakes indicates otherwise. "I want you to take me now. To be yours. Just please, take them too."

John goes utterly still, though one glance at Michael in his arms keeps him from protesting.

The ladder rattles.

"You see, that's the problem, Wendy Darling. You're already mine."

My heart is pounding. "Please. I can't—I can't let them die. If you've ever cared for me at all, just bring them with us. I promise I'll be a much more amiable prisoner knowing they're safe."

The shadow pauses. It's hard to tell, with only the distorted moonlight highlighting his edges, but it looks as though he glances toward the rattling ladder.

"You don't know what you're asking. The freedom of theirs you're bargaining away."

I falter, but when I think of my parents, my resolve increases. "My parents did the same for me. Saw I was dying and borrowed time. That time might have come to a close, but I'm still grateful for it." And besides, I'll find a way to get John and Michael out of this, I don't add.

"All right, then. But as you're already mine, and I could easily take you by force, I'll need something in addition to yourself."

"What else is there possibly to give?" barks John, to which the Shadow Keeper snaps his head, before slowly turning back toward me.

"A bargain," he says.

My heart sinks, but somewhere down below someone is yelling that he sees us.

The Shadow Keeper flicks his fingers, and out shoot spindly

tendrils that snake down the ladder. Someone cries out, and his outburst is echoed by the pirates.

There's the crash of splintering wooden crates at the base of the tower.

And then the captain's voice. "Fine. I'll get her myself."

My stomach rolls over as the ladder shakes again.

"What sort of bargain?"

"What sort of bargain are you offering?" the Shadow Keeper teases.

I blink. What else am I to give other than myself? I suppose I'm the heiress to this manor now, as sick as that makes me. Somehow I doubt the Shadow Keeper concerns himself with such mortal cares as wealth.

"Anything," I finally settle on. "Anything you want."

The Shadow Keeper places a veiling hand to his chin, thinking. "Anything I want?"

Then he shoots out the same hand.

"What's the bargain?" asks John.

"The bargain," says the shadows, "is just as your sister proposed. Anything I want, whenever I choose to call this bargain in. Anything I want, and I'll bring your brothers along."

John opens his mouth to protest. "Wendy, you don't have to—"

But I've already taken hold of the shadowed hand.

CHAPTER 9

J'm not sure what I was expecting from the moment my flesh finally grazed the shadows. Perhaps to meld with this creature of the night, for my body to break apart like the ash of a crisp sheet of parchment held over the fire.

Instead, the inner crease of my right elbow stings. Two white-hot ovals appear, separated by an untouched patch of skin between them.

I hardly have time to consider the implications of the mark that signifies this new bargain, because before me the shadows thicken, compressing until they turn solid. In the dull glow of the distorted moonlight, the creature before me shifts, color blooming within the previously vague elements.

Pale skin knits itself over sinew, copper hair lengthening at his skull. The shadows coalesce to reveal a man—fae, given his pointed ears—with a lean build and chiseled shoulders, though his eyes remain black as coal, dyeing even the whites.

Dark patagium forms his wings, which fold in at his side, expanding as he stretches them. He's dressed from head to foot in black leathers, a strap across his back and a pouch at his hip. The same brand that marks me for our recent bargain now settles onto the knuckles of his right hand.

None of that is what catches my attention though.

It's the playful smirk on the edge of his lips.

It's the type of smile that should make me want to shrink back, but I'm familiar with the shadows, and all it seems to do is invite my forbearing spirit on an adventure.

The Shadow Keeper is beautiful.

Where the captain is all sharp edges and dark corners, the Shadow Keeper is the glow frolicking in his mischievous eyes, glinting off his copper hair.

"Hello there, my Darling," he says, allowing my hand to drop limply at my side.

I'm not sure what to say to that, but the Shadow Keeper's attention has already been diverted to the rattling ladder where the pursuing captain now climbs.

"Best hurry then." He grabs the pouch from his waist and tosses it to John, who catches it out of the air. "Just enough to coat your forefinger should do for the young one. Might need two for yourself."

John peers skeptically down at the pouch, then unties it and dips his finger inside. When he withdraws it, it's brushed in a shimmering gold powder. "This is concentrated faerie dust. It's not edible," he says.

The Shadow Keeper shrugs. "Says who?"

John frowns at him from behind his spectacles. "Says anyone who knows better than to drink from the tank of a faerie dust lamp."

"Wendy Darling," says the Shadow Keeper, turning to me. "You didn't mention in your bargain that your brother would be so difficult to convince."

This seems to incite John, because he groans and presses the powder to his tongue. His expression shifts ever so slightly, like he's surprised by the taste. Quickly, he goes for another. When he seems satisfied with the fact he hasn't dropped dead, he goes to hand some to Michael, but Michael, who has always had an affection for shiny things, has already dug through the pouch and brought the faerie dust to his lips.

After a moment, John's eyes widen, and his feet lift off the ground.

One would expect a nineteen-year-old boy to be thrilled at flying, but John just whispers, "Fascinating. I wonder how this works," as he stares at Michael, who is now spinning in circles in the air.

"Not really the time or place, John," I say, reaching for the bag. As John tosses it to me, the Shadow Keeper snatches it from the air.

For a moment, my heart sinks. Does the Shadow Keeper intend to leave me to the pirates?

"Don't worry, Darling," says the Shadow Keeper. "I don't like the idea of those men touching you."

"Then why not let me take the faerie dust?" I ask, eyeing the bag, well aware of how close the captain is to gaining on us.

"Because," says the Shadow Keeper, slipping back into shadow form, then reappearing behind me, his arms wrapping around my waist, pulling me into his chest as he leans in to whisper in my ear, "I like to keep what's mine close."

In midair, John tenses across from me, but the Shadow Keeper nods for him to go on ahead.

"Where are we supposed to go?" asks John, staring up at the closed ceiling above us.

"We'll have to teach that one to have a bit more imagination, won't we, Darling?" the Shadow Keeper says. "Tell me, where's your imagination leading you?"

Before I can answer, a golden-laced hand appears at the top of the ladder. The captain pulls himself halfway up, a curse on the tip of his tongue, rage flashing in his sharp and beautiful face.

His eyes search the landing for me.

He finds me sure enough, but he finds the Shadow Keeper, too.

I've lived my entire life adjacent to the shadows, but I've never seen one overcome a man's face so fully.

"Peter," the captain whispers.

The Shadow Keeper traces his thumb around my hip. "Hello, old friend."

Fear seizes my heart, but the captain is momentarily stunned by the Shadow Keeper's—Peter's—arrival. With a beat of his wings, our feet escape the ground, and we shoot toward the glass clock.

I let out a scream, sure that the glass will slice my skin, but Peter curls his body around mine.

We burst through the glass.

Glass rains down, coating the landing below us, showering the captain, who throws his arms up to cover his head. Shadows twirl around the shards falling toward my brothers, catching them before they pierce their skin.

John's eyes go wide, but his gaze quickly finds Michael, and something resolute overtakes his features.

He grabs onto Michael's hand.

And my brothers fly.

The captain rights himself, lunging onto the landing, his fingers grabbing hold of Michael's ankle. John lets out a yelp and kicks at him. The captain roars as his grip loosens and Michael slips free.

Wind beats at my face as Peter and I soar upward, but only when John and Michael clear the broken face of the clock tower do I allow myself to take in my surroundings.

The city of Jolpa is lit up in the gentle glow of faerie lamps cutting through the fog. The same material now works through the bodies of my brothers, keeping them afloat.

We rise higher and higher until the glass clock tower is barely a yellow glow in the distance, its broken face only a memory.

When I glimpse the houses shrinking into tiny dots below us, I let out a gasp.

"Frightened?" asks Peter, his breath warm on my ear.

"Yes," I say, my words breathy.

"Good."

For years, I've dreaded the Shadow Keeper's possessive nature. Now, I try to take comfort in the fact that he's not likely to drop me.

As we fly, I open one eye to peer down at the Estellian landscape below us. Twinkling lights speckle the ground, a mirror reflection of the starlit sky. I'd gaze at the stars too, but Peter has us flying almost perpendicular, his body a firm wall between me and the sky as he clutches me close. My head is still dizzy with the height. I'm used to climbing, but I've never been without a sturdy foothold, and now my entire lower body feels as if it's being pricked with needles.

"Where are we going?" I ask once the kingdom of Estelle fades from view and the dark and swarthy mountains overtake the landscape.

"Tell you what, why don't we play a game where you ask me five questions, then once your questions are up, you can guess where I'm taking you?"

"And what am I to gain if I win?" I ask.

"The answer, of course."

"And if I lose?"

"Then I drop you."

My heart stops in my chest, my vision tunneling as I stare at the ground so far beneath us, at the craggy tips of the mountains, the boulders that would break me upon impact.

"What do you say, Wendy Darling?"

I let out a chuckle that doesn't at all sound like the scream I'm unleashing inwardly. My poor mother didn't know what a terrible trait she was passing along to me, the inability to express my displeasure.

"I'd say I'm a rather patient person and do believe I can wait."

"Well, that's no fun, now, is it?" The teasing still tinges Peter's voice, but there's something sinister that's crept into it. Something dark that I don't dare disturb.

"What doesn't seem fun is breaking my body upon the rocks." I fight to keep my tone casual, steer the Shadow Keeper away from his madness.

"True. But think of the thrill of the game. Don't you want to feel, Wendy Darling?"

I want to tell him that I do feel. That terror creeps up my spine like spiders carrying their silk egg sacs on their back. That I feel his grip around my waist, firm for the moment, but with no promise anchoring it.

I want to tell him that I'm well acquainted with feeling. That I've felt nothing but fear and anxiety all my life, all because of him.

But as I consider it, it hits me that this isn't entirely true. Fear terrorized me, overcame me as a child, but over time I learned to tuck it away, to sear my soul with a white-hot iron until fear could not touch me. Until the haunting shadows no longer stirred much of anything in me, except for perhaps the longing that one day they would either end the numbness or fulfill it.

I open my mouth, almost ready to play this maniac's game, but then I think better of it, changing my question. "The captain. He knew you. He called you Peter."

"Did you think you were the only person ever to be haunted?"

"No, but..." I bite my lip. "I don't think you haunted him the way you haunted me. He knew your name."

"You never asked me my name."

I suppose that's true, but there's something not right about this. "Did you know him...before you were the Shadow Keeper?"

"Careful, or I might be convinced you want to play a game with me after all."

I clamp my mouth shut, frustrated. There's a stubborn part of me, the part of me that expected my life to end this very evening, who's brave enough to risk it to get answers. After all, I'm just on borrowed time now anyway, aren't I?

But then I glimpse my brothers soaring several feet below us, John leading Michael along by the hand, all the while glancing up at me every few seconds to make sure I'm okay.

I can't risk my life. Not when my death would crush them. Not when I need to devote my energy to finding a way to get them out of whatever horrid place Peter is planning on keeping us. Besides. If I'm cursed to be Peter's slave, I should have plenty of time to question him in whatever life he has planned for me.

A chill snakes through me at the idea of what this lunatic, intent on taking me since I was a child, might do to me once we reach our destination. Black dots swarm my vision, panic spiking at every part of my body he touches. I fear if I ponder it too long, I might pass out. But then Peter strokes my belly with his knuckles, and calm instantly seeps back into my veins.

So I pivot my questions. "If you know the captain, do you know why he wanted my parents dead?"

My stomach clenches at the question, and Peter's hands tighten at my waist, his chest tensing at my back. Our flight path dips a bit before Peter rights it with a steady beat of his wings.

"I'm many extraordinary things, as you'll come to discover. But I'm no mind-reader."

"Disappointing indeed," I say, realizing too late the ease with which I say it. I'll have to be careful in this man's presence.

I'd never met a fae until tonight, but so far the legends about them seem to be true. There are several tales of humans becoming enraptured by the fae's beauty, entangled in their glamour. Walls of self-preservation crumble in the presence of these beings when they should grow more fortified.

I've already experienced the effects on myself while dancing with the captain, the ease with which I found my heart bending toward him despite the awful words he spouted my way.

I'll have to keep a check on myself to avoid stumbling similarly with the Shadow Keeper.

As Peter leads us toward the stars, I glimpse a shadow hanging over us. One that blots out the light of just two of them, distorting their shimmering like the glass of the clock tower did to the light of the moon.

"Wendy, my Darling little thing," says the Shadow Keeper. "Would you believe that you're finally home?"

CHAPTER 10

*P*eter's fingers curl possessively around my waist as we soar toward the stars that seem moments from twinkling out. Around them is a gentle haze that distorts the misty black of the evening.

In the legends of the ancients—the ones John found during his research, prompted by the night I broke down and told him of my curse despite my parents forbidding it—there's a story of a Fate who takes slaves for herself, slaves whose mortality she wraps into the Fabric of time itself.

The only price they must pay is their soul.

My thoughts are cut short as my fae master stops in midair, his ebony wings still flapping.

"The children first," he says, the taunting in his tone evident as he gestures toward John, whose jaw is ticking. Michael pays him no mind. He's simply whistling, spinning in circles in the air. As if the faerie dust has put him in the most wonderful trance, releasing him from the ground that has proven to be a shackle to how he'd prefer to move—smooth and untethered by space or time.

"Come on, Michael," John says, taking our younger brother by the hand and leading him toward the distortion. He stops as he approaches it.

"A warping," he says, peering at it through his round spectacles. "I wasn't sure these actually existed."

Peter yawns behind me, and John shoots him a menacing look. "You really expect for us to just enter a hole in the realms without questioning you?"

"I suppose not," says Peter. "What I do expect is for your faerie dust to wear off shortly. As much as it would amuse me to sit back and watch you fall, dashing your mortal flesh upon the rocks below, I'm afraid my little pet here might cry over your deaths. And that truly would put a damper on my spirits. So I suggest you go on ahead."

John grits his teeth, glancing at me. When I nod, he pulls Michael close and floats toward the distortion.

In a moment, a blink of the eye, my brothers disappear. As if they'd never existed at all.

"What do you think, Wendy Darling? Do you wish to follow them or would you rather dally in the outside world for a moment longer?"

Peter's fingers play at my waist, flexing so that only a few hold me at a time.

Fear crawls up my throat. "I'd like to follow them now."

"But you don't know where we're going. You never played my game. Tell me, don't you ever wonder what it might feel like to fall?"

"No," I say, the lie seeping through my clenched teeth.

How often did I forsake the clock tower's rusty ladder to scale the outer facade, wondering just how many moments of sheer euphoria I would experience if I simply let go? If those fleeting seconds would be enough to cut through the watery numbness that had crusted over my soul.

But now that I'm this high up, the peaks of the mountains glimmering like the edges of white-hot blades, my toes are simmering with static, an unpleasant tingling overcoming my limbs.

"You're shaking," he whispers in my ear.

"Why are you doing this?" I ask. "I'm yours now. Why insist on torturing me?"

"Turn around, and I'll tell you."

His demand has my stomach roiling, but I'm at the mercy of his fading grip, so I do as he tells me.

I twist around, feeling his hands slip around my ribcage and toward my back as I roll in his grip, until my arms are wrapped around his neck, my chest tucked into his.

I squeeze my eyes shut, the pain of keeping myself in this position, my legs dangling at an odd angle, making my torso feel as if it's about to shred apart.

"Open your eyes, Wendy Darling."

"I can't."

"Open your eyes, or I'll drop you and not bother to watch you all the way down."

Fear lances my ribcage, and when I open my eyes, I meet his. Black and glinting with cruel mischief.

"Tell me, why did you not wish to open your eyes to look at me when you were so content staring at the ground below? Isn't the ground more dangerous?"

His smirk is bitter, and a shiver snakes up my spine. I know good and well why I wished to keep my eyes shut. Because this close to the Shadow Keeper, his scent of amber and pine threatening to intoxicate me, his firm chest flush with mine, I can't help but admire his beauty.

It's tantalizing, like the flame that devours the moth, and the way Peter's smiling down at me tells me he knows as much. Is well aware of the crippling effect his fae aura has on me as a human. It's why the humans rose up and banished the fae all those years ago. Why so many humans blinded themselves in the war effort, so as not to be seduced by the fae's tempting beauty.

"See, that's not so bad, now is it?"

I notice now how long his dark eyelashes are, how they graze my forehead as he presses his face close to mine.

A calm sweeps over me, and it's more terrifying than anything

I've ever experienced. There's a moment when I grasp for it, for the fear, but it's slipping from my grip. As hard as I cling to it, it cuts free just the same.

"Do you remember the promise I made to you, Wendy Darling?" asks the Shadow Keeper, righting us in the sky so that we're no longer perpendicular to the ground.

"No," I lie.

A soft smile curves on his beautiful lips. "I promised I would take the fear away."

That's not entirely true. He said he'd take the pain away. Though I suppose to some, to me, they're one and the same.

"What if I'm not ready?" I ask as we drift ever closer toward the distortion in the sky.

"Just let it go," he tells me.

And his voice is so soothing, so intoxicating, I do.

I feel it fall, the fear I've carried so long on my shoulders. It drops like the contents of a package whose strings have come untied. I'm not sure how long it falls. If it ever hits the sharp edges of the mountains beneath, or if it's caught by the wind and driven into the crashing waves. I don't look down, because I can gaze at nothing but the engrossing pits of his eyes that I might just let swallow me.

"See? I told you that would feel better."

CHAPTER 11

*W*hen we slip into the distortion, it's as if the world flips upside down.

Something silky coats my limbs, then something smooth and leathery as Peter's wings fold around my body, encasing me in their gentle but firm cocoon.

The stars turn into streams around us, breaking into dancing rivulets as we spin.

A cold gust of air, and the world comes back into focus. Except this time we're underneath a night sky that glows not with stars, but with swirling pinks and greens. It reminds me of the aurora I've seen pictures of in science books.

"Entranced, Wendy Darling?" asks Peter.

He hasn't told me to move, so I'm still cradled in his arms, facing him.

"It's beautiful," I say.

"And to think you were frightened of the shadows all this time. Welcome to Neverland."

"Is it always like this?"

"When it's nighttime," he says, though the teasing in his voice has returned, replacing the taunting. "You know, this would be more comfortable if you wouldn't dangle your legs like that."

I blush, realizing the awkwardness of how I have myself positioned against Peter. I've already pulled my legs up, linking them around his waist, tucking my ankles together around his back, before I realize this is much, much worse.

"Your cheeks are reddening," Peter says, glancing at me with a twinkle in his eyes. I'm taken aback by the change that's washed over them since entering this new realm. Where before, black ink coated even the whites of his eyes, the darkness has drained away, leaving behind eyes so deeply blue I feel as though I could float in them.

"This isn't the most ladylike of positions," I say, conscious of how my ball gown flaps open beneath me, threatening to expose my legs.

"You really wouldn't have liked it if I'd dropped you, would you?"

Fear contorts my gut, so much so that it takes me a moment to realize he's joking. He must either glimpse my reaction in the widening of my eyes or the way my thighs tense around his waist, because he leans in conspiratorially.

"You'll have to forgive my lack of manners out there," he says, gesturing his head backward toward the twin-star distortion in the sky quickly fading from view as we fly.

"I'm afraid I don't understand."

"There are certain qualities I find...more tame when I'm not in shadow form," he says, a casual grin appearing on his beautiful mouth. "I'm afraid the darkness brings out the worst in me."

Were I the type to speak my snark aloud, I would inform him that this tendency doesn't exactly make him unique. "But you haven't been in shadow form since we clasped hands in the clock tower."

"The effects linger. They take time to wear off."

That would explain the change in his eyes, the shift from black all over to the sparkling blue eyes that now dance over my features. My stomach twists, considering the wickedness Peter expressed only moments ago still swarms within him, even if he possesses a tighter grasp on it now.

"Well, as long as you don't threaten to drop me again."

Peter leans in. "Only when you ask me to, Wendy Darling."

I promptly suppress the shiver running down my spine and divert my attention. Instead, I search the sky for my brothers.

When I don't find them there, panic wells within me, but then Peter nods toward the ground. "Down there. Don't fret. They seem to have landed safely."

Indeed, I'm relieved to find the silhouettes of two boys gracing the beach below, their forms filling out as we approach them. Peter lands us on the beach. I must have lost my heels in the clock tower, because my bare feet sink into the gently pebbled sand. It's difficult to tell in the dark, but I believe the sand itself is the color of charcoal.

The crash of the waves sends water foaming up the shore, issuing a chill between my toes as it soaks the hem of my skirts.

"Wendy, look!" Michael cries with delight as he crosses a section of tiny pebbles barefoot. There's no telling at what point in the night he alleviated himself of the burden of shoes. I reach out instinctively to snatch him away from the jagged stretch of beach. When Michael was smaller, the servants had to be especially attentive to glass bottles or saucers should they break, lest Michael step atop them. For a while, my parents wondered if Michael struggled to feel pain in the soles of his feet, but over time we grew to understand that he craved the sensation.

As soon as I go to grab Michael, John puts out a hand and stops me. "I already checked this area for glass or debris. The pebbles themselves are fairly smooth. I wouldn't want to walk across them barefoot myself, but I don't think he'll hurt himself."

I sigh, my mind set free from at least one worry.

Now that I know my brothers are safe, at least for now, I turn my attention to our surroundings. The beach itself backs up to a cluster of pine trees, their scent giving away their type even in the dark.

"There's something strange about this place," says John. "Something that's not quite right."

If John plans on explaining, he's cut off by heavy footsteps as Peter approaches, his wings now tucked behind him.

He says nothing, and with a glance between John and me, we grab Michael by the hands and follow the Shadow Keeper into the darkness.

TRUDGING through the forest proves to be an ordeal barefooted in the dark. Michael seems unbothered by the ever-changing terrain beneath our feet, though John, who actually managed to hold onto his shoes, gives in and launches Michael onto his back after the former steps on a thorn branch.

All the while, the shadow of a winged figure leads us deeper and deeper into the forest.

"What's to say that fae don't feast on the flesh of humans? Or sacrifice us to their gods?" John asks.

"You're quite the skeptic, you know," I tease my brother, to which he lets out a wry but knowing laugh.

"And you're not skeptical enough."

My memory flashes back to the captain. John had known by looking at the man he was trouble, yet I'd been drawn to him like a mouse to a trap, the gold of his Mating Mark like the shiny end of a hook, begging the gaping trout to swim just a tad closer.

The memory of the captain's hands on my waist dances over me, and I have to shove it away, focus instead on putting one foot in front of the other. If I think of the captain's hands on me, I'm afraid of what will come up, that the feelings I let him muster within my inner being will prove me a traitor to my parents, unwittingly aiding their killer.

Now that we're in the quiet of the forest, Michael's humming coupled with our footsteps the only noises, I can't seem to block out the sounds of tonight's—has it only been a few hours?—horrors. Every snapping twig is the slice of the blade against their exposed necks, every glance I take at the crescent moon, my mother's grin, or the curve of blood against her exposed throat.

When I slip my hand into my gown pocket, I find it empty. My hope sinks as I realize my pocket watch must have fallen out during the escape. It might not have been my favorite memory of my father, but it was the last bit of him I had left. Or, thought I had.

It's no use distracting myself, so I glance over at John and try to decipher whether the same images and sounds berate his mind. He's blinking furiously underneath his glasses, his lashes damp, though he doesn't let the moisture spill past that point.

My heart aches for my brothers, and I wonder what will become of both of them. What sort of life of servitude have I sold them into? Does John resent me for it already? Will Michael one day hate me for it, or will his mind ever develop to the point of understanding what has happened to us? Why Mama and Papa no longer roll him snugly in his pile of sheets at night.

My thoughts are interrupted by the snapping of a twig and a gentle glow in the distance. As we follow the Shadow Keeper, he leads us into a clearing, in the midst of which towers a great oak tree the size of the clock tower. The glowing comes from the holes within its great trunk, where something must be producing light from the inside. Clusters of lichen let off a gentle pinkish hue as they cling to its bark. The canopy spreads high above us, blocking the swirling light of the heavens from reaching us.

Peter spins on his heel to face us, propping himself lazily against the thick trunk of the massive tree as he examines our trio, assessing whether we can be trusted.

"I don't let you leave after this point."

"You've already claimed me for yourself, haven't you?" I say, somewhat shocked at how resigned the words sound as they come out of my mouth.

Peter's eyes flash with amusement. "It was never in your fate for me to let you go, Wendy Darling. But your brothers have a decision to make."

John glances back and forth between me and Peter. Then shrugs. "It's not as if there's another logical option for us, now is there?"

"That's the spirit," says Peter. "And the little one?"

John and I exchange a look.

"Michael..." I hesitate, not wishing to give Peter the wrong impression—that Michael doesn't think for himself or deserve choices in life. "It's going to be difficult for us to explain to him what's happening."

Indeed, Michael is whistling to himself, his curious brown eyes enraptured by the lights coming off of the tree. I remember Mama weeping when Michael was younger over the fact that he never seemed to look at her like he looked at his lights. Part of me understands why it grieved my mother so. The other part of me has always figured that Michael just has his own way of making us feel seen. He might rarely look me in the eye, but I can tell when he clings to my arm or places a toy in my hand that he's seeing me. Even if it is just out of the corner of his eye.

"I see," Peter says, looking Michael up and down for the first time. "Well, then. In that case, Michael can have longer to decide."

I blink, not sure I heard the fae Shadow Keeper correctly, but before I can ask him to clarify, he turns toward the tree and beckons us to follow.

When we reach the tree, Peter holds a hand out to Michael. I'm a little shocked. Usually Michael swats away hands of people he doesn't know, but Peter somehow knew not to grab it. Just to extend his as an invitation. Michael sways a bit, then puts his little hand into Peter's, who leads it to a knot on the log.

It's strange to watch, when usually it's Michael leading us by the hand to whatever he needs.

As soon as Michael's palm touches the knot on the tree, it starts to glow, tendrils of light spreading through the cracks in the bark.

"How do we see? We see with our eyes," whispers Michael, and the words are so familiar, I almost hear them in my father's voice.

But then, slowly, the tendrils of the tree multiply. They slip over Michael's hand, consuming it like a disease.

Michael's shriek is the most horrible sound ever to reach my ears.

Panic strikes my brother's sweet features. He begins jumping up and down, slamming his open palm against the tree in an attempt to break free.

"No," I whisper, wishing to yell but afraid to spook Michael further. Tears sting my eyes as I watch my terrified brother struggle. I go to grab him, to yank the horrible flora off of him, but Peter's shadows restrain both me and John.

What have I done?

"Bad bad bad bad bad!" screams Michael, now clutching at his hair and attempting to rip it from his head.

"Please," I beg Peter. "Please, let him go."

If Peter's listening to me, he doesn't show it. Instead, he dips a finger into the pouch at his hip and presses the faerie dust to Michael's lips. Michael must have bitten him, because when Peter withdraws his finger from my brother's mouth, a droplet of blood wells at its tip. At least some dust must have made it into Michael's mouth because a palpable calm comes over him, and his poor little body goes still as the branches overcome him, wrapping him in their dreadful cocoon and drawing him into the base of the tree.

"What did you do?" I cry, but to my surprise, John takes my hand, his voice rather devoid of the rage I would have expected.

"It's a reaping tree," he explains, as if that's supposed to comfort me after just having watched it consume our little brother. "It provides shelter to those it deems…" He stops, glancing toward me, then at Peter.

"It's not going to take me," John says matter-of-factly.

Peter cranes his head to the side, back to leaning against the tree with his arms crossed like he enjoyed watching our panic, enjoyed drugging my little brother to calm him down. "Is that so?" Peter asks, scanning my brother like he sees something in him that's surprising.

"Well then," says Peter. "If you've educated yourself about the reaping tree, then I'm assuming you know what must be done to win its favor once you've lost it."

For the first time tonight, I glimpse John tremble under Peter's gaze.

"Sure you don't wish to turn back?" Peter asks.

John glances between me and the tree, but I know he's looking at where Michael just disappeared. He bites the inside of his cheek. "No. Family sticks together," he says, echoing a sentiment of Mother's.

My heart aches, but dread is brooding in my stomach.

"What does the tree want from you, John?" I ask.

John blinks, hesitating. "The reaping tree accepts those it perceives as having something...missing. Michael has his difficulty communicating." A pang strikes my heart. Part of me resents the tree for believing there's anything lacking in my brother. The other part of me considers my father's blatant refusal to acknowledge my brother's struggles by making light of them or pretending them away. I'm not sure which mindset hurts Michael more in the end. If there's an in-between to be had that accepts him as he is while still acknowledging the invisible challenges he faces in the world he lives in. "You have—" John blinks, and my chest tightens. There are several wounds to which John could be referring, though I'm unsure which ones he knows about. "Unfortunately, I'm painfully normal."

"Then what does the tree want from you?"

John shrugs. "It wants something to be missing, I suppose."

Peter's brow raises, like for the first time my brother has actually succeeded in sparking his curiosity. I don't realize what John is planning to do. Not until Peter laughs and tosses John an object.

John places his hand flat upon a tree stump nearby, and before I realize what's happening, slices his pinkie finger at the knuckle.

I hardly register it.

Not until the bulb of his finger hits the stump, blood spattering across the moss.

John doesn't even cry out. He just clutches his hand to his chest, his eyes rolling back in his head, the sight only magnified by his thick-rimmed glasses.

"John." I call out my brother's name, but he puts out his other hand to stop me. Like he doesn't want me taking on his pain, lest I make it my own. Slowly, I back away, at a loss of how to help as my brother wraps his wounded hand in a strip of cloth he's ripped from his coat, before stumbling over to the tree trunk.

When he unwraps his wound and spreads his blood across the ripples in the bark, the tree itself seems to drink it in, absorbing the scarlet liquid. Slowly, the vines come and consume John, until it's just Peter and me left in these forsaken woods.

Peter cocks his head to the side, examining where the tree is knitting back together in the shape of John's absorbed body.

"I have to say, I wasn't sure your brother had it in him—the older one, I mean. Seems like the stuffy sort."

I tense, my head swimming with rage. I can hardly look at the tree stump where John's severed pinkie remains.

I think I might lose the contents of my stomach.

"I must say, you Darlings are more entertaining than one could ever hope for from a family so terribly sheltered."

"You're vile," I say, but it comes out shaking, pitiful.

Peter flashes me a disarming grin. "Remember that, Wendy Darling, lest you be tempted to forget."

Then he gestures his head to the side. "Should you go in first, or should I?"

I wish I could say I step forward out of sheer bravery, but the idea of being left behind alone in this forest that seems to breathe villainy has me shivering. Besides, I'll always go where my brothers go.

So I step toward the awful tree, its lights looking more like the bulbs that hang off an angler fish at the bottom of the ocean, and place my hand against the knot. From deep within the bark comes a thrumming, one that beats like a pulse against my open palm. Hungry, the vines skitter toward my outstretched fingers, diligent ants readying to swarm their prey.

For a moment, I hope that maybe the tree won't accept me. That like John, there won't be anything in me that's missing. Not that I want to cut off my own finger, of course. But just this once, I think I'd like to be told I'm not lacking.

The tree does no such thing, and in an instant it snakes its tendrils around my body, binding me in utter darkness before swallowing me whole.

CHAPTER 12

There's a moment when I'm being swallowed by the tree where I feel the vines reach down into my throat, and take.

I'm not sure what they're possibly taking, given they accepted me because of the part of myself that's missing.

Like Michael, I thrash against the wretched plant as it gags me with its tendrils, but after an agonizing eclipse that threatens to last an eternity, it withdraws, releasing my body like vipers fleeing a den.

Gentle golden faerie light floods my vision, and when my eyes adjust, it's to a room too spacious for the size of the tree trunk. At first I have the absurd thought that perhaps the tree is larger on the inside—which I suppose can't be that absurd as the tree did just swallow me and force my brother to slice off a finger. But the walls are made of the tangle of roots and earth, not hollowed bark.

We're not in the reaping tree. We're underneath it.

Whispers reach my ears. I spot John in the corner, holding Michael to his chest as he rocks him back and forth, fisting his hands at Michael's chest to put pressure there the way Michael likes.

Instinctively, perhaps because I'm used to it, I prepare to scold whoever's whispering and giggling about Michael. But when my eyes find the offenders, no one is staring at my brother.

Nine sets of eyes stare directly at me.

They're children—all of them boys, most of them looking to be about sixteen. They're of all heights and builds, their skin colors ranging from pale as the beaches back home to as dark as Neverland's charcoal sand.

"That boy looks funny," says the youngest, the only one who looks to be about ten. He points directly toward my breasts, which I realize are showing slightly from how my gown has gone askew during flight. I flush, pulling my neckline up to cover myself, at which point a boy—the one with light brown skin and silky black hair—just chuckles.

"That's cuz that's a girl, Smalls."

Smalls, the youngest boy, whose body is rather cushioned around the edges, opens his mouth wide. "No way, Simon. I thought you were making those up."

Simon grins, though only he seems at all comfortable with my presence. The rest of the boys are glancing at me shyly. Like they can't tell whether they should greet me or ignore me.

What kind of life these boys have lived so that the youngest has never seen a girl before, I hesitate to even ponder.

"What's Peter going to do with you?" asks a redheaded, pale and freckled boy whose frame is slender.

Instantly, John tenses in the corner, still holding Michael.

Heat blotches my cheeks and neck.

"I—" I'm not sure how to answer when a clump of roots from the ceiling drifts downward. They soon retreat, setting Peter on the dirt floor. His wings flutter lightly as he shakes the dirt from them. There's a cacophony of hoots and hollers from the boys. The youngest, Smalls, runs up to Peter, looks like he's considering hugging him, then thinks better of it and gives Peter a hearty salute.

Simon follows, clapping Peter on the back in a swift embrace.

One by one, all the boys file up to him, beaming like he's their returned savior. Like he's a father, home from a long day of work or a faraway journey.

The image of my father's neck streaked with blood flashes across my memory.

I blink the image away behind muddied tears, focusing back on the reunion before me. When Peter greets the boys, it's the first time I've seen him offer a smile that isn't a smirk. He uses all the muscles in his face, complete joy written all over his beautiful features as he clasps the boys' hands like they're the oldest of friends.

Something threatens to shift in my perspective, but I refuse to let it.

"All right, Pete," says Simon, once all the boys have gotten a chance to greet the Shadow Keeper. "Who're the new kids?"

"This, Simon," says Peter, gesturing toward my brothers, "is John and Michael."

Interestingly enough, none of the boys comment on the way Michael is rocking back and forth, whispering something I can't make out.

Simon nudges Peter in the shoulder. "I think you're forgetting someone." He winks, his copper eyes glinting in the light of the torches lining the walls.

Peter's brilliant smile falters a bit, but he regains his casual disposition quickly enough. He spins toward me, bowing low as he nocks a mocking grin like it's an arrow. "This, boys, is your new mother."

A chill runs up my spine, confusion at the Shadow Keeper's words rattling my bones. Is this what the Shadow Keeper has wanted from me all this time? A kidnapped woman only fit for raising this group of boys?

Questions bombard my mind. Do they see Peter as a father figure? *Is* Peter their father? He certainly doesn't look old enough to be, but he's fae. If he's from any other realm than mine, it's likely he's not cursed with mortality, so it's possible he could be hundreds of years old.

I glance at the faces of the boys, searching for any resemblance to the copper-haired fae who's haunted me since childhood, but other than the pointed ears I find none. Besides, from what I remember, fae have difficulty procreating. It would be unlikely that Peter had sired all of these boys.

So who are they? And where did they come from?

If I'm flabbergasted by Peter's expectations for me, then the boys are even more so. A silence settles over the dark space, confusion wrought over each face. Even Simon, who practically exudes confidence, has a smile barely hanging onto his lips.

"What's got it into your head that we need a mother?" says a solemn boy in the corner. Shadows underneath his eyes provide a stark contrast to his ghostly face.

Even the charming Simon looks concerned and grabs Peter by the shoulder, leaning into him to whisper something into his ear. "Pete, if this is about Tom—"

Peter swiftly removes himself from the boy's grip. "Don't get your corset tangled, Simon. I was only checking to see if the lot of you are still as gullible as when I left."

"That was only a few hours ago," mumbles the redheaded boy.

"I didn't bring you a mother. Wendy's much too young and beautiful for that. Simon," he says, taking the dark-haired boy by the shoulders, then nodding toward two others, "Joel, Victor" —I note the boy with shadows underneath his eyes—"you're hardly boys anymore. And men need mates to look after. I brought Wendy here for the three of you to compete for. Winner gets to make her your bride."

My stomach turns over, horror wringing my insides as I consider the boys standing before me.

John jumps up from the corner. "You'll do no such thing—"

Peter releases a whirl of shadows, keeping John in place.

He's not looking at John. He's not even looking at the boys, who hardly dare to glance at me, their faces blanketed with mortification. The Shadow Keeper is looking at me. For a moment, it seems the cruelty he apologized for earlier has returned, despite having taken his fae form.

"What do you say, Wendy Darling? You up for a game?"

My mouth goes dry, my tongue too. I want to cry, to hold back the tears. This is a nightmare, the worst sort. It was bad enough when I thought I was being kidnapped as the slave of the Shadow Keeper, but for him to auction me off to adolescent boys...

Peter sighs, his trickster eyes glinting with mischief. "I didn't think so. You, Darling, and the three of you boys by the looks of you, will be glad to know I'm just teasing. Wendy will live here like the rest of you, and you'll treat her as one of the Lost Boys."

Lost Boys?

A set of grumbles fills the room, but Simon at least looks relieved. When he glances my way, there's a softness in his eyes that makes me feel the tiniest bit safer.

Then, without deigning to acknowledge me any further, the Shadow Keeper stalks through the nearest darkened hallway hewn from the earth.

I stand there stunned for a moment, but I'm tired of being immobile while the world moves around me. Taking me and leaving me at everyone else's whim.

You're the type of girl who allows life to happen to her.

I grit my teeth, pushing the swarthy captain from my mind, and shove past the gaggle of boys huddled around, gaping at me.

A few of them whisper, and John starts to follow me, but I shake my head. "Just give me a moment," I say.

Then follow Peter down the dark hall.

Part of me expects not to find him, anticipates he'll have already cloaked himself in shadows, blended into the darkness that's so clearly his natural home. But then footsteps sound in my ears, and I pick up my pace until I'm running. The soles of my bare feet pound against loose roots along the way. I can only hope I don't step on a vine of thorns.

A turn of the corner, and I slam into a firm, warm figure.

I'd know it was him even if I hadn't been chasing him. The

amber and pine scent of shadows is so distinct, burned into my memory from the flight over Estelle, I would recognize it out of context, a world away.

"Stalking me from the shadows, Wendy Darling?" asks Peter. "I didn't take you for that type, but I have to admit, I'm intrigued."

I realize then that I've run straight into his chest. He must have heard me coming with that fae hearing of his, and turned around to catch me in his arms. One cradles the small of my back, the other hand follows the path of my shoulder until he's stroking my cheek with the back of his palm.

He leaves a chill everywhere he touches. Like breathing the fresh winter air after being stuck in a smoking cabin.

"You just left," I say, and immediately realize it was the wrong thing to say.

Peter cranes his head, an amused smirk flickering on the edges of his mouth. "Perhaps I liked the idea of *you* following *me* for once? Just how far into the shadows are you willing to trail me, Wendy Darling?" In horror, I watch as Peter's wings turn to shadows, wrapping in front of him until they cover my eyes with the gentlest touch. "Do you crave the dark?"

Everything is black, magnifying the feel of his hand against the skin of my face.

"The only thing I crave is the truth."

From the darkness comes a chuckle that has my spine crawling, a haunting that's as familiar as the silk of my pillowcase back home. "We both know that's a lie."

My throat tightens, my body stiffening underneath his touch. A million questions swirl in my mind. For years, all I've expected from the Shadow Keeper is to steal me away. To make me into some melding of slave and concubine. I've spent years expecting him to strip me of everything I am, of my identity, my very being, until the memories of who I once was fade away and there's nothing but a fragment of me left.

But now that I'm here, I'm beginning to wonder if the anticipation of such a fate hasn't been chipping away at me already. Sanding me down until I'm barely a shadow of the woman I might have become had I been ignorant of my future.

I've made peace with the emptiness in my soul. I've embraced the nothingness.

"I'd just like to know what I'm to expect from you. Grant me that at least," I say into the darkness, surprised by how my voice doesn't shake, even if it does scrape my throat on the way out.

"Whatever do you mean?"

Frustrated with the Shadow Keeper's fingers stroking my cheek, I pull away, wincing. "I thought—" My throat tightens. I can barely get the words out. This isn't the type of thing I've ever spoken to anyone about. "I was under the impression you wanted me. That I was supposed to be a gift."

The air turns stagnant. "Is that what you want, Wendy Darling? For me to want you?"

"No." The word comes out just emphatically enough not to sound convincing. A blush rises to my cheeks, and Peter must sense it, because he retracts his shadows into his back, where they take the solid form of wings once more.

Peter scans the blotches spotting my skin, then says, carefully, "The woman your mother bargained with doesn't have friends. Only lovers and slaves. Sometimes both. You, Wendy Darling, are no gift."

When he removes his hand from my cheek, the refreshing chill disappears with it, leaving behind the numbness of extreme exposure to the cold.

CHAPTER 13

By the time I wander back to the main living room, the boys are gathered around John, besieging my brother with questions.

"Where are you from?"

"Why did Peter bring you here?"

"Don't be stupid, Freckles. He doesn't remember."

"Nettle says he remembers."

"Nettle is an attention-seeking idiot."

The blond, spindly boy in the corner, whose nose looks like it's been punched enough to be permanently crooked in the upward direction, sneers.

So that one's Nettle.

I mark him to question later.

"I can't answer a dozen questions at once," says John, whose face grows paler with each word. He's clutching Michael's shoulder with his uninjured hand.

"It's a shame you had to slice that off just to get in," says a boy with dark brown skin and coiled black hair cut close to his scalp. He points at John's stump of a finger.

"I think it's pretty diehard," says Smalls.

"Yeah, all of us are missing something already," says Freckles, before flicking his neighbor on the skull. "Up here."

"If you idiots don't shut up, the new guy is going to pass out from that wound of his before we get any answers," says Simon, who appears very much to be the head of the group, all dashing smiles and charisma.

John glances at me from behind the swarm of adolescent boys, exasperation written all over his face. It would be humorous if we hadn't been dealt so much tragedy today. If I couldn't read the pain of loss on my brother's face so easily, in the weariness that sits like stagnant water behind his glassy eyes.

He looks so, so tired. And John has never been one to enjoy crowds.

I take a step forward, making sure to step on a twig this time. It snaps, and slowly the host of boys crane their necks over to me.

Honestly, the way the teenage boys look at me, you would have thought none of them had ever seen a girl before. John seems to notice it too, because he clears his throat to redirect the boys' attention. It's to no avail.

Only Victor, the boy with shadows underneath his eyes, seems uninterested in my presence.

Simon's face lights up in a smile, and he crosses the room, bowing low before me, taking my hand and kissing my knuckles with a sparkle in his eyes. "My lady."

"You don't know she's a lady."

"Yeah, she could very well be a peasant."

"Nah, Peter wouldn't bother bringing back a peasant."

"You'll have to forgive us. We're motherless orphans, after all," says Simon. "Welcome to the Lost Boys."

"The Lost Boys?" I ask, slightly endeared by the nickname this group of outcasts has come up with for themselves, though I have plenty of questions for them.

Simon's grin is dazzling, the type that instantly makes you want to be his friend. "Yep, I'm Simon, but I'm assuming you already figured that out." He winks, amused by his own presumptuousness.

"This"—he points to the boy with dark brown skin who expressed lament over John's injury—"is Benjamin. Nettle's the one in the corner with his nose glued to the ceiling. Smalls is the baby. This is Joel"—I note a handsome boy with lightly tanned skin and shrewd green eyes—"Victor over here's the one who looks like he's been infected with vampirism. And these are the Twins." Simon gestures to two boys in the corner, both with shaved ivory heads.

"And what are your names?" I ask.

Neither of them answer.

"Don't bother trying to figure out their names. We've lived with them for years and can't tell them apart, anyway."

"What are their names, just in case I figure it out?" I ask.

Simon shrugs. "Not sure. We've called them the Twins for so long, we've all forgotten by this point. I'm fairly sure even they can't remember."

Again, something twists in my stomach. "How did you all end up here? And...what is this place?"

The boys let out amused laughs, but the noise dies down when they witness the confusion on my face.

"That wasn't a joke, stupid," says Freckles, slapping Smalls on the back of the head.

"I knew it wasn't a joke."

Simon is the only one who doesn't look amused. He raises an eyebrow. "You remember how you got here?"

I frown, exchanging a glance with John. "Of course I do. We only just arrived."

A frown flickers across Simon's features, but he schools it into a smile quickly enough. "Well, that just made you three the most interesting thing to happen to Neverland in well, ever, I suppose."

"Did you come to Neverland very young, then?" I ask, imagining Peter rounding up a band of street urchin toddlers, though the image is as ephemeral as the shadows themselves.

"Not exactly," says Simon, his pointed ears flicking.

"We just don't remember what happened to us before," pipes up Smalls from the back.

"Well, except for Nettle," Joel snickers.

Nettle doesn't appear amused, but he doesn't defend himself to the other boys either.

"You'll have to tell us some stories from the world you hail from," says Simon. "We get pretty bored around here. Would do us some good, especially the younger ones."

My throat goes dry. "I don't have any stories."

It's not true, not in the least, but I'm not ready to tell these hopeful, excited-looking boys about a world that's just as dreary as the one they inhabit.

"That's a shame," says Simon, disappointment flickering in the corners of his smile. "Well, I suppose we should get you oriented to your new home, then. This is the Den. There's an extra room at the end of that hallway right there that the three of you can share. That is, unless you'll be staying with Peter."

My cheeks flush scarlet. "No. No, I won't be."

Simon nudges me. "Just checking. Wasn't sure if Peter had kidnapped himself a bride or something."

My stomach twists with unease, which Simon must pick up on, because he winces apologetically, then swiftly changes the subject. "We're the Lost Boys—sorry, I think I already said that. Probably don't have to do much imagining to figure out how we came up with the name. It's not all that original, despite what Benjamin will tell you."

I examine the surrounding boys, some barely two years younger than me. Though each one of them has a set of pointed-tipped ears, so even the youngest, Smalls, could very well be ten years my senior.

Fae in my world were cursed with mortality during the War, but from what I've read in books, fae from other realms live several centuries, to the point that some scholars believe them to be immortal, as one has never been known to die of old age. Granted, it's not all that surprising none of them make it that long, when they tend to be bloodthirsty deceivers who rack up enemies faster than a drunk does a tab at the local tavern.

Once Simon is done with the introductions, the boys bombard me with questions, having given up entirely on John and Michael.

"What's your world like?"

"Did you bring any food in your pockets?"

But then Victor, the sullen one in the corner, speaks up. "I take it you're orphans too."

Not a question.

My blood runs cold, the memory of my parents' deaths still fresh, the scent of their spilled blood still caking my throat.

Orphans.

I feel as if I might throw up.

"I think we'd like to be shown to our rooms now," I say.

Simon flicks a quieting glare at the other boys, who slowly cease their rambling.

Then he leads us to a dingy room where I wonder if we'll live out the rest of our days.

If we even make it through them.

THERE'S no door to the room John, Michael, and I are to inhabit. Just a curtain of leaves draped over a cavity dug into the wall of earth. Now that we have a moment of quiet, devoid of the boys' incessant questions, tonight's events encroach on me. Just like the realization that the world is up there, and I'm stuck here, beneath the surface. The ground itself feels as if it's suffocating me, like it might cave in on me at any moment. For years, I've sought escape from the shadows, secretly craving the shadows themselves. But never once did I consider darkness would come from the earth itself, cutting me off from the sun and the brush of fresh air against my skin.

There are no windows down here for me to crack. No shadows to cast a lantern on and pretend to banish. The shadows are not as alluring when there's no light around to distinguish them, no illumination to flee into when the darkness gets too close.

The room itself is simple, decorated with a bear-skin rug on the floor, nothing on the walls.

There are three cots in the room, bare except for the blankets Simon had the other boys fetch us. Michael curls up on his and goes to sleep. I imagine he needs to recharge after expending so much emotional energy with the reaping tree, even if the faerie dust did work to calm him. He's always done that. Escaped the room and hidden away for a while until he regains control over his body, at which point he'll wander back to us.

All my life, everyone has acted as if there's something strange about Michael, but I wonder if he's the only one who has any of this figured out.

John doesn't curl up on his cot. Instead, he sits on the earth with his back propped up against the wall, his elbows resting on his knees as he peers at his bandaged hand.

He's staring at his finger, but that's not the loss he's contemplating.

"I'm so sorry, John," I whisper.

Slowly, he cranes his head up to me. "Don't go and try to make out like this is all your fault," he says, his voice heavy, resigned. "It's the type of thing characters in dramas do, and it makes it seem as if the world is concerned with them above all else. It's insufferable and inaccurate," he says, matter-of-factly. But then a cool smile tugs at the wrinkles beside my brother's eyes, magnified by his spectacles. "I've had a rather bad day for you, a supporting character, to go and make it worse by pretending this isn't all about me."

I let out a laugh, one that frosts the air in front of my lips, and soon my brother and I are laughing so hard, we're both clutching our stomachs. But then our gazes lock onto John's wounded hand, the way he's so poorly wrapped it. The laughter explodes into something more manic, until it's indistinguishable from our sobs.

Eventually the hysteria fades, and the silence between us takes us with it, lulling us precariously close to the edge of despair.

"I know it's just a truth my mind has to work through," says my brother, "but I can't seem to wrap myself around the fact that they're gone."

"It's someone else's blood," I say, nodding in agreement.

"Lookalike actors they hired in advance, knowing the pirates would attack."

"They must have paid them quite well to die in their stead," I say.

John shrugs. "It would surprise you what people would do for money."

I chuckle, and the air scratches my throat. Eventually, we settle into a quiet that feels treacherous. The kind that might consume us whole. John's right, the death of our parents doesn't quite seem real, nor do the events of the evening. Which is strange, given the way this night ended the way it was always supposed to.

One would think I would have been prepared.

But I suppose it's only natural to assume the inevitable can't in fact happen to us. Isn't that what humans do with death all the time? Set aside the only thing in life that's actually guaranteed to happen. Determine to think about it later, then feign shock when it appears at our doorstep, just like it always promised it would.

"Permission to take up the role of the person around which the world revolves?" I ask.

"Permission granted."

"Do you think he killed them because of me?"

My question hangs in the air for a moment.

"I think it's probably down to how you define 'because of.'"

My stomach sinks, but I appreciate my brother's honesty. It's always been the raw sort, the kind that others find coarse, but John's mind is technical. He sees truth and filters out the lies that would attempt to warp it, dilute it.

There's a kindness in that as well. To hear the truth spoken, with all the pain it carries with it. It's not as if I don't know the truth deep down anyway. It's not as if I can't feel it scraping against our insides.

John just surrenders a blade to it, so it can actually cut its way out.

"He claimed they wronged him. Took something—someone—of

his away. He thought killing me would hurt them the same way it hurt him."

John peers down at his wounded hand, not looking at me, then shrugs. "The man was a disillusioned captain turned pirate. Or *privateer*, as most haughty pirates prefer to think of themselves. He probably ran a merchant voyage for Pa and Ma at some point. More than likely, they ran into trouble at sea and someone he loved was lost. Then he spent years unable to grapple with the truth of what an unfair realm we live in and decided it was easier to blame our parents."

"He didn't seem completely illogical when I spoke to him. Do you think he might have had a legitimate complaint?"

John looks at me knowingly.

"What?" I ask.

"You do this thing where you betray what you believe in the form of questions."

A knot forms in my throat. Not because I feel exposed, but because my brother has taken the time to get to know my tells.

"What's your hypothesis, Wendy?"

I sigh, burying my face in my hands. "I don't know."

John shifts, and I know he's staring me down. Challenging me.

I'm always so afraid the truth will hurt others. I forget that some people crave it, while others possess the ability to examine it without feeling.

"I wonder if somehow they were more at fault than we'd like to believe. The looks they exchanged when he asked if they knew who he was... They were hiding something."

When I glance up at my brother, he's thoughtfully picking at the bandage on his hand. "I got into some of Father's accounting books last year. He'd run up quite a bit of debt in the past few years. With as much enthusiasm as he has—had—for life, I could see him making rash decisions in an attempt to pay off the debts, assuming all would work out fine. The most reasonable conclusion is that Father pressured someone to set sail under treacherous conditions. Perhaps he sent the captain off during a storm, or worse, in a vessel that had no business being in the water. And then Father's enthusiasm wasn't enough to carry it through to its destination. The captain must have lost someone along the way."

"I didn't know Father was in debt."

John doesn't explain why that might be. He doesn't have to. Not with the weight of my failed dowry hanging around my neck.

"Did you figure out what the Shadow Keeper wants from you when you chased him down?"

I shake my head. "That's the strange thing. He's always tried to convince me to come with him. But now that I'm here, he acts like he doesn't want me at all. Like..."

John cranes his head. I know better than to think I'm a match for my brother's curiosity.

"Almost like I'm meant to be some sort of punishment."

"You do have that gaping Mark on your face. Perhaps he displeased whoever cursed you and she hopes he'll fall in love with a woman Marked to another. That he'll be eaten alive with jealousy."

"Perhaps," I say.

"As long as whatever it is keeps him away from you," John concedes.

I can't help but agree. Little has gone my way tonight, but at least I'm not being forced to bed a stranger. At least I have the comfort of having my brothers nearby.

"I'll figure out a way to get us home," I tell my brother.

He looks at me a long time from behind his spectacles, his hair disheveled. I can practically feel the pain in his heart, like I'm the one with the missing finger, and it's my pulse pounding. "I'll be impressed when you make that happen, considering we don't have a home to go back to."

CHAPTER 14

The next morning at breakfast—a spread of wild berries, roasted pine nuts, and spindly red citrus fruits—Simon recites The Lost Boy code of conduct to us.

First, and most importantly: There's no trying to escape Neverland. Apparently, this rule is to do with safety and not the fact that Peter is a maniacal overlord intent on kidnapping the young.

John seems less than convinced.

"Most of the island is free range, but we're to be back in the Den by last light, no exceptions," says Simon.

"Makes sense," says John. "I assume the wildlife is most active at night. Do you set traps during the day?"

Simon appears impressed, if not a tad annoyed that John is a know-it-all. I can't blame him.

John is a know-it-all. Always has been.

"And what of the part of the island that's off-limits?" I ask.

"Ah, Wendy Darling, always looking for the boundaries in which she can cage herself," says an amused voice.

Those at the table go quiet in reverent awe. Except for John, who bristles, and Michael, who couldn't care less about Peter's entrance.

He waltzes in like a prince, flicking a few of the boys on the ears on the way, stealing the plumpest berries off their plates. But he doesn't stop with them. Instead, he appears behind me, pressing his fingertips into my shoulders.

There are legends of fae males claiming human females. Of the gentle glamour they seep into their prey over countless touches, their magic building up over time.

If there's a wall to keep it out, I raise it. But there's no ignoring the gentle flare of delight that crops up in my belly at Peter's obvious claiming. In the hushed corners of my mind, I know that as soon as he lets go of me, the thrill will dissipate and dread will seep in to fill its gaps.

"Did you tell our guests what the last rule is?" Peter asks Simon.

I expect Simon to flash a smile. Instead, he glances at me and blushes.

I can't help it. I crane my neck up toward Peter, drinking in his every word.

"No girls," Peter says, flashing me a smirk.

As soon as he releases his grip, the dam holding back my good sense bursts. Fear of him, of my reaction to him, drenches the tantalizing attraction that swarmed me just moments ago. How long until Peter's glamour finds a foothold? How long until it overcomes me so completely, there's no flushing it out when he leaves the room?

"Obviously, we're happy to make an exception for you," says Simon, placatingly, if not apologetically. I can't help but notice the way his shoulders relax when Peter steps away from me.

John rolls his eyes. "And how glad we are for that."

"How very glad indeed," pipes up Michael.

WHEN THE BOYS set off to hunt and set traps along the island, I volunteer to go with Simon.

Most of the boys give me an unsure look, but Victor speaks up dryly from the corner. "Please. The lot of you act like because she's a female, she can't tie a knot."

I neglect to add that I could learn to wield a bow and arrow if given the opportunity. My entire life's purpose up to this point has been to snare a husband rather than dinner. Given I'd failed miserably at that, I need to prove myself *to myself* before worrying about anything else.

Simon seems rather pleased that I asked to accompany him, though John is less than thrilled. My brother might be brave, but he's practical and levelheaded enough to know it will only cause more problems if he tries to hunt with the others before his knuckle heals over, so he stays behind to keep watch on Michael.

In the end, Smalls volunteers to come with us, which doesn't seem to surprise Simon at all. "He'll be enthusiastic but utterly useless," he leans over and whispers to me.

"I'll go too," says Victor, at which Simon blinks several times.

"What? You don't want the help?" asks Victor, folding his sturdy, pale arms across his chest.

Simon clears his throat and the casual charm returns. "Of course you're welcome. You can keep Smalls in line."

Smalls, who has just dropped his fork and is scurrying to find it underneath the table, doesn't seem to notice.

OUR ESCAPE from the reaping tree is just as unpleasant as our entrance. At least I'm prepared to feel suffocated and strangled this time.

Victor and Smalls separate from us quickly, headed to check a few of the smaller traps toward the center of the island, though they'll meet up with us at the traps meant for larger game in case we need to drag a boar back to the Den.

By the time Simon and I reach the beach, the sun is mostly risen, which I find a tad disappointing.

"What's wrong?" Simon asks good-naturedly.

"I just thought it would be nice to catch the sunrise."

"You act as if you won't get another chance," he says, nudging me in the shoulder.

"Are sunrise privileges a perk to eternal captivity, then?" I ask dryly.

"Oh, don't look at it like that," says Simon, though he's clearly wincing underneath that bright smile of his.

"How should I look at it, then?"

He gestures toward the sun. "Well, I look at it as an opportunity to sleep in late for the rest of my existence."

A soft smile frames my lips. "I suppose there's that. But then you miss the sunrise."

"Trust me. Get used to the feeling of sleeping in as long as your heart desires, and you won't be worried about missing anything."

I nod, standing in the bright sun for a moment and letting myself soak it in. I always imagined that being captured by the Shadow Keeper would mean never feeling the gentle caress of sunlight on my skin, but it's here. Granted, it's cold on this island, and Simon has to give me his overcoat to supplement the little my ball gown does to protect me from the elements.

"We've got to get you some furs or something," he says. "Though that would be unfortunate, considering how pretty you look in that dress." I scrunch my nose at his shameless flirting, causing Simon to shrug. "Worth a shot. You probably are the only female I'll ever get a chance with."

"Simon, I—"

"Just teasing," he says, nodding for me to follow him down the shore. I do, reveling in the way my feet feel pressing into the dark sand. I was right last night; it's the color of charcoal. Between it, the steady spray of the frigid ocean water, and the dark cliffs in the distance, there's a sort of gloominess here that feels comfortable. Like it's the same color and scent and texture as my soul, and I could melt right into it and finally be one with something, even if it's not a sentient being that would know me back.

I follow behind Simon for a while, allowing the crash of the waves to drown out his vibrant chatter. After a while, we veer off the beach and into the forest, where Simon shows me how to set a trap aiming to capture a wild hare. When I make one on my own and it snaps shut at the gentlest touch, the slightest thrill ripples through me.

I'm not fond of the idea of coming back here and finding an animal dead in my trap, but just the feel of my hands doing something other than embroidering, or playing the pianoforte, or any number of things my fingers only learned to do so that someone might place a ring upon one of them—it sets something aflame within me. It's barely a flicker, but it's pleasant against my listless heart all the same.

"Are you going to cry when we come back and there's a cute little bunny wrapped up in this?" Simon asks.

"Why? Did you the first time?"

Simon laughs. "Most definitely."

We set a few more traps as Simon shows me how to spot where the underbrush is matted, marking paths where animals frequently travel. Once we're finished, we trace our own footsteps back to a nearby clearing and meet up with Victor and Smalls, who've come back empty-handed from their traps.

"No luck?" asks Simon.

"Not for us, at least," says Victor. "Though the rabbits might beg to differ."

I let out a nervous chuckle, but Simon must not appreciate Victor's joke, because he ignores him and instead shows me how the boar trap works.

There's a hole in the ground covered by a lattice of sticks, upon which is perched the bait. Above the hole is a trapping system that keeps a considerable log suspended by rope—until the boar steps on the sticks, that is. We spend at least an hour with Simon and Victor showing me how to assemble and disassemble the trap.

"Who knows," says Victor when I finally get the trap assembled correctly. "Wendy here might just kill something yet."

I offer him a noncommittal noise that falls short of my intended laugh, and Simon looks up apologetically through his long, dark eyelashes as he pushes himself from the ground.

. . .

"IF WE'RE NOT CAREFUL, someone is going to come along and track us," I say, pointing at the footprints as we make our way across the beach.

"Nah," says Simon, "but even if something did, Peter would protect us."

"Is that what he's doing?" I ask. "Protecting you?"

"Of course," says Simon. "What else would he be doing?"

He says it with such nonchalance, he must be genuine. I want his confidence in Peter to be comforting, to put me at ease and convince me my brothers are safe here, but it's a monumental task to believe something so counter to everything I've been raised to think.

"It doesn't bother you that you're not allowed to leave?" I ask.

"Where you came from, were you allowed to leave?"

I stop, my mouth going dry. "I'm not sure that I ever asked to."

"Exactly. Why would we want to leave when we have all we could ever want here?"

"I thought you said you wanted to pursue a woman," I tease.

Simon gestures open-palmed at me. "Like I said, everything I could ever want, right here."

I don't miss the way his jaw ticks on the side.

I can't help it. Years of keeping my thoughts to myself have helped me hone my skills at interpreting people. Making others comfortable. I suppose some would call what I'm about to do manipulation, but I don't know the harm of it when all it does is make someone else feel seen.

"You're telling me you never think about swiping some of Peter's faerie dust and getting out of here?" I ask. When Simon bunches his brow, I add, "Just to see what it's like, then sneak back, I mean. You don't dream of finding a pretty girl you visit once every full moon or something ridiculous like that?"

Simon's shoulders relax. "I might have tried once, a few years back. Snuck into Peter's supply of faerie dust. Got my hands on a pouch, too, before a nightstalker jumped out of the trees and attacked me." He pulls down the neck of his shirt to show me the scar sliced over his collarbone. It must have been deep if the scar still mars Simon's fae skin. Then again, legends of nightstalkers claim they rip their victims' minds apart along with their bodies. It's a wonder Simon's speaking to me at all. "Peter tore it to shreds, of course. Ripped it straight out of its pounce. Started hiding the faerie dust in a storehouse on the cliffs after that, where only he can fly to get to it. He was...well, Peter doesn't ever let it show when he's upset. But he wasn't happy. All the good-natured teasing—that was all gone. At first I worried he was angry at me, but then everything went back to normal after that." Simon turns to me, examining me. "I know you're afraid of him, but you shouldn't be."

"Well," I say, tucking my hands into Simon's coat pockets. "I'm at least not afraid of you."

Simon offers me a toothy grin, then nods his head and leads us to the next trapping location.

On the way, Smalls lets out a yelp. Simon and I spin around to find him screaming and red-faced as a crab dangles out in front of him, its pincer sunk into his fingernail.

Victor keeps his hands in his pockets, unaffected by the younger boy's pain.

"You're really not going to help?" asks Simon, shooting Victor a patronizing glare before prying the pincer from Smalls's finger.

Victor shrugs. "I told him not to mess with it. He wouldn't listen to me."

Smalls whimpers, red blotches refusing to fade from his usually white cheeks. The way he clutches his hand reminds me of John after he sliced off his pinkie, so though I'd never admit it to Victor, Smalls's dramatic reaction is wasted on me as well.

"Nettle told me crabs can't reach you if you grab them from behind," Smalls attests between gasps.

"And that's why we don't listen to people who think they know more than they do," says Victor.

"Well," says Simon, examining Smalls's bleeding fingernail. "There's plenty of antiseptic at the Den. We'll at least get it cleaned up so it doesn't get infected. Victor, Winds, think you can handle the last trap?"

I'm about to protest—there's something about Victor that sets me on edge—when Victor says, "I'm sure we can manage, isn't that right, *Winds?*"

Before I can come up with an excuse to return to the Den, Simon and Smalls are gone.

VICTOR IS quiet as he leads me deep into the forest. His hands remain pocketed, his footsteps casual yet sure. He doesn't seem to be in any rush to reach the trap, though I tell myself that's probably a by-product of living on a remote island, away from the hustle of port life.

"I wouldn't be so quick to cast off that healthy skepticism if I were you," he finally says at the same moment I step on a dry twig. The combination of his voice and the snapping has me flinching, to which he offers me a wry smile. "I guess I don't have to tell you to keep your guard up, then. Though you shouldn't have agreed to come into the forest alone with me."

Slowly, I turn toward Victor, panic seizing my mind, my limbs. I fist my hands, as if that's going to do anything against a fae. I can't tell if it's a trick of the light redirected from the canopy overhead, but the shadows underneath Victor's eyes deepen.

"I'm not going to hurt you," he says, his gaze dipping to my fist. "All I meant is that you don't know that."

"Are we talking about you?" I ask, my mind flitting back to my conversation with Simon on the beach. Was Victor listening in? "Or are we talking about Peter?"

"Simon's a trusting fellow," is all Victor says.

"And you're not?"

Next to him, a butterfly lands on a flaking tree trunk. He stares at its lightning-colored wings. "I used to be."

A breeze ripples through the leaves, tiptoeing down my spine. "But then something happened."

Victor doesn't look at me. For a moment, he seems as petrified as the tree upon which the butterfly has landed.

If this were either of my brothers, or any of the other Lost Boys, for that matter, I might have reached out my hand and placed it on his shoulder. But there's a clamp on my limbs keeping me from touching Victor, from drawing any closer. "Did someone hurt you, Victor?" I whisper. "Did Peter hurt you?"

The spell over Victor snaps, and his caustic snort sends the butterfly fluttering away. "Trust me. Peter did nothing."

When I don't answer, he gives me a grim smile. "Listen. All I meant is that you need to be careful. This island isn't your friend."

"I wasn't under the impression that it was."

"Good." Victor cranes his neck, beckoning me deeper into the forest. After his ominous comment, I'm even more reticent to follow him. But we're already far enough from the Den that no one would hear if he tried to hurt me anyway.

"Victor? Can I ask you something?" I say, my throat going dry.

"Sure."

"Did you...when you lost your memories...did it happen gradually? Or had you already lost them by the time you got to Neverland?"

Victor furrows his brow, considering. "I can't remember a time in Neverland when I could recall what my life was like before. But the first several weeks we got here are hazy anyway. I'm not sure I can trust what I remember from that time."

"So you just woke up one day in Neverland—no memories of who you were?"

Victor's jaw bulges. "Something like that. Except I remember being feverish when I first got here. Throwing up all the time. Sweating through my sheets. We all were. If I still had my memories at that time, I would have been too ill to care."

I work my lip, thinking. "How long were you ill?"

Victor wipes his black hair from his brow. "Could have been a week. Could have been a year, for all I knew."

Dread settles in my stomach. Did Peter take the boys' memories or did the island? I've heard of merchants falling terribly ill when first arriving in new lands, their bodies unaccustomed to the illnesses that inhabit specific regions. It's dreadful, but I'd be more comforted if I knew for sure that the boys lost their memories before they came here. Otherwise, if it really is the work of a strange illness or a devious magic that inhabits the island, what's to stop the same thing from happening to me? To John and Michael?

For the rest of our trip, I take account of every memory I can muster. The feel of the clock tower bricks, the rust of the ladder. The sound of Michael's high-pitched screams when he was a baby. Every story Mother ever read me before bed. The face of every tutor I strove to please.

The memories are still there—but for how long?

When we reach the trap, it's already caught our meal for the day. A hare is snared in its coil, its body hardened in death, its black eyes wide and glassy.

Later, when Simon asks me if I cried, I lie and tell him I did.

CHAPTER 15

*E*ver since I was a little girl, people have had a tendency to spill their secrets at my feet. Drunk middle-aged women over for dinner at my parents' manor would tell me that their husbands had never touched them, not even on their wedding night. Men would wander off to the balcony to smoke, find me perched atop the railing, my feet dangling over the edge, and confide in me that they'd never felt successful enough for their titles. Or they'd tell me about the working-class woman they let their aristocratic parents talk them out of marrying. Every one of them had a gaping hole in their soul, one that success and riches had never even begun to fill.

I guess I have one of those faces. Gentle eyes free of judgment. Or perhaps I've always seemed the type of girl with too few friends to risk telling their secrets.

Either way, people do not hold their tongues in my presence.

Guilt taps against my soul as I remember the walk earlier today with Simon. He's a nice boy, one I think might wish to be a friend to me here.

But it had worked.

All it had taken was asking him if he'd ever wanted to escape, and he'd told me exactly where Peter keeps his faerie dust reserves.

Besides, I have to get John and Michael out of here. Something is off about this island, these boys. There's a grisly truth hiding in the shadows, crawling in the canopy, waiting to strike. I'm not sure what happened here that has Victor so embittered—that has Simon so nervous around Victor—but I keep replaying something he said.

Peter did nothing.

He'd almost told me in the forest, but something had stopped him.

I keep counting up my memories like I'm a vendor in the market numbering my stock to make sure a petty thief hasn't run off with anything.

There are memories I wouldn't mind this island taking from me —the feel of velvet underneath my fingernails and hot, greedy breath against my flesh. The last flash of light in my parents' eyes before their spirits slipped from their bodies through the gashes in their throats.

But I won't let this island take my brothers' memories.

I won't let it make me forget who Peter is.

I'm afraid of what I might succumb to if I let myself forget his dreadful shadows, the way they taunted me as a child.

As if thinking of them invited them in, the thought of shadows caressing my skin slithers through me, tantalizing me with their beautiful lies.

I could take away your pain.

If I can't remember, I'm not sure I'll have the strength to resist.

It's a shame Peter doesn't keep the faerie dust in the Den. Although, the idea of sneaking through Peter's quarters sends chills against the lining of my stomach. Perhaps it's better he hides it in the cliffs.

I've been wracking my brain all day to figure out a way to scale the cliffs at the edge of the beach. I almost asked for John's help. He has the sort of mind that would probably engineer a system for us to scale the cliffs twice as quickly as mine will take. But I don't want John coming with me. He's sacrificed enough already for our family. Not just his finger, but the time and mental energy he spent—wasted—on trying to find a way out of our parents' bargain.

Besides. Someone needs to stay behind to watch Michael.

So I wait until night falls, though I have to guess at it since there are no windows in our room, and for John's and Michael's breaths to deepen.

Then I sneak on the pads of my feet and make my way outside.

EVERY TIME I pass through the reaping tree, the process is shorter. Like there's less and less for the tree to take from my innermost being.

I try not to think about that as I break into a run across the wet sand of the beach. The tide has come in, swallowing up most of the beach's surface, but there's still enough of a path for me to run down without having to worry about clambering barefoot through the brush, though occasionally I have to traverse piles of rocks.

The kelp that lines the beach during the day sloshes up with the tide, wrapping its slimy claws around my ankles. Simon told me earlier that the awful-looking plants with shiny bulbs for heads are actually edible, but even the idea of that makes me nauseous. Every time one grazes my skin, I can't shake the feeling that their tendrils are like those of the jellyfish, just waiting to wrap around my limbs and drag me paralyzed underneath the sea.

The bluish moon has already traversed a quarter of tonight's black sky by the time I make it all the way down the beach and to the cliffs that bar it from the rest of the island.

I stare upward, frustrated at how difficult it is to see out here. I had counted on the darkness, grabbing a lantern from the hall, but it does little to illuminate my path with the thick fog that creeps up from the surface of the crashing water.

Waves slap against the stubborn facade of the cliffs, whipping the rocks into a slow submission.

Luckily, the cliffs themselves are rather jagged. Not only does the texture provide plenty of handholds, but as I stare upward with my hands on my hips, I glimpse alcoves and small plateaus that will make for adequate rest stops.

So I loop my lantern through my belt—Simon supplied it to me along with a set of trousers and a tunic after commenting on how impractical my ball gown was—and climb.

The rocks at the base of the cliffs are still slick from the waves lapping up and staining the bottom surface, but once I scale several feet carefully, the rocks dry out.

It's effortful work, and I can't help but thank my past self for climbing the clock tower's outer brick facade all those years.

John doesn't know about that, of course. He thinks I only ever climbed the ladder.

It's a strange thing, thinking about my younger self partaking in such recklessness. But there's something about the pounding of blood against my temples, the way my lungs fight for breath, that clears my head of anything besides what's directly before me.

Not falling—I can focus on that.

I never was able to banish the fears of what all might transpire in the future. But climb high enough, and the simple need to survive drove them out for just a moment.

Eventually, our excursions to the top of the clock tower didn't affect me like they once did. The ladder felt too stable, too easy, the rungs a tether that kept me from floating away from the knowledge of what my future held.

I was twelve when I first climbed the clock tower from the outside.

It's positioned in the center of my parents' manor, in the middle of a gardened courtyard. Meaning I had to make my climbs in the middle of the night. That wasn't so much of a problem, though. Sleepless nights made my acquaintance from a young age.

The clock tower is styled with bricks stacked perpendicular to one another. The alternating pattern looks expensive, but it serves the unintended functionality of making it possible to scale. It had taken years for me to build up the strength and endurance to make it to the top, of course. I'm not sure how many nights I spent on one of the decorative platforms jutting from the tower, mustering up the courage to climb back down.

One time, I slipped and landed on a platform below. I broke my ankle and told my mother I'd tripped down the staircase.

Still, scaling the outside of the clock tower did what the inside ladder could no longer accomplish. It allowed me to drown the fear of something I couldn't control in the exhilaration of something I could. There's something empowering about using a fear you choose to smother the one you don't.

Of course, the clock tower wasn't quite this high.

When I come to the fifth alcove, I'm sweating so profusely my palms have gone slick and I have to rest on the platform for a while until my hands dry again. It takes longer than I want it to with the humidity fighting against me.

But I slowly fall into a rhythm. Climb, rest, climb, rest, until I finally reach the top of the cliffs.

There's part of me that longs to gaze down, to take in the great heights which I just climbed, but wisdom reminds me that if I don't find the faerie dust, I'll have to climb back down. So perhaps looking isn't in my best interest.

The cliffs themselves jut out over the water and come to a point. It's there at the tip I find a ramshackle warehouse. I can hardly believe my luck as I race over to the dingy structure. When I reach the door, I find it locked, but that was to be expected.

I pull out one of the many hairpins left over from how my hair was styled for the ball. I haven't been able to bring myself to take it down. Not when it was my mother who insisted on running a brush gently through my tresses before the maids set to work on their task.

I can't think of my mother now. Not when John and Michael are still alive and I need to keep my focus honed on saving them.

When we were ten, John and I got on a spy kick and read all the books in our parents' massive library on the subject. It took us several weeks of sheer determination to learn how to pick a lock. Looking back, I realize it was quite impressive for ten-year-olds, which is likely why my parents allowed it to persist. Eventually, after many grueling fights and bickering and tears that rendered John's glasses smudged and useless, we successfully picked the lock to our father's study.

Of course, as soon as he found us roaming around in there, we were sentenced to grounding for a month. During our imprisonment, we continued to practice from our separate rooms. By the time our punishment was over, we'd become rather proficient at the process.

I tenderly place the two pins into the lock, feeling for the gentle give that will tell me the first is in place. Nurturing the lock takes a while, especially since my hands are still shaking from the exertion of my climb, but eventually it sends the feedback I'm looking for down the little pin. Like it's pressing a gentle hand to my shoulder to urge me to continue.

There's a rhythm to lock picking that reminds me of strumming my fingers against a harp, losing myself and my thoughts in the gentle hum of its strings. My excitement builds as I feel the tension of my pick, indicating I'm about to succeed, but then a sensation I haven't experienced in a long while washes over me.

A cool dread seeps through my veins, begging me to let it in. And now I'm not the one breaking in but the one being broken into, the walls around my mind and heart crumbling as the darkness seeps into the cracks, threatening to overcome me.

Someone, a woman, cries out in the distance, her beautiful voice ringing in my ears.

The makeshift picks fall to the earth, lost to the dust that's the same shade as I cover my ears with my palms to drown out the sound.

Horror, damp and dark, slips through the spaces my fingertips can't seal, whispering atrocities in my ears. Begging me to come and see, to come and lay my eyes upon its terrors.

Shadows, dreadful and fierce, take shape around me, forming

into shapes of people, tall and small, adults and children chanting words I can't grasp. And through it all, a woman's voice slices deep into my soul. Screaming, begging for me to listen, to drown in her sorrow with her.

They urge me to turn around, to face them for what they truly are, to hear their stories, but I know these kinds of stories. The ones that will torment me until I'm paralyzed, feverish.

Except now, my mother won't find me seizing on the ground. My father won't pick me up and carry me to the soft comforts of my bed, where my mother will place a cool cloth against my head and nurse me back to health, reassuring me that the shadows aren't real. That my nightmares, the visions, aren't real.

The nightmares beg to differ.

CHAPTER 16

I'm paralyzed, my hands clutching the door handle for support, my knees digging into the dirt as I kneel, refusing to turn around.

Something moves behind me, something with padded feet and a growl that reverberates in my very bones.

The shadows are crying out, though whether they want me to face them or run, I can no longer tell. Their grief is so devastating, it pierces through my chest. I can't breathe, much less move.

The woman shrieks again. Her agony rips through me, conjuring the beginnings of a scream on my lips.

A hand wraps around my mouth, pressing a palm to my lips. Faintly, I taste something that reminds me of plucking honeysuckles from the hedges at the manor garden.

"Dangerous here at night," Peter whispers into my ear as, quietly, he pulls me into his arms, forcing me to rest my weight not upon the door, but upon his heaving chest.

And then he turns us around.

"See?"

My eyes go wide, my breathing ragged as my sense of the

present returns to me. The shadows drain from the edges of my vision.

And then I see it.

The feline creature stalks us in the moonlight, its silky black coat glossy and tantalizing. Fangs protrude from its ebony lips, dripping venom into the earth beneath.

Nightstalker.

Dreamwalker.

"What do you say, Wendy Darling? Would you like for me to hand you over to it? Were you looking for a quick end when you snuck up here, away from my protection?"

Fear seizes me, but this time it doesn't paralyze me. I shake my head softly underneath his grip.

"You have to remember to look behind you, Wendy Darling. You can't ignore what might be stalking you from your blind spot. Do you understand?"

I swallow and nod.

"Good," Peter says, and I can feel the way his lips curl into a treacherous smile, the tips of them grazing my ear.

And then Peter moves.

It's so fluid, I wonder if he morphs into shadows to pass through my petrified body before materializing in front of me. Long, leathery wings stretch out behind him.

The feline creature whimpers, ever so slightly, as it realizes what a large foe it's come across, but it digs its haunches in, nonetheless.

It pounces, its lithe body cutting through the air, but Peter is faster. He jumps, his wings spreading out above him, obscuring the night's moon as he flies above the creature, digging his fingers into the nape of its neck and plucking it from the air, mid-pounce.

With the grace of a panther, he slams it to the ground, landing atop its exposed belly, his boot against its throat as it writhes.

Peter shifts his weight, and something crunches.

I watch as the feline struggles for breath, but it's too late. Its throat is already crushed beneath Peter's boot. Slowly, the writhing of its limbs turns to twitching, until before us the petrifying creature lies dead.

"Wendy Darling," says Peter, eyes like coal as he turns toward me and extends his hand. "That bordered upon unpleasant. I'd rather you not make me do that again."

THE FLIGHT back to the tree is more terrifying than the ascent.

It's the sensation when your body finally catches up to the fact that it was almost severed from your soul. The anger and betrayal it harbors toward your mind for carelessly placing it in harm's way.

Of course, then there's the fact that I'm back in the arms of the Shadow Keeper. And that's dangerous in and of itself.

If Peter is angry, he doesn't show it. Really, he hardly shows anything except for a mild disdain for my foolish actions. He says nothing the entire flight back. It's not as if I have anything to say either.

I think it's fairly obvious what I was attempting. No need to address it, except to say, "John didn't know what I was planning to do."

"That much is obvious, or he would have been at your side."

Something twists in my belly. That my brother's loyalty to me is so obvious to even a creature as unattached as the Shadow Keeper.

When we reach the reaping tree, Peter lands, then gestures for me to go on ahead. Once the roots deposit me in the Den, I try to scamper away, but Peter is right behind me. Before I can escape down the hall, he sidles in front of me, blocking my path.

"Why did you try to escape?"

I shuffle on my feet. "Because I don't like being kept a prisoner."

Peter cranes his head to the side. "You don't?"

I bristle. "Of course I don't. Who would?"

A knowing look concentrates Peter's features as he crosses his arms. His eyes are back to blue now. I suppose he wasn't in his shadow form sufficient time for the effects to linger long. "Explain to me why you don't want to be my prisoner, Wendy Darling."

"Because I'm not free. Because my brothers aren't free."

"Free to do what?"

"Free to..." I stop, something catching in my throat.

Peter advances, though he doesn't touch me. Instead, he examines me with those glinting blue eyes of his. "What is it you'd so love to do out there that you can't do here?"

"That's not the point. The point is that I can't leave."

"Where can't you leave? This island? Neverland? Your manor? Estelle? Or..." He places his thumb on my temple and caresses it. "Is it here you long to escape?"

I swallow, wrapping my arms around my waist and turning away, brushing aside his touch as if that will sweep away the thorns his words leave behind.

"Getting off this island won't free you from what's lurking in your own head."

A lump rises in my throat. "You have no idea what's in my head."

Peter raises an amused brow. "Is that so? Tell me, what was it that had you so paralyzed by the warehouse that you couldn't even support your own weight? What had a woman fearless enough to climb a cliffside with bare feet keeled over with terror? It wasn't the nightstalker. You didn't even know it was there when I arrived. So tell me, I insist, what makes you believe I'm the one imprisoning you?"

I blink away tears, and though anger rises in my throat, I can't form the words to answer.

"Goodnight, Wendy Darling," says Peter, before disappearing into the shadows.

Faintly, in the edges of my memory, I remember a voice caressing me from the chaise in my bedroom.

I could take away your pain.

I DON'T GO BACK to my room. Not yet. Not when I'm barely holding back sobs. I don't know if it's the aftermath of my adrenal response to almost being ripped to shreds, or if it's the dread of having my memories slip away from me. The eerie anticipation of what Peter might make me into once there's nothing left of my mother's careful warnings, once the little bit of myself I managed to tuck away, to salvage during my upbringing, is gone. Will I forget that John and Michael are my brothers? Peter wasn't keen on bringing them to Neverland. It could very well be that if I forget they exist, he could dispose of them without worrying about me giving him trouble over it. Our deal was that he would bring them to Neverland, not that he would allow them to stay forever.

Of course, I suppose if Peter wanted me to forget, he could make good on the bargain I offered him.

Anything. A blank check, for him to use as he pleases. Absent-mindedly, I run my thumb over the silvery ovals that mark the crease of my inner right elbow.

I suppose if he hasn't used it to wipe my memories, it's only because he has something more strategic in mind. Or perhaps because the island will do the memory-wiping for him.

"Winds?" someone asks from the doorway to the Den. I look up to find Freckles standing there, shuffling between his feet awkwardly.

I'm not sure when the Lost Boys convened and decided to call me Winds. Maybe I'm just sensitive right now because I feel my memories, my control, slipping like oil through my fingertips, but I snap, "That's not my name."

His eyes widen, and guilt instantly pierces my chest.

"I'm sorry. I didn't mean—"

I sigh, wiping tears from my cheek, embarrassed by my outburst. "I know. I'm sorry. You can call me Winds," I say, remembering how I didn't mind when Simon said it only a few hours ago.

Freckles actually smiles at that, and my chest cracks open a little bit. He's tended to be a tad prickly in my estimation, but there's a softness in his cheeks I haven't noticed until now.

"Are you missing home?" he asks, approaching me like one might a stray kitten hiding in a gutter.

My throat bobs, stinging. I don't know how to answer that question, so I don't. "It's not that, so much as I don't like the idea of—" Propriety stops me. Freckles probably doesn't want to hear me complaining about the potential of losing my memories when he's already lost his.

"You're afraid of what the island might do to your head, aren't you?" Light from the dwindling fire in the hearth dances across the smattering of freckles on his nose and cheeks.

Hindered from replying by the throbbing pain in my throat, I nod, clutching my knees to my chest I huddle against the wall.

Freckles pivots back and forth on his feet for a moment, then holds out a finger. "Wait here," he says, before scrambling off.

He returns a few minutes later with his hand behind his back. When he sits cross-legged on the floor in front of me, he whips the hidden object out and presses it into my hands.

The wrapping is hasty at best, a broad leaf bent around the object's edges and secured with twine. When I open it, out falls a leather journal.

"Peter got it for me on one of his missions to the outside realms," says Freckles, undoing the leather strap and opening the journal for me. When he notices me staring at the rough edges on the inner spine where it's obvious several pages have been ripped out, he blushes. "I thought maybe if I had a pen in my hand, wrote stream-of-consciousness-like, the memories might come back to me. They never did. But hey—you still have your memories," he says, flicking me in the temple. He must instantly regret it, because he offers me a wince and tucks his hands back into his lap. "This way, even if you forget, you'll have a record of your life before that you can always go back to."

When I let out another choked sob, horror fills Freckles's face. "I'm sorry. I didn't mean to upset you."

I launch myself over to him and wrap him up in a hug, my face settling into his coarse red hair.

"Oh," he says, chuckling nervously as he pats me flat-palmed on the back.

· · ·

FRECKLES FINDS me a quill and ink before he returns to bed, leaving me curled up with the journal. I fill the first ten pages with every detail I think I might need if I wake up tomorrow with my memory wiped. It's mostly simple things: my name, that John and Michael are my brothers, that my parents died at the hands of a man named Captain Astor, but my scribbling soon turns to Peter, and once I've started, I can't seem to stop.

Every detail I include has a single purpose, which I underline and circle once my eyes start to droop with weariness.

Peter is dangerous.

As I finally crawl into bed, I clutch the journal to my chest, too afraid to set it out of sight, lest I forget that it exists tomorrow.

WHEN I WAKE the next morning, my memories remain.

It's Michael who's gone.

CHAPTER 17

*M*ichael is missing. It takes a moment to register as I jolt from bed, stuffing my journal underneath my pillow.

Panic seizes me as I consider all the worst-case scenarios as to where my brother might have wandered off to. John is still asleep, looking peaceful and drooling a bit on his cot, his spectacles tucked neatly by his pillow.

I pace back and forth, wondering if I should wake him. Together, we could cover ground more quickly. But it could very well be that Michael is just outside in the hallway. If that's the case and I'm simply overreacting, there's no reason to worry him.

In a split decision, I grab the fur coat Simon lent me and tuck it around my shoulders, determining that if I don't find Michael within the next several minutes, I'll come back to wake John.

Scouring the tunnels does me no good. It's early—Michael's internal clock has always woken him at least an hour before the sun thinks it a decent time to rise—so none of the boys are out and about either.

Except for Joel, whom I happen upon in the dining room as he squats by the hearth carved into the walls.

"Pardon me, but have you seen Michael anywhere?" I ask.

Joel flinches, which I find odd until I tell myself it's probably just because he's not used to anyone else being up this early. When he turns from the hearth, I can't help but notice the way he keeps his shoulders huddled toward the fire and away from me.

"Haven't seen him, but Peter walked by that way a little bit ago. Might could ask him," he says.

Glad for a lead, I make off toward the tunnel Joel indicated. Quickly, my mother's lessons overtake me, and I spin on my heel to thank the boy. From this angle, I can see what he's messing with in front of the fire.

It's a rodent, one he's managed to trap in a twig-knit cage. I don't much like rodents and am not sorry to see one terminated, but it's what Joel is doing with the cage that has unease piling in my gut.

Propped open with a stick is the cage door, positioned in front of the fire. The little rodent is curled up on the opposite side of the cage, trying to escape the heat. It squeaks in protest as Joel prods its bloated belly with his whittled stick, forcing it to flee directly into the fire or be skewered.

"Perhaps you could try breaking its neck instead," I offer, trying and failing to keep my voice casual.

Joel turns to me, color blotching his tanned cheeks. I can't remember if his flush was already there from the warmth of the fire.

"Good idea," he says, though he doesn't remove the cage from the proximity of the hungry flames.

I feel as if I'm going to be sick, but I can't be worrying over the fate of a rodent that's stealing our food supplies and probably carries diseases. Not when Michael is missing. So I swallow my trepidation and make off to find Peter.

Halfway down the hall, I hear the gentle and familiar sound of Michael singing. Relief washes over me, and I slow my pace. If he were frightened, his pitch would be much higher and more urgent. As it is, Michael sounds content.

I follow his voice until I reach the corner and peek around.

I got in the habit of peering in on Michael when he was young, mostly because he does some of the most clever and wonderful things when no one is watching. One time I found him cross-legged in a circlet of Mother's crystal chalices. He'd filled them to varying levels and was tapping them with a nail he'd found. To this day, I don't know where he learned you could make music that way. I like to think he just discovered it himself.

As I peer around the corner, I'm shocked to find Michael isn't alone.

Michael's standing across from Peter, who's pulled up a little stool and perched upon it. Peter's a large enough man that it hardly makes him eye level with Michael, but it's pretty close.

I tense up, immediately distrustful of this interaction. Peter can be cruel, and even if Michael is less than likely to pick up on the subtlety of Peter's humor, I've always despised it when people talk to Michael as if he's not in the room. As if he doesn't understand.

"We don't know that he doesn't understand us," I remember telling my father one day. "Even if he doesn't always grasp the meaning of the words or the metaphor, he picks up a lot through our pitch."

But there's nothing mocking in Peter's voice as he plays with Michael.

Michael's gotten his hands on a wooden toy train, but instead of placing it on the tracks, he's disconnected all the boxes, leaving the majority of the train in a horizontal line on the floor. The caboose has always been his favorite. He's got it upside down in one hand, spinning the wheels as fast as he can with the other.

I wait for Peter to take it from him, to try to make him put the train back together and play with it "the right way"—on the tracks.

Instead, Peter just takes the train engine from Michael's line, flips it upside down in his hand, and starts spinning the wheels along with Michael. At first, Michael pays him no mind. But then something extraordinary happens. Without looking at Peter, Michael sets the caboose to the side and takes the engine from Peter's hands, testing out those wheels, too.

It's complicated to explain why that snags on my heart like it does. I know it's silly, tearing up over Michael paying attention to the engine of the train instead of the caboose. But there's something about Michael wanting to explore an object because someone else did that has my heart twisting up.

Eventually, Michael goes down the line of the train cars, testing the wheels of all of them. I watch as Peter sneaks away the last car, popping the wheels off and hiding them behind his back before returning it to the line. When Michael reaches the broken toy, he stares at it, unblinking.

The two of them sit in the quiet for so long, it takes everything in me not to jump from the shadows and give Michael the words to ask for help, like I'm so used to doing.

But then he pushes the toy into Peter's lap and says, "Do you want me to fix it?"

A smile brushes across my lips. Michael's always used questions that way, but I don't have to explain as much to Peter.

"Let me fix it for you," Peter says, snapping the wheels back into place.

"It's all better now," Michael whispers, smiling pleasantly as he continues to play with the wheels.

It's so odd watching him. It's not that people outside the family have never attempted to play with Michael. It's just that, typically, they have a set way they think Michael should play, and they can't seem to understand when he isn't interested. Why would he not toss a ball back and forth with them or make the horse go to sleep in the barn, when that's how other children might do it? They mean well, of course. Everyone wants to teach Michael something. But sometimes I wonder if perhaps Michael might have more to say than others give him credit for.

I can remember countless men attempting to court me, boring me to tears with the state of their financial conquests. Often, I found I had nothing to say, not because I couldn't possibly communicate about such things, but simply because I had so little interest, my will to converse about such things dried up.

So I watch in wonder as Peter plays with Michael, yet allows my brother to take the lead.

"Wendy Darling wants to play," says Michael, and I jolt in place. I didn't realize he knew I was here, and I'm not sure I love Michael calling me by my full name like Peter does, but I emerge from the shadows, nonetheless.

"Of course I want to play."

Peter offers a hand, and when I take it hesitantly, he pulls me to the ground next to him.

"Michael here was just showing me a new way to play with the train set," he says. "I must say, I'm rather partial to it."

"The Lost Boys are on an adventure." Michael tosses the train to the side. Taking a stick from the ground, he jabs Peter in the torso like it's a sword.

I don't see him do that often—pretend with objects that don't look exactly like what they're trying to be. I can't help the smile that encroaches on my lips.

Once Peter is sufficiently stabbed, Michael loses interest in playing with us and grabs his pile of stick swords, retreating to the corner to play quietly, organizing them from shortest to longest.

Just then, Benjamin strides into the room, a knife and oblong block of wood in hand. "Oh, great! Michael is playing with the swords," he says, bouncing on his heels as a smile stretches across his deep brown cheeks. He turns to me to explain. "Those are too small for the rest of us to spar with. Beginner mistake on my part. But I'm so glad Michael's here now to play with them. It would have been dreadful if all that hard work had gone to waste. I can't help but notice that he likes the train set I made as an experiment two months ago. Perhaps, if he prefers toys with wheels, I can craft him a wagon as well."

"Benjamin here is a genius with a blade," says Peter. "He made all of our spoons and bowls."

"And forks," corrects Benjamin.

Peter smiles softly. "Those too."

When the conversation lulls to silence, Benjamin turns toward

Michael. "I noticed he doesn't talk much, but when he does, he uses quite peculiar turns of phrase. Peter says I didn't talk until I was five, but that I make up for it now."

"Yeah, now we can't get you to shut up," says Freckles, his red hair poking in all directions as he appears around the corner and chucks a wad of parchment at Benjamin. "Come on, you're supposed to be helping me chop firewood today."

Benjamin throws his hands out. "We already did that yesterday."

"Yeah, and then half of it disappeared. Wonder where it went," Freckles says, chuckling as he stares pointedly at the block of wood in Benjamin's hand.

I glance back and forth between Michael and Benjamin, who is now holding the block of wood behind his back. Something deep inside me swells with warmth.

"Thanks for playing with him," I tell Peter once Benjamin and Freckles leave, offering Peter what must be the most uncomfortable smile ever to grace my face after the horrible encounter Peter and I suffered last night.

Peter smiles, dimples forming in his cheeks. "No need to thank me. Michael is my favorite of the Darling siblings. Much better to play with him than the others, who both seem to have pretend swords stuck up their rear ends."

His jab is meant in jest, but it pricks and lodges itself right between my ribcage.

"John and I had to grow up faster than most children."

"That's possibly the most depressing thing that could happen to a person, don't you think?"

I remember last night, his thumb caressing my temple, like he somehow knows the darkness that creeps there, how it leaves my soul sodden and damp until I feel as if I'm breathing through a wet cloth.

"I'm sorry about last night," I say, though as soon as the words are out, I feel a creeping of shame at the skin of my neck for apologizing. Peter is my captor, not my friend. No matter how clearly he sees me.

Lying awake, scrambling for a response that would satisfy his question, had gotten me nowhere. I'm no closer to figuring out what I would do with freedom if I had it.

"Well, I'm not sorry," he says, his eyes dancing as he watches me intently. "It's rare that I'm as entertained as I was watching you scale that cliffside. You had my heart pounding, wondering if you would fall."

My throat goes dry. "I didn't realize you were watching the entire time."

"I like to keep my eye on you."

"And if I'd slipped?"

He jerks his chin to the side, gesturing toward his wings. "I have these, don't I?"

"Would you have used them, though? Or let me fall?"

There it is, that cruel smile that overcomes his face that I find so grounding. Perhaps because it reminds me not to trust him. "Isn't wondering half the fun?"

I swallow. "Perhaps for you. I'm not certain I would have enjoyed becoming spatter against the rocks."

"No, I imagine you wouldn't have," he says, standing and stretching his limbs and wings. The action itself is so boyish, so reminiscent of something Michael would do, I fight with a smile tugging at my cheeks.

He turns to leave, but I find myself speaking up without the permission of my good sense. "You would have caught me."

Peter turns slowly, curiosity brimming on his face. "What makes you think that?"

"Because you could have let that nightstalker rip me to shreds, and you didn't."

"But Wendy Darling," he says in a voice that has a shudder snaking through me, "that's not nearly as satisfying as watching you fall."

. . .

MICHAEL REFUSES to leave the room until all the toys are sorted from smallest to largest in the nearest closet.

Closet is probably too generous a term. It's more that there's a woven pine needle curtain covering a hole in the earth.

"A clean room makes Mama happy," Michael says. I can't count how many times our mother said that to him while teaching him to clean his messes.

Unfortunately, while Michael no longer leaves toys strewn across the floor, he now knows the subtle joys of having a pristine organization system, and once he sees the havoc of the closet, there's no turning back.

We spend the rest of the morning reorganizing.

I'm about to give up and go find John to ask him to relieve me when a sheet of parchment tucked behind one of the shelves catches my attention. It's rather small, about the size of a piece of letter paper, but someone has sketched on it with charcoal. It's a beautiful portrait, the type that my parents would have paid good money to be professionally done back in Estelle. When I look closer, I realize it's a drawing of the Lost Boys, each of their faces immortalized on the smooth side of this thin piece of hide.

The resemblances are uncanny, and I find my gaze lingering over how the artist managed to capture Simon's toothy grin, Freckles's dimples, Victor's scowl and the shadowlike bruises that frame his eyes. Even the cunning glint in Peter's expression.

As I examine the boys' faces, my gaze halts and retreats back to one of the figures.

He looks to be the same age as the others—excluding Smalls—no older than sixteen, with messy hair and a captivating grin, though I can't help but think his face looks distorted compared to the other boys'. As if the artist didn't know it as well as the others.

As I stare into the boy's smile, something cold and scaly slithers in my belly.

Because I've never met him.

CHAPTER 18

While the fear of my brothers and I losing our memories still lingers, my mind clings onto the face of the missing Lost Boy. Stories weave themselves into my dreams—all of them tragic, most of them bloody and reeking of death.

He becomes my new obsession, and I can't help but wonder if he has something to do with Victor's warning on the day we went trapping.

To my shame, it's not the fear over what happened to him that grips me, so much as the dread that my brothers might meet the same fate. I try to get Victor alone, but he's been elusive. Mealtimes make up our only interactions, and he usually leaves the table early, disappearing to who knows where.

Speaking of our dining situation.

After several meals with the Lost Boys, most of them featuring boar meat so tough I fear I'll break a tooth, vegetables that are so underdone they're chilled on the inside, and liberal use of sea salt that causes inflammation in my throat, I decide something must be done.

At first, I thought the meals were only so horrid because the boys rotate who's on cooking duty for the day. I figured Smalls and Benjamin must simply be dreadful at it.

But days have passed, and I fear Smalls might actually prove to be the most talented of the group.

I can handle many things in life.

Knowing even as a youth that I was born to be given over to the shadows? Handled. Well, sort of.

But if I'm to be a prisoner, I intend to eat well if I have anything to say about it.

It's certainly not that we don't have the facilities to make an excellent meal. I peeked in the kitchen, and it's complete with a cast-iron oven, its vent carved into the earthen ceiling. There are also plenty of knives, spices, cedar cutting boards, and pots and pans. Some appear to have been shaped by Benjamin's blade. Others appear aged and like they might have been stolen from the kitchens of the unsuspecting.

One day during our trapping excursion, I ask Simon if I might help him with his cooking shift. Simon appears thrilled, though I'm not sure if it's for my company or my assistance, but at this point I can't worry about these things.

Later that day when I arrive at the kitchen, it's Nettle who meets me, his blond bangs already sweat-soaked from the heat of the stove.

"Are you on duty with Simon?" I ask, confused.

Nettle shakes his head. "Simon's got a bad stomach. He's holed up in the outhouse, so I told him I'd trade shifts with him."

I examine the thin boy. "That was kind of you," I say.

Nettle gives me a bemused look. "Why do you sound so surprised?"

"No reason," I lie, as Nettle has certainly not struck me as the kind and selfless type. Although, I'm unsure whether my impression of him is based off his actions or what the other boys have told me.

"You're right though," he says. "I didn't do it out of kindness. Simon was bragging earlier about how you asked to help him tonight. I figured if I traded with him, I'd only have to do half the work."

I let out an exasperated laugh. "And here you were, making me feel bad about my assumptions."

Nettle turns to me, a smile threatening the edges of his mouth.

"Well, you'll be displeased to discover that I have slightly higher expectations than you might be used to," I tell him.

Nettle whisks out a kitchen knife. "Just tell me what needs to be cut."

By the end of our first hour of preparation, Nettle is muttering something about regretting switching with Simon, but I flash him a smile and tell him he'll be reconsidering that when he tastes the fruit of our labor.

Actually, I tell him we'll be tasting the vegetables of our labor, at which point he almost boos me out of the kitchen.

As the heiress of a grand estate, it wasn't within my training regimen to learn to prepare meals. Only to delegate them. But, same with climbing the clock tower, I found the intricacy that goes into cooking, coupled with the head chef's outlandish stories, to be a welcome distraction from the dreadful future that plagued my mind.

After beating the boar meat until it's dead all over again with a mallet I found in the hunting closet and teaching Nettle how to properly salt the meat, I'm rather pleased with how my—our, I suppose—labor is coming along.

"Nettle, can I ask you a question?" I ask as we work on slicing the vegetables.

"Sure. If you agree to finish the rest of this on your own," he says.

I ignore him and ask anyway. "The other boys say you remember what your life was like before Neverland."

"That doesn't sound like a question to me."

I bite the inside of my cheek. "Do you really remember?"

He looks up at me, blue eyes watery as he slices into the onions. "Sure I do. The rest of the boys claim to be orphans, and maybe they were, but I think they like the romantic notion of it. I'm not an orphan, though. My father's a duke. Owns a massive estate out in Hestershire."

"Hestershire?" I ask, trying to hide the way my pitch rises. Our nanny used to sing us a nursery rhyme about Hestershire, but that's all it was. A made-up place only named as such because the lyricist needed something to rhyme with the next verse.

"Yeah, it's at the farthest corner of the world."

"Where the sea is blue as sapphire?" I ask, thinking of the rest of the nursery rhyme.

"You've heard of it?" he asks, eyes brightening. I can't tell if it's the heat from the stove that's blotching his pale cheeks with color.

Sadness and guilt pinch my chest. "Yeah, I've heard of it."

Nettle smiles, and I feel as if I might weep. "Well, you'll have to tell the others then. They think I made it up."

My heart hurts when I remember then the third verse of the rhyme, the one about a rich duke who owns the city of Hestershire. I don't know what magic wiped these boys' memories, but obviously the nursery rhyme left something planted deep in Nettle's mind.

I quickly change the subject. "Where do all these vegetables come from anyway?"

Nettle offers me a sidelong glance, before saying, "The ground."

When my elbow collides with his ribcage, he lets out a startled laugh. "Joel tends to our garden. It's in a clearing north of the Den."

My brow curves before I can stop it. "*Joel* is your gardener?" It's hard to imagine the boy I caught ushering a rat to its agonizing demise tending to any sort of life.

Nettle is careful not to look at me, his voice even as he collects a pile of sliced carrots onto the center of the cutting board. "Peter thought he'd be better suited to it than hunting," is all he says.

My skin crawls, and because I don't want to talk about Joel anymore, I say, "There sure are a lot of onions."

Nettle's nose turns up. "I hate onions. They're not proper food for nobility"—I try to avoid cringing as I recall that verse of the rhyme—"but they're real easy to grow here, so Peter makes us eat them with everything. Doesn't like us to waste anything. But I always give mine to Simon."

"Well, I happen to love onions. Maybe you could share yours with me instead," I laugh.

Nettle gives me a conspiratorial glance. "But then you'll stink just like the rest."

I TRY to work up the courage to ask Nettle about the missing boy from the sketch before dinner. The entire time, I'm telling myself this would be the best time, when he and I are alone. But something's gnawing at my gut, anxiety trapping my tongue behind my teeth. Every time I come close to asking him, my mind comes up with a reason I'm being ridiculous. That there's some completely reasonable explanation for why I haven't met the boy in the picture.

Perhaps he's not real at all. He looked more distorted than the others, after all. Perhaps the artist attempted to draw the face of a boy conjured by his imagination, and this boy simply wasn't as clear as those for which he had a visual reference. Perhaps he's a lost memory from one of the boys' past lives.

These explanations do little to soothe the constriction in my chest, though they do delay me from asking Nettle about them. Eventually, I lose my shot when the other boys clamber into the kitchen, claiming they're starving and don't see what could be taking us so long.

So Nettle and I pile the plates high with food, and my moment to question him fades into the prison of my indecision.

THE ROAST IS A HIT. Part of me is delighted when all the boys go back for seconds. Part of me feels a bit guilty when there's only enough left for half of them.

Michael must be hungry, because while he normally only picks at his food, he wipes his plate clean tonight. Granted, I did give him an extra portion of potatoes and kept the roast in a separate bowl so they wouldn't touch.

Even Nettle clears his plate, though he piles his onions on Simon's. I check Simon's face for any sign of queasiness, considering he had to switch shifts with Nettle earlier, but if he's still feeling ill, I can't tell underneath that dazzling smile.

"We should make Wendy cook from now on," says Victor, which might be the closest he's ever come to paying me a compliment.

Freckles nods. "Yeah, you're much better at it than the rest of us."

"Can you make us breakfast too?" asks Benjamin.

Oh no. This is definitely not what I wanted. Sure, I don't mind cooking. Even like it to some degree. But sharing in the task differs greatly from taking on the entire responsibility.

Besides, if I'm in the kitchen all the time, I won't have time to go hunting with Simon. I've come to look forward to our little excursions—the feel of the black sand against the balls of my feet. The spike of pleasure in my brain when I test a trap and find I've set it just right.

I would have never thought it, growing up in the aristocracy, but there's something about working for everything I've got, removing the wall of riches between myself and the very nature that sustains me, that provides me a sort of inner peace.

"I'm not confident that's the best idea," I say, warily setting my fork down.

"Oh, come on, Winds," says Freckles. "You've been here long enough to know that none of us are any good at it. Nettle, did you even help at all?"

Nettle shrugs. "I mostly just followed instructions."

Freckles gestures with both palms open toward the sky in a sweeping motion, then props himself back in his chair on only two of its legs and crosses his arms. I suppose he thinks his point well made.

I glance at John for help. He's sitting next to me, playing with the gristle left on his plate with a wooden fork. When he finally shrugs at me apologetically, he pours salt on the wound by adding, "This is the best meal we've had yet."

I groan, the sight of which has the boys cackling. I seem to have stoked the fire, because now I'm pretty sure they're just picking on me.

"All right. That's enough of that. As delicious as this was, we won't be chaining Wendy's ankles to the stove anytime soon," says Peter as he waltzes into the room.

I go tense. Peter rarely eats with us. Tonight, Nettle dropped off a plate by Peter's room, which is down the long hallway toward the east of the Den.

"As much as it would serve to boost our morale," he adds, winking at me.

I fight not to blush under his attention, reminding myself that one pleasant conversation doesn't make him any less of the monster I've always known him to be. Doesn't make me any less of a prisoner. Besides, I still have the drawing of the unfamiliar boy scraping at the back of my mind, giving me a fresh set of chills when I think of him.

This time, it's the Lost Boys' turn to groan.

Freckles laments that he shall never taste a properly salted piece of meat again.

"Oh, I don't know about that," says Peter, before turning to me. "What do you say, Wendy? Would you consider teaching the rest of us your ways?"

I go rigid, but it's no use. The Lost Boys concur that this is the best alternative if I'm not going to agree to become their cooking slave.

"I could do that," I say, not for Peter, but because I actually did enjoy instructing Nettle tonight.

And besides, the boys aren't the only ones who benefit if the quality of meals around here increases.

Cheers erupt from the table from everyone except for Joel, who, though smiling, is doing so half-heartedly. We make eye contact from across the table, one I wish he would break, but he's examining me like he wonders if I'll tell anyone what I saw regarding the rodent by the fire.

I can't help myself; my gaze darts to the hearth across the room. Of course, there's no trap there.

When I glance back at Joel, a coldness has overtaken his stony expression.

The image of the boy in the drawing flashes against my mind once again.

AFTER DINNER, Simon agrees to help me clean dishes, explaining that he feels guilty for forcing me into Nettle's snooty presence. I try to tell him Nettle wasn't so bad, to which Simon appears suspicious. I can't exactly tell Simon that Nettle's memory of his past life is wrapped up in the boundaries of a nursery rhyme. Pity and compassion might be the reaction I'd be going for, but I'm not confident those won't be lost on the pointed ears of a sixteen-year-old boy.

"Oh, even you must not hate him so much," I say. "You take his onions, after all."

Simon chuckles. "I would take onions from a loose convict. I love them."

I smile slightly before finally working up the courage to ask him about the boy. Rather, I pull the folded picture from my pocket and show it to him.

"I found this tucked away in the closet. It's pretty impressive. Which one of you draws?" I ask, careful not to actually mention the boy.

"Oh, it's Victor who draws," says Simon without looking at the picture, as he's focused on scrubbing a piece of gristle off one of the pots. But then he wipes his forehead with his clean wrist and glances my way. As soon as he sees the picture, his entire body goes still, his eyes flickering quickly away from the left corner of the page, where the unfamiliar boy's likeness lies.

"Does this look like one of Victor's?" I ask innocently.

Simon pales. "Um. I guess so. It's not like I pay attention to his drawing style or anything."

There's a defensiveness in his voice I've yet to hear.

"Oh, I was noticing, too—who's this boy? I don't think I've met him yet."

Simon isn't looking at the picture anymore. In fact, he's looking anywhere but the picture, his eyes darting around, searching for somewhere to land. He runs his hands through his glossy black hair, seemingly unaware that he hasn't washed the dish soap from them yet. It leaves grimy little bubbles in between his thick strands.

"Simon?"

When he says nothing, I ask, "Victor didn't draw this, did he?"

He clears his throat. "We're not supposed to talk about Thomas."

Thomas.

Something about the name fits the boy's face. His vibrant grin and round cheeks.

"Thomas was always sketching stuff like this," Simon says, turning his attention back to the parchment.

I pause. We're on shaky ground here, and I don't want Simon to shut me out. But now that I have momentum, I can't help but push. "Who's Thomas?"

Simon's attention snaps back to me. "I said we're not supposed to talk about him, okay?" He must realize how harsh he sounds, because he blushes, the ire draining from his face. "I'm sorry. I just— can we drop it?"

I bite my lip, nodding.

The worm in my stomach is still gnawing, but this time, it's not anxiety alone feeding the sensation.

Because now I've got a name for the Lost Boy.

ON THE WAY to my room that night, a hand grips my shoulder. I go rigid underneath the touch, but then a voice swims out of the darkness.

"I just wanted to thank you."

I turn to find Joel behind me, his hand still on my shoulder.

Worms gnaw at my insides at the feel of his touch. The faint singe of burning rat hair taps on my memory.

"For what?" I ask, wriggling myself from his grasp.

He clears his throat, tucking his hands behind his back. "For not telling anyone about what you saw." His green eyes flicker. "You… haven't told anyone, have you?"

"About what?" I ask, wondering now if there's rat remains in the hearth.

He lets out a relieved smile, running his hands through his silky black hair. "Good. You haven't snitched. I just…I'd really appreciate it if you kept it our secret." He scrunches his forehead as he squeezes his eyes shut. "I'm not exactly proud of my little problem. It started after Peter taught me to hunt. He doesn't let me do that anymore, though. Says I'm better at tending to the garden, but I know it's because he started to notice…" Joel swallows, his eyes glazing with tears. "Anyway, I don't want to be this way. I don't know what's wrong with me, but I'd rather them not think I'm a freak."

After my conversation with Nettle in the kitchen, something tells me the boys already know, but I'm not about to share that suspicion.

"Of course, Joel," I say.

I don't notice until he's gone that I'm clutching the sketch of Thomas behind my back.

CHAPTER 19

riting in Freckles's journal proves to be difficult in the room I share with my brothers. First of all, Michael is drawn to the feel of the leather binding. When he's not rubbing his palm over the back of it, he's trying to snatch my quill from my hand. Already, two of the pages are no longer useable after Michael got a hold of the quill and scribbled all over them, collapsing into a fit of giggles that instantly melted my irritation with him.

Since Michael sleeps the best in complete darkness, I don't want to disturb him by kindling a lantern. When he finally crawls onto his cot, dreary-eyed and yawning, I flick the lantern off, bid John goodnight, and pad down the hall toward the Den area.

Unfortunately, the Den is already inhabited when I arrive.

Peter sits on a bench propped up against the far wall, the glow from the dwindling fire in the hearth highlighting the copper tinge to his hair, the subtle freckles on his nose.

Before I can scramble away, he flicks his devastating blue eyes toward me, peering at me through long eyelashes.

"Stay," he says, casually gesturing toward the couch across from the fire. "No need to let me scare you off."

Personally, I'm of the opinion I have every reason to let him scare me off, but I don't say as much. Instead, I say, "I don't want to bother you."

A sly smile curves his lips. "Then don't leave."

Something hitches in my throat, and I glance over my shoulder and down the hall. If I knew what was good for me, I'd stay out of Peter's way.

Yet.

The pad of my thumb finds the leather of the journal, the crisp edges of the pages. I'd been planning on mapping out my ideas about what happened to the missing Lost Boy, compiling a list of questions and who best to ask them to.

But if anyone can tell me what happened to Thomas, what happened to the boys' memories, it's the fae sitting across the room from me.

I trace my feet across the dirt floor, finding my seat on the wicker chair furthest from the Shadow Keeper.

"So proper," he says, his eyes tracing the straight line of my back, as if he can see through me to the ripples of my spine. "Surely that's not the posture you intended on taking to settle down for the night."

I let out a nervous chuckle, then pull my feet onto the chair, propping my back against the armrest as I tuck the journal into my lap.

"That's better," says Peter, lifting something from the bench next to him—a flute, I now realize, made of bamboo tubes progressing in size.

I divert my eyes to my journal, but my attention is soon swept away by the gentle hum of the flute as Peter plays. Its low vibrato fills the room, echoing easily off the bare walls. There's an effort-lessness about the beautiful tune, one that seeps into muscles I hadn't even noticed were tensed, letting them out like a masseuse to a knot. My shoulders slump as the rest of my body sinks into the chair.

Blinking to revive my heavy eyes, I try to look like I'm focusing on my journal, but my mind is elsewhere—trying to devise the best way to extract the information I want out of Peter.

"Wendy Darling, you're not writing," says Peter, my attention snapping up to him as the music halts. "Do you find me distracting?"

Shaking my head out, I push myself upright in the chair. "No," I say. "Sometimes I just like to gather my thoughts before I write. To make sure I say it the right way."

He yawns. "Sounds boring."

I flinch, but if he's bothered by hurting my feelings, he doesn't show it.

Irritated, I finally find the will to ask, "Will you take my brothers' memories?"

He cocks his brow. "And what of your memories? You're not concerned about those?"

I huff. "Of course I am."

"That explains the journal then. But it's unnecessary. Trust me, the Darling memories are safe."

My pulse flutters, and I can't tell if I believe him. "Truly? There's not some disease on the island that wipes them away? Some magic you possess that...feeds off them? Nothing like that?"

Peter rests his smirk against his knuckles. "Nothing like that, no."

I slam my journal shut. "What about the Lost Boys? Why can't they remember their pasts?"

Peter examines me carefully. "The Lost Boys are in a unique situation."

"What situation?"

"A situation that doesn't apply to you or your brothers. Is that not enough to comfort you?"

"I care for the Lost Boys too. I don't want to see them hurt."

Peter places his hands on his knees. "I'm glad to hear it, Wendy Darling, as that's a goal we share. Everything I do, I do to protect them."

"Is that what you did for Thomas? Protect him?" The words are out before I can gather them back in.

Peter's pointed ears flick, but other than that, his face remains impassive, his casual smirk unaffected. "Who told you about Thomas?"

I chew on the inside of my cheek. "Why? Are you going to punish whoever it was? Is that about protecting them, too?"

Peter shakes his head and stares into the fire. "No," he says, softly. "I suppose you're right; I'd rather not know."

He sinks into a silence I have a feeling further questions won't breach, so I return to my journal, pondering whether I should be relieved that Peter claims my and my brother's memories are protected, or if I should believe him at all.

Peter moves so quietly that I don't hear him until he's behind me, bent over the back of my chair with his mouth hovering at my ear.

"Oh, and Wendy Darling?"

I snap the journal shut. "Yes?"

"You said you like to think through what you write beforehand. But should you ever write the thoughts that first come to your mind, should you ever cease filtering out those lovely little atrocities before there's physical evidence that they exist—well, should you ever do that, I'd hide that journal from me if I were you. I might just succumb to my inclination to peek."

CHAPTER 20

*B*enjamin lets it slip during breakfast that on the full moon, Peter goes away for a while. This lines up with what I might have expected. The shadows always spoke to me more frequently when the moon was at its brightest.

I can't help but wonder if Peter's trips will end now that he has me in his possession. Given he's yet to seek me out since I arrived, I doubt it. The Shadow Keeper might as well be a child who spent months begging for a puppy for winter solstice, only to toss it aside upon the realization that having a pet paled in comparison to their anticipation.

I suppose that's me, Wendy Darling, always coming up short of expectations. Granted, usually it's my Mating Mark that does that for me, though I'm unsure that's what's keeping Peter away. Fae males are known for being possessive, and I can see my Mark turning Peter off of me.

One would think that the fact that he has me secluded, tucked away within a mostly abandoned realm, would diffuse some of the jealousy.

Apparently not.

Not that I'm complaining.

It's been to my benefit that Peter rarely comes near me, a blessing I didn't expect from my captivity.

Still, I watch Peter stride past the dining table and allow the reaping tree to form clots of vines around him, stealing him from our sight.

LATER THAT NIGHT, when I'm certain John and Michael are both sleeping soundly, I sneak out of our room and down the long hallway where Peter's room lies.

It's lit dimly by the gentle glow of green lichen that line the walls. In the dim lighting, my shadow diffuses, cresting the earthy ceiling above me as I creep through the tunnel.

For a moment, when the divots in the wall rise and fall, it occasionally appears as if my shadow is the one creeping, moving and dancing in ways my limbs cannot. Fear threatens to turn me back, but I don't let it, not when I don't know if I'll get another chance like this within the next month.

The image of Thomas has been eating away at me at night. His laugh echoes in my ears anytime I traverse down a dark tunnel in search of materials from a closet. His happy-go-lucky grin warps into a scowl in my dreams, fangs ripping from his full lips.

I have to know. If only for the peace of mind that whatever happened to him won't befall John and Michael.

People have a tendency to blame the victim when calamity befalls them. When I was young, I thought it a by-product of some innate cruelty, but when I matured, I recognized it for what it was— a symptom of fear.

We like to think victims had something to do with their own pain, fault to take in their own misfortune. Because if that is true, then, so long as we avoid walking the same path, we need not worry about suffering the same fate.

Perhaps that's what I'm looking for. Reassurance that there's something I can do to keep John and Michael from turning up on a charcoal parchment, their lopsided smiles smudged in the crease of its folds, collecting dust.

PETER'S ROOM is the only one that actually has the luxury of a door. It's wooden, as opposed to the leafy curtains that separate the rest of the rooms from the outside tunnels.

At first, I worry it may be locked. It's not that I'm concerned about my ability to pick it, but last time I was that focused on an activity in the dark, I had an episode. And with my shadow playing tricks on me, it's not as if this is the optimum environment for things to go any better. Except that this time I'm pretty sure I'm not being stalked by a wild animal, so that's a mild comfort.

As it turns out, my apprehensions are for naught. A gentle push on the door knob results in a creak as the door opens up for me. Peter's room is...well, cluttered. It's the neat sort of clutter. The type where no one can accuse you of being a hoarder, because at least everything has its preordained place and there's nothing in the walkway. But it's cluttered all the same.

Trinkets line the walls, decorate the tables. Silver candlesticks, wax still dripping down their sleek bodies. Pocket watches, much like mine and John's, though varying in color and size. Saucers, painted with cherry blossoms and tigers and everything in between. They're all organized about the room in clusters. There's even a book on etiquette sitting atop Peter's bedside table. It's not even collecting dust because of course it's not. He probably only keeps it to maintain his aura of being unpredictable.

Unfortunately, I have the feeling Peter will notice if one of his many trinkets goes out of place. This might be more difficult than I thought. Oh well. I'll just have to be careful to put everything back where I found it.

As I rummage through Peter's belongings, I realize I'm not sure what exactly I'm looking for. Another likeness of the Lost Boy, perhaps? Or maybe I'm looking for some type of journal that might explain the circumstances surrounding the boy's disappearance. A token of Thomas's that Peter keeps to remember him by?

There's also the possibility I discover something explaining why the Lost Boys are in Neverland. The idea of uncovering such information fills me with as much trepidation as it does a thrill.

As I'm searching, a shadow flickers in the corner. I jump, but I'm pretty sure it's just my own shadow, bouncing back and forth against the undulations of the candlelight. Still, my imagination warps the shadow into that of a tattered wing.

I need to stop. Spooking myself isn't going to help anything. And I certainly don't want to have another episode like the one at the warehouse.

I return to examining the chipped teacup in my hand, but for the second time, something shifts in my vision.

When I turn around, I'm too late to avoid the flashing, bared teeth.

CHAPTER 21

W hoever's with me in this room is obscured by the shadows, but that doesn't dampen the pain as fingers wrap through the hair lining my skull and twist. Hard.

Teeth gnash before my vision, glinting in the eerie glow of the lichen.

Again, my tongue gets trapped in my throat.

I open my mouth to scream, but nothing comes out.

And then I'm seeing them again, my parents falling to the floor, blood streaking their throats, Michael being taken by the burly henchman, but I still can't get any sound out, can't get my voice to obey.

Sparks erupt in my skull as I'm knocked over the head, but my assailant doesn't stop there. Pain needles my face as talons, long and sharp, scrape across my cheek, digging into my skin. Blood dribbles down my face, but my attacker doesn't seem satisfied.

In a dizzying haze, my eyes adjust. In front of me, dragonfly wings begin to glow, lighting up their owner. She's relented for a moment, pleasure cutting across her lips as she examines the damage she's done to my face.

She's a faerie, her insect-like wings betraying as much. Unlike

Peter's leathery wings, hers are see-through, little veins glowing as they course through delicate skin. Strange, they couldn't have been glowing when she approached me from behind, or I would have seen her coming.

The faerie's hair is golden, cut close to her scalp, long enough to dip down over her pointed ears. She has a slender face, one that looks narrower than her bone structure might prefer, and dazzling blue eyes. She's dressed in frayed sacks, perhaps the very type the Lost Boys store food in.

That's not the only thing that's frayed. Her wings look as though they've been shredded at the bottoms by a wild beast, bits of them hanging loose at her back.

My only advantage is that I'm slightly taller than she is.

Blood drips from her sharp fingernails. She slowly brings the blood to her lips, then smiles.

My stomach turns over.

Move, Wendy, I tell myself, but my limbs are sutured in place, frozen in terror. A possum rolling over and playing dead as its predator stalks.

Except that this predator already has her claws in me.

If I don't move, I'm going to die, but I can't seem to make my body understand that. Perhaps it does understand; it simply doesn't care.

There's hunger in her gaze. There are legends, rumors that the unseelie faeries feast on the flesh of humans. Not quite cannibals because of the difference in species, but close enough.

No. No, I've come too far, avoided too much peril to die like this.

It's like slogging through the marshes in iron-soled boots, but eventually my will overcomes my fear.

And I scratch back.

It's not the noblest or most honorable of ways to fight, but it's the only way I know to inflict damage quickly. I go for the faerie's piercing blue eyes. She's faster and jerks her head to the side in time for me to miss, but I draw blood at her cheek.

My nails dig in deep, but no scream comes. Just a hiss of displeasure as the faerie swats my hands away, then grabs my wrists, wrestling for control as she attempts to force me to my knees. I writhe in her arms, remembering what it's like to try to console Michael when his body is out of his control. How taxing it is to hold him to my chest when his movements threaten to cause him harm.

So I fight back like Michael would, flailing my limbs and allowing the weight of my body to become more cumbersome than my mass should allow.

All the while, I try to force the scream from my throat, but it won't come.

The faerie lands another blow to my face, but this time I'm ready for it and thrash out of her way, allowing her momentary shift in balance to release me from under her grip. Again, I aim for the eyes, sure that's the only place I have a chance to inflict damage upon a faerie.

I miss, but this time my fingernails find a handhold in the faerie's throat.

It shouldn't be as debilitating of a wound as it is. It's not as if I've ripped out her larynx or anything. But as if by instinct, the faerie's limbs freeze. Her fingers go limp, and I fall. I use the opportunity to crawl backward on my forearms, my legs still trembling too much to support me.

She clutches the scratch, cradling it as if I inflicted the sort of lacerating wound that might cause the contents of her throat to spill out. She blinks rapidly, momentarily stunned. So am I, confused by the reaction this faerie has had to a scratch that, though dripping blood, might very well heal up on its own within the next few minutes.

The faerie blinks herself back into the present until the fog in her gaze disappears. She homes back in on me, but then her pointed ears flicker upward and back as she senses something I cannot.

Panic overtakes her features, pretty now that she's not flashing her teeth at me. Before I can push myself off the floor, she slips out the door and into the hallway, leaving behind a trail of glowing light.

Moments later Peter rushes in, his dark form taking up the entire space of the doorway. Wings rattle as he pushes his way into the room. His gaze flickers with rage when he finds me on the floor.

"Where'd she go?"

I raise a trembling hand to point to the left, where the faerie escaped down the tunnel.

Peter's out of the room faster than I can blink. I coax myself onto my feet. My heart is racing so quickly I have to prop myself against the wall for support as I stumble away.

I've no idea what Peter will do to me when he returns from hunting the faerie, but I can't imagine it will be anything good. He might have tolerated my ascent to the cliffside where I tried to steal his faerie dust, but I know I've crossed a line by pilfering through his room. The Lost Boys might look up to Peter. Simon might consider him their protector. But I'm familiar enough with those who use good-natured humor and dazzling smiles as a mask. I've witnessed the smirks he flashes them, the way he ruffles their hair and picks food off their plates and uses every ancient trick to put them at ease.

I know those tricks as well as I know my parents' faces.

Even as I try to conjure them for strength, I find the edges fading, warped and distorted, slightly off like the sketch of the missing Lost Boy.

I'm halfway down the hallway when a dark figure appears before me. Peter's still in his physical form, though his shadows wrap themselves around me as fury blazes in his blue eyes.

A mischievous grin cuts across his beautiful face. "Now, where do you think you're going?"

CHAPTER 22

I don't resist as Peter lifts me into his arms and carries me back to his rooms. The meager fight I had in me I expended struggling with the faerie. Besides, I know better than to fight back against the Shadow Keeper, the very being who, if I attempted to land a blow, could simply slip into shadows and out of the grasp of my doomed attempts.

In a way, it strikes me as exactly what should have happened when I first arrived here. The behavior I always anticipated from the Shadow Keeper. To carry me in chains of shadows to his rooms and steal my very will to live from my bones as he pillaged the last tendril of agency I still possessed.

But when Peter brings me to his rooms, he doesn't place me on the bed as I expect, but in the wooden, knotted rocking chair in the corner of the room. He then lights the lantern I'd brought in, which had toppled over in my struggle with the faerie. Casually, as if nothing odd has occurred tonight, he props himself atop the footrest in front of me, bracing his elbows on his knees, his chin in his hands.

There's something so boyish about the position, it's almost charming.

Almost.

I search for anger in his face but find none. Faintly, I notice my pulse throbbing where the faerie scratched at me. As if reading my mind, he pulls a linen from the dresser nearby and presses it gently to my face, dabbing carefully at the wounds.

"I have to say, the last thing I was expecting this evening was to find a lady waiting for me in my chambers."

I swallow, trying not to feel how close his fingers are to stroking my skin through the thin linen. "Technically, you came home to two women in your chambers."

Peter's smile is dazzling. "So the timid heiress knows how to tell a joke after all."

"Only when prompted."

"If that's the case, perhaps I should send a bloodthirsty faerie after you more often."

I actually roll my eyes. It was evident by Peter's reaction that he had no clue the faerie had broken into the reaping tree, much less his room.

"So. What were you doing in my chambers, Wendy Darling?"

My throat goes dry, but Peter's beautiful eyes don't meet mine as he focuses on treating my wound.

"I would have thought you'd be more concerned with the cannibal faerie who made it into the Den."

Peter's jaw somehow manages to go stiff without corrupting the confidence in his smile. "I'm more concerned about the girl who dances with the shadows and pretends she doesn't like it."

A thrill thrums through my chest, but I stifle it in practicality.

"And I'm more concerned with the faerie who wants to eat me. Or lick my blood, or whatever she wants. Who is she?"

Peter laughs. "You should talk this openly more often."

"I talk this way to the boys all the time."

"I meant to me."

Again, my face flushes, and it's amazing that my blood doesn't start pouring more profusely from my cheeks.

"You're avoiding my question," I say.

"And you're avoiding mine. What an amusing set of dance partners this makes us, constantly going about in opposite circles."

My mind tries to transport me to the masquerade ball, to my dance with the captain, but I don't let it wander there. Instead, I ground myself to the tether of Peter's thumb propped against my jaw.

"A question for a question then," I say.

"I'm not sure I like those rules," says Peter.

"You can be comforted in knowing I probably like them less."

He laughs, then withdraws his hand, though I can't help but notice that his gaze lingers on my Mating Mark. Now, he's looking me square in the face as he leans back and folds his hands over his chest.

"The faerie you had the immense pleasure of meeting is Tink. She's...disillusioned."

"You know her?" I ask, something sharp stinging at my chest that I refuse to acknowledge.

Peter glances toward the ground. "I'm afraid not half as well as she would like."

The stinging in my chest is definitely becoming more pronounced. He sighs. "There are a few ways to end up in Neverland. Tink's reason for being here is unique, to say the least. She and I developed a relationship before...this. When it came time to transition to Neverland, Tink followed me. But the burdens of the realm were too much for her. She eventually resented me for bringing her here. It was clear our relationship was destined for disaster. Despite the fact she hated me for what she perceived as ruining her life, she refused to let go. Still does. Ever done that, Wendy Darling? Refused to let go of the very thing you claim is poisoning you?"

My throat goes dry, an acidic taste on my tongue. "But why attack me?"

Peter actually blushes. "I doubt it was Tink's intention to attack anyone this evening."

"Then why?"

Oh.

Embarrassment needles me all over. I take it Tink had other plans when it came to visiting Peter's chambers, and those likely didn't include finding another woman in them.

My upbringing doesn't allow me to speak so directly of these matters, so instead I say, "That explains trying to disfigure me, then."

"Indeed. In the future, perhaps simply tell her the truth, and she'll leave you alone."

"What truth?"

"That you find me repulsive."

There's a hint of smugness lingering on Peter's lips. The way the right side of his mouth lifts slightly more than the rest. It's probably not for the best that I'm staring.

"I'll have to try that next time. Though I imagine it would be more soothing to her if instead you told her you find me repulsive."

"That's different," he says. "It wouldn't work at all."

"Why not?"

"Because it's not the truth."

Again, a shudder snakes through me. In relation to Peter, the sensation typically stems from fear. Somehow, fear doesn't feel quite so unpleasant this time.

"How did you end up in Neverland?" I ask.

"Second star to the right."

I frown. "No, I mean, why did you end up in Neverland? Why are the Lost Boys here, and why don't they remember anything about their lives before?"

Peter blinks, then leans forward, propping himself on his elbows and knees. As he stares up at me through those thick copper eyelashes of his, my heart gives a lurch. "Because, Wendy Darling, don't you think it's more fun this way?"

A chill scatters up my arms, prickling gooseflesh bulging on my skin, but I won't let him disarm me, so I ask, "Do you?"

Shutters snap into place over Peter's expression, darkening it at the edges. There's no anger in his expression, no hurt. Just gentle numbness, a lack of feeling so close to my heart, I can practically taste it coming off of him.

"Of course I do. I don't do anything unless it's fun. That's my secret."

Something tells me it's not.

CHAPTER 23

⧼⧽

The boys must have heard about Tink's attack, because when I return to my room after setting traps the next day, I find an assortment of gifts on my bed.

None of them left a note with their gifts, but they didn't have to.

There's a whittled wooden lock for my journal from Benjamin, along with a fresh quill pen from Freckles. Simon has gifted me another one of his shirts, which is probably the most practical of the gifts, since Tink shredded mine at the waist last night.

There's also a palm-sized bag of crushed leaves—that one actually does have a note telling me it's rushweed and can be used as a paralytic if necessary. As it also says, *I told you this island was dangerous*, I'm assuming that one came from Victor. He's also left me a warning. *Don't soak the leaves. It'll delay the effect. Unless you're trying to poison someone and don't want the effects to show up until later. But be careful—soaked, it causes breathing difficulties.*

It's a peculiar way to express affection for me, but I decide to take the gift in the manner it was intended.

John is livid, of course, that anyone would dare hurt me. I try to laugh it off and tell him it was only Peter's suspicious ex-lover, jealous for no reason at all.

This doesn't appear to comfort my brother.

That night, when the Lost Boys ask me for a story, I finally agree.

We huddle in the Den. Peter drags over the same stool he sat upon while playing with Michael for me to use. My youngest brother comes and crawls on my lap, playing with a bracelet of beads Peter must have gifted him. Thankfully, none of the boys snicker about him being too old for such things.

"I'm really not the best storyteller," I say.

"She's right," says John, propped up against the wall, paces away from the rest of the boys. "She gets the inflection all wrong."

I crinkle my nose at my brother, and when he laughs, it's not the wry dismal sort I've gotten used to hearing over the past few weeks.

"Oh, shut up," I say, though there's no truth in my words.

John sticks his tongue out at me playfully. When I glance at the boys, all crowded on the floor in front of me, I can't help but suppress a smile. They're all gangly limbs.

And then there's Peter. He's the only one standing, propped up against the doorframe of the hallway that leads to his quarters. Like he's already planned his escape when he grows bored of my story.

Still, there's a twinkle in his eyes when he examines me unabashedly from across the room.

I clear my throat and avert my eyes from my captor. "In ages past, there were three Sisters. The eldest two loved one another dearly, though they never seemed to find connection with the Youngest. She had been created centuries after her Sisters and lacked the camaraderie the eldest two shared so deeply. Still, the love the eldest two Sisters shared for one another was enough, and they paid it no mind that the Youngest always lingered outside their exclusive ring of trust and devotion.

"You see, the three Sisters were created for a specific task. Each realm the Creator had formed was beautiful, but they had a tendency to meld together, to cave in on one another, until beings from one land might find themselves thrown into another, causing chaos. It was the task of the three Sisters to weave the Fabric that now separates the Realms, that keeps them from bleeding into one another.

"It was a pleasant life, if not a dull one, so the three Sisters found ways to entertain themselves. A favored pastime included weaving their own stories into the Fabric. While it started innocently, they soon found their stories reflected in the lives of the beings who lived in the various realms. Fascination sparked in the hearts of the three Sisters, though the Youngest was skeptical. She warned that, should they allow themselves to be swept away, there would be dire consequences to meddling in the lives of fae and mortals.

"So the Sisters designated roles. Only a select few of the beings would they exert control over, and only in certain areas. The Eldest Sister was a romantic at heart. She took it upon herself to find individuals, split apart by great distance, though who, if ever to meet, would surely fill the gaping hole in the other's soul. Into these she wove her golden thread, marking them for one another. That way, should their paths ever cross, they would be at no risk of allowing their true love to pass by them unnoticed on a crowded street."

The fire crackles in the hearth. As I tell my story, the boys' eyes trace the Mark across my cheek in wonder. In vibrant curiosity.

"The Middle Sister was more practical-minded. Or so she thought. She often lamented over the injustices committed by the sentient beings who roamed the realms. While some injustice was to be expected and even tolerated, it was those who committed great atrocities that she desired to thwart. Rather than staking her claim for love, she took up the mantle for death. Learning that some wove themselves on a path bent for destruction despite her attempts to redirect their stories, she took it upon herself to exterminate those whose intention was bent toward evil."

"What about the Youngest Sister?" asks Smalls, who immediately receives the brunt of the most aggressive hushes I've ever heard.

"She's getting to that," says Nettle.

In the back, hiding in the shadows of the dimming light, Peter's eyes laugh.

"The Youngest Sister was the most practical of them all and

sensed that meddling in the lives of those below would end in great tragedy. She vowed to keep watch on her elder Sisters, to steer them away from great trouble, for she knew the elder two would not dare dissuade one another from the musings of their hearts, misguided as their hearts may be.

"For many years, the Sisters worked in harmony and found contentment in the roles they had undertaken. But over time, the Eldest Sister, after watching countless humans and fae find their mates, began to long for a mate of her own. She found him, though whether he was truly meant for another is still under question to this day. He was a beautiful man—a farmer—kind of heart and brave of spirit. She'd seen him coming years ahead, through the threads of her tapestry. One night, she used the very golden thread upon which she'd marked his skin, and took it to her own flesh, threading it into her forearm.

"Instantly, she felt the immense connection to the farmer. She had thought herself infatuated with him before, but this? This was love."

Smalls gags. "You didn't tell us this was going to be a love story."

"I get the feeling it's not," drawls Peter from the back, and I can't help but meet his mischievous grin with one of my own.

"The Eldest Sister soon began making visits to the object of her affection, hoping to woo him. Of course, the farmer was hardly immune to the Mating Mark that wove their souls together, so he found himself captivated by her immediately.

"The Youngest Sister questioned the ethics of the Eldest's choices, but she remained quiet in the matter. The Middle Sister, of course, only cared for the Eldest Sister's happiness, and it would have never crossed her mind to oppose her.

"But something else bothered the Middle Sister. As she wove the Fate of a certain mason she'd been keeping an eye on, one predisposed to great atrocities, his threads kept creeping ever closer to the section of the Fabric occupied by the Eldest Sister's lover. The Middle Sister had seen its like before, and she fretted that when the path of her murderous mason crossed that of her sister's lover, tragedy would ensue.

"Seeking to save her eldest Sister grief, she crossed over the Fabric and into the realm in which both the farmer and mason inhabited. For years she'd attempted to redirect the path of the mason, but his will was too forceful, and she often woke from slumber to find that he had rewoven the threads she had plucked from his path. There was nothing else to be done; she must end the man, the threat to her Sister's happiness, with her own hands.

"When the Middle Sister arrived at the mason's cottage, she found him not at all as she'd imagined. It was one thing to peer at the likeness of a man through the tapestry, but now that she was in his presence, there were details she realized the tapestry could have never captured. The musky scent of hard labor on his clothes, the texture of his dark beard, the way the firelight glinted off his beautiful eyes, the deep gravel of his voice when he spoke to her. Most of all, the fire that lit in her heart when he laid eyes upon her.

"Over time, the Middle Sister came to discover that the mason was gentler, kinder than she had expected. Unfortunate circumstances had led him to harden his soul. He needed only true love to spark in his heart to steer him in the correct direction."

Benjamin shakes his head in the corner, placing his forehead in his hand.

"The Middle Sister found herself visiting the mason often. It wasn't long before she knew with all her being that her immortal heart belonged to him, his mortal heart to her. She didn't need the validation of golden threads marking their skin to know they existed for one another. All she needed was the soft press of his lips to hers and the caress of his adoring words against her ears.

"Up to this point, there was no joy in life that the Middle Sister had ever refused to share with her Eldest Sister. Though she was happy with her lover, she found herself wishing for the Eldest to know of her newfound delight. Now that the mason's heart had been mended by love, there could be no evil in him. With that in mind, the Middle Sister determined that she would introduce him to her Eldest Sister.

"The path to the farm that the Eldest Sister's lover inhabited was an arduous one, but the Middle Sister did not mind the journey as long as her mason's hand was in hers. When they arrived at the cottage, the Eldest was overjoyed to discover her Middle Sister at the door. Even more so, to find her sister in love, for the Eldest valued romance above all else. The four ate, drank, and were merry. And all was well.

"But in the middle of the night, the Middle Sister rose to the sound of the Eldest crying out in anguish. When the Middle Sister reached her, she found the body of the farmer dead on the floor, the mason's knife jutting through his chest.

"The Middle Sister knew not what to do, for she was sure her eyes were deceiving her. Her mason, now truly a murderer, stood over the corpse with rage glinting in his eyes. He explained that the farmer had once cheated him out of his family's estate. Horror overtook the Middle Sister. She cried out, lamenting that she had helped to fulfill the very fate she'd been attempting to thwart. The Eldest Sister let out a shriek, and taking hold of the mason by the throat, determined to kill him. But even in her anguish, she knew that such pain would not be punishment enough for her Middle Sister, with no golden thread binding her sister to the mason's soul. She could not possibly know the misery she had caused.

"So rather than killing the mason, the Eldest Sister set upon him a curse. That his heart would be knit to that of another woman. He would fall so ardently in love with a girl, the Middle Sister would be but a distant memory to him in comparison. One would think this would have provoked enough pain. But the Eldest Sister was certain her own pain would last an eternity, and as she wished the same for her foolish Sister, she added to the curse. The mason would fall in love and bear children. Should he sire a son, the Middle Sister would be cursed to love his eldest male offspring, for all generations.

The Eldest Sister, in turn, made it her mission to ensure the offspring never loved her sister back.

"And thus is the story of the three Sisters. It is said that the Eldest, to this day, weaves the hearts of Mates together as a tribute to her dead lover. The Middle Sister has gone mad with rejection as she seeks the male offspring of her mason, never to receive their affection in return."

"And the Youngest Sister?" asks Peter from the back.

"It's said that she minds her own business, occasionally cleaning up messes made by the other two."

"Sounds familiar," he says, and I press my lips together to hide my smile. "Though I've always heard she assists the dying with letting go."

My heart thuds as a conversation of my mother's I wasn't supposed to overhear taps at my memory, begging to be let in. But I don't want to relive my childhood panic in front of the boys, so I just say, "If you mean that she poisons them, then yes."

Peter cocks his head, examining me. I break the stare.

Huddled in a semicircle on the floor, the Lost Boys appear as young as ever. Faintly, I'm aware that developmentally, they're only a few years younger than I am. Though I suppose I still don't know how old they really are. Not when I'm unsure as to how time works in this world or when the fae stop aging. But as sleep encroaches on their expressions, it softens them, giving them all boyish qualities.

Even Victor, with his harsh features and shadows framing his eyes, seems to have softened a bit.

"That's a dreadful story," says John, tossing a loose twig he picked off the walls my way.

I feign shock. "I always thought it was your favorite."

I could name off John's complaints with the story using all ten of my fingers, but the rest of the Lost Boys are beating me to it.

"Yeah, it's kind of creepy that the Middle Sister falls in love with her lover's sons and grandsons," says Nettle.

"That's the point of the curse, stupid," says Freckles.

Benjamin frowns. "I thought the point of the curse was to make the Middle Sister miserable."

"Wouldn't you be miserable if you fell in love, then were cursed to be a creep who pined after your lover's descendants?" scoffs Nettle.

Simon places his hands behind his head. "Yeah, it's basically incest."

"It's not at all incest. It's not like they're related," says Joel.

Benjamin scrunches his nose. "They might as well be."

Grunts of agreement rumble through the boys.

I try not to, but I find myself glancing at Peter every so often. As always, his expression is unreadable. A mask of quiet amusement obscures whatever's prancing through his mind. I can't help but wonder how he feels about the way the Lost Boys have taken to me. If he's still thinking about the conversation we shared while playing with Michael, or if he's contemplating what it would have been like to watch me fall from a slick cliffside.

Unsettled by the notion, I return to the comfort of the Lost Boys' bickering. Something in my heart unfolds, and it's possibly the most dangerous thing I've experienced yet—the sense of peace that's settling over me as, without my express consent, my mind reframes my prison into my home.

CHAPTER 24

'm up early the next morning, unable to sleep because of the lost boy Thomas's face hovering in the corners of my mind, his beautiful smile haunting my sleepless nights. If it were just me who'd been snatched out of my home and brought to this island, I'm not sure I'd want to know what happened to him.

But it's not just me. I've roped John and Michael into my fate.

So I'm rummaging through ideas at the same time I'm walking about the Den, picking up leftover orange peels and trash that the boys left lying around, when an amused voice pricks my ears.

"You really don't know how to have fun, do you?"

I spin on my heel, surprised to find how close Peter has managed to get without me realizing it. He's near enough that I can smell the casual scent of amber wafting off of his shadows, his smirk highlighting the dimple on his left cheek.

"Someone has to clean up around here," I say.

Peter raises his brow. "And that has to be you?"

I stiffen, but I have nothing to say.

"What if..." Peter rolls his words over his tongue as if he doesn't know exactly what he's about to say. "You just...didn't?"

I stare down at the orange peel below my feet.

"Then this is going to rot here."

Peter shrugs. "Maybe. And why should that be your problem?"

"Because someone is forcing me to live in this space."

Peter's eyes flicker. "If memory serves me correctly, you're the one who brought up the bargain that ended you up here."

I stiffen. "Yes, and you were quick to remind me that I had little to bargain away, given I already belonged to you."

His eyes glitter in the torchlight, raking every last inch of me. "I suppose that does sound like me. I'm rather possessive in my shadow form. So I'm told, at least. Given how you looked the night of the masquerade, I'm not exactly shocked that I would have wanted to stake my claim to you."

The bargain I made with Peter in the clock tower tingles against the crook of my elbow, so naturally, I deflect the pleasant sensation with a snort. "I looked ridiculous. My mother..." A bulge forms in my throat, even bringing her up. "She thought it would place matrimony into the minds of the suitors."

Again, Peter examines me. It's like he's no longer seeing me as I am, standing before him in Simon's gifted clothes, baggy enough to obscure my curves, but in the silk wedding gown I'd donned that night. A bride prepared. "Well," he says, voice dropping an octave, "I'd say your mother knew what she was doing. I doubt there was a man who saw you that night who wasn't contemplating whether life was worth living if he couldn't make you his."

A wry laugh escapes me as I consider the captain's harsh words. "If only you knew."

"Oh, I know."

Red blotches swarm my arms. I hug them to my chest to hide my body's reaction to his words, his lingering gaze, but it's no use. Peter reaches out, trailing his finger over the fresh blemishes on my skin, the evidence of the effect he has on me.

Lightning courses through me at his touch, sending my hairs on end, further condemning me. Peter must notice, because he flicks his gaze toward my face, staring at my mouth through those long copper lashes of his.

And because I'm afraid of what I'll allow my captor to do, what I'll *welcome* him to do, if I let this moment draw on any longer, I drop the orange peel on his boot. If nothing else, it diverts his gaze, if not his attention.

"What was that for?" he asks, though I can barely hear him over the roaring in my ears from where his fingers still trail the skin of my arm.

"I'm proving you wrong," I say, voice shaky even as I muster every bit of stability left in me to keep it level.

"You think throwing an orange peel on my shoe proves you know how to have fun?"

"No," I say. "But it does prove that I'm not content being your slave."

Peter slips his fingers from my skin, returning his hand to his side as he steps back, putting distance between us. If I expected space to allow me to breathe again, I was wrong.

When he turns to go, my heart is still pounding.

"You shouldn't have done that," he says on his way out, placing his hand on the doorway with his back to me. It's then I realize I've made a mistake. Tried to take hold of the reins without considering the repercussions.

"And why not?" I breathe, trying and failing to keep the panic out of my voice.

"Because," he says, "proving me wrong is dangerous, Wendy Darling."

"What, because you don't like to be proved wrong?"

When he turns to look at me over his shoulder, his eyes flash. "Just the opposite."

LATER THAT DAY, Smalls and Benjamin get into an argument over who ate the last of the pine nuts Benjamin harvested. The matter has since devolved into a wrestling tournament under the canopy of the reaping tree, the Lost Boys eager to avoid their chores for as long as possible—all but Simon, who sits out.

After brushing aside the twigs littering the ground, I settle cross-legged beside him. "You don't like wrestling?" I ask.

Before Simon can answer, Victor, who's cracking his knuckles in preparation to wrestle Nettle, says, "Simon thinks he's outgrown having fun."

Simon's tanned cheeks redden, so I nudge him softly. "That's okay. I prefer it that way."

He lifts a questioning brow.

"It means I have someone to talk to," I say, to which Simon flushes again.

In truth, I'm thankful to have a few moments to speak with Simon while the other boys are distracted. The image of the missing boy berates my mind, but as Simon seemed so unwilling to talk about him last time, I try a different approach.

"Simon," I whisper, hoping the boys' hollers will obscure our conversation, "why are you here? You and the Lost Boys, I mean? I know you don't remember your life before, but surely there's some explanation for where you all came from."

Simon shrugs. "I don't know. None of us know. Well, Nettle says he knows, but you've met him." He shoots me a knowing look.

I bite the inside of my cheek, shrugging noncommittally. Hopefully Simon has more of an idea about their past than the clinging fragments of a nursery rhyme.

"That doesn't bother you? Not knowing who you are?"

He flashes me a pearly grin. "Who says I don't know who I am?"

I smile softly at that. I suppose he's right. Sure, Victor's comment clearly embarrassed him, but typically he's about the most self-assured person I've ever met. Except for perhaps Peter, but Peter seems steeped in something much less stable than Simon.

"I still think it would bother me, not knowing," I say.

Simon just picks at a twig on the ground in front of him. "Only Peter knows. He keeps it to himself so we don't have to bear it."

I swallow. "So you think it's something that might bother you if you knew?"

Simon goes quiet. After a few moments, he rubs his hands down the length of his thighs. "Well," he says, standing up, "some of us actually have to get work done today."

When he strokes the bark of the reaping tree and disappears into its tendrils, I maneuver my way over to Freckles, who's the first to be cut from the tournament after being pinned by both Nettle and Benjamin.

"Hey, Winds," he says, offering me a bright smile. The brown of his freckles has deepened with exposure to the sun on this uncharacteristically sunny day, where even under the shade of the reaping tree, light filters in through the leaves. "How's that memory of yours?"

I let out a small laugh and wrap my knuckles against my skull. "Still there, as far as I know."

He shrugs, a goofy smile on his face. "Entirely my doing, I'm sure. You'd probably have lost them now if it weren't for my journal. Don't worry. You can repay me by doing my chores for a month."

I flick him on the ear, and he swats me away dramatically.

"Hey, Freckles, did you finally find an opponent you actually have a chance of beating?" yells Joel from the center of the ring of boys. He's drenched in sweat after having pinned one of the twins.

I turn around, expecting to find Freckles red and fuming. Instead, he's shrugging, palms to the sky, a mischievous look on his face. "What do ya say, Winds? Winner does the other person's chores for a month?"

The laugh that escapes my lips surprises even me. The freedom of it. "You're delusional if you think I'm going to agree to that."

"If you go for his ankles, you actually have a decent chance of winning," concedes Benjamin.

I'm not sure what comes over me—perhaps this island is messing with my head after all—but I lunge for Freckles's ankles. He sidesteps me with a shocked laugh, and I end up with a mouthful of earth.

Motivated now by the boys booing me, I push myself up.

"That was pretty pitiful, Winds," says Freckles. "Come on. Try again," he says, beckoning me with his hand.

This time, when I launch myself at him, he catches me by the waist and tosses me over his shoulder, spinning me around before setting me giggling back on the ground.

"I'm not doing your chores, though," I say, to which Freckles feigns outrage.

"She's right," says Benjamin. "Technically the rules state that you don't win unless you pin her."

Freckles snorts, a flush climbing his neck. "Yeah, well, I'm not doing that."

I'm still laughing, dusting my pants off, when I notice the emptiness in my pocket. Panicked, I slip my hands into my pockets, but it's no use. I spin around to find Victor plucking the folded parchment from the dust.

"Oh. What does Winds have here?" he asks.

There's no time to snatch it from him before he unfolds it, the shadows underneath his dark eyes deepening as soon as he glimpses its contents.

His hands tremble as he snaps his gaze up to me. "Where did you get this?"

"I—"

He doesn't wait for me to respond as he wads it up and chucks it at me. I have to shield my face, the edges of the parchment stinging as they make contact with my forearms.

When Victor storms off, the rest of the boys remain wide-eyed. Freckles shoos them off before picking up the parchment and pressing it into my hands.

"What's in it?" he asks.

When I show it to him, he nods knowingly.

"Oh, that's Thomas."

"What happened to him?" I ask.

Freckles shrugs. "We're not really supposed to say. Peter warned us when you first got here. Well, right before he went to fetch you, I guess."

"Can you tell me what Thomas was like, at least?"

Freckles pinches his forehead, considering whether this technically breaks Peter's rules. Something tells me it breaks the intention, but I'm not about to make that argument to Freckles.

"Everyone practically worshipped him," he says, blandly.

I raise my brow. "And you didn't?"

"He was just an orphan like the rest of us. There's nothing special about any of us. Not sure why everyone acted like he was, except that he was the oldest."

The acid drips off Freckles's tongue with such ease, I'm somewhat shocked. Even among the aristocracy, the dead were always much more amiable than their living personas. Death turned a drunk into a "jolly ole fellow, always up for a good time," a cheater into a charmer, a miser into a conscientious businessman.

But I suppose jealousy is sharp enough to cut through even the flattering haze that lingers over our memories of the dead.

"I wouldn't go around saying that," I say.

Hurt flashes across Freckles' face, the playful boy who just pretended to wrestle with me replaced by a sullen adolescent. "It's not like they don't already know. It's not a secret that I wasn't exactly an admirer while he lived. And I'm not going to go around shedding fake tears just because that's what everyone expects. Everyone acts like they have the right to dictate how I feel about his death. If I bring up anything negative about Thomas, Simon says I'm being insensitive. The Twins just stare at me like I've grown an extra set of eyes. Nettle acts like I've transgressed some ancient ducal code of conduct." Freckles rolls his eyes. "Smalls...well, it makes him cry, so I do feel kinda bad about that." Guilt pinches Freckles's features, red creeping up his neck. "You probably think I'm awful, don't you?"

Because it's difficult for me to imagine sweet Freckles, the boy who found me crying and gifted me his journal, being truly awful, I shake my head. "I'm sure you have your reasons for not liking him."

Freckles shrugs. "I never could put my finger on it. Something about him...well, he just seemed...off, I guess."

"Off how?"

Frustration rims Freckles's brow as he struggles for the words and fails. "Too friendly, too likable to be real, I guess. I dunno—that doesn't make any sense, I know. Forget I said anything."

I offer him a gentle smile. "Just maybe don't mention that around Victor," I say. "He and Thomas must have been close."

"Close?" says Freckles, snorting. "Victor practically worshipped Thomas. But I suppose I can't blame him."

"Why not?" I ask.

Freckles scratches the back of his neck, actually looking sympathetic. "Because they were brothers."

CHAPTER 25

*D*ark, wet sand pounds against the bottoms of my feet, slugging through my toes as I run.

It's not quite climbing. I don't get the same high that I do from scaling a tower or edifice, but since I fear that climbing the cliffs will end in another encounter with a nightstalker, running it is.

It's not as satisfying as I'd like for it to be. The sand on the beach is packed in from the tide last night, but it's still soft enough against my feet that every step feels as if I'm expending way too much effort for how far I've traversed.

Still, it's better than nothing.

It's better than the tightness in my chest. The exertion, the gasping for breath, unravels the cord wound around my ribcage. At least when I'm running, I have an excuse for why my heart pounds, unlike when I lie awake at night, my pulse accelerating wildly despite being sedentary.

It's not climbing, but it makes the images of my parents' deaths not seem so vivid. It leaches the crimson from their bloodstains, douses their gargling underneath the lapping of the waves. It takes the touch of Peter's hand against my skin, the way it lights me on fire, and allows me to blame the sensation on the burn of my body gasping for air, my muscles tearing and rebuilding themselves.

Mostly, it just makes everything go quiet.

Over the horizon peeks the sun, coming up from the nighttime bath in the salty water, reinvigorated and ready to start anew.

The waves are frigid when they bounce against my feet, but there's a part of me that wonders if that would help, too. Submerging my aching body in the freezing waves. Allowing them to chill the rot threatening to decay my muscles. Do to my throbbing heart what a physician might do to a wound before it's amputated.

These are the kinds of things I get to thinking about when I'm alone.

"Have you ever just *lain?*"

I hear the voice just in time to go crashing into a set of firm arms, to feel the weight of a sturdy chest. I know who it is before looking up, recognize the scent of amber and shadows, the casual amusement in his voice.

I stop, staring up at Peter's beautiful face, lit in orange from the rising sun as he smirks down at me. His hands coax my shoulders, though as soon as his eyes land on my Mating Mark, it's like he remembers I belong to someone else. He drops his arms, stepping back and placing space to breathe between us.

My pulse races, my head spinning. I tell myself it's from halting mid-run.

"Excuse me?" I ask.

"Have you ever just lain? Out on the beach, maybe? Or even in bed until the sun was already high in the sky?"

The answer is yes. The answer is that I've lain in bed with the covers pulled over my head, praying for just a few more moments before I had to rise, foolishly pretending my blankets into a set of armor, ready to protect me from the assaulting demands of the coming day.

"It's too cold to lay out on the beach," is what I say instead.

"I'd keep you company," says Peter, his voice tinged with teasing.

He flexes his wings. "Laying in these makes for great protection against the wind. Then there's the body heat…"

"I thought you were staying away from me."

Peter cocks his head. "Somehow, I don't remember saying that."

"You didn't have to."

It's true. Peter's been avoiding me since the moment we shared in the Den, the memory of which still lingers, tingling my skin where he traced the blotches on my arm.

"Where would be the fun in staying away from you?" he asks, still avoiding my question. It drives me insane the way he does that. "Though it seems you're inviting adventure by running out here by yourself. I seem to recall a golden-haired faerie about who's thirsty for your blood."

I gesture to my waist, where I brought a knife I borrowed from Simon.

"Now that, I'd love to see."

Irritation swells in me. I don't much like being interrupted in the middle of a run. There's something about having the feeling of peace swept away from me before I'm finished that leaves me in this heightened state. It feels suspiciously like teetering on the edge of a cliff.

"Seems to me you're running from something."

"I'm not running from anything. I'm just running to run."

Peter quirks his brow.

"It's become a popular source of entertainment among the aristocracy," I say.

Among the men, I neglect to add.

"You cause yourself literal pain and call it entertainment?" says Peter. "And here I was, thinking you might have a point about me having a warped sense of what makes for good fun."

I cross my arms over my chest, shivering as my body temperature cools and the wind from the waves laps up my sweat.

"This isn't pain," I say, letting my eyes avert to the dark sand beneath my feet.

I can take away your pain.

"If you say so," says Peter, eyeing me warily. Then he leans in and whispers in my ear. "But it's not fun, either. I'd be happy to teach you my ways, if you'd let me."

He pulls back but extends a hand all the same. The same hand I took out of desperation in the clock tower that night. The same hand whose shadows seeped in through the windowsill for years. The same hand that pulled me to his chest and flew me high above Estelle, where the city lights speckled like dewdrops on the ground and the whirl of the wind stole the air from my lungs and took the pain out of breathing.

The same hands that threatened to drop me in the name of fun.

That thought sobers me right up. I need to get Peter away from me before I succumb to his allure, his tempting promises. Pain has planted its roots in my soul. If I allowed him to pluck it out, he'd shred the very muscle that keeps my blood pumping.

So instead of taking his hand, I slip mine into my pocket, withdrawing the soft, leathery slip of parchment I know will wipe the teasing from his voice. Will remind me just who it is that wants me to entrust him with flying me above the ground.

Peter still appears amused, and he snatches the parchment from my hand playfully. "What could this be? Wendy Darling's list of painful activities she convinces herself are pleasurable? Do you also include passing a bladder stone on this lis—"

Peter's voice disappears. He snaps his gaze to mine, peering over the now unfolded parchment. "Where did you get this?"

There's no anger in his voice. No emotion at all.

"What happened to him?" I counter, repeating the question he refused to answer the night I found him playing his flute by the hearth.

A cruel smile overtakes Peter's lips. "Maybe he went running by himself."

Anger stings at my heart, riling me. When I speak, my voice warbles, which only makes me more frustrated. "Is that what you told the other boys?"

Something odd overcomes Peter's body. A sort of laxness where

I would have expected tension. It's like watching a sink drain of water.

Peter quietly folds the sketch in his hands and tucks it back into my palm, closing my fingers over it gently. "Thomas wandered too far. Too far for me to protect him," is all he says.

Judging by the way his eyes glaze over, go unfocused, by the way his voice doesn't change in pitch, I get the feeling I'm not the only one who has strategies for drowning out the pain.

I'm debating whether to mention as much when Peter's ears flick. My gaze follows his, curious as to what has snatched away his attention.

Simon approaches, feet bare and kicking up the steely sand. When he reaches us, he bends over, catching himself on his knees. Strange, considering he's fae. I can't imagine how fast he must have been running to get winded like that.

He gulps in the salty air, and at first I think that's what has the whites of his eyes tinted red.

"What's wrong?" asks Peter, wings going taut, readied for flight at his sides.

"It's happened again," Simon says, panic trilling his voice. "We found him over by the cove... His face..." Simon's eyes go in and out of focus.

"Who?" Peter and I shout at the same time. The plea in his voice is for his Lost Boys.

Mine's for my brothers.

CHAPTER 26

*S*imon loses the contents of his stomach twice on the run back to the cove. Normally, I wouldn't be able to keep pace with a fae, but Simon's normally tanned face has paled to a ghoulish white, his limbs trembling. His shoulders sag, his limbs kicking through the earth, freshly muddied by the mist that's overcome the island. It looks as if he might topple over any minute, and he often does, disappearing into the brush to hide the vomit from me.

We don't say much on the way to the cove. Peter launched into the sky as soon as the boy's name left Simon's lips. I can't bear to think of his name right now, his face, one I only just saw...

My legs ache, pulling me back to the Den. But I have to see for myself, or else I'm afraid I'll pretend it away like Peter and this poor boy's memory will be lost to the grim past, just like Thomas's.

There's the guilt too, pinching my chest. The gaping hole taken out of my soul when Simon told me who it was, and I rejoiced inwardly that it wasn't John or Michael.

When we finally reach the edge of the tree line hemming in the cove, Simon props himself against a tree and leans his forehead against it, breathing in the cool isle air. I squeeze his shoulder, and he acknowledges me with a feeble grimace.

FOG DUSTS the crystalline blue waters of the cove. Minerals drip from the glacier resting between the mountains into the water, giving it its vibrant hue. From a distance, it almost looks like someone dumped a lake's worth of sky-blue paint into a hole in the ground, the water appears so thick, palpable.

But as I approach the shore, several dark figures cut through the fog—one winged, the others huddled, their figures merging like crowded shadows.

Only one shadow lies parallel with the shoreline, a dash of gray paint. An accident, swept in the wrong direction.

Murmurs bounce across the black-pebbled shoreline, a few quiet sobs joining them. I scan the crowd of Lost Boys but don't see John and assume he stayed back at the Den, watching over Michael.

I would have done the same. Michael shouldn't see this.

Only once I reach Peter's side do I let myself examine the body. You would think my brain would have had time to process it on the way, but seeing him slack-jawed and bloodied steals the wind out of me the same as if I'd happened upon him unsuspecting.

Freckles's eyes are closed, but there's no mistaking him for a sleeping boy. Not with the blood that coats the belly of his shirt. Not with the lacerations carved into his face.

Cuts trace his freckles in a meticulous pattern, one that stirs a memory in me I can't quite place. Still, there's no mistaking that the pattern is premeditated.

I feel that my stomach should turn over, but it doesn't. The alienist my mother hired for me when I was a child said I had a tendency of disassociating with my pain.

He was wrong, of course.

I don't disassociate. I just tuck it away for later. It simply lurks in the shadows of my mind, waiting to assault me when I'm alone, like a lioness waiting for the straggler to become separated from its pack.

A quietness has overcome the boys since I arrived. I sense their stares boring into me, surely wondering when the only girl among them will faint.

Unnatural. That's the word my mother's alienist had used for me when he completed his evaluation. He'd shown me pictures, sketches taken from grueling crime scenes. Bodies—usually women —dismembered.

Doesn't have the womanly instinct for compassion within her, is what he'd told my mother.

I suppose I'd been supposed to cry. Vomit. Shake. Something other than blink. I had, of course, once night fell. But I'm sure the alienist was sound asleep in his own bed by that point.

Part of me must believe the alienist's accusations, because I make myself examine my memories of Freckles. His bashful, goofy smile. The feel of leather as he tucked his journal into my hands. Our mingled laughter as he taunted me to wrestle him, then picked me off the ground.

I feel nothing.

Victor is the first to speak up. "You going to try to convince us this was an accident, too?"

Peter swivels his stony gaze upon the boy with shadowed eyes. "No, I'm not."

"As both Thomas and Freckles were found with unnatural wounds, it stands to reason that they were both murdered. Most likely by the same individual," says Benjamin, his analytical gaze unwavering from Freckles's wounds.

Fear ripples through me, and it's visible in the Lost Boys too. The way they shudder and tremble.

"Someone's after blood," says Joel, his gaze tracing the lines on Freckles's face.

"Someone," says Victor through gritted teeth, "killed my brother."

The Twins tense simultaneously, but Peter doesn't back down from Victor's stare.

"Why don't you go back to the Den, Victor?"

"Why, so there won't be anyone around to say that you were wrong?"

"No, because we all know how you get when you're emotional."

Victor's face and neck take on a crimson hue. "I'm not emotional."

"Sure, if anger isn't an emotion," whispers Nettle under his breath.

Victor snaps, lunging for Nettle, but Peter steps in his path, catching Victor by his wrists. "Go back to the Den," he says, his voice calm, emotionless.

Victor looks like he's about to fight Peter, but instead he turns and spits on the ground. "Fine, but when you find my body slain in the woods, I hope it makes you think twice before trusting him again."

He stomps off, but Peter calls after him, "I don't want you going by yourself."

"I'll go," offers Simon, finally regaining some color as he steps off the tree where he's been leaning.

Peter nods, and even Victor doesn't argue. I can't help but think Simon, with his calming presence, is the best person to pair with anyone who's tottering on losing control.

"Who found him?" Peter asks, glancing around at the boys. The Twins both raise their hands.

"When?"

"An hour ago," says the first.

"And what were you doing out by the cove?"

Both twins flush, but the second lets his gaze slip to his bag on the ground. It's half open, a gill net so large it hardly fits into the bag pouring out.

"You know better," is all Peter says. The indifference in his tone is enough to make both boys hang their heads.

I want to ask what they were trying to catch, but this doesn't feel like the right moment.

"Which begs the question, what was Freckles doing out here?" asks Nettle.

Benjamin peers down at the body. "And who did he run into on the way?"

"Is anything missing?" asks Joel. When I shoot him a questioning glance, he shrugs. "Thomas..." He goes quiet, glancing up at Peter as if he wonders if he'll be punished for speaking the boy's name. "He always wore this red and blue beaded bracelet. Couldn't find it on his body."

I frown. "Wait? You found Thomas's body?" I'm not sure why, but I'd assumed Thomas had gone missing and been presumed dead.

Peter opens his mouth, but Smalls beats him to speaking. He hasn't said anything yet, just stared at Freckles's body, slack-jawed. "He had bruises all over his throat," says Smalls.

Without thinking, I shoot Peter a glare. One that's meant to say, *And you tried to convince the boys it was an accident? Do you think they're stupid?*

Peter averts his gaze.

Baffled, I check Freckles's neck, but there's nothing nefarious there. Whoever killed him, it's clear they did it with a blade to his belly. When I kneel closer to Freckles, wiping his red hair from his brow, another scent cuts through the blood. Singed hair crinkles to ash in my hands. Like the killer took a match to the tips of Freckles's hair. The scent tugs at a memory, one I can't quite place.

"Was Thomas's hair burned?" I ask.

The boys look around at one another and shrug. "If it was, none of us noticed," says Benjamin.

I glance up at Peter, who's peering down at the body thoughtfully.

I bite my lip, wishing John were here. He's always been my sounding board, helped me organize the thoughts swarming in my head.

"Victor thinks the same person who killed Freckles killed Thomas too," I say. "But if that's the case, why are the wounds so different?"

Everything I know about repeat killers is that they almost always kill using the same method.

Joel's the one who answers. "Maybe the killer is just honing their technique."

I glance up at him, his sparking green eyes.

Suddenly, I realize which memory Freckles's singed hair is tugging on.

CHAPTER 27

We e bury Freckles under a mound of rocks off of the shoreline of the cove. It takes long enough that Benjamin and Joel go back to the Den to ask Victor and Simon if they want to take part. I don't realize Benjamin is wandering off with Joel until they're already gone, and Smalls tells me. The next half hour is spent with me digging my nails into my palms, wondering if I should tell Peter to run after them, that Benjamin is in danger. But they return soon enough, Benjamin unharmed, Joel glancing at me often—or am I imagining that?

Either way, they both report that Victor turned them down.

I can't help but wonder if Victor knew about Freckles's disdain for Thomas. Part of me fills with unease thinking about Victor's tendency toward violence, but he'd seemed just as rattled as the other Lost Boys at the sight of Freckles's body. Perhaps he doesn't wish to help bury Freckles because of the emotions it brings up of burying his brother.

Once we've finished the burial, Peter turns to fly off. I go to him, calling his name, but he blatantly ignores me—I can tell because I glimpsed his ears flick at my voice—and launches into the sky.

I stand there with my hands on my hips, watching as he disappears toward the northern bluffs.

"He goes there sometimes, when something bad happens," says Simon, coming up beside me, brushing his arm against my shoulder. "Went up there after Thomas died, too."

"Bearing the secrets so you don't have to?" I ask, not managing to hide the accusation in my tone.

Simon shifts uncomfortably. "Come on. Let's go home," he says, gesturing back in the direction of the Den, where the other boys are now heading.

I nod, following the others from behind, but I can't shake the feeling that my brothers are in danger here, and that there's only one person on this island who has any answers that might save them. It's a risk, not warning John about my suspicions regarding Joel. Possibly even Victor. But John's more skeptical of the Lost Boys than I've been. I find it unlikely he'll follow any of them to remote sections of the island.

Besides, I've been unable to coax any information out of Peter up to this point. It's cruel of me, but I'd be foolish not to recognize that getting to Peter while he's emotional over the death of one of his Lost Boys might be my only shot at garnering information to help my brothers.

So when Simon catches up to the others, I lag behind, then slip into the trees.

NIGHT FALLS SWIFTLY. I'm sweating and brambles pierce my skin by the time I reach the top of the bluff.

Peter sits atop a rock across the way, watching me as I struggle to pull myself over the side of the cliff. He doesn't rise to help, but it's not as if I expect him to.

The far-off look is still in his eyes, even as he stares at me. Like he's not looking at me, but through me.

I recognize it. The grief that empties instead of overcomes, drowns instead of burns.

I put myself through pain to mask what's inside, hoist myself toward a baseline that I can convince myself is normal. Peter runs away from his. Well, flies away, sweeping it under the rug of frivolity and riddles and games.

But happiness can't drown out pain. It simply isn't potent enough, or else my mother would have managed it. So I scramble over to Peter and wipe the dust off my clothes as I confront him.

"You shouldn't have followed me up here," says Peter, and the way he swivels his head around to meet me makes me wonder if he's drunk, though I smell nothing on him, and I've yet to witness any wine on the island.

"You're hurting," I say, hugging my chest and fiddling with my loose sleeves, which are too long given that this tunic was originally Simon's.

A wry smile casts a shadow over Peter's face. One that's outside of his control, not a by-product of his magic, but of his demeanor. "I can assure you that's not the case."

Frustration boils up within me. "You love those boys. Adore them. Fight for them, for their protection. And you're hurting from losing two of them."

"And what use would that be, Wendy Darling? To hurt? What has that dreadful emotion ever done for you, as much as you like to keep it close to you, as much as you like to cloak yourself in it? Tell me a single time in your life that pain saved you from anything. Did it keep you from being swallowed by the shadows? Did it protect your parents from slitting their own throats? What did it ever do for you to hurt?"

I pause, my words thick and slimy, caught there in the stinging pain of the lump forming in my throat.

"You like to think your pain makes you noble, but it doesn't hold you in the same esteem, Wendy Darling. You care more for it than it cares for you."

My mouth goes dry. "You've lost someone very dear to you," I whisper. "You need time to heal."

"What for? To get patched up in time for the next death to occur, the next person to be ripped from my hands? Those who keep their pain close only do so because they're too weak, too dependent to let it go. They're incapable of admitting it doesn't make them any better, any stronger. Too weak to lift their sorry chins up and look to the future."

I could take away your pain.

I venture a step forward. Peter doesn't tense. Doesn't react at all.

"If you're not hurting, why did you fly up here by yourself?"

Peter doesn't look at me. He just stares into the sky above. "Thomas liked the stars. Before…before Neverland, he must have pored over books about constellations, because he had all of them memorized. That kind of memory wasn't taken from him. He knew constellations I'd never heard of, though he could never tell the stories that go along with them."

Finally, Peter turns to face me. "I came up here because the picture you showed me reminded me of that, and I wanted to remember sitting up here with Thomas as he traced patterns in the sky."

"Oh," I say. I can't help but notice how he doesn't mention Freckles. Like he can't stand to even approach a pain that lingers so close. Like it's easier to ignore it and focus on something more distant.

Peter raises his voice. "Come on, Wendy Darling. No comment about how my way of remembering my friend is somehow inferior to yours?"

There's no acid in his tone—it's still flat. Bored, almost.

I shake my head, shame wafting over me, tingeing my cheeks in unpleasant warmth.

"No. No, I'd rather not do that," I say, though it makes me uncomfortable how right he is to assume judgment on my part.

Peter points, and I follow the line of his finger. I stare up at the sky, remembering the lessons my tutors gave me about the stories written in the sky.

"That one's the Reaper," I say, identifying the constellation of a robed figure holding a scythe above us.

"Are you familiar with the tale?"

I think back to the story behind the formidable constellation and nod. "The legend is that, when we die, the Reaper comes with his familiar—a fox, I think—to escort us to the afterlife. Some time ago, the Reaper fell in love with a living woman. But he soon grew lonely, desperate for her company as they could only meet one another during the brief moments surrounding a nearby death. Impatient, the Reaper took the woman's life, slaughtering her with his sickle. But the Reaper was never supposed to take life, only to lead souls as they transitioned from bodily to spiritual form. By killing her, he'd inadvertently tied her soul to the earth. When she rotted, the ground took her as its own, and in the spot she was buried grew a tree. An oak so great it burst through the headstone her family had used to mark where she lay. They say the branches were barren and formed the shape of a hand—the woman's spirit reaching above, hoping to grasp hold of her lover, but never able to bridge the gap between the earth and the heavens, the physical and spiritual."

"And what of the roots?" asks Peter.

I scrunch my brow, confused, until the memory returns. "It's said that if you see a fox digging at the base of a tree, it's the Reaper's familiar seeking the woman's soul in the roots. But...oh."

I choke back a sob, recognizing now why the pattern carved into Freckles's cheek looked so familiar. "It's a fox. *The* fox." I search the sky, finding the constellation just below the Reaper.

"I gather you see the resemblance now," Peter says, voice dry.

"Do you think it's a coincidence?" I ask. "I could see a killer marking his victim with the Reaper's familiar anyway, but the fact that Thomas, the first victim, adored constellations..."

"You seem to have answered your own question. And the fox was Thomas's favorite."

My mind races. On the shore of the cove, I'd wondered if there were two different killers, given the different causes of death. But the murderer practically bragged about killing Thomas by cutting the Reaper's fox into Freckles's skin. "Peter, if the killer knew Thomas..."

He cuts me off. "Why exert all that effort climbing up here?"

I'm so taken aback, the rest of my question gets caught in my throat. "You were hurting. I thought you might want some company." It strikes me how true the words are. How I'd convinced myself I was doing this for John and Michael.

Peter's face is devoid of emotion as he finally turns to look at me. "I thought I already told you," he says. "I don't want you at all."

CHAPTER 28

"So you think the same person killed Thomas and Freckles?" John asks, tapping his fingers against his knees as he sits at the side of his cot, directly across from me. An hour of trekking down the bluffs and across the forest to reach the Den had left me exhausted, but that had done nothing to deter John from bombarding me with questions about Freckles's murder.

I bite the inside of my cheek. "It seems that way, doesn't it? With the way the killer carved Thomas's favorite constellation into Freckles's cheek?"

John shrugs. "Sure, but technically, there are other explanations. It could simply be a coincidence. It's not too far-fetched to think someone who murders for fun might take on the Reaper's fox as their symbol. Though now that I'm thinking about it, one would think a killer would prefer the symbol of the Reaper himself. Another option is whoever killed Freckles might wish for us to believe that his murder is connected to Thomas's."

"Like if he killed Freckles out of anger?" I ask.

John reaches across the cot and scratches Michael's back, our youngest brother sleeping soundly in his cot. "You did say Freckles didn't keep his disdain for Thomas a secret. It's likely Victor knew about it."

"Yes, but is that really a motive for murder?" I ask.

"It would make me mad if I overheard someone bad-mouthing our parents," says John, somewhat distantly. "Besides, if Freckles wasn't sorry that Thomas was dead, Victor could have gotten it into his head that Freckles was the one who killed him. Maybe he lured Freckles out to the cove and stabbed him in revenge."

"I don't know," I say. "There's also Joel. He seems to have an affinity for torture."

"Carving a constellation in someone's face is a bit of an escalation from coaxing rats into the fire, don't you think?"

We let that settle between us for a moment, gooseflesh prickling my forearms. John reaches out, placing a hand on my shoulder. "Hey," he says. "You okay?"

I blink, despite the fact that my eyes are dry. "Yeah. Yeah, I'm fine."

John crinkles his brow. "You know that's just as concerning, right?"

I close my eyes and nod. "Does it make me a freak?" I ask. "If I didn't feel anything when we found Freckles today? I mean, he was my friend..."

John stares at me, his brown eyes magnified by his thick spectacles. "Wendy?" He says my name like it's a question in and of itself. "Can I ask you something?"

No! my mind screams, dread rattling me at the idea of what secrets of mine my clever brother might have unlocked.

"Of course," I say, and it's my mother's tenor I hear in the words.

John isn't looking at me anymore, but at my hands, folded in my lap in front of me. "One time, during your second season out in society, I passed the smoking parlor, and I thought I heard—"

"No," I lie. "It wasn't what you think."

My brother looks at me, cocking his head to the side as sorrow and pity crinkle in folds around his eyes, his brow. "I didn't say what I thought it was."

He says it like my reaction is answer enough, but I can't allow it. Can't allow John to know what happened in that parlor, not when he wouldn't understand. Not when he's just lost our parents and knowing the truth might give him the wrong impression.

"Don't worry about me. I'm fine," I whisper, pleading with him not to press further.

John frowns. Opens his mouth, then shuts it again.

Michael lets out a violent snore, causing John and me to spring off of our respective cots, shaking.

"Goodnight, John," I say, retreating into my blankets like they're impenetrable enough not only to protect me, but also John's memory of our parents.

He's quiet for a minute. When he speaks, I fear he hasn't dropped the subject, but then he says, "We'll see if anyone saw Joel around the time of the murder."

I SPEND the evening soaking my sheets with tears. I wish I could say I shed every one of them for Freckles, for Thomas, for the Lost Boys. For the boy whose love of the stars surpassed any magic worked on his mind. For the boy whose hand sketched the features of others with such love and precision, yet barely knew his own.

For the freckled boy who longed for nothing more than the attention of his peers.

Grief might not have assaulted me on the rocky beaches of the cove, but only because it was stalking me from the shadows, waiting for the darkness to descend.

My mind tortures me, trying to replay every interaction I've ever had with Freckles. I clutch his journal to my chest like it contains the soul of my sweet friend. Like, if only I keep it close, I won't forget the already fading chime of his laugh.

I cry for myself, for witnessing the bloodied wounds that sing of the way my parents died, that carve themselves into the backs of my eyelids as sleep evades me. For the fact that I have to live with the answer to John's question of what used to happen in the parlor. I cry because of what my parents felt they must do to save me.

I cry for John and Michael too, for trading their safety from the pirates for life on an island that craves their blood.

But I'd be lying if I didn't say I was hoarding some of the tears for myself. For the stinging bits of flesh flaking off my heart as Peter's words pierce my soul like tattoo needles into the flesh.

I don't want you at all.

I don't want you at all.

I don't want you at all.

They're the same words whispered on sneering lips as eligible men take in my Mating Mark for the first time. The same javelin to my chest as when Captain Astor scoffed at the idea that he might wish to dance with me, when I'd hoped perhaps my Mating Mark had finally found its match.

They're tears not only for the lack of being wanted, but for the guilt of letting such a petty thought scrape the emptiness from my soul. It's not as if I grew up loveless, the unwanted daughter that so many of the old faerie tales paint alongside disappointed fathers who wished for a son as an heir. Never did my family act as though I was any less worthy of their love than John or Michael. In fact, they protected me more fiercely.

In their own misguided way.

So why do Peter's callous words sting like adders' fangs at my sternum?

Shouldn't I be rejoicing that the villain whose attention, whose wanting I dreaded for years, isn't interested in inflicting evil upon me?

It hits me that all this time, Peter was the one person I never counted on losing interest in me.

It's sick and repulsive and I hate myself for letting a man who's never cared about me delve his claws so deeply into my identity.

The girl who men never wanted, but the shadows always did.

What does it say about me if even the shadows turn away?

Despite myself, I find my fingers trailing my cheek. The spaces between the freckles of my Mating Mark are marred by the scars from where Tink dug her fingernails into my flesh, her jealousy lining my skin. I'd laugh at the irony if it wouldn't wake my brothers.

Tink clearly has nothing to be jealous of.

Still, as my hands trace the raised golden mark, I allow my thoughts to wander. I let them off their leash and toward a past rewritten by a foolish heart. Let them daydream of a future that was never to be mine.

I wonder where he is, the male who owns my heart. Not Peter, who owns my body and freedom, but the man whose soul is knit with mine.

It's not as if I ever expected to meet him. Sure, with every suitor my parents picked out for me, I allowed that little sliver of hope lodged in my chest to jut out, like a buried splinter being expunged by the body as it slowly reknits itself.

I'd never as much as laid eyes on another Mating Mark until I met the captain. And that man had dashed my hopes in more than one way.

As I think of the captain's face, of his coarse voice masking the pain, but not nearly as well as Peter, I think of his hand on my waist, the flicker of warmth and connection that had fired there.

I think of the captain, and that beautiful, perfect moment, and I hate him for it. I hate him for stealing my attention away from my misery, just for a moment. For making me feel safe, even in the wake of his brusque words and blunt temperament. I hate that we shared a moment of agony together, both victims of our own lost loves.

I hate him for making me like him, then shattering me.

And I hate myself right now for allowing my mind to wander to the man who killed my parents.

My fingertips become wet where they linger on the Mark as tears slip down my cheeks and the quiet sobs start. I muffle them with my blanket, my body shaking and trembling.

It's not long before tiny footsteps pad over to me in the dark, a drowsy Michael wiping his eyes of sleep before slipping onto my cot with me, curling up with his head on my chest.

"Don't cry, Michael," he whispers. "Mama's got you."

I shake harder, clutching onto my brother as if to life itself.

When sleep finally overtakes me, it's with the nightmare of Captain Astor's voice in my ears, quietly seducing me to slit my parents' throats.

"YOU LOOK like you got stung in the face by a wasp," says Smalls, looking across the breakfast table at me as he scoops a spoonful of berry-speckled oats into his mouth.

Next to him, Benjamin elbows him in the side. Hard. "That's from crying, stupid."

I can't help but note how they don't mention the way all of their eyes are puffy underneath the lids, too. How scarlet veins thread the whites around their irises.

I suppose for them, it's easier to focus on the crying girl.

I might take more offense if I didn't know they'd been mourning along with me, separated only by the roots of this wretched tree. I'd wept myself to sleep, and when I woke, it was to a puffy face and constricted sinuses. But it was also as if someone had poured chilled water over my soul, washing the pain from my heart like a stain from cloth.

Of course, exhaustion lingers, making my muscles heavy. I might have stayed in my cot today, slept until noon, except that Michael's internal clock had him up before the sun and trying to tiptoe on my back.

Next to me, John nudges me ever so slightly. When I glance at him, there's a silent question in his thoughtful eyes. *Are you okay?*

I give him a soft smile and nod quietly.

It doesn't feel like as much of a lie as it is.

Simon gives me an apologetic glance, then opens up discussion around the table about when the boys think the frostbugs will first appear.

It's a clear attempt to distract the conversation away from their pain. The kind of thing Peter would do. The kind of thing Simon has likely learned from Peter.

I'm asking what the frostbugs are when Peter strides in from the hall.

He stops in his tracks when he sees me, the same blankness in his expression that was there yesterday. His eyes linger on the deep lines cut into and below my eyelids, the blotches that must remain around my cheeks, the shine of my eyes that deepens their blue hue.

He turns back around and disappears down the hallway.

"Frostbugs are like fireflies, except they come out when it's cold," says John.

Benjamin almost smiles. "Joel and I were looking for their dens yesterday. They're easier to catch when you can find them sleeping. If you can trap them in a glass jar, they'll bring you good luck."

I'm about to ask why frostbugs would bestow luck upon their captors when John asks, "How long did it take you to find any?"

Joel cuts his eyes to John, but Benjamin just laughs. "I do wish we would have found some. We spent all day looking. Well, early in the morning until..." He trails off, eyes going glassy.

I try not to make eye contact with John, but I can tell he's staring at me.

It seems Joel has an alibi.

THE WEAKNESS BROUGHT on by yesterday's murder has yet to leave my limbs by the day's end. Simon pestered me about what was bothering me during our hunt today, but I found it didn't feel quite fair to complain to him about my before-Never when he has no memories of his.

I'm sitting by the fire in the Den, curling the corner of Thomas's sketch in my hand, when I hear a voice.

"Winds?"

I get the strangest sense that this moment in time has overlapped with a moment from the past, but when I turn around, of course it's not Freckles I find.

Because Freckles is dead.

Nettle approaches, hesitantly, his blond hair, usually combed neatly at his forehead, mussed. "Can I ask you a question?"

I'm too exhausted for questions, but I don't feel that I can say as much, so I nod.

"That night you helped me cook," he says. "Remember how I told you about my father being a duke?"

The muscles in my hand tense. I don't think I can bear telling Nettle that the memory he clings to with all his might is the remnants of a nursery rhyme.

"Of course I do," I respond, trying my best to sound chipper.

"It's okay," he says, kicking at the corner of the rug. "You don't have to pretend. I heard Michael singing earlier. And as it seems a little far-fetched to assume that your little brother made up an entire song about my family..." He offers me a pained wince.

"I'm sorry, Nettle," I say. "I should have told you."

He shakes his head, his blond hair rustling as he does. I suppose I now know why he's stopped bothering to comb it like he's an aristocrat. "No. I'm glad you didn't. It was nice getting to believe something spectacular. That I have a family out there missing me. Thanks for letting me hold onto that just a little bit longer."

Tears well at my eyes, and he offers me a sad smile.

"Does this mean you can eat onions again?" I tease.

He lets out a startled laugh. "Not a chance," he says. "Aristocrat or not, it doesn't change the way they taste."

Nettle sits with me by the fire for a while. By the time he leaves, I feel as if I've given him the last bits of my dwindling energy reserves, he at least leaves smiling.

I'm about to return to my room, when someone speaks.

"Get your coat."

I spin around, stunned a little by the enthusiasm in the voice. It's almost as if I expect it to be Simon, though I know better. My eyes check for me, but there he is, propped against the doorway, his entire body giving off an aura that hums with adventure.

"Pardon me?" I ask, not at all attempting to hide the disinterest in my tone.

"Come on, Wendy Darling," Peter says, offering me a smirk. "Get your coat."

My mind buzzes, whiplash overtaking me at the sudden shift in Peter's mood. Though, I suppose I haven't seen him since this morning, so it might not be as sudden as it seems. "What for?"

His eyes twinkle with amusement. "It's a surprise."

I quietly fold the sketch and tuck it in my pocket. "I'm not sure you and I like the same kinds of surprises."

I expect hurt to flash in his eyes, but he's undeterred. "I apologize for being cruel yesterday, Wendy Darling," he says. "I'm not often challenged in my way of thinking."

I bite my lip. It's nice that he's at least acknowledging what a scoundrel he was yesterday. How unnecessarily cruel.

"I'd rather you not be angry with me forever. We are, after all, doomed to inhabit this same island."

When I say nothing, Peter shrugs, though not dismissively. "I'll be at the mouth of the tree," he says.

I wait for the pounding of his feet to echo into silence down the hallway, my heart racing as I listen for him. I shouldn't go. Shouldn't trust the fae, in general. Isn't that lesson number one in being human? And I especially shouldn't trust the Shadow Keeper, especially not after how he treated me yesterday.

Then again.

I suppose I dredged up the pain he'd been suppressing. Obviously I could have done nothing about his loss of Freckles, but it's clear how much he cared about Thomas, how much it pained him to lose both boys. People deal with pain in different ways. Some embrace it, wallowing in it. Others shut it out completely.

Who am I to judge the way Peter handles his grief?

Sure, he could have been kinder about it, but as much as it stings, he wasn't entirely wrong about my intentions—my insistence that he was grieving incorrectly. Now that I think of it, sitting in the spot where he once shared wonderful memories doesn't seem like an inappropriate way to treat the boy's memory.

In a warped way, it makes sense he'd clung to an older pain, the loss of the first boy. I'd learned from the alienist that grief is felt first as denial.

Again, not an excuse for cruelty, but a reason.

And it's nice to be apologized to.

That's something my father never quite got down. He was a kind and cheerful man, most always, but on the rare occasion he did treat us unfairly, he never acknowledged as much.

As much as my heart still stings when I think of Peter's words, *I never wanted you*, it's not as if the words are untrue. Not as if I've earned his wanting of me or am entitled to it. The simple apology does wonders to soothe the aching.

And besides.

My other option is curling up on my cot and facing nightmares where the devastatingly beautiful captain steals my heart, then makes me slit my parents' throats.

So I dash down the hall to get my coat before I can convince myself otherwise. I'm grabbing it from where I left it folded on my cot when John speaks up from where he's sitting in the corner.

"Where are you heading off to?"

I bite my lip, slipping my coat on slowly so I have time to collect my thoughts before I turn to face him. "The stove fire burned out, so it's freezing in the kitchen, and I've still got half the dishes to wash."

The lie tastes foul, like vomit staining the back of my teeth. It's not even my night to do the dishes. I'm not sure why I lied, except that John is so protective of me, and I worry he'll talk me out of letting go for once.

John pushes himself from his chair. "Let me help you. It'll go by much faster."

I wave him off. "It was your duty last night. Besides, I don't want us to have to bring Michael in there. You know how much he detests the cold."

John frowns, but there's no suspicion in his face when he sits back down.

My gut is still sour with the lie when I slip into the hall.

WHEN THE TREE deposits me out in the cold, my heart sinks as I realize no one is there.

I search back around the wide trunk, wondering if perhaps Peter meant the other side, but he's nowhere to be found.

Did I take too long and he left on his adventure without me?

Or worse, was inviting me up here just another one of his cruel little games? Like threatening to drop me from the sky or waiting for me to fall from the cliffs. My stomach turns over.

"I was starting to think you'd never forgive me, Wendy Darling," says a voice, and my heart jumps into my throat. I jump too, stumbling over a root in front of me. There's a carefree laugh echoing from above, and I glimpse Peter peering down at me from where he's perched in the branches above.

"I'm still debating," I say, and I can't help the way my heart thumps at the pleased smile that spreads across his beautiful face.

"Is this the adventure, then?" I ask, gesturing up toward the reaping tree. My heart lights with anticipation at the idea of scaling it. I hate the tree for what it did to John, what it assumed about Michael, but that doesn't mean I don't long for the feel of its bark underneath my fingertips.

"This?" Peter says, glancing around. "Have you not already climbed it? I would have expected as much from a girl who makes a habit of climbing things she wasn't supposed to."

I shrug. "In all honesty, I've considered it. But I wasn't sure the tree would tolerate it. Forgive me if I'm hesitant of climbing into the branches of a tree that..." I stop, thinking of John's pinkie left to rot upon the stump.

My throat goes dry.

"That's probably wise of you," says Peter, jumping down from the high branch as if he's hopping off the railing of a bridge onto the walkway. His wings expand ever so slightly, slowing his descent. "But no, we won't be climbing the tree tonight. Unless that's what you have your heart set on, of course."

I shake my head, curiosity threatening to eat a hole in my gut.

Suddenly, he's close, and his gaze flicks to my shoulders. I wonder then if he'll slip his arm around me, but he doesn't. Instead, he tilts his head to the side and beckons for me to follow him into the dark night.

I do.

WHEN WE REACH A CLEARING, he spins on his heel and extends a hand to me.

I keep my hands clasped behind my back. I'm hoping the stance comes across as casually disinterested, but really my fingers are twisting around one another, fidgeting with excitement.

I shouldn't be thrilled to be out alone with the Shadow Keeper. Not when I belong to him. Not when he holds a blank bargain over me.

I try to swallow that thought down, push it to the back of my mind. So far Peter's shown no indication that he intends me harm.

"You act as if we haven't done this before," he says, his grin wicked in the shimmer of the moonlight. I'm transported back to my little window, the shadows beckoning me. To the night in the clock tower when Peter extended his hand, and I took it without deliberating.

I'm deliberating now, and when I place my hand in his, it's intentional. Immediately, he whirls me around, spinning me in a pirouette. I let out a laugh, but he stops me as my back faces him and pulls me close.

Anticipation whirls under my skin, not just from his touch, but from the realization of what he's about to do.

"Are you ready, Wendy Darling?"

He doesn't wait for a response before he shoots into the sky.

CHAPTER 29

The wind whirls through my hair, whipping it into my face as Peter launches us skyward. The stars are out tonight, painting streaks of light across the sky as we race toward them. It's stunning up here, and exhilaration fills my chest, opening my lungs from their usual constricted position as we soar up and up and up.

We're so high now. High above the troubles and fears and aches and pains that compel me on the ground below. If I peer hard enough, I can see the speckles of light glowing from the reaping tree. Can see the stretch of sand where I pound my feet into the ground to stomp out the pain.

Peter tightens his powerful arms around me, and we leave them all behind, until they're fading speckles on the shore. Just as small and indistinguishable as one grain of sand from the next.

Light streaks around us, the colors of the painted night sky filling my head, my eyes, my chest, my everything, until Peter and I swim in a world of color, one that's only our own.

This is his world, I realize. The world above the ground, the world of escape and joy and bliss and...

And laughter.

That's the sound coming from my lips. Free and joyous and

bursting from my lungs that have held it captive for so long. I'm laughing, and the sound is so unfamiliar to me, it's like hearing music for the first time. The plucking of a harp string to a soul that's never tasted the depths of its tremors.

I'm laughing, and the sky is swarming with color.

I'm soaring.

Rather, Peter is soaring, and he's taking me with him, allowing me to taste the chill of the air as it whips against my face. It's not that I haven't flown in his arms before. But the night he stole me away from the clock tower, I'd just witnessed my parents' deaths.

No.

I won't think about them now.

Not when, for the first time since my mother told me my body belonged to the shadows, my lungs swell to their capacity. No weight bears against my chest, squeezing me until I can't get a full breath of air.

Up here, my feet don't touch the ground, and there's a weightlessness to me that's intoxicating.

There's something about Peter that's intoxicating, too.

I'd forgotten when I grabbed his hand the effect his fae glamour has upon me. The way it seeps into my veins like brandy into the bloodstream, filling me with a buzzing, limitless warmth.

I'd forgotten, but I'm glad I forgot.

Because once, just this once, I want to let myself feel this. I want to drink up the blissful attraction that is Peter and not deprive myself of the intoxicating sensation just because I'm afraid.

"You're beautiful, Wendy Darling," says Peter, whispering something wonderful into my ear, his cheek grazing mine as he does, undeterred by the Mark against my skin.

"You can hardly see me the way I'm turned away from you," I whisper back.

"I don't have to see you. I feel you."

I laugh, this time nervously. "That's hardly the same thing."

"I'm not talking about this," he says, stroking my belly where he has a firm grip on me. "Or this," he says, burrowing his face into my neck so that his lips almost graze my skin. "I'm talking about you. About the aura you're putting off."

"Humans don't have auras."

"Not the boring ones," he says, gently amused. "You, though— you've got that little bit left in you."

"Perhaps it's from communing with the shadows," I say.

"Perhaps."

I'd say I want to drown in how it feels to be tucked into Peter's chest, to stare down at the ground far below us and feel my toes tingle with that pleasant numbness. Like my feet have fallen asleep, but without the pain.

There was a time in my life where I'd have let myself drown in a sensation like this.

But I don't want to drown. I want to drink. I want this moment, this feeling, to slip down my throat and fill my empty, starving belly.

"Wendy Darling," Peter says, leveling out as his wings send a gentle, constant breeze flapping into my face.

"Yes?" I ask, breathless.

"I'm going to ask you a question, and I'm going to need you to trust me enough to answer yes."

"Okay."

"Would you like me to drop you?"

My heart should plummet, and it does.

But I think I might like how it feels to fall.

"Yes," I whisper. And it's as if I'm parched and he's asked me if I need fresh water. As if I'm starving and he's offered me a plate of hot bread, freshly pulled from the oven and buttered.

"That's what I like to hear," he says.

Then Peter lets go.

ALL MY LIFE I've climbed. Higher and higher, chasing that raging numbness that would waft over my body, my limbs.

All my life, I thought it was the scaling I was grasping for.

All my life, I've been wrong. Sidling up to the precipice, too afraid to grasp what my heart truly desired. I've been scaling, thinking the top of the mountain was what I sought.

When all I ever truly wanted to do was jump.

Fall.

Plummet.

Feel my body cut through the air in a hasty descent toward the ground. Hear nothing but my heart pounding against my ears from the inside, the wind from the outside. A steady thrum in a world of color and chaos. To see the ground coming ever closer, closing in on me.

To stare down my future and feel the thrill rather than the fear.

It lasts for a few seconds and an entirety. A moment frozen—no, separate—from time. Like the space distinct from time I've always searched for in my bed, not wanting to wake from my slumber.

A place where the ticking minute hand can't get me.

Steady, warm hands catch me, and then I'm floating in Peter's arms, my breathing labored with exhilaration as I stare into his beautiful face.

A smile breaks across it, and I imagine it's as crazed and wild as mine.

"Again," I gasp.

Peter shakes his head in wonder, as drunk on the high as I am.

"Whatever you say, Wendy Darling."

THE NEXT TIME Peter drops me, I'm prepared. I use the descent to twirl in the air, noting how my body feels with absolutely nothing touching it other than my clothes. Nothing bearing down on me from above, no weight tethering me to the ground below. It's like iron shackles have been weighing my weary body down for years, and now I'm free.

By the time Peter and I take a break, I've lost count of how many times he's dropped me.

How many times he's caught me.

"I should have let you do that the first time you asked," I admit, and that only incenses the mischief in his glowing blue eyes.

"I'd say I wish you had, but then would it be as thrilling tonight?" He brushes a finger through my hair as he says it, tucking my hair behind my ear. Then he spins me around to face him. I have to cross my ankles behind his back to keep my feet from dangling awkwardly.

"Would you do me the pleasure of allowing me a dance?"

"I don't know how good of a dance partner I'll be up here," I giggle.

Peter's eyes twinkle. "Good thing I have a solution to that."

He dips one hand into the pouch at his side, keeping me fastened to his chest with the other. When he removes his finger, it's coated with glimmering dust, though I can't help but notice that it's less than he commanded either Michael or John to take when it was time for them to fly.

"This should be enough to keep your feet steady," he explains, pressing his finger to my lips, his eyes flickering when my tongue touches his fingertip.

A shattering warmth washes over me, cleansing me of the pain of Freckles's death, of my parents' deaths, though I'm not sure if it's from Peter's touch at my mouth, or the effects of the faerie dust, or a combination of both. When I gaze behind him at the sky unfolding beyond us, I can't help but notice that the colors seem sharper, though the shapes of the objects on the ground below are less defined.

Definitely the faerie dust then.

I now see why he keeps it away from the Lost Boys, only using it on them in emergencies, like with John and Michael or when the nightstalker assaulted me at the warehouse. He'd given me such a minuscule dose then, I'd hardly registered it.

I can't help but wonder if he'd give me another taste if I asked him. Before I can make my request, he interlocks his fingers through mine, keeping the other firmly at my hip.

And then we dance.

It's like no dancing I've ever done, the carefully calculated waltzes of the aristocracy. Peter whirls me around like I'm a puppet at the end of his string, spinning me in a blur of dizzying streaks of starlight.

There's nothing at all. Nothing but warmth in my chest and lights glittering around us and Peter's touch.

It's lovely and wonderful, and I never want it to end.

It's his glamour enchanting you, says my mother's voice, warning me nightly as a child, well intentioned as she filled my soul with dread.

But nothing my mother feared was as dreadful as what has actually come to pass. She spent her life warning me of Peter, when she should have been warning me of sullen captains and their sharp edges and their thirst for retribution. She should have warned me about the necessary evils that I'd be subjected to as someone whose life depended on ensnaring a husband.

I don't want to think about that either.

So I don't.

I dance.

CHAPTER 30

When the dance is over, Peter pulls me back into his chest and flies me to the top of a tree on a nearby cliff. We settle into the shelter of its branches, Peter slipping his arm around my shoulders as I lean into him.

It shouldn't, but it fills me with an assurance of safety I can't describe, can't quite get a grasp on. While the joy in the sky jolted the melancholy out of me like lightning fraying a mast, nesting in Peter's arms smothers the heaviness in my chest in the blanket of his embrace.

His wings are too large for our resting spot, so he cocoons them around us both, casually tracing my shoulder blade with his thumb. I'm as high on excitement as I was plummeting through the sky, and all it takes is his wayward touch.

"How did that feel?" he asks, his voice a whisper riding the breeze.

My attention is so focused on the warm trail of his touch, it takes me a moment to realize he's talking about flying. Falling.

"It felt like letting go," I say, and I'm reminded of entering Neverland, of Peter's command. I hadn't considered it much before now.

Perhaps that's due to the glamour he used on me. "Did you use magic to take away my fear of you when we first arrived?" I ask.

"It's not quite as simple as that," Peter says. "I can't compel you with my glamour. Only suggest. Whether my suggestion takes root depends entirely on whether you let it. And even then, it doesn't work on everyone."

"Why does it work on me?"

He pauses. Considers. "It only influences those who already want it to."

I bite my lip, waiting for the horror to skitter up my spine. It doesn't. All my life, I've been afraid, and though there's part of me, the part my parents trained into me, that screams I should quake at Peter's power over me, it's not *my* fear. Not really.

"I was frightened of you, you know. They wanted me to be frightened." For the first time, I wonder how my childhood would have gone had my parents not taught me to be afraid of the dark. Would I have learned to dance with the shadows earlier? Would I have set aside the vain pursuit of finding a husband and lived out my youth like the other children, unconcerned with the future?

There's something else, though. Something that threatens to steal away the enjoyment of how it feels when Peter touches me. And I'm so very tired of the pleasure being leached out of everything I do.

"I suppose I was frightening," Peter responds, his voice light, though it's softer than it normally is. His hand twitches ever so slightly. I wonder if he's as uncomfortable as I am, if we're thinking the same thing.

Probably not. The fae from the ancient stories had a tendency to steal their human brides away at an age rather younger than what aristocratic society would deem appropriate.

"Wendy," Peter says, his voice knowing.

"Yes?" I ask.

"Is it possible that something is bothering you?"

I bite my lip. "What makes you think that?"

"Oh, I don't know. Perhaps the way you're staring off into the distance."

"What can I say? It's a beautiful view."

"And you're avoiding my question."

I scoff. As if Peter isn't the prince of avoiding questions.

"Let me guess. It has something to do with my shadows visiting you when you were a child?"

I gulp. "It's not just that."

Peter chuckles, his hand stroking my shoulder. "Then a combination of my shadows visiting you as a child and the way this," he says, caressing my shoulder, "makes you feel." True to his word, a shudder reverberates on the skin he so casually touches.

I clear my throat.

"It's a fair question," says Peter.

"Then why aren't you answering it?"

"Because you haven't asked."

My chest tightens, my face paling. I want this so badly—for the way his touch makes me feel to be okay. Acceptable. Real. But the doubt in the back of my mind claws at me now that we're not swimming in the thrill of the sky. Now that the taste of faerie dust has faded from my tongue.

"My master," he says, his throat dry, "wished that I keep an eye on you as a child. Mark your whereabouts. Make sure your parents weren't trying to sneak you away, hide you in some remote place of the world."

My heart thuds against my chest. "By master, you mean the Fate. The Fate who healed me. Cursed me."

It's nothing more than a guess, though one I've had years to educate myself about. My mother never told me it was a Fate who came to her. Maybe it was the way my imagination ran away with me as a child, but I always thought—hoped—it was a Fate. As if that would somehow imbue my suffering with meaning.

Peter nods, and my breath hitches at this subtle confirmation of a question that's been rattling me my entire life. I remember what he said about his master, how she has no friends, only lovers and slaves. How quickly it had become apparent that Peter never wanted me to be enslaved to him. It was her idea all along.

"I kept in my shadow form because..." He draws in a breath. "I'm not myself then. I suppose I'm parts of myself, but not entirely. In some ways, it's a curse, but in other ways, it helps me stay detached. Even my memories of what happens when I'm in my shadow form are hazy. It's like how dreams seem clear in the moment, but then you have trouble reconciling the details when you're awake. You were never real to me, Wendy. Just fragments of a memory. It must feel strange to you, like I've known you since you were a child. But to me, I didn't know you until the moment you took my hand in the tower."

My mother's voice warns me, claims I shouldn't be swayed by what he's saying, but I can't help but wish for it to be true. I want so badly for our night in the stars to be a beautiful memory, one I can cling onto in safety. A night where I became brave, the type of girl who soars through the night, not one who teeters on the edge, too afraid to jump.

That's the thing.

I'm tired of being afraid.

My fear is a weariness leaching my soul from my bloodstream, the blood from my already sallow cheeks.

I don't want to fear Peter anymore.

"Tell me about her. The Fate." I hate how breathless my voice has gone, how thirsty I am for the story of the being who set my life on a path I couldn't escape.

Peter's face goes blank again, and I wonder if I've struck a nerve, picked at the crack in the dam of his larger-than-life exterior.

"You have to understand, growing up in the orphanage I did, there wasn't much to look forward to in life. They'd keep us until we grew up. Reaching adulthood was about as good as having a noose tied around your neck for kids like us. Tossed out on the street without the orphanage to feed us. Most turned to thievery, made the wrong noble angry, and ended up on the wrong side of a noose. I can't tell you how many of the older boys I saw hanging from the juniper tree in the middle of the town square, just weeks after they'd come of age. Growing up was a death sentence," he says.

"Isn't it always? At some point, I mean."

The smile he offers me is almost sad. Almost. "I can't imagine why you seek out such thoughts."

I shrug, pulling my overcoat into myself, stroking the furs of my sleeve. "I like to know what to expect, what I should anticipate. Even if it's pain, it's not quite as frightening once you get a full view of it. Take it in for what it is."

"Like me?" Peter says, swiping his hand with a flourish down his lithe body, wrapped head to foot in black leathers.

"No," I say. "You're just frightening. Only, in a different way."

Peter's eyes light with mischief, but he continues on with his story. "I wanted so badly never to grow up when I was a child. I'd seen death. My..." He blinks quickly, then pivots. "Well, I suppose you don't have to have too grand of an imagination to figure out why I ended up in an orphanage. I'd seen death wrap its slimy fingers around someone I loved, seen the breath stolen from her sunken mouth. Seen the boys I used to play cards with and make bets with swollen with after-stench in the town square. I figured I'd find my way out of it, if I could."

I wonder then if such dread of death is worse for the fae. From what I know of the legends, the fae used to be close to immortal, living hundreds of years. Their lifespan was cut short due to a curse a century and a half ago, though the curse only applies to fae born after the curse was enacted. But most of the fae were wiped out in the War, so if there are any with immortal lifespans, they're likely few in number. I wonder what it's like knowing your body possesses the capability of living a thousand years, but magic is keeping you from it. It stands to reason that Peter would try to outdo the curse through magic. As a child, he wouldn't have been able to see that beating the curse, never growing up, would not save him from the cruelty of his society.

"I searched for a Fate, tried to trap one through all the clever means I could devise, but never once was I successful. When I came of age, I convinced the warden to give me a position on the orphan-age's staff. But then," he says, his throat going hoarse, "one night, everything changed. The children were asleep, but I was never a good sleeper. Not after years of training my body to stay up all hours of the night, watching for a Fate. I'd given up my search by then, but I heard a draft from the window, and she just…appeared."

Peter's eyes go glassy now, his awe still peeking through the surface. "She was hideous and beautiful and hidden in the shadows, but I knew she was one of the Fates. I was so sure she had come for me, after all those years. I called out to her as she approached the bed of one of the boys. It must've startled her, because she whipped around, and it was only then I realized she hadn't come for me at all, but the boy in the bed across from me, still sound asleep. At first I suppose I was jealous, but now that I had her attention, I was sure I could keep it. I was always good at finding and keeping attention," he says, an affectionate smile for his younger self playing on his face.

"The Sister appeared intrigued that I didn't cower from her pres-ence and that her sleeping spell had not worked on me. Upon further examination, she realized it was because I had been waiting for her, expecting her, that I was immune to her glamour. I begged her for a chance to prove myself. Promised I'd make any bargain she wished, if only I didn't have to be thrown out onto the street where I would surely become a bloated corpse. You see, there was talk of a new warden overtaking the facility after unflattering rumors had circulated about the current warden. I wasn't sure it would be as easy to convince the new warden to keep me on staff."

"Why not?" I ask.

Peter blinks, then continues on with his story. As if he didn't hear me at all. "The Sister stared at me a long while and informed me my aspirations were too meager. That they wouldn't protect me from that which I truly feared. This confused me, but she had already turned back to the boy across from me. I scrambled out of my bed and followed her, watching as she unstoppered a vial of shimmering liquid."

My heart pounds as I hang on every word of Peter's. My mother never told me this part of the story, but one night I overheard her telling my father she'd had a nightmare that the shadowed woman had come for me. That Mother had consented as she'd pressed a vial, dripping with opal liquid, to my lips. My mother had instantly regretted it, but it had been too late. The potion had already stolen the color from my cheeks, the blood from my lips. I'd gotten the impression that, in reality, before the Fate had offered my mother a bargain to save my life, she'd offered to put me out of my suffering.

When I first read the story of the Sisters in a tattered faerie tale book caked with dust, I imagined it had been the Eldest Sister who had healed me. I'd been young and thought that since the Eldest Sister was obsessed with love, it had to have been her who promised me to her Shadow Keeper. Only after I learned of my mother's nightmare did my attention shift to the Youngest Sister, who had appeared at my sickbed not to heal me, but to usher me to the grave without pain.

Peter continues. "She lowered it to his mouth, but I defied her, grabbing the vial before the liquid could brush his lips. I knew I had forfeited my life, then. I just expected the Sister to end me with a true death. Never did I anticipate the punishment that ensued, though even then, I didn't realize it was a punishment.

"She told me I was a fool. That she was a Fate, and she could see that which I could not. Killing the child in his bed, in the middle of a deep slumber from which he would not wake, a full belly and a heart full of bedtime stories—that path would have been a mercy, she told me. She told me she was the most compassionate of her sisters, and that she had seen what their dark hearts had worked for this child. She told me there was a plague within the walls of the orphanage, one that had already infected the boy. A disease that he'd already spread to some of the others."

I think of the way my parents described the plague to me. Sailors waking in the middle of the night to the sound of scraping metal, thinking someone was unfurling the chains that held the anchor, only to discover it was coming from their bunkmate's chest. The ill losing limbs to a sickly necrosis.

"The Sister claimed death was a mercy. When she told me what the boy's future held, my whole body trembled, the vial with it. I couldn't imagine such a fate for my friend, and I immediately had to run to the latrine and unburden my stomach. She appeared pleased, at first, that I had heard of the pain to befall the boy and been affected by it. Perhaps she felt my reaction justified her perception of mercy. But I couldn't bear to poison my friend, even knowing the future it would spare him.

"I refused to give the Fate her vial back. Instead, I offered an idea. It wasn't too hard to come up with, not when it had been part of my dream all along. I asked her if the boy could be cured, his fate changed, but she said it could not. The illness had already taken hold."

My stomach writhes, my breathing labored. "But he wasn't showing symptoms yet, was he?" I ask. It doesn't make sense to me, why the Sister could heal me, but not the boy, when I was a step away from death.

"According to the Sister," Peter says, "it was about more than just the matter of a plague. The boy's fate was already woven. Had been rewoven a thousand times and still ended with the same horrific result. The sickness would spread, eventually wiping out the entire village.

"I asked her if his fate would change if he were taken far away, quarantined outside of the village, but she said she'd already tried as much in his tapestry. The boy had to die. All other paths led to the same destination.

"I could feel myself desperately grasping for a solution that would spare his life. So I asked, what if we took him out of the realm? What if we wove him somewhere different, somewhere his fate could not reach him? Perhaps then he'd have a fair chance to recover. This, it seemed, struck a chord with the Fate, and I glimpsed a flash of regret in her shadows. It seemed clear to me she didn't enjoy bringing swift death upon children, even if she perceived it to be a mercy. She said it was indeed possible, though it would not guarantee keeping the boy from meeting another miserable fate. Perhaps the same one. But she agreed it increased his chances of a better life. She faded away, and when she returned, it was with a loom and thread. I watched her all night as she wove.

"When the time came to weave the boy in, I stuck out my hand to stop her. She couldn't very well put him in a tapestry all by himself. That would be the worst torture of all. According to the Sister, this boy wasn't the only one who had been infected. She'd come to the orphanage intending to take the lives of several boys, but there was a condition for saving them.

"She needed a Shadow Keeper. Someone to watch over not just the boys, but the realm itself. It was experimental, she said, and she was less than confident that this plan would work. So she agreed only under the condition I would become the Shadow Keeper and watch after the boys she planned to weave into the tapestry."

"So that's what Neverland is?" I ask. "A tapestry created by a Fate?"

"More or less," he says, "though it operates differently from the rest of the realms. It was made under a sense of urgency, so if you were to travel across the sea, you'd find a void where the sea ended."

"Like a tapestry left unfinished," I say.

"Exactly like that," says Peter.

"And the Lost Boys? They're here because each of them was infected? And when you brought them here, they recovered?"

Peter nods. He doesn't say whether all the boys he brought to Neverland recovered. It makes me wonder if something about being in Neverland bolsters the body's immunity, or if the Lost Boys are just a remnant of the group he tried to save from the orphanage.

The unsaid statement hangs between us, swelling in the humid air until I can hardly hold it in. "And Thomas? He was the original boy who got sick, wasn't he? And he died anyway. And Freckles too."

Peter turns away from me, staring blankly into the canopy. "The Fate warned me that our plan would not protect them from all possible woes. But even Thomas's death—this will sound cruel, but if you knew what was to become of him in our original realm, you would likely find his premature death a mercy."

"Peter," I say, hardly able to get his name out, "do you think that's why they're dying? Because they were supposed to die in their own realm? Because they weren't supposed to escape?"

"I hope not," is all he says, which isn't at all comforting.

"And their memories? Why can't they remember their time before Neverland?"

"The Sister and I thought it would be for the best, considering the things that happened to them in that orphanage." He says it so flatly, it almost doesn't register. Like when he wouldn't answer my question about why the first warden had been easy to persuade.

I feel sick, but it seems wrong to pry about such private matters. So I pivot to the other question still rattling in my mind. "So why me? If this is the very Fate with which my parents made their bargain, why did she wish to give me to you?"

"That is a mystery, isn't it?" says Peter.

"You said when you first arrived it was meant to be a punishment. What is the Fate punishing you for?"

Peter's eyes twinkle. "Funny. I don't remember saying you were a punishment."

"It was implied."

Peter just smirks, avoiding my question by saying, "The Sister has her own reasons for doing things. If I were to guess, it likely has more to do with something she wants than anything to do with me or you."

A thought churns in my mind. I don't love the idea of that creature having something she wants from me. "But if she wants something, why make a bargain with humans at all? Why not just weave it into my fate?"

"Human and fae fates are more complex than that. The Sisters themselves have some control over them, but you have to remember that there are three of them, so when the will of one diverges from that of the other two, she must become crafty to get her way. You see, we individuals sometimes move the threads ourselves in the Fates' sleep. I imagine they find it quite frustrating indeed," he says. A lovely defiance winks in the corners of Peter's expression, in the way he clings to me all the more tightly.

"So you gave up your life in your original realm to watch over the Lost Boys?" I ask.

Peter shrugs. "It's not as if I had much of a future anyway. At the end of the day, I got what I wanted, didn't I? Not to find myself cast out on the street, begging and stealing food until I turned up in the ground, facing whatever horrible fate awaits me."

I frown, sorrow for Peter overcoming my chest.

"And your shadow self?"

"I can only return to the other realms if I'm in that form, but it takes something away from me. The last bit of reason and self-control that keep my less desirable qualities in check."

"Unless?" I say, remembering the night he took my hand in the clock tower.

"Unless I'm touching you, so it seems," he says, his thumb drawing circles on my shoulder. "Though why I was provided that lovely little loophole, I can't say."

My throat goes dry. "That hardly seems necessary. The part about only being able to visit the other realms in shadow form, I mean."

"I don't believe the Sister ever wanted me to leave here willingly." He winks at me. "She's been known to think I'm flighty."

"But you'd never leave the boys."

Peter shakes his head, then after a moment, says, "I apologize for how I treated you when in shadow form. As I said, it's me, but without any restraint. Without a moral code guiding my actions and desires. I am sorry for frightening you as a child, but I hope you believe me when I say I am not that being. Not always, at least. Not now."

Again, I feel that swell of indecision surround me. There's a gentle trust ebbing between us. There has been since the moment I not only let him drop me, but begged him. He caught me, didn't he?

Every time. If he meant me harm, at least in this form, he would show it. Still, the vision of the shadow creature that dwells inside him lurches through my memories, cutting through his words and swathing them in darkness, so I can't tell which way is up. What is the lie and what is the truth.

My mother used to tell me that I had an uncanny gift for seeing everyone else's perspective. She said I could tiptoe into their minds and peep out from behind their pupils. From the way she spoke, you would have thought it was an asset, but it's not as simple as that. It's having to rethink everything I believe each time a new point is brought to my attention. It's evaluating everyone else's opinion, everyone else's story, with equal seriousness, regardless of whether they've earned it. It's forgetting myself every time another person opens their mouth, then waiting for my own opinions to return to me only in the safety of quiet loneliness.

"I need some time to think," I tell him, because I can't trust my own thoughts with Peter's voice in my ear, his hands on my waist.

With what I now know, I want nothing more than to comfort him. But what if I were to tell John the truth? Would he offer a perspective I hadn't yet considered, one that sounded as convincing as Peter's? I don't doubt that John wouldn't trust Peter's tale, but how much of that is because John will never trust Peter, no matter whether Peter deserves it?

Peter presses something into my palm, leathery and sure. The hilt of the curved dagger is weighty, the leather supple against my chapped fingertips.

"I want you to keep this with you," he says, nuzzling his face into my hair. "The shabby one Simon sometimes lets you borrow wouldn't protect you from a wild hare."

I fall asleep like that, in Peter's arms, the very ones I once feared. We're high above the ground, but I no longer fear falling.

I fall asleep with a dagger clutched to my lap.

CHAPTER 31

I wake up in a panicked haze, hair mussed from where Peter's been combing his hands through it. After insisting he take me back, I barely make it to the Den before the sun rises fully. Anxiety plagues my chest as I sneak back to my rooms.

Just as I'm about to crawl into the cot, someone clears their throat in the corner. I turn to find John propped at his usual position against the wall. Faintly, in the glow of the faerie light from the hallway, I glimpse him fidgeting with a twig in his fingers, twirling the stem and crushing the leaves between his fingertips.

"Where were you?"

"You were already asleep when I finished the dishes. Then I had to relieve myself." I'm shocked by how easily the lie slips out of my mouth.

"I hate to hear it took you several hours. Must have been quite unpleasant."

I can't see John's expression in the shadows, but I don't have to. His voice, typically cool and even, is trembling.

"John."

"You were out with him, weren't you?"

I swallow, sitting on the edge of my cot to face him more fully.

Like that will somehow help to make him understand, even when he can't see my face in the dark.

"I was," I finally say.

John goes very, very quiet for a moment. "I'd think he forced you, except that you're lying for him. You lied to me last night about the coat, seemed so excited to be off. Your cheeks were flushed. I thought it was from the heat of the stove and the hot water from cleaning the dishes."

Guilt pricks at my stomach. "I'm sorry I lied to you."

"He's our captor, Wendy. He's the enemy."

I shift again on my cot, my heart breaking at the way my brother, the boy who didn't hesitate to slice off his own finger, is trembling. I understand what it is to fear Peter like this, to dread the day the shadows will come and take away everything you hold dear.

"All my life I knew he'd come and take you away," John says. "All my life. Half of the time, I worried you'd go eagerly. I heard you talking to the shadows when we were children. There's no telling how many times I caught you, hand outstretched to meet his. I used to sleep outside of your room in the hall, bring a blanket to drape over myself so I could listen. So I could hear if he came to take you, if you started to sound as if you'd been convinced."

"Peter's not exactly what we anticipated," I say. "Even you have to admit that. We feared him for our entire childhood..."

"No," snaps John. "I feared him. You..." He trails off, like he can't bear to say the words himself. "You've always possessed an affinity for the darkness."

Anger pricks at my stomach, but I tamp it down, remembering John is only looking after me. That he hasn't seen the difference between the Peter of the shadows and the Peter of the light. John doesn't know what Peter sacrificed to keep the Lost Boys alive.

"He hasn't hurt us," I say.

"Oh, yeah?" says John, holding up his stump of a pinkie finger. I can barely see its outline in the dim light.

"You did that to yourself, to be completely fair," I tease, hoping

John will join in on our usual game of being as morbid as possible, but he doesn't.

"Wendy, it's like he casts some spell over you. Like he always has."

I cringe. I thought so too, when we first arrived. That Peter had some glamoured hold over me that forced me to drown in his aura, to cling to my attraction to him. Sure, he used his glamour to calm me when I first came to Neverland, but it's not as if he did it to hurt me. I realize now that most of what I ascribed to glamour was just denial, me wishing to blame magic for the intense draw I feel toward Peter. That I've always felt toward Peter.

"He protects the Lost Boys," I say. "You have to admit, he cares for them."

"By keeping their pasts in the dark."

"Maybe their pasts aren't worth remembering."

"And whose opinion is that? Yours or Peter's?"

Uncertainty twists in my gut, but I hold my resolve. I've seen the agony in Peter's face over the boys, especially over Thomas. He wants nothing but the best for them, and Peter is just as trapped here, just as chained here as they are. There's no doubt in my mind that Peter's only trying to keep them from pain.

"Peter's not the only one at work here," I say. "You're forgetting about the Sister. He called her his master," I say, the word thick on my tongue, like mucus.

"That's convenient for him. A being on which he can rest all the blame for his actions."

"Peter saved us the night of the masquerade," I snap.

John cocks his head to the side.

"You're forgetting what you handed over to him to get him to take me and Michael with us."

My stomach caves in, my mind returning to the unconditional bargain I'd given Peter the night of the masquerade, like a blank check for him to cash at his leisure. I shouldn't have forgotten, not with the mysterious ovals marking my skin.

"He's asked nothing of me," I say.

"Yet."

I stiffen.

"Wendy," John says, rubbing the space between his eyebrows. The motion causes his spectacles to ride up. "I know you don't want to talk about what happened to you in the parlor that night. And I'm not trying to imply that you can't make your own decisions about men, but I worry that, just perhaps, it affected the way you—"

"No. No, I'm not talking about this." Flustered and unable to come up with a response other than that, I jump out of my cot and grab my coat, twisting it around my shoulders.

"Where are you going?" asks John, but my attention is fixated on the smallest of phrases. *That night.*

Because John is under the impression it only happened once.

"To take a walk."

"I thought you just had one of those."

No, I think. *I flew.*

I GO LOOKING FOR PETER, regretting making him fly me back to the Den. I should have stayed with him, shouldn't have let John take a needle to my perfect night. Now I'm left alone with my thoughts, and they're as hostile as ever. Peter's confession about the origins of Neverland quelled my anxieties surrounding him, at least the idea that he's been manipulating me. But they awakened new fears within my soul. They swarm in my head, keeping me on edge.

This place should not exist. Neverland should not exist. Simon was right when he said that Peter keeps the memories of their pasts so that they don't have to, but dread crawls in my belly when I think of Thomas. Of Freckles.

No matter what Peter attempted, he couldn't protect them from their fates. Sure, they survived the plague, but only to be handed over to death anyway. Thomas, strangled. Freckles, stabbed and disfigured.

The morning air is frigid, the fog obscuring my view of anything well past the shoreline, but I follow it toward the northernmost tip of the island, where I confronted Peter after Freckles's death. When Peter dropped me off at the Den, he flew off in this direction.

It's raining, the clouds a mist of gray overshadowing the island. I can't imagine that Peter fares well on days like this, when the weather itself feels as if it's bearing down on your soul. I tell myself that's why I search for him, to make sure he's okay. Because he's the only source of protection the Lost Boys have, and I need to make sure he's okay to make sure they're okay. Because if Peter is distracted by his own gloominess, something could happen again, like what happened to Thomas and Freckles.

I tell myself it's not because Peter has left a shard in my heart, a stitch on my soul. That I can feel his presence tugging at me. That after Freckles died, I knew in my very being where Peter had gone.

I don't want to feel this draw toward Peter, toward the male who finds himself cloaked in shadows, hardly able to restrain himself from his whims. I tell myself that's not the man I'm following into the fog. That I'm following the orphan who gave his life up to protect the children destined for misery. The man who holds the burden of their pasts on his shoulders so that they don't have to. I tell myself I'm running toward the male who plays with Michael like his way is just as legitimate as any other child's.

That's what I tell myself as I wander into the fog until it swallows me up.

PETER'S not on the cliffside, but there's an outcropping of rock beyond the shoreline. A boulder amongst the waves. I can see the faintest glimpse of Peter's outline in the fog as he perches atop it. It's the type of rock that might be simple to get to, the type I'd be tempted to climb on any day other than today, when the waves warn of an approaching storm, lapping at my feet and begging me to run back to the safety of the Den.

But there Peter is, and I can't seem to take my eyes off him.

He's perched atop the rock, and when the wind clears the fog in short bursts, I can see the way the spray of the sea speckles his tanned cheeks with droplets. At least, I tell myself I can see that. Perhaps I'm imagining things. With Peter, imagining never seems so far off from reality.

I open my mouth to call to him, but then a large wave crashes against his boulder, and the sound drowns out his name on my lips. I falter, wondering if perhaps I should leave him be, allow him to retreat into his sorrow in his own way.

It must have been difficult for him last night, telling me about the bloated corpses hanging from the juniper tree, about the life he bargained away to save the Lost Boys.

His name is still on my tongue when I go to retreat, all my bravery swallowed up in the deafening echo of the waves that quelled my voice moments ago.

Some people are brave naturally.

Others of us have just enough courage for one shot, and even then our voices shake with trepidation, never quite loud enough to be heard over the bustle of a world that's bolder than we are.

I turn to go, but then I glimpse something out of the corner of my vision. A shadow. At first, I think it must be Peter shifting into his shadow form, but as I turn to look, I find another silhouette on the rock. This one's climbing the edge, directly behind Peter. Battering waves obscure the sound that the figure must be making as he breathes heavily with the ascent.

At first, I'm sure the man—I'm certain it's a man now, though probably fae—will fall on the slick rock, but his ascent is steady, determined.

As he climbs, I feel the wet and jagged surface underneath his hands as if they're my own.

I scan the man's features for something familiar. Perhaps one of the Lost Boys come to fetch Peter. My eyes scour the man's figure, trying to force it into the shape of one of the Lost Boys. I tell myself it could be Victor because of the sturdy build, but I know I'm kidding myself. Even from here, I can tell his hair is cropped shorter than Victor's, his hair lighter, his skin a shade darker. Besides, he has the bulk of a man, not a boy, and the movements of one too.

Why is a man on this island?

Why is there a man in Neverland?

I know the Lost Boys aren't the only ones here. Tink, for example. But she came here with Peter originally, though I remember now that he left that part out of his story about the orphanage.

Before I can follow that train of thought, Peter whirls around, like he senses something. I wave at him, and he waves hesitantly back, probably less than thrilled that I've come out here to disturb him.

He still doesn't see the man climbing.

The lump in my throat crawls upward, touching the base of my tongue and making me gag.

Something is very, very wrong.

"Peter, look out!" I call, my tongue finally unfastened from its restraints, but Peter only shakes his head.

I point toward the man, but of course, he's lower than Peter's scope of view. Peter must assume that I'm asking him to fly me up there, because he adopts a teasing stance and beckons with his hand for me to come to him.

The man continues to ascend.

"Peter!" I call, tears stinging at my cheeks now, because I know. I know. Something is terribly wrong. That man is not supposed to be here, and Peter doesn't know what he's facing. What's creeping up to meet him from below.

I flail my arms, jumping up and down, hoping that will convey my panic as I point toward the strange man.

Something about Peter's silhouette stiffens. He must have gotten my message. His shadow widens as he steps forward, craning his head to peek over the rock.

The stranger lunges.

He's fast. Faster than any human man. He wasn't yet to the top of the rock, but somehow his agility allows him to fling himself up and into Peter, knocking both figures to the flat plateau of the rock, a tangle of shadows struggling for purchase.

My feet bob in the hard, cold sand as I search for any way to help. I can't reach the rock. Can't even swim to it, not without the waves beating my body into submission and dragging me into their otherworldly den.

I can't do anything but watch as the stranger attacks Peter, as a knife flashes above Peter's chest.

Panic swirls within me, mimicking the waves around my feet, but I back up. The last thing I need to do is get caught in the undercurrent and risk distracting Peter or dying.

I should run back to the Den. Alert the Lost Boys that Neverland has been compromised. I've about convinced myself to do it when Peter grabs the other man by the neck, and in a feat I can't quite make sense of, shoots both men into the air.

Peter's dark wings flap around him, but the storm has intensified, and the pelting rain seems to be weighing them down. I watch as his wings fight with the howling wind to keep him upright, but even while being held by the throat, the man's thrashing keeps Peter from being able to maintain control.

I can sense the panic rolling off of Peter, though I can't explain how—perhaps I'm simply attributing my own state to him. Peter pivots, tightening his wings at his back as he attempts to bring the fight toward the shore. I watch as Peter attempts to drop the man upon the sharp rocks, but the man wrestles for a grip around Peter's neck and manages to hold on.

I know what Peter's going to do before he does it.

My heart plummets, ripping a hole in my stomach.

Peter feints, then dives headlong for the patch of jagged rocks below them.

I don't let myself watch as Peter drives both him and the stranger directly into what might as well be spears sticking up from the ground. There's a horrible absence of sound, of their bodies landing against the terrain as the storm drowns out all evidence of the fight.

My bare feet pound against the stiff sand as I sprint for them.

By the time I'm able to make out the features of the man, I'm out of breath. Peter is splayed out above the rocks, face-down with his wings sprawling out behind him. I think I glimpse where the tip of a sharp boulder is protruding through his leathery wing.

I want to retch.

But I don't have time for that.

Not when the man, who landed several paces away from Peter, is stumbling toward Peter's limp body, a dagger flashing in his hand.

I don't have time to think. I just run, urging my body to go faster. I scream, hoping to distract the man from his intentions just long enough for Peter to whirl on him, but my voice is lost to the current.

As I reach the rocks, jagged pebbles splinter into my bare heels, but I hardly feel them. I hardly feel anything except for the urge to push faster. The knowledge that if I don't reach them in time, that shining dagger will make its way into Peter's heart.

His heart of flesh. And then Peter will die. Will succumb to the fate he feared so much as a child.

I didn't think to ask him if he still feared death like he did then.

I might not get the chance.

Thankfully, the man was injured in the fall. He's stumbling toward Peter, holding a bleeding and crooked leg with one arm. I'm almost in awe of the determination in his movement, when his pain must be intense enough to make most men pass out.

Then again, I don't much feel the cuts on my feet either.

I suppose that happens when you're running toward something you crave with all your being.

There's a moment of hesitation when I don't know that I can do it. There's only one path to saving Peter, and I have never been the brave sort. Never been the type who thought I could ever take a life, even in the service of saving another.

Feet slogging into the wet sand, I close the distance between myself and Peter's assailant, moments from reaching him.

The man readies the dagger over Peter's back, aiming for his chest.

It's the minute hand in my lost pocket watch clinking in alignment with the hour hand at the stroke of midnight come early. It's an explosion of blinding light.

It's everything I've ever desired with a blade to his heart.

I don't get there in time to throw myself between the blade and Peter.

But I don't have to.

I unsheathe my dagger—the one Peter gifted me to protect myself. And I plunge mine first.

The storm drowns out the sound, but I don't need it to feel the breaking of flesh against my blade when it makes contact with the man's back. The man freezes for a moment in surprise, and I realize I didn't put enough force into the motion. Not with a band of ribs protecting the man's heart like armor. I want nothing more than to place my fist into my mouth and scream in agony, but I need both hands for what I have to do.

I thrust again, this time throwing all my weight into it.

In faerie tales, when a person stabs another in the heart, it's a swift motion. A clean cut that's over with in the span of a few words.

Killing this man is not like that.

I'm not strong enough to stab him thoroughly enough on the second blow, so I have to grit my teeth and strain. I feel everything, and it's agonizingly slow. The crunching of ribs, the splicing of flesh reverberating through my blade. There's a dreadful squishing sensation as the tip of my blade finally, finally, punctures his heart, but even that bit of muscle puts up more resistance than I'm expecting.

He falls forward.

The man is screaming. Screeching.

That, the storm allows me to hear.

IN THE END, he doesn't die swiftly, and I'm too much of a coward to slice his throat and grant him that.

I tell myself that's not what I should be doing anyway. That I should be getting information out of the man I've now rolled onto his back as he moans and screams, the obsidian sand around him no darker as it licks up the blood from his wound.

"Who are you?" I ask, because that makes me feel better about not granting the man mercy. Not when I can't bear the idea of my blade slicing against flesh yet again.

"Who are you?" I demand, but the man's eyes are rolling back in his head, his pointed ears immune to my voice.

Finally. Finally, the Fates are going to grant me mercy and let this man die.

His hand lurches, and my eye catches on something I hadn't noticed before. Something on his wrist.

It's a bracelet.

Alternating red and blue beads. The one Joel said they couldn't find on Thomas's body.

Panic surges over me now, and I feel as if I'm going to be sick.

I watch until the murderer who's been haunting Neverland takes his last breath.

His lungs rattle when he does.

CHAPTER 32

*N*earby, Peter stirs. I hardly notice.
I killed a man.
I killed a man.
I killed a man.

It's as if I think repeating it to myself will punish me somehow. Will make me believe it. I feel as if I should need to vomit, but nothing comes up. My hands tremble, black sand embedding itself underneath my fingernails as I stare at the open-mouthed corpse.

"You're going into shock," says Peter, scraping his cheek against the sand as he hefts his body to turn and look at me.

"I suppose that makes sense," I say quietly, unable to take my eyes off the man I just killed.

Just a few moments ago, he was climbing. His robust body was scaling the rock in the midst of the storm. Strong and lithe and agile. It's amazing what the human body can do, but the fae body even more so.

What is equally amazing is how quickly all that ability drains away. It doesn't seem like it should be possible. To die that quickly. That easily. Of course, it wasn't quick, I remind myself. It wasn't some strange accident that removed the man's head before he had time to register that death had come for its prey early.

I drove my dagger into his back.

No. Drove is too definite a word. I hacked into his organs, carving his flesh, his very life, from his chest cavity.

"He was going to kill me," says Peter, his voice too even, too sure.

"Right," I say, shaking my head back and forth. This was a madman. Not only was he going to kill Peter, he had Thomas's bracelet. The one that they never found when they recovered Thomas's body.

This man had killed an innocent boy. And I had killed him.

It was only right.

"You did the right thing," echoes Peter.

It sounds true on his lips, so why is my soul so skeptical? Perhaps it's forever imprinted from the plunging of my dagger into his flesh, the awful crunch of ribs and burst of fleshy cardiac muscle underneath my blade's too-dull point.

"Wendy Darling, I need patching up," Peter says, flicking his tattered wing to emphasize his words.

I nod my head like doing so will shake out the shock paralyzing my body. It doesn't feel as though it should work. I can't feel my limbs, a horrible numbness settling over me so completely it's a wonder they move at all.

I watch my fingers as if I'm not the one guiding them, as if I'm an apprentice gazing upon another's hands at work. It's someone else's hands that follow Peter's instructions to get the stitching material out of the pouch hanging from his belt.

I take a breath.

I can do this.

Luckily, the motion of stitching is familiar to me, having taken so many lessons in embroidery as a child. Peter's hide is tougher than cloth, but I tell myself it's not the flesh of his wings. That I'm simply stitching a crisp pattern into leather.

Leather is already dead.

My mind repeats these words as if they'll help, but I find it's the familiar task that steadies my quivering fingers. I thread the needle in and out, paying careful attention to the section where a flap of wing hangs, almost separated from the wing itself. The man must have struck while they struggled in the sky. No wonder Peter dove.

As a fae, Peter should heal quickly, though I'm sure it helps if all the pieces that need healing are in the correct place. Likely, that makes it even more imperative that I stitch Peter up quickly.

"You're not even flinching," I say.

Peter cranes his neck, his cheek dusted with black sand, and winks at me. "I have an abnormally high pain tolerance."

I think he's trying to make me feel better. That much is obvious. Or perhaps he's keeping himself from flinching because he knows if I feel the slightest indication that I'm causing him pain by ripping into his skin, I'll lose the contents of my gut.

At least, that's what should happen.

I'm not sure why it's not happening. I just killed a man, after all.

Peter closes his eyes and breathes deeply throughout the entire process, not even clenching his jaw to brace himself. I read once that fae wings are highly sensitive to both touch and pain. I'm not sure what to make of it that Peter is pretending this isn't excruciating for him. Maybe he innately knows what I need right now.

"The man..." I say, hoping if I say this aloud, maybe I'll feel something. Maybe the words will get stuck in my throat and I'll sob. I don't, so I continue. "I found Thomas's bracelet on him."

Peter goes still as the surface of an undisturbed pond.

"Why..." I swallow. "Why do you think he hurt him? Why was he trying to hurt you?"

Peter's breathing isn't quite as even anymore, and from where I have one hand braced on his wing, I can feel his pulse accelerate.

"How did he even get here?" Finally, my voice breaks, though it's not with guilt so much as anger. Anguish ripples through me each time I make a puncture in Peter's skin. Each cut feels like piercing my own flesh.

It's not only Peter I'm angry for. I'm angry for me. Angry at the stranger who forced me to shed blood, who stole my innocence.

Whose back did not break easily, whose ribs protected him and forced me to linger longer in the moment than I should have.

I hate the stranger for ripping my soul from my chest, almost as much as I hate him for doing worse to Thomas and Freckles. For leaving those poor boys' bodies mangled for their friends to find.

A scream riles at my throat, but I hold it back as Peter takes a breath to respond.

"When the Sister formed this realm, she warned me it was unnatural. Different from the rest. That its pull would attract lost souls. It's one reason she sent me to watch after the Lost Boys. She warned that her other Sisters would not like that their fates had been tampered with, their threads pulled. It's not so easy to rewrite a fate that has been set several times. Because of Neverland's origins, there are lost souls who find themselves wandering in."

"But how do they get in?" I almost choke the question out. It's hot in my throat, on my chapped lips, in the freezing air.

"There are other ways into Neverland besides just the second star," says Peter. "The second star is one of many gaps. The Sister had to make Neverland in a hurry. From how she's explained it, there are gaps in the Fabric, holes and mistakes she made as she wove it under a time restraint, racing the boys' fate. Those are how the wild ones slip in. I'm usually able to find them, to deal with them before they get anywhere close to the Lost Boys. Our Den is as far away from any of the mistakes in Neverland as I could get it. But I told you...Thomas strayed too far for me to protect him. So did Freckles. He was never supposed to go near that cove. They both must have wandered close to the gaps."

I think of what the wretched stranger did to the boy who happened to be in the wrong place at the wrong time.

"Peter?" I ask, my heart thundering wildly.

"Yes?" he says, though his voice is cold, like he knows what I'm about to ask.

"You said all the Lost Boys were infected, right? That everyone here was supposed to die?"

Peter swallows, and that's answer enough.

"Does that mean..." I pause, taking a breath. "Do you think the other boys are in danger? That their fates will come to find them too?"

"I don't know," says Peter. Why does that sound so much like a lie?

I'm about to confront him about it, but just as I'm about to open my mouth, someone yells from across the beach.

At first, I think it's just the howling wind, but when I turn to look, I find a group of boys scrambling over the rocks. The Lost Boys approach us quickly, Simon running at the front, John taking up the rear as he holds Michael's hand.

Why John brought him out given the weather we were experiencing only a few moments ago, I have no idea, but the storm itself seems to have died down. Like it changed its mind after it saw that its fun was over, that the mercenary it sent to do its dirty work was dead.

Simon glimpses the dead body first. His first inclination is to turn around. I watch his gaze bounce atop each head of the group, counting.

Sweet Simon.

As soon as he's done counting, relief swarms his face.

Then he picks up his pace and runs.

"Peter, what ha—"

Simon's eyes slip over the corpse's wrist, landing on the bracelet.

The rest of the boys have caught up to us now. I go to call to my brother, but he's lost in thought.

John's attention is fixated on my hands. Or rather, the blood staining them.

EVENTUALLY, we get Peter upright, though his wings are already healing around the stitches I made.

"How did you know to come after us?" I ask Simon.

The boys all huddle around in a circle, some of them tending to Peter. Victor alone stands above the corpse, his eyes locked to attention on the dead man. I wonder if he knows. If it's worth telling him that this is the man who killed his brother. Perhaps he'll hate me for stealing the kill that was his right.

"Peter never stays out this long in a storm," says Simon, a teasing grin on his face as he looks at Peter. "It's because he's a princess about his wings. You would think they were made of cashmere."

I consider how that's not entirely true. He'd stayed out in the rain the day Freckles died.

Peter, now propped against a rock, shoves at Simon's knees, but Simon dodges well enough.

The Lost Boys look back and forth between Peter and the corpse, an unspoken question hanging in the air.

"Well, if the rest of you are too much of obedient cowards to ask, I'll do it," says Victor, his voice hoarse as he looks at Peter. "Is this the man that killed my brother?"

Instead of answering, Peter nods toward me. Lip trembling, I pull the bracelet off the man's limp wrist and hand it to Victor, placing it in his shaking palm and closing his fingers over it. As soon as he feels the press of the beads against his palm, he lets out a horrible strangled sound.

Rarely have I witnessed a man cry. There's John and Michael, of course, but even John stopped the habit when my father told him he was a man now, and that men don't show weakness.

Victor must have gotten the same message because he clasps his hand over his mouth as if to shove the wretched noise back in, as if he can swallow the sound, force it into his gut until the bile in his stomach churns it into excrement.

It doesn't work, of course, and only serves to make Victor sob louder, thick tears blanketing his face, larger than the beads of rain that trickle down his cheeks. The other boys don't seem to know what to do. Most of them have tears running down their faces as well, though they're the quiet sort. The type that would be indistinguishable from the rain if one wasn't looking carefully.

"Victor," I say softly, advancing, but he shakes his head, holding a palm out to keep me from coming any closer. The beaded bracelet is still looped around his thumb in the shape of a noose.

"The rest of you go home," says Peter.

The boys open their mouths to argue, but are stopped when Peter, in a tone more forcefully than I've ever heard, says, "*Now.*"

Dejectedly, the boys turn and huddle in a group to walk back. Only John and Michael linger, Michael's voice high-pitched as he repeats, "And the monster was slain, and the prince and the princess lived happily ever after. And the monster was slain, and the prince and the princess lived happily ever after."

"You should get him away from the body," I say, my throat dry.

John nods, somewhat absentmindedly, moisture fogging his glasses. He offers me a gentle twitch of his head that tells me he wants to talk later.

When he and Michael leave, it's just me, Peter, and Victor who remain.

"I want to know everything you do," says Victor. The sobbing has subsided now, his voice dipping into a register I've yet to hear from him. "Don't think you can leave anything out. I deserve to know."

I listen as Peter explains that there are holes in Neverland where sometimes others can fall through. He makes a point to say they only work one-way. That strikes me as odd, but perhaps he forgot to mention that to me earlier. Then he tells Victor that sometimes the evil, the lost, are drawn to the pull of Neverland. He leaves out the part about why. About the Sister who wove the tapestry specifically for these boys.

He leaves out all information pertinent to their past.

"But why Thomas?" Victor asks, his question a plea.

I want to tell him that there will be no answer to satisfy. That nothing will make the brutal murder of an innocent boy make sense. But I think Victor probably already knows that. Saying so would make him out to be a fool, and Victor is no fool.

He's just a boy.

And a brother.

"Thomas was in the wrong place at the wrong time," says Peter. "There's no rhyme or reason to it other than that."

Victor's face goes placid, and I recognize the utter resignation in the way the fight seeps out of him. "I thought there might have been a reason," he says, somewhat distantly, under his breath.

He blinks away tears, like this is his last shot at them. Like it's time to put away such foolish things.

"What are you going to do with the body?" Victor asks.

Peter looks at me, hand on his knee, but addresses Victor. "I thought I would leave that up to you."

Victor nods, placing his fists on his hips and glaring down at the man who murdered his brother. "I want to leave him in a shallow grave. Just like he left Thomas. That way, the crows won't have any trouble finding him."

My stomach feels as if it's going to be sick, but what am I going to do? Tell Victor that letting this corpse rot openly won't bring his brother back?

I think he probably already knows that.

IN THE END, we don't bury the man on the beach. Victor doesn't want to risk the tide washing away the body. I get the sickening feeling that he wants to come back for it. That he wants to watch it rot, bit by bit. As if he'll gain some peace of mind from witnessing the worms wriggle and writhe through the rotting corpse.

"When we found Thomas," Victor says as he stares at his brother's killer, "the bugs had already gotten to him. He had marks on his neck from where he was choked. I keep wondering how long it took him to pass out. How long he had to live with the realization that he was going to die."

I say nothing.

I just dig. It doesn't take us long. Not when the intent is to leave the grave shallow. I dig with my trembling hands next to Victor, whose tears mingle with the rainwater dripping from the canopy overhead, forming mud clots in the dirt.

We dump the body in.

Victor spits on the corpse's face.

WHEN I GET BACK to the room, my belly is empty, leaving a gnawing feeling like it's eating itself. But even if I wanted to sneak food from the kitchens, even if I had any appetite, I'm not sure that I could keep it down.

I find the communal bathroom, a room consisting of a bucket and a spigot that siphons water from the underground streams, and scrub at my bloodied hands until they're raw. When that doesn't rid me of the stink of the stranger's blood, I rub so hard that I draw my own blood, hoping that at least it will mask the stench.

It doesn't. It smells the same as the murderer's. Like there's no difference between him and me. Like even my nose is aware of the fact that both of us are tainted, poisoned with the fact that we've stolen a life from this world, severed a soul from its body.

I have to turn the spigot off, because the dripping makes me think of blood. I already have to deal with the sound of crunching ribs echoing in my skull. The sound I know I didn't actually hear, due to the raging of the waves, but my mind seems to have filled in the gaps of my memories.

When I bite down on my sleeve to stifle a scream, something moves in the corner. I spin around and clutch the water basin, only to find John standing in the shadows. His face is pale, more so than usual. Like all that's happened has scoured the color right out of his cheeks. Like he's a sketch being erased by an artist struggling with confidence in his work.

"I hate what he's done to you," John says, his voice even, though not the type that indicates calm.

The faerie lantern light flickers on his face, gone gaunt at the cheeks. I hadn't noticed before how conspicuous his cheekbones have become, how he's all sharp lines and angles.

It reminds me of Captain Astor, for some reason, but I don't want it to, so I push it away.

"It's not Peter's fault," I say, sticking my hands back into the frigid water behind me, hoping that this time the cold will cleanse them. And if not, at least it will numb them. At least it will keep me from feeling the resistance of the man's flesh carried up through the hilt of the dagger.

"I'm not talking about Peter," says John, his eyes glassing over.

"Oh." My mind flashes back to the night of our parents' death, and I realize that to John, this isn't the only time I've been forced to shed blood. Granted, it wasn't my blade that took to our parents' throats, but it happened because of me. Even if I don't understand all the reasons, it's because of me that my brothers are orphans.

I wonder then if secretly John hates me, despite himself. I wouldn't have thought it possible, but then again, I wouldn't have thought I could draw blood, halt its pulsing, much less.

"What did it feel like?" John asks, blinking until his eyes come into focus. "Taking that man's life?"

A shiver ripples through me.

"Horrible," I say, though that's such an understatement it feels like a lie.

John nods, then frowns. "Did you know he'd murdered Thomas when you killed him?"

I shake my head, my throat dry.

John nods again, thoughtfully. "It makes sense then, why you feel guilt over it."

"He was going to kill Peter," I say. "I had to save him. I want it not to have been me who did it. I want something else to blame, but it was my hands, my fingers, my panic."

John comes over and reaches behind me, taking my numb hands from underneath the chilled water and handing me a rag to dry them off. "It's because of how you feel about him. About Peter."

I nod, because that explanation stings less, though something about it still doesn't sit right with me.

"If he had succeeded in killing Peter, do you think you would have enjoyed killing him more?"

I freeze, that chill rippling through me again. "John, I—"

John stares at me with mournful eyes. "Please don't look at me like that," he says.

"Like what?"

"Like you're disappointed in me. Like you don't at all understand what I mean. How I could want..." He sighs, letting his shoulders droop, then runs his fingers through his hair. "I dream about it sometimes," he says, "forcing the captain to slit his throat with his own blade."

I nod, ashamed of myself for not noticing the bitter hole that's burned its way through my brother's chest.

"I doubt it would feel as satisfying as you think," I say.

"What makes you say that?"

"Victor got his revenge on his brother's killer. He buried him in a shallow grave so the ravens could pluck out his eyes and the worms could eat his flesh. He spat on the corpse of the man who stole everything from him. And he was still weeping on his knees when we left."

John stares at me. His voice doesn't waver when he says, "Victor didn't get to feel the soul leave that scum's body."

My breath catches as I'm transported to that moment. The moment when I knew the man was dead at my hands, when his spirit cried out at me.

"You don't want that, John. Trust me when I say you don't want that."

"*Don't tell me what I want*," he snaps. It's the first time he's ever raised his voice at me since we were children.

Just then, Nettle and Benjamin barge in, both cramming themselves through the doorway like they've been racing to the bathroom. Confusion swarms their faces as they glance back and forth between me and my brother. The tension in the room must be palpable because Nettle murmurs an apology about not knowing anyone was in here and scurries out, dragging Benjamin with him.

John clears his throat.

I pick at the hairs at the base of my skull, sighing as I try not to take his outburst personally. "John, to take another person's life..."

"You did it when it needed to be done."

"Taking a life to save another's isn't what you're talking about."

"Is it not? What if I need it to save mine?"

John's blinking away tears now, and for a moment, it strikes through the leather barrier covering my soul. I throw my arms around my brother, pulling him closer, sorry for the pain I let him drown in without my help.

"Don't let him eat at you from the inside," I whisper. "I miss them too, but we're never going to see him again. Fantasizing about revenge, it's only going to leave you wanting. Empty. Do you understand me?" I ask, pulling away and gazing into my brother's face. For a moment, I'm shocked when I have to look up at him, not down. It's silly, because John has been taller than me for several years now, but in this moment, I'd felt like we were still children, John coming to me crying after he'd scraped his knee.

But John hasn't scraped his knee.

I can see it in the way he looks down at me with pity. Like, though the care I have for him has touched him, he thinks there's something I'm missing. Something that could set both of us free.

I'm starting to wonder if my parents aren't the only family members that I lost to the captain that night.

CHAPTER 33

I hardly sleep that night.

I hardly sleep for several nights.

The man is there, the man who took Thomas's life, and every time I close my eyes, he's waiting for me behind my darkened lids. He's sneaking in the shadows, slipping his hands around Thomas's neck, digging his fingernails into the boy's flesh. Fashioning the Reaper's fox into Freckles's cheek. And then I'm there, clawing at the man, begging him to tell me why. The man only laughs, and then he rips away the picture of Thomas I keep folded up in my pocket, shredding it to pieces with yellowed claws that turn into talons. He's taking the talons to Peter's wings, carving gash marks in his flesh in the shape of a smile. It bleeds and bleeds and bleeds, and the sand laps it up as if it's parched from only ever consuming the salty waves, the water that's too heavy and thick ever to quench thirst.

Somehow, the blood always ends up staining my hands.

I'm tortured every night until the visions slip into the daytime.

I wake, though is it truly waking if I never fall asleep? If I wake to bleeding palms from where I've tried to scrape the man's death off of them? From where I've tried to pry my own fingers from the blade.

John worries about me. So does Michael, who often wakes in the night sobbing as he tries and fails to shake me awake from the awful dreamscapes that haunt me.

I haven't brought up the nightmares to Peter yet, but he watches me carefully, his eyes often darting to my hands, which are never quite able to scar.

One night I wake to wrestling Michael to the floor. He's scratching my face, John screaming at me as I press my hands into Michael's throat, trying to strangle the stranger before he can sneak up behind Thomas. Before I have to watch the boy die again.

Shock and shame overwhelm me when I come to my senses and realize what I've done. Michael scrambles away from me, his body writhing this way and that, like he doesn't know what to do with his limbs in space. Doesn't know the difference between the ground and the ceiling. The difference between my damaging touch upon his throat and the collarless neckline of his shirt, into which he now claws his fingers, trying to rip it away. Like he thinks it might choke him as well.

I loose a scream, covering my mouth with my hand lest the sharp sound harm Michael further. He covers his ears, wailing, until John drags me by my armpits out of the room and into the hall.

"Wait for me here," he says calmly, though there's a hint of panic in his voice. I catch the downward twitch of pity on his face as he looks over me. Then he returns to our brother, where he'll surely wrap him up tightly in his arms until Michael knows he's safe again, until he stops clawing at his neck, at invisible hands that no longer choke him.

I sob, my tears staining my palms. My palms that I hate. I hate them for driving the knife into that man's back. For placing themselves on Michael's innocent skin, for strangling the air out of my sweet, innocent brother.

Regret and shame and self-loathing beat at my insides, threatening to tear me apart, and though I try to keep my voice down as to not upset Michael further, the sobs puncture my throat in pulsing staccato, the panicked labor of a war drum.

A hand finds its way to my shoulder, and when I look up to find John, I find Victor instead. His long, dark eyelashes frame eyes black as soot, but there's understanding in them. Ink curving into letters meant to be read.

"I'll get Peter," he says, then goes sprinting down the hallway.

It feels like hours later when the dark silhouette appears. At first I think Peter is in his shadow from, but it's just a trick of the light. His eyes are the same familiar blue when he kneels down and lifts me into his arms and carries me away.

"No, not me," I whisper. "Michael. I hurt Michael. You need to help him."

"John's taking care of Michael," says Peter, a softness in his voice I've yet to hear. There's no lighthearted teasing in his tone, nor is there that utter lack of feeling.

"I hurt him. Michael. He'll never forgive me."

"You're his sister," Peter says. "Of course he'll forgive you."

"No." The word grinds past my teeth. "You don't know him like I do. He won't understand when I apologize. I won't be able to explain to him why I did it. That I didn't mean to. I can't tell him it was an accident. All he's going to know is that I hurt him."

"He'll forget."

A shudder ripples through me. "Michael never forgets."

Peter carries me into a dark room. I don't have to glance around to know that it's his. I can smell the scent of amber and incense— the same scent from the night I snooped in here and Tink attacked me.

I find myself wishing her claws had run deeper. That she had succeeded in her purpose of killing me. Then I never would have killed that man.

I never would have hurt Michael.

The memory of my hands on his throat wrings another scream from mine.

"Wendy," Peter says, voice uneven. It's the first time I've ever heard him sound like he doesn't know what to do.

There's someone else in the room. Victor, judging by his soft whispers. He must have waited here for Peter to return. "Can you help her?"

"I—" Peter's at a loss for words, and when another vision of the man hits me, it's like he's here, in the room with us. I writhe my limbs, seeking to free myself from Peter's grip, because now Peter is the stranger, and he's going to kill Victor.

"Run, Victor," I say, shadows whirling around my vision.

"What's happening to her?" I faintly hear Victor say.

"She's had a traumatic experience," says Peter.

"We've all had traumatic experiences. None of us started hallucinating," Victor spits back.

Peter pauses, grabbing my hand as I go to pluck out his eye. His grip feels constricting, makes me lash even harder. Shadows swirl around him, but they're not his shadows, they're the shadows from the storehouse where he keeps the faerie dust. They've come for me again, come to swallow me in my sleep. They wriggle themselves into my throat and choke me. I start retching, and Victor's pitch soars. "Peter. You've got to do something for her."

Footsteps as someone else runs into the room. "I heard screaming. What's—Wendy?"

Simon appears above me, horror plastered on his face. Shadows crawl into his nostrils, turning his beautiful eyes crimson.

I claw at him, too.

And then the shadows take me under.

For a moment, all is dark. And then I see him—a dark figure clutching, overpowering a struggling boy—Thomas. A tendrilled arm shackles his neck from behind as the boy kicks and writhes, then goes limp. Faintly, I think I hear crying, but Thomas is already dead, and his killer is shaking over his body.

"YOU HAVE TO DO SOMETHING," someone bellows.

I'm still trying to decipher the killer's face, when something soft like powdered sugar and sweet like honeysuckles blooms on my tongue, and my entire being is blanketed in the sweet oblivion of light.

. . .

FAERIE DUST IS MORE beautiful than I'd ever imagined it.

The night I danced in the heavens with Peter, I'd only gotten a taste, the smallest droplet of nectar. He hadn't wanted to give me too much, and I'd understood as soon as he pressed it to my tongue.

I don't understand anymore. I don't understand why Peter held any of it back.

It starts on the wet tip of my tongue, but it blossoms everywhere. I feel it before it even hits the back of my mouth. I trace it tingling in my cheeks, where it enters my bloodstream. It's a kaleidoscope of colors, like the kind my father used to make for me when I was a child.

Most importantly, it's nothing at all.

Because that's what color is. It might seem like something, but it's only perception. You can't reach out and touch color. You can't hold it in your hand. You can attach it to something else, but you can't run your fingers through the rainbow, only ever chase it.

I don't have to chase it anymore.

Because it's inside me.

It is me.

I'm weightless. Must be, by the way Peter's muscles have to tense to hold me down.

I don't want to be held down. I want to be set free. Contentment keeps me from worrying about telling him as much.

Faintly, as if it's happening to someone else, I sense him tuck me into the bed and pull the covers over me, but as I said, I'm weightless, and soon my body floats over the bed, my mind lost in a whirl of light.

I don't mind. Because I'm the only one here in this clover field of blinding color.

Slowly, I feel the blanket, which is not at all weightless like me, slip off my body.

"Is she okay?" someone asks. I don't hear the answer, but I'm not exactly listening.

Something warm wraps around me. Two warm somethings.

Arms bring me to a firm chest, then lower me until my side hits the soft mattress again.

The sturdy body lands there with me, though more intentionally, anchoring me when I so wish to soar. Again, I'm too content to bother telling him as much.

"She'll be fine," says a voice that doesn't sound like he believes himself. "You can go now."

I don't hear footsteps.

"Now," says the voice, and there's a hesitant shuffle before the boys leave.

Light shuffles behind me on the other side of my eyelids, but here is timeless, and I can't tell for how long. I don't really care to count. Eventually, the darkness of Peter's bedroom begins to leak into the corners of my vision. I'm not upset by this. They're just the regular sort of shadows. Not the types that whisper of murder and scream in anguish.

I can feel him next to me. The unsteady rhythm of his chest against my back tells me he's more alert than I am.

CHAPTER 34

J wake to the taut curve of muscular arms tethering me safely within the soft sheets, the ebbing of Peter's chest pressed to my cheek. He's awake. I can tell by the pattern of his breathing, even in my haze, the come-down from a high I hate to think I'll never reach again.

My body feels worn out. A beaten rug that's been slapped against the doorstep one too many times. Still, my sore flaccid limbs find comfort in the arms of the shadows.

"Have you slept at all?" I ask.

"Couldn't," Peter says, shifting me slightly so I can face him. His eyes are out of focus, and at first I wonder if he took the faerie dust, too. Perhaps he's simply drunk on our nearness, high on the thrill of protecting me. I think I like that. "If I had, you would have simply floated away."

"Are you being literal or figurative?" I groan.

"The poets had a tendency of being both."

"You speak of poets like they're an extinct species."

Peter chuckles. "When was the last time you read a poem from this century that made you feel like this?" He trails a finger down my spine. My skin isn't exposed, but it might as well be for how sensitive it is to his touch.

A soft smile tugs at my lips. "I don't think a poem's ever made me feel like this."

"Then you haven't read enough poetry," says Peter, leaning in so that his mouth barely brushes my forehead. He lingers there for a moment, and my heart stops with the idea that he might kiss me, but he doesn't. He just plays with the curve of my spine, teasing me in the most torturously wonderful way.

I'm not high from the faerie dust anymore. I don't think so, at least. But the calm that seeps into my muscles isn't natural. Not for me, at least. I'm not sure if it's normal for anyone else, how others go about their day inhabiting themselves.

For years, I've successfully maintained the facade of calm, but it's come at the cost of not feeling much of anything. Delicate happiness swells in my chest now, but even in Peter's arms, it feels fleeting. Like a hummingbird buzzing in my chest, one that I feel I must trap in the cage of my ribs, suturing the gaps with tough and implacable skin lest it flutter away, leaving me wondering after it forever, grasping at this moment of peace for the remainder of my days.

"Why do you have a book on etiquette sitting on your bedside table?" I ask him, glancing at the leather book I noted the time I searched his room.

"I needed a reliable source on what it was to be a gentleman," he says. "That way I could be certain I'd never turn into one by accident."

"You did drug me, I suppose," I say teasingly. "Not very gentlemanly."

"You didn't seem to mind too much." He says it nonchalantly, but that doesn't change the fact that until last night, Peter had been hesitant to give me any more than a minuscule dose. My throat goes dry remembering the shadows swelling over me. "Why do the shadows come after me?" I ask. "Why have they always come after me?"

Peter's throat bobs.

"You weren't always the shadows that whispered to me, were you?" I ask, breathless, thinking of the night terrors I experienced as a child, the ones that often sent me into a fever, from which I'd awake to my mother pressing a cold rag against my forehead.

Peter swallows, then shakes his head. "No. When I'd come to speak to you from the window, that was me. Or, my shadow self, at least. But I wasn't the one who caused your nightmares."

"Why did you let me believe that you were?"

"I didn't want you to be frightened," he says.

I shift. "I was still frightened. Just of you. Just of..." I stop myself before the words come out. The words that admit the spark in my chest I've stoked for longer than I care to admit to myself.

Peter averts his eyes, and I fight with the discomfort swelling in my belly. "I don't want to ruin this moment," Peter says, and I almost wonder if he's sad.

I offer him a weak smile. "I don't know when else I'm going to feel much safer."

Something lights in his eyes, and it might be my imagination, but I feel as though he holds me tighter, claiming me in defiance of the shadows that so desire me.

"I've suspected since the night I found you at the warehouse that you might be a shadow-soother," says Peter. My rounded ears perk at the term. It's unfamiliar to me, which is a bit shocking given how much reading I did on shadows as a child. "Not all shadows are simply a by-product of an object blocking the light. Sometimes, shadows become infused with magic."

"Like you?" I ask.

Peter shakes his head. "I'm a fae who was given a shadow form. What I'm speaking of...it's almost like the opposite. A shadow coming to life."

"How?"

Peter grins. "Magic."

I frown. This isn't exactly the type of answer that would assuage my brother John, nor am I fond of it.

Peter's grin falters, and I get the sense that he doesn't want to tell me.

"You don't have to protect everyone around you from pain, you know."

Peter smiles, wiping my hair from my forehead. "But it's such a naughty thing, pain."

"Sometimes necessary, though," I whisper, though in my heart I don't know if I believe it. Not when a night soaring in the blur of faerie dust has me wondering if pain is imperative to living at all.

My mouth salivates. Embarrassed, I swallow the craving, untangling myself from Peter's arms and propping myself on the edge of the bed, hoping sitting upright will clear my head. Peter follows my lead. When he maneuvers next to me, our legs brush.

"It's a dark sort of magic that creates Wraiths," says Peter. "Shadows infused with life. It often requires someone or something to undergo such agony that the pain becomes palpable enough for the shadows to latch onto, to feed off of. Those who wish to create Wraiths often do so by sacrificing living beings, though some Wraiths are made through happenstance. An eager shadow that happens to be in the same place where intense pain occurs. They're often found in old houses, where many have suffered agony as they watched at bedsides as their loved ones passed."

"Makes sense as to why they were everywhere in our manor," I say. "It's been in our family for generations now." I think of the ballroom and wonder how many shadows were brought to life on the night of the masquerade. My stomach rocks at the thought.

Peter nods, contemplatively. "There are some fae gifted with the ability not only to speak to the Wraiths, but also to wield them. If you can hear them, you likely have fae somewhere in your bloodline."

I jut my chin backward.

"What? Disappointed?" Peter asks teasingly.

"No, just surprised. I didn't know fae..." My cheeks blush.

"You didn't know fae what?"

"I was always under the impression that the fae of old found humans undesirable. I'm surprised one took a liking to my ancestor, that's all." I'm not sure why, but my mind flashes back to the captain, to his utter disgust as he beheld me approaching him. *Why would I be interested in dancing with a spoiled heiress who looks as if she's hardly been weaned?*

My stomach sours, but I tuck the memory away. No reason to let it crawl through the snug hold Peter has on me now.

"Who gave you that idea?" Peter asks, his eyes glinting.

My blood turns up the heat a few notches, so much so that I almost feel feverish. "Just a few books."

"First the poets, now you're believing fiction. We need to get you better read, Wendy Darling."

"They didn't tell me much about Shadow Keepers, either. Or, they did, but now I'm wondering if they could have provided false information. Perhaps you could educate me," I say, breathless.

"Do you think I deserve that honor?" Peter asks.

"I think you deserve so much more than you give yourself credit for." It's not the couth flirtatious response my mother would have taught me. Not the type of thing you say to a man whose attentions you'd like to capture. It's too honest. Too raw. Too open. The type of thing that makes men lose interest.

But I was never good at maintaining men's interest, anyway.

Peter's eyes flicker with something I don't recognize. "You're wrong, you know."

"How do you figure that?"

"You think I can be more for you. Someone I can't be. You think I'll be your knight in shining armor."

"I'm tired of knights in shining armor. They never came to rescue me from my tower. Only you did that."

"Did I rescue you, Wendy Darling? Or did I steal you away?"

Our lips are close now. It's a feat they don't touch with how I'm trembling. "I'm starting to think that perhaps I needed to be stolen."

The edges of Peter's lips twitch. "I'm inclined to agree. You're mine, Wendy Darling. Don't ever start thinking otherwise."

My breath catches.

"Does that frighten you?" he asks, blue eyes lingering on my mouth.

My answer comes without hesitation. "Yes."

"And what about this?" he asks, brushing his lips over the edge of mine. "Does this frighten you?"

I don't answer. Don't have to. Because the way I'm trembling brings a sly grin to his face.

"Good," he says, lingering so close it's almost more intimate than actually touching.

"I thought you said you didn't want me," I breathe.

"I say a lot of things."

When I can't stand it anymore, I lean in.

Peter's mouth is ready for mine, and his lips drag me into the kiss, suffusing me with a greedy abandon I can't quite contain.

It's lightning and falling and crashing and picking up my broken bones to do it all over again. Something slides into place within me, the rightness of it all, but also the wrongness. The wrongness that this is the first time I'm tasting his kiss, when it should have occurred long ago. When I've been his since the moment he extended his hand in that clock tower.

It's the first time we touched all over again, except this time, instead of my touch stitching his shadowed form into flesh, it's the other way around.

His touch unravels me. I'm the spool, his kiss what sends me spinning across the floor, the tight thread around my heart unwinding. When Peter fists the fabric of my shirt at my back, I feel as if he'll never let me go.

"I want to hear you say it," he whispers to me between kisses.

I don't even have to ask what, because my lips are already forming the words. "I'm yours."

Peter's ravenous grin presses against my mouth in answer.

"Wendy?"

Shock barrels through me at the sound of my brother's voice. I startle, my limbs doing their utmost to put as much distance between myself and Peter. But Peter's hands are still firm on my back, keeping me close though he pulls himself away from the kiss. It's probably for the best that he doesn't let me go, given I was lurching straight for his bedside table, where I might have hit my head.

"John, I—"

"I thought you were drugged." His words are directed at me, but his stare is locked on Peter.

Unsteady laughter rattles through my chest as I wipe sweat from my brow. "Obviously, the effects have worn off."

"Is it—obvious?" John asks, sweeping his gaze over to me. I watch his attention linger on my trembling hands, but we both know the shaking has nothing to do with the faerie dust.

"Yes, it is," says Peter, though he slips his hands off of me, pushing himself off the bed. "What do you need?"

John blinks, caught off guard by the way Peter doesn't try to argue with him. "Simon wanted me to remind you that tonight's the blood moon."

Peter actually blanches, but the effect only lasts for a moment. He spins on his heel, taking my hand and planting a kiss on my knuckles that has my face heating even more than it is already. "I'm afraid we'll have to continue this later," he whispers to me with a wink.

He grabs a satchel from his closet, then turns to leave. I jump from the bed, but that turns out to be a mistake because my legs are still weak from the aftereffects of the faerie dust. In a moment, he's at my side, catching me before I fall.

"Where are you going?"

"I'm afraid my tasks as a Shadow Keeper aren't limited to Neverland." He says it with a quick glance at John, so I assume he'll tell me more once we can be alone again.

Then he sets me gently on the side of the bed and dissipates into shadows. In a blink, he's gone, leaving me alone with John.

I open my mouth to explain, but he beats me to it. "Glad to see what happened last night actually worked in your favor," he says. "At least one of us ended up having a pleasant evening."

His words puncture my throat, but it's his caustic tone that twists the blade. John never speaks to me like this. I bite my lip. "How's Michael?"

John snorts. "How do you think?" He crosses his arms, highlighting streaks of red across his forearms. The lantern light flickers, revealing more scratch marks on his neck.

Guilt pricks at my stomach, but anger, too. "I thought you were going off the assumption I'm too drugged up to think. You can't have it both ways, you know."

"Fine," John says. "I'll let you choose for me: Should I hate Peter for taking advantage of you when you're not in your right mind? Or should I hate you for having a tryst with our captor while I spent the evening trying to console our brother after you almost choked him to death?"

"John—"

"I'm fine either way. You just let me know."

CHAPTER 35

*a*fter the dreadful evening when my mother and father sat me down at the foot of their bed and shattered my world by telling me of a sickly girl and a bargain struck with a shadow, I didn't sleep for weeks.

When my young, restless body finally succumbed to slumber, I began walking through the house at night, screaming when I would awake to find myself lost in the wailing shadows.

My mother, as incapable of handling my pain as she was the dreadful night I fell ill, came up with a solution.

One night as she tucked me in, she waited for John to fall asleep —Michael was yet to be born—and tipped a cold goblet to my lips. She told me it was juice. I knew how juice was made, by squeezing the liquid from a grape, but as soon as the foul liquid hit my tongue, I knew there had been a mistake. The grape must have soured before the juice had a chance to be made.

I remember gagging as the vile liquid stung on its way down my throat. After several seconds, the sensation of being lowered into a freshly heated bath washed over my body. Like having a fever, except without the sweats and chills and body aches that make fevers so unpleasant.

Not only that, but the shadows in the corner that had just seemed so looming, so terrifying, now appeared like regular shadows.

I didn't fight my mother after that. Instead, I asked for another sip.

PETER DOESN'T RETURN that night. Or the next. Or the night after that. I ask Simon about it, and he says when there's a blood moon, it's not unusual for Peter to be away for weeks.

Peter took his pouch of faerie dust with him.

He left some behind with Simon. Enough to keep me protected from the shadows, Simon explains. But he's on strict orders not to give me more than a pinch. The burst of color I get from my daily dose is the pinnacle of my day, but it's never enough.

My blood feels as if it's scraping through my veins. I try to distract myself, volunteering for half the boys' chores. While it endears me to them, it does little to soothe the sandpaper feel of my veins.

John doesn't come to visit me, and he certainly doesn't bring Michael. I've been sleeping in Peter's bed, seeking solace in the amber and pine scent of his sheets.

Episodes of feverish sweats wake me during the night, but so far the shadows have yet to return. By the third day, I'm positive that if I don't get more faerie dust in my system, my blood will run dry and I'll shrivel up.

Presents show up at the foot of Peter's bed. A whittled set of figurines—a farmer, a merchant, and three women with hoods. Wildflowers from the edges of Joel's garden—I'm pretty sure they're weeds, but their blue hue and delicate petals make them beautiful. Nettle brings me my meals, always making sure to tell me when the food was prepared by him, thereby making it superior. Simon brings me a change of clothes to replace the ones I sweated through. The Twins afford me their quiet company, and I often wake to one of them reading silently in the corner, though I'm never sure which one. Even Smalls comes to check on me, though he darts out of the room anytime he realizes I'm awake.

The small acts of kindness touch my heart, but I can't help but wish they were coming from my own family.

Once I feel well enough to walk, I go back to my room to seek solace in my brothers, but as soon as I enter the room, Michael slinks away from me, hiding in John's arms.

So I grab my coat and sneak out of the Den and into Neverland.

THE PLAN IS to scale the cliffs to Peter's storehouse. Guilt writhes in my chest for plotting to steal from him. Though I remind myself that it's not really stealing. Not when Peter would happily provide me with more if he were here.

Well, perhaps not happily. But he would give it to me. I'm certain of it.

As I walk along the beach, the sorrowful wind howls, though what it's mourning, I can't say. Beach air sprays in my nostrils, filling my lungs in a way that's refreshing, clearing my head.

The more I walk and the more my blood flows, the more my one-track mind clears, and it hits me what exactly I'm doing. I'm sneaking out of the Den in the middle of the night to get a fix.

My hands tremble, though I'm not sure whether it's from withdrawals or terror at the thought.

This happened to me when I was eight. My father discovered me in his wine cellar in the middle of the night, nursing a bottle of aged faerie wine.

I'd downed an entire bottle, and had yet to fall over.

My father was furious, I'm sure, though he wasn't the type to fight with my mother in front of the children. He didn't speak to her for months after that.

Apparently, that behavior was considered appropriate in front of the children. Like we wouldn't notice that Papa suddenly couldn't hear Mama's questions at the breakfast table.

Truth be told, it's amazing I did notice. The doctor had to be called when, after several days without the wine, my body fell into shock, my limbs shaking as I broke into a cold sweat. I vaguely remember shouting obscenities at my parents, words that had never left my mouth before that day and haven't since.

I remember not being Wendy.

I remember waking up as myself and being terrified.

The aching for the wine stayed with me and remained for a good while, though I found myself slipping into the old habit around courting season. Or in the winter, when the shadows lingered longer.

I recognize it now, the vicious tapping against my skull, my body demanding that which it doesn't need. It threatens to drown out all rational thought, which is why I'm out on the beach in the middle of the night.

In the middle of a storm. I blink, finally noticing the raindrops needling my skin. The murky sky above, clouds obscuring the stars.

How desperate had I been for faerie dust that I hadn't even noticed it was storming?

It's a physically arduous task, but I turn myself back around, the magnetism of Peter's storehouse screaming at me.

That's when I see it.

Further down the beach, a silhouette lies prostrate in the sand, highlighted by the moonlight.

My steps accelerate into a run. Thoughts of who might be laid out on the sand bombard me. Is it a Lost Boy, or perhaps Peter?

No, it wouldn't be Peter. I don't see any wings.

When I approach, I find the man face-down in the sand. When I go to turn him, I'm throttled with a horrible flashback to flipping the murderer's body in the sand. I hesitate, then tuck my finger into the crook of the man's jaw. It's stubbly, rough against my skin, but I feel a faint pulse there, begging me softly to save the stranger. I bite my lip. I can't make out the man's features, but he's dressed in soaked breeches and a white shirt.

What had Peter said?

That Neverland attracts those with darkness in their souls?

My heart flutters, racing faster than it should even under stress due to the faerie dust, but I defy my better judgment and loop my arms underneath the man's torso, struggling with his limp body as I flip him over.

His back thuds against the ground at the same moment the moonlight flashes across his face, like the sky itself is intent on exposing him.

My gut turns over, my head whirling. Blood painted in the shape of open smiles streaks across my vision, my memories, but none of them obscure his hauntingly beautiful face.

Because the man who lies before me is the one who forced my parents to take their own lives.

Captain Nolan Astor.

SAND LODGES itself between my toes as I pace up and down the shoreline. My fingers are in my mouth as I bite at my nails, something I haven't done since that first time my father took the bottle away from me. My heart thuds against my chest, Peter's storehouse calling to me even louder than before.

I need more. My throat bulges with pain, pain that just a drop against my tongue would whisk away, but no.

The captain is here, in Neverland, on the beach with me, and I have to figure out what to do about it.

My belt digs into my flesh as I fumble for my dagger. Even the weight of the hilt against my palm feels like a judge's gavel, resoundingly permanent. It's heavier than before, like it absorbed the resistance of the murderer's flesh, and now I can sense the reverberations of his crunching ribs reaching out to me from the past.

It would be easier this time, I tell myself. Captain Astor isn't moving.

The very thought makes me want to vomit, but I crawl next to him on my hands and knees anyway. Then I place the tip of my blade to his chest, allowing it to follow the curve of his ribs until I find the soft, open flesh between.

There. I'll just aim there.

I lift the blade, but my hands are trembling so violently, I lose my place. I don't know if I can bear to strike him twice, no matter how my hate for him surges in my chest. So I touch the tip of the blade to his chest and determine to throw all my weight into the hilt.

I push there lightly, too lightly. Sweat beads on my forehead, mingling with rainwater, as I remember just how much pressure I'm going to have to apply to actually pierce this fae through.

I close my eyes and try again, but it's like an invisible hand sneaks in through the past, from the beach where I killed the stranger, and stops me.

I can't do it.

I can't do it.

My mother slitting her throat.

I can't do it for her.

My father crumpling to the floor in a pool of his own blood.

I can't do it for him.

My scream.

I certainly can't do it for me.

I had one kill in me, and I spent it on the murderer on the beach.

Panicked, I wipe the sweat from my brow and try to calm myself. It's okay that I can't kill the captain. I'll just find Peter, and Peter will do it for me.

Except Peter isn't here.

Perhaps I could recruit some of the Lost Boys for help, but they've become closer to John lately, and I don't think I can bear for him to know the captain is on the island. I remember him finding me by the sink basin and asking if I enjoyed putting a blade through Thomas's murderer. My brother has bloodshed in his heart, a stinging sense of vengeance in his eyes. If he finds out Captain Astor is on the island, he'll drive a blade through his neck. Or make him cut his throat with his own hand.

And then he'll be a killer like me.

I don't know that the shadows will haunt John at night like they do me, but there's something wrong on this island, in this realm that was rushed to be made. Grief comes in torrents, and where I could hold it at bay in my home world, here it topples over me, consuming me.

So letting out a tiny sob as I do it, I sheathe my dagger and loop my hands underneath the captain's armpits.

And drag him away.

CHAPTER 36

*T*he cave I find to dump the captain in is off the shoreline. The tide has come in, so I have to drag his body over the jagged, wet rocks to get there, water sloshing inside my leather boots. I get a sick catharsis every time the captain's shirt tears, the sharp rocks digging into the flesh of his back. Every time I have to tug extra hard to get his limbs unstuck.

I don't know how he's here, in Neverland, but the captain must have been hunting me. He'd wanted to kidnap me the night of the masquerade, though for what purpose, I don't know. Fear threatens to overtake me, and just before reaching the mouth of the cave, I consider whether I should leave the captain face-down in the water.

I'm not sure what all kills the fae anymore. They rarely make an appearance among humans, so all I have to go on is what I've read in the old faerie tales. So far, they haven't steered me correctly. When the fae were cursed with mortal lifespans, did it make them easier to kill too? That seems likely given the fact that I was able to take the life of the murderer with my dagger.

I bite my lip, a sharp pain stinging at my lower back from where I slipped and had to overcompensate on my right side to keep the captain from falling into the water.

What am I even doing?

Even if I manage to hide him in this cave, there's no telling how quickly he'll come to his senses. How quickly he'll be able to escape.

I release my grip on his arms and let the captain slump.

As if hearing my call, a wave consumes the captain's body, covering his mouth and nose in the ocean's froth. The ocean itself tries to pull the captain into its watery grave, its treasure store of corpses and bones and waste, but the jagged rocks provide a barrier upon which the captain's limbs become stuck.

I watch as the waves retreat, leaving a gargling half-corpse upon the rocks as the captain's body fights for air. It sounds like choking on your own blood. The sound my parents made when their throats were slit.

I should revel in this male's pain. His agonizing death should fill some gaping hole in my chest, but I make the mistake of looking at his face.

He's devastating. That alone might be enough to let him drown here. People with wretched hearts shouldn't get to be beautiful. Not when he ripped mine from my very chest. But it's the pain on his face that gets me. The slight wrinkles around his eyes betraying years of suffering he has over me.

Another wave splashes against the captain's face. I might as well be pinching his nose shut while covering his mouth in a cloth. But even in his passed out stupor, he reaches for his hand.

The hand with the severed Mating Mark.

With a jolt, I remember the hatred and desperation with which I dug my dagger into the murderer's chest cavity, even thinking he might lay a hand on Peter. I tremble to consider what I might have done had he succeeded. And Peter isn't even my Mate.

The captain had been married to his Mate, I remember from the night of the masquerade.

What sort of madness had the captain been driven to when the Mark on his hand withered and died, following the death of his wife?

This time, the crashing waves succeed in lifting the captain from his safehold behind the rocks. In a moment of anguish and folly, I lunge after him, splashing myself up to the waist as I struggle against the sea for the captain's body.

Heaving, I drag him across the rocks and into the mouth of the cave. I drop him onto the ground, wondering if he'll drown despite my effort. But the man's mouth begins to foam with saltwater. He chokes and gargles, coughing it up as it spews past his lips and down the sides of his cheek.

I stand there for a long while, staring at him, until I realize I don't have time for such things. Not when he'll wake eventually and persist in his quest to kill me. Or whatever it is he has planned for me.

My mind is racing, and I rub my hands on my hips absentmindedly. As I scan the cave, my gaze lands on the purple-leafed plants that jut out rebelliously from the sand.

Rushweed.

The same herb Victor gifted me after Tink's attack.

It's not faerie dust by any means. Back at home, it's what doctors used to keep their patients still while they operated on them.

If only it helped with the pain.

For now, I'm glad it doesn't.

I left Victor's pouch back at the Den, so I'll have to make do with what I have on hand. My hands trembling, not just with fear, but from the muscular exhaustion of dragging the tall and broad captain across the rocks, I grab a handful of rushweed, then grind it between two rocks. The leaves are brittle and dissolve easily into a powder, which I press to the captain's lips. They're softer than I imagined, and the feel of them against my skin brings an unwanted fantasy to the forefront of my mind—the reaction I'd expected from the mysterious man with the golden Mark when I approached him at the ball. I'd thought he'd press his lips to the back of my hand, hold my gaze in a trance.

I'd been a stupid girl then.

I'm probably still a stupid girl, but at least I know better than to blush like that.

I swallow my reaction and watch as the captain's tense face goes lax, his breathing stabilizing. In hindsight, I probably should have waited to make sure he coughed up all the water, but I'm still not convinced I *don't* want the captain to die. I just don't want his blood on my hands.

It's still several hours until the sun rises, and I can't very well go back to the Den. If any of the Lost Boys see me quaking like this, they'll think I'm as high as the clock tower, and Peter will find out I went looking for faerie dust. Even if I did turn back.

Besides. Now that I have the captain subdued, I have so many questions. Questions I buried when we crossed into Neverland. I'd accepted the fact that I'd left the answers behind in my home realm. But now that Captain Astor is here, they're flooding back in with such urgency, I have to restrain myself from grabbing the captain's shoulders and shaking him awake.

Instead, I sit and wait.

I'm not sure how much time passes before the captain's long, black eyelashes flutter and reveal those stunning green eyes.

They're awash with confusion. I watch as realization slowly overcomes him. It's in the way his fingers tense in an attempt to curl together, but fail. In the way his boots flick as he tries to move his legs. I've been dosed with rushweed before, and it feels as if the doctors poured concrete into your limbs.

Painfully, the captain squeezes his eyes shut—I suppose in an attempt to contain his frustration.

Then, effortfully, judging by the way his neck muscles flex, he cranes his neck to look at me.

The breath whooshes out of my lungs when those ivy irises pierce my very soul. As with the first time we met, I feel as though I'm naked. Not because he stares at me as some of my suitors did, as if they were undressing me in their mind. It's more like I showed up at a gathering having forgotten to don clothes, and the captain is the first to notice.

I fight the heat crawling up my cheeks.

I don't have to be intimidated by this man. For once in my life, I'm the one in control.

Then why do I let him be the first to speak?

"You didn't kill me," he says, slowly. I can't tell if he's testing out the words, careful not to startle a rabid animal, or if the drugs are just making him have to focus more on speaking. "Tell me why."

My response catches in my throat, and I fumble for an answer. "I—"

No. I shake my head. "I'm the one who has you subdued, not the other way around."

"Forgive me if your tone isn't convincing."

Okay, so the captain isn't having difficulty finding his words, after all. He's right though; my voice is shaking terribly, coming out in short screeches at parts. His pointing it out only causes my tongue to grow thicker in my mouth, a stumbling block for any witty response I might have come up with.

"Now tell me why you didn't kill me," says the captain.

My heart stills.

My father used to say that I was the most compliant child in the world. That I'd do anything I was asked.

Being told to do something, on the other hand?

That's when I would dig my heels in. I wouldn't tantrum like some children or outright refuse like others. But if it was a chore I didn't find fair, I'd do it poorly. If it was schoolwork, I'd do it so slowly, force my tutors to suffer through a long afternoon with me.

So no.

I don't have a clever response to the captain, but I'm sure one will come to me in my dreams tonight. When I sleep exceedingly well, knowing I have this man underneath my thumb.

Instead, I just crane my head to the side and smile softly. Waiting.

After a moment of staring me down, the captain actually gives an approving laugh, though there are remnants of the gurgling ocean in it. Even now, in my resolute state, I can't help but notice the way the laughter softens his harsh features, warming his eyes as they come to a fresh simmer.

"So you can be stubborn, after all."

"I can see you struggling," I say, nodding toward his feet, which are wiggling, though not with much success.

"Come now, Darling. I was just coming to terms with the fact that you're not as dull as you let on. Don't go and ruin it by stating such obvious facts. Of course I'm struggling."

I flush, anger roiling inside my throat, silencing me and holding my tongue against my will.

A cruel smirk slices against the captain's beautiful features. "Oh, but I forgot. You're not the type to struggle against your chains, are you, Darling?"

Tears spring up in my eyes, but I blink them away hastily. "How did you find me?"

This time, it's the captain who offers me a cruelly placating smile, mirroring my own from earlier. I fear his probably appears more sinister than mine.

"How did you find me?" I repeat.

"Why do you assume I was looking for you? Slightly presumptuous of you, though I suppose that's to be expected from a girl whose parents taught her from a young age that she was the only thing that was important in the universe. That her life was so much more valuable than anyone else's."

"Please don't talk about my parents," I whisper.

The captain's cheek ticks. "Please?"

Again, my throat bulges, and I find myself nervously digging my fingers through the black sand underneath me.

"I don't do please. Or do you think that would have been a kinder way to ask your parents to slit their own throats?"

I'm not sure what happens to me, but I lunge, the anger I've been stuffing down finally building up enough resistance, like a metal spring that's been pressed and released, propelling me to my feet.

I find myself above the captain, my dagger unsheathed and glinting against his throat.

"Your hands are trembling, Darling," he taunts.

"You know what you don't need a steady hand for? Slitting a man's throat."

"But do you know what you do need?" says the captain, sighing. "Courage. Guts. And that, Darling, is something I'm afraid you're utterly lacking."

"I've killed before," I say, and the words feel like a betrayal. Like holding up a medal I won by slicing off the hand of the person who earned it.

The captain cocks his head, though barely, searching my face intently. "Have you now? I'm impressed. But if you believe that makes you courageous, you're sorely mistaken. Courage isn't found in what you're willing to do once. Courage is knowing what it feels like to get your hands slick with blood, to have your soul chipped away at. Courage is to know what it is to steep in that kind of pain, and to still be willing to do it again. Are you willing to do it again?"

I try to dig the blade further into his throat, but it's like I've hit a wall—the resistance of his skin that begs me not to go forward, not to rip through it like I did the stranger. Or maybe the resistance is in my limbs. Possibly even in my soul itself, begging me not to sacrifice yet another piece of it to this island.

With haste, I retract the blade from the captain's throat and bite down to stifle my frustrated scream.

When he finally answers my question, it feels more like a failure than anything else. A reminder that he only answers me on his own terms. "If you must know, you left your pocket watch behind in the tower. There are some talented Seers out there who can locate people by their possessions. Especially possessions that evoke emotion."

My father gifting me the glass pocket watch dances before my memory. The present of a father tainted by what the object meant— a reminder that my time was running out.

"Where is it then?" I ask, mouth dry.

"Wouldn't you like to know?"

. . .

As I SLOG my boots through damp sand on the way out, hoping the tide will come in and fill the cave and drown that horrid man in its wake, his last words pound at my skull.

"Wendy Darling, always letting life happen to her, never brave enough to take the helm."

CHAPTER 37

I intend to tell Peter about capturing the captain as soon as he returns from whatever mission the Sister has him conducting in the other realms.

A week goes by before he gets back, and after several trips to the cave to force-feed Captain Astor more rushweed, as well as offer him actual food I sneak from the kitchens, I decide I won't tell Peter.

I saw what Peter did to the nightstalker that dared to hunt me on the cliffs that one night. I can't imagine what he'd do to the man who killed my parents. Though part of me welcomes such violence, I'm not ready for the captain to die. Yet.

I want answers. The fact that Peter puts more value in protecting the Lost Boys than restoring their memories has me inclined to believe he won't hesitate to usher the captain and his secrets to the grave. And later, when I weep over never uncovering the truth behind my parents' deaths, he'll tell me I'm probably happier not knowing.

I am not happier not knowing.

When I first arrived on the island, I managed well enough by pushing queries about my parents aside. It seemed the reasonable thing to do, aware that, cut off from our home realm, there was no chance of discovering why the captain held such a grudge against them. Why whatever they did caused him to hate me.

I want to believe John's theory, that my father simply sent the captain on a dangerous expedition that resulted in his wife's death. It's not a flattering theory, but it's the kindest we can come up with. It could very well be that my father was misinformed by an expert in sailing conditions. My father never sailed in these expeditions himself, after all, only funded them. Maybe forcing the boat out under poor conditions was a misguided mistake rather than a greedy attempt to stuff his coffers at the risk of the crew's life.

Still, I need to know this is the case.

Something tells me it is. But perhaps that's just my heart wanting it to be so.

Funny how gut feelings have a tendency to tell us the kinds of things we want to hear. Some people's do, at least. They talk to them like they're oily merchants trying to sidle up and earn their favor with flattery.

My gut feelings are generally not so complimentary.

They prefer the blunt approach. The panicked what-ifs of the worst-case scenario. The scenario where the captain took revenge on my parents because of a cruelty for which they truly deserved their fates. A cruelty that has something to do with me.

My stomach turns over with anxiety when I think of it. It consumes my every thought, stealing me away. At breakfast this morning, Simon had to poke me in the shoulder to get my attention after calling my name several times.

John is getting suspicious that something is off. If I don't want Peter knowing about the captain, I want John knowing about him even less. Peter would kill the captain to protect the Lost Boys and would walk away from the murder, soul and conscience unscathed, believing he was only fulfilling his duty.

John would not be so lucky. The scent of blood would wake him in the middle of the night, the sound of the captain gurgling on his own lifeblood. Hatred and revenge might be rotting John's bones, but at least his soul isn't yet broken.

Then there's the problem of my cravings.

They're worse at night, exacerbated by the lack of sleep I'm getting. Though, I'd be lying if I said I wasn't fixated on the storehouse all hours of the day. I worry that the shadows—the Wraiths—will return before Peter does and that this time I'll have no armor against them.

There's only one activity that provides me any relief.

I can only visit the captain at night when I'm sure everyone else is asleep. This proves to be problematic, but I make it work.

He's yet to answer questions about my parents. He's yet to answer any questions, really, but I still feel as though we're making progress. Each time he scalds me with his words, the pain sears my heart a little less. I become a tad more numb to the insults, the slights on my character.

I have a feeling that by the time this is over, I won't hurt at all.

I'M COLLECTING rushweed along the beach near the cliffs when a dark figure forms in the sky. As he approaches, limbs and wings come to focus in my vision, along with a smile that knocks my breath from me.

"Hello, Wendy Darling." Peter sweeps to the ground in front of me. He's in his solid form, though he allows his shadows to nip at the waistband of my pants and curl around my shoulders, making me slip off my feet and into his arms.

"Hello, Peter," I say. The grin that tugs at my lips comes without forethought, a smile I don't have to practice like the ones I used to offer to my countless suitors.

"Where's my favorite Darling running off to?" he asks, though I don't think he intends for me to answer, given the way he pulls me into his kiss, pressing his lips to mine until I'm lost in the feel of him.

It's a good thing, too, because I'm not keen on answering his question.

When Peter pulls away, he seems to have forgotten he asked anything. He wheels me forward by my hand, twirling me in circles.

"Where are we going?" I giggle, though I can't help but glance toward the cave where I've trapped the captain. It's not terribly far off, but I worry it's within hearing distance for Peter, though the rush of the waves should keep sound from traveling.

Besides, surely the captain knows better than to alert Peter of his presence.

"On an adventure," he says, swinging my arm in his. There's a buzz about him, the flicker of a glow. Like he's the center of a particle of faerie dust, making everything around him just a few shades brighter.

At first, I think he'll take my hand and fly me heavenward, so I let out a gasped shock when he backs me into the cliffside, the jagged rocks jutting underneath my shoulder blades.

I don't have time to protest before his mouth meets mine, desire threatening to whisk me away.

But as his hands roam my body and find the waistline of my trousers, the world shifts, and I'm sixteen. I'm no longer in Neverland, but in my parents' smoking parlor, heady incense filling my nostrils as I try to sever my mind from my body. My pale pink fingernails dig into the velvet lining of my father's favorite chair, while a man whose name I haven't bothered to remember…

"Peter. Peter, stop," I say, my breathing ragged as I pull myself from his hungry kiss and grasp at his wrists, now playing with the buttons on my pants.

He blinks, and it takes him a moment to seem like he hears me. When he raises a brow in confusion, a host of dreadful memories bash me over the back of the head, swirling my vision.

"What's wrong, Wendy Darling?"

The words teeter on the tip of my tongue, but they refuse to go any further, muted by the warnings of my mother never to tell a soul. So I offer Peter a half-truth instead. "I promised myself I wouldn't."

He cranes his head to the side. "Ever?"

I let out a nervous laugh. "No. Of course not. Just not..." My cheeks heat, and I try to hide my embarrassment—unsuccessfully, I might add—by taking Peter's hand and wiggling it. "Not until I see a ring on your finger."

Peter's pointed ears flick, and for a dreadful moment, he says nothing. I wait for him to laugh, to tell me I'm being silly. That marriage has no meaning in a realm tucked away from the rest, a world all our own.

I'm already preparing a defense that will keep me from having to tell him the truth, but when he removes his hand from mine, there's a weight left behind, a metallic chill wrapping around a finger on my left hand.

My gaze drops, and so does my heart.

The ring is forged of silver, a dazzling emerald shimmering amid a halo of sparkling diamonds.

"Peter."

I glance back up at him, at his beautiful face. His shining copper hair. His perfectly tanned skin. The ever-present twinkle in his eyes. He's just smirking, that smug arrogance playing into his features perfectly.

"Is this one of your tricks?" I can't help the way my voice falters, but Peter just shakes his head.

"I told you, Wendy Darling. You and I are going on an adventure. That is..." He extends a hand. "If you're brave enough."

A breathless smile tugs at my lips, and I pinch the band of the ring between my forefinger and thumb, rotating it over the skin where my finger meets my palm. It fits loosely, just a tad too big.

That's what Peter was doing while he was away. Procuring a ring from one of the realms.

I forget to breathe.

Peter twists his head to the side, examining me with vague curiosity. "You don't like it?"

"No," I laugh. I laugh because it's a ridiculous notion. Because it's absurd to imagine any sane girl *not* cherishing the moment a beautiful boy gifted her a beautiful ring. "It's just..."

He swivels me into his chest. "It's just what?"

"It's just...don't you think it's a bit...hasty?"

"Says who?" he asks, his eyes gleaming.

"Says...well, says anyone with an ounce of sense, probably."

"If you're looking for the sensible sort, I'm afraid you're with the wrong man."

I bite back my smile.

"Wendy," he says, taking my hand. "I just got back from a harrowing journey to the other realms. Where men and women are slaves to time, constantly chasing ambition until the clock ticks down, the sand runs out. They watch what they love slip between their fingertips because they wait too long. They strive and work by the sweat of their brow, then their heart gives out on them before they can enjoy the pension they've set up for themselves. I don't want that for us. You and I? We don't have to heed time. What we do today, tomorrow, it doesn't make a difference. We're on whatever schedule we desire here. Just you and me. We make the rules."

"I have to admit, I like the sound of that."

"I thought you might. But you still look disappointed. Why?"

I gaze up at him, openmouthed as I grasp for the words. It's a silly notion, but it's tugging on my heart, causing the slightest ache of disappointment. "It's just that I always imagined that the man asking for my hand would be kneeling."

"You want me to kneel?" Peter's scoff is tinged with playfulness. "Why?"

"Because. It's just what's done," I laugh, my nerves coming through. "It's how I always imagined it would happen."

Peter bites the inside of his cheek as he grins. "Were you imagining me proposing to you, or was it all those suitors of yours?"

"It was usually a faceless man proposing to me," I admit with a chuckle.

Peter knits his brow playfully. "I do fit that description on occasion."

"I suppose." My fingers interlock with his, swinging his hands back and forth. "But it's what I've always dreamed."

"My, my, you are traditional-minded, aren't you?"

My face flushes. Peter's such a free spirit; I don't want him to see me like he did before. I don't want to go back to being the girl who teetered on the edge, clinging to the surface without ever letting myself jump.

Peter must note my embarrassment, because he slides his thumb over my finger, slipping his hand over the metal, then pocketing the ring. My stomach plummets as I lose sight of it, but then he pulls me close and brushes a kiss on my forehead. The salty breeze picks up, meaning his kiss is the only warmth around. "What if I have a better idea?"

Before I can answer, he shoots us into the air, the black sand beach a streak of charcoal against a blue and green canvas below us.

Thousands of feet above Neverland, he asks again. "Wendy Darling, will you marry me?"

"Of course," I say, as I lose myself in his kiss. The rush of his lips on mine is so intoxicating, I almost can't feel the ring he slides back onto my finger.

CHAPTER 38

"Thinking about someone?" The captain's voice breaks me out of my wandering thoughts, of Peter kissing me breathless in the sky. I've got him propped against a boulder in the back of the cave. I've been spoon-feeding him cold boar stew for the past several minutes. Normally I'd be pestering him with questions, and he'd be pestering me with insults, but today my mind has been elsewhere.

"What makes you say that?" I ask, the affront obvious in my voice.

The captain's eyes wander, tracing the golden freckles of my cheek with a precision that makes me feel as if he's glimpsed more flesh than just what's on my face. "Because you're trailing your finger over that Mark of yours like it's the wooden notches on the casket of a loved one you're about to bury."

I wrench my hand from my cheek, embarrassment flooding me.

"You didn't realize you were doing it, did you?" There's a taunting condescension in his gaze, but that might just be his face. Now that I think of it, I can't think of a time he's ever looked at me like I had any semblance of a brain.

I ignore him, then go back to stirring his stew.

"I used to do it too, you know," he says, rubbing his thumb against the ruined Mark on his wrist. That's about all he can manage with his hands right now, because of the rushweed. "Hated what a hold a girl I'd never met had on me."

Irritation springs up in my chest. "Doesn't matter. No one ever meets their Mate anyway. Except for you, I guess. And you already told me it was a misfortune."

"So he's not your Mate, then?"

My heart drops out. It's just a question, but I feel like I'm an animal who's just stepped in a lure and been yanked into the trees. "You could have just asked me directly if you were so interested. No need to trick me into it."

Captain Astor's smile is almost sickeningly innocent. "Yes. Because I'm sure a clever girl like you isn't used to being tricked into things you don't want to do."

He holds my stare. A silent challenge.

One that I lose as soon as I let my gaze slip toward the emerald ring on my finger.

"I saw that the winged boy took you on an adventure in the sky earlier."

My heart skips at the same time a rock forms in my gut. I shove the spoon into his mouth, hoping to shut him up while I regain my composure. His throat bobs as he swallows. Dark stubble flecks his neck, his chin, reminding me of how it felt scraping against my cheek as he commanded my parents to take their own lives.

I would prefer to watch him choke on a piece of boar meat, but that wouldn't get us any closer to clearing my parents' names, would it?

"How did you manage to see us from the cave?" I ask, unable to hide my apprehension.

"Well, when you have the misfortune of being chronically poisoned by a pretty girl, you start to entertain yourself by trying to find pictures in the clouds. Imagine my horror when a perfectly good cumulous unicorn was shot through the chest by a pair of lovesick children."

Something stabs at my gut, but my shoulders relax. I don't want to think about why I'm glad the captain didn't hear the entire proposal.

"Why call him the winged boy when you know his name is Peter?"

"Because it bothers you, and that's the other source of entertainment I've found. It's almost more interesting than finding shapes in the clouds."

"Yes, well, it's hard to beat a cumulous unicorn."

The captain chuckles, his smile lazy. "That was almost funny, Darling, but I'm afraid you stole half the joke from my lips."

An uncomfortable knot forms in my belly, so I redirect. "How do you know Peter?"

"How do you know I know Peter?"

"Because you said his name in the clock tower that night."

"What night?"

I shoot the captain a glare, and his grin is just as sharp. "Why don't you ask him yourself? It appears the two of you have grown..." His gaze lingers on the sparkling ring. "Close. Though, tell me, does he give rings to all the girls he steals from their beds at night?"

My fingers flex in irritation. I don't even rise to his bait. "Only the ones he steals from clock towers, I'm afraid."

"Mm."

"You didn't answer my question."

"Get an answer from your lover, and I'll help you come to a more accurate understanding of the truth based off what he says."

I direct the spoon toward the captain like it's one of the pointers my tutors used to use. "I'll hold you to that."

"I wouldn't hope for anything less," he says, his eyes silently taunting me. But then he has the audacity to add, "Why the headlong rush into matrimony?"

I chew on the edge of my tongue. "That's not really any of your business, is it?"

The captain ignores my cue to end the conversation. "Oh,

come now. We both know swift engagements are the by-product of only two situations: a significant dowry or a child forthcoming."

I snort. "I assure you, in this case, it's neither."

The captain examines me carefully. "You say it with such confidence."

I turn my attention to stuffing the empty bowl and spoon into my satchel. It doesn't matter that I'm not looking at him, though. Even the air around the captain curves into a taunting grin, one I don't have to glimpse to feel creeping over my skin. "You haven't slept with him, have you?"

Wooden spoons clank as I slam the satchel into the ground. "Must you always be this crass?"

"I'm afraid I must, given your love life—or lack thereof, as the case may be—is all I have to keep me entertained during my solitary confinement."

My hands are trembling so hard with my eagerness to remove myself from this conversation, I'm struggling to tie the knot securing my satchel.

But the captain isn't done. "Tell me—what about the winged boy revolts you so much?"

"It's not for lack of desire, I assure you," I say, smug satisfaction settling in my belly when the captain has the audacity to look annoyed by my response.

"Well, if you're denying his advances until marriage, I suppose that explains the ring."

"At least he respects my decision," I snap. "Because no one is touching me again until I see a ring on his finger."

Captain Astor stills, his throat bobbing slightly.

Sand bulges underneath my fingernails as I dig them into the ground to steady myself. Slowly, I feel the pain in the beds of my nails tether me back to reality. Reminding me I'm here, not in my parents' dark and smoky parlor. Not in the arms of yet another...

"Again?"

I blink. "What?"

The captain's breathing quickens. "You said no one is touching you *again*."

Outside the mouth of the cave, the stars blur together. "You already saw what happened with Lord Credence."

"But it happened before."

"I wish that's all that had happened before," I say, and I tell myself to end this conversation there, but for some reason, the words start to spill out. Because I'm so angry, furious at the captain for making me remember. Angry enough to pelt him with the grimy details of the past, so he'll have to sit in my discomfort with me. "When it was time for my coming out into society, my parents relied on my beauty and charm to win over suitors. They knew my Mark would be a hindrance, but that didn't stop them from assuring me I'd have several proposals to choose from by the end of my first season.

"They were right to assume I'd attract attention. Men were always calling on me, lining up to ask me to dance. We thought our fears that my Mark would drive them away had been all for naught. But then the end of my first season came, and I was without a single proposal. My parents chalked it up to my youth—I was only fifteen at the time. But I knew they were just saying as much to make me feel better.

"My nightmares grew worse after that—almost as bad as when I was a child. Once my second season rolled around, I was more motivated than ever to win a man's heart. But my motivation couldn't have matched my mother's. The night before the season's first ball, she visited me in my rooms and said it was time that we talked. Woman-to-woman."

A lump forms in my throat. It feels like a betrayal, telling this story to the person responsible for my mother's death. But it's as if the story has taken the reins of my mouth, and I'm simply listening, a bystander like the captain, hanging onto every word.

"She assured me that things would have been different if not for my Mark. That I would have had several proposals the previous year otherwise. As our hopes had proven vain, she suggested it was time we employed a more shrewd approach in securing me a husband.

"My mother said…" I draw a square in the sand with my finger, but then erase it because it makes me think of Michael. "She said there were other ways to entice men, besides good manners and etiquette. I thought…" My throat stings, and I have to talk around the lump swelling in my throat. "I thought she was going to suggest that we lower my neckline. Cut slits into my skirts, which was starting to come into fashion. That wasn't what she meant.

"There were things a woman could do with a man that could leave him wanting more, later, she said. Things that would leave behind no evidence." My cheeks go hot, and I flip the collar of my coat up so the captain won't see. I still don't know why I'm telling him this, except that suddenly, though I've refused to think of the parlor in over a year, I feel as though, if I keep it to myself a moment longer, it will gnaw my flesh from the inside out.

"I told her I didn't want to have to do those things. Most of the men who courted me in my first season were—well, they hadn't seemed so bad when I'd thought marriage meant living in the same manor and having a baby magically appear in one's belly once every few years." I chuckle nervously.

The captain does not.

"She hugged me. She didn't want me to have to do any of those things either. But she said once the Shadow Keeper took me away, he would make me do all those things and worse. At least this way, I'd have my mother just outside the door, listening for me to cry out in case the suitor wanted more than we were willing to give him."

At the sound of the word *we*, the captain's jaw bulges.

"That first night, she bullied a man attending the ball to come speak with us in the parlor. I remember having to tug at my collar because the incense my mother was burning made my throat scratchy. The man seemed annoyed to have been cornered by yet another mother wishing him to give up his bachelorhood for the sake of her daughter. My mother went to pour him a drink, but the wine bottle was empty."

My hands are sweating now, so I rub them on my trousers. "She'd left an empty bottle on the cart on purpose, of course. She jabbered on about how silly she'd been, that she'd have to make a trip to the cellar to get more wine. Before she left, she made sure to mention how long it took for her to make decisions. How if she ended up trapped in the cellar for hours, I was to keep the suitor entertained."

A tear, salty as the ocean breeze wafting into the cave, scrambles down my cheek. "I did what I was told. When it was over, I just remember racking my brain trying to make sure what I'd let him do was within the parameters of what my mother told me. We waited all week for a proposal, but it never came. I believe my mother threatened him with exposing what he'd done to me, but he told her to go ahead. No one would blame him for not wanting to marry a Marked girl. Exposing him would only ruin my already meager chances of finding a husband.

"I was relieved, to be honest. I thought that would be the end of it, but my mother insisted the flaw was not with the methods, but the suitor. By the next week, she'd found another man to abandon me in the parlor with. She always smiled at them, even afterward. Always beamed at them like they were our last hope.

"I got used to it after a while, but I was relieved when my second season came to a close. I thought it would mean a break, but my parents had other ideas. They made it a ritual to invite over a bachelor for dinner at least twice a week. We'd go back to the parlor, but only after a few drinks, of course."

My tongue goes parched at the memory of faerie wine. Father wouldn't let me drink any of it. Not after I almost died from it as a child. But I remember watching it sparkle in the crystal, hating the suitors who got to be rid of their inhibitions when I had to remember *everything* that happened in that parlor.

I blink back tears. "I got used to it eventually. But then a man came by for dinner, and when he smiled at me, butterflies swarmed in my stomach. When he told jokes, I didn't have to pretend to laugh. The parlor didn't seem like such a dreadful way to end the night, and I found myself looking forward to the moment she abandoned us."

I go silent, the will to form words having died out. I don't have the energy to tell the captain about that particular suitor—the first night a man's touch felt pleasant against my skin. I'd cried after he left, just because I hadn't known women had the capability of enjoying being touched. For the next week, I stalked my parents' valet, waiting for the letter petitioning my father for my hand.

In the end, all I can bring myself to say is, "He didn't want to marry me either. So I promised myself no more nights in the parlor. No more letting men touch me. Not until I saw a ring on his finger."

I glance at the captain, just for a second, waiting for him to mock me. There's a tick in his jaw, the only movement in his body.

"You shouldn't have told me that," he says, and it feels as if my heart is falling out of my chest, all the air being wrung out of my lungs.

Stupid. Stupid of me to open up to him. "Well, I figure better you than anyone else, considering you'll be dead soon enough," I practically spit.

The captain stares at me, murder limning every sharp feature. "No," he says slowly. "I mean you shouldn't have told me that. Not if you ever wanted me to feel a twinge of guilt about spilling your sorry parents' blood."

His words skewer me, twisting and taking bits of my flesh with them on the way out. The manifold facets of my pain fold atop one another, murky and opaque and impossible to differentiate. Is my hatred toward the captain because he killed them, or because he killed them before I grew brave enough to scream at them for what they'd done to me? Did he steal my parents, or my chance at hearing their ardent apologies? And is my hatred for the captain, or have I only directed it toward him because that seems less complicated than aiming it elsewhere?

"Why are you here?" I ask, wrenching my racing thoughts from their destructive path.

"I think you know the answer to that question."

I grit my teeth, shaking my head. "No, I know you're here for me. But why? What do you want from me? You've already gotten your revenge for whatever it is you think my parents were to blame for."

"If that's your subtle way of trying to get me to tell you why I killed your parents—excuse me, had them kill themselves—I've met possums that were slyer."

"Or you could just tell me," I say, sitting on the ground next to him, a careful distance, then folding my legs over one another. "Wouldn't that be the best revenge of all? Knowing you spoiled their memory for their daughter they so adored?"

"The best revenge of all was watching them take the blade to their own throats. Besides, it seems as if they already did the spoiling themselves."

I breathe through the way his words puncture my chest, lodging in my sternum. Slowly but surely, I'm learning not to let his cruelty tie my tongue in knots. "But it's all you have left now, isn't it?"

The captain's eyes flicker with something I can't quite read. "I already told you, Wendy Darling. You'll suffer enough as it is. No need to add to your load."

A chill rattles my bones. The last time Captain Astor predicted my suffering, it had come at his own hands. I find myself clenching the pouch of rushweed powder stuffed in my pocket.

"I see nothing around that might harm me," I say, placing my words with care.

"That's because there's no seeing the shadows when you're blind." Captain Astor says it with a smile, though the words have to make it past his clenched teeth.

Now that he's done with his food, I gather my things to go. It's clear the captain is done talking anyway. Before I leave, I fish a pinch of rushweed powder out of my bag with the tip of my spoon, then offer it to the captain. He stares at me for a moment, but he must know I'm offering him a chance at dignity by not shoving it in his mouth, because he closes his lips around the edge of the spoon.

His thumb, still stroking his Mating Mark, goes limp.

287

"So, was it better?" asks the captain on my way out.

I turn around, furrowing my brow in confusion. "Was what better?"

"Whatever it was that the Shadow Keeper persuaded you was so much better than kneeling?"

CHAPTER 39

*t's almost morning by the time I make it back to the Den. That concerns me, mostly because I don't like that I lost track of time while telling the captain my story.

His words still grate on me, the way he took my pain and used it as yet another reason to justify what he did to my parents.

I've worked myself into such a fury that I don't notice Joel until I run straight into him.

"Winds?" he says, placing his hands on my shoulders as he looks down at me with a sheepish grin. I fight the urge to recoil at his touch. Joel has always been kind to me, but I won't easily forget his tendency to torture animals.

"What are you doing up so early?" he asks, noting the satchel slung across my body.

My heart pounds, my mind searching for an answer that will satisfy him. I'm so exhausted, it takes me a moment to realize that he asked what I'm doing up early rather than why I was out so late.

"I'm about to go gather…" I stare at my satchel. "Herbs. Today's a busy day, so I thought I'd get an early start."

This seems to satisfy Joel, because he nods and says, "Makes sense. Especially since you have cooking duty with me tonight."

"Right," I say, neglecting to mention that I'd forgotten all about that.

"Hey, I'm glad I ran into you." Joel plunges his hand into his own satchel. When he pulls out a furry white mouse, I cringe, which he immediately misinterprets as pity for the disgusting creature.

"No, it's not like that," he says, eyes wide as he clings to the wriggling animal. "I'm not going to hurt him. I've been keeping him as a pet. Found him in the garden a week ago, caught in the tomato vines. I've been taking care of him ever since. I thought..." He stops, swallowing, desperation haunting his sallow cheeks, begging me to understand.

"You're replacing a bad habit with a good one," I say, though keeping a rodent as a pet isn't exactly what I would normally classify as a good habit.

Joel's face lights up. "Yeah. And it's working, too. But it's all because of you. Knowing that there was someone out there who knew about my...well, problem, but didn't treat me any differently. It helped, somehow."

My stomach sinks as I recall all the times I've had to school myself to hide my fear of Joel.

"Anyway," he says, extending his hand to me, "I wanted you to have him."

I blink, staring at the squirming rodent. "You what?"

I END up back outside the reaping tree with a splitting headache and a mouse named Benedict squeaking in my satchel.

When I'd turned to go back to my room, Joel had reminded me that I was supposed to be out picking herbs, so now I have to find a way to kill time before I return to the Den.

I'm not sure how it happens. At first I tell myself I'm just taking a walk.

The route is circuitous, but I need time to think anyway, time to clear my head. Walking does nothing to cleanse my mind of the captain's cruel words, though, so I end up climbing a cliffside, hoping the exertion will distract me.

I don't even realize I'm by the shed until I'm standing at its door, picking the lock, my hands and fingers more steady than they ever are these days.

The door creaks open, and there's a blissful moment when the scent of faerie dust wafts through the air, already filling my lungs with a gentle, pleasant numbness, a weightless euphoria that feels like nothing, nothing at all.

It sounds like the absence of Captain Astor's voice in my head. Smells like velvet untouched by lingering incense.

I don't wait until I'm outside the shed. I convince myself it's because I'm afraid of the shadows attacking me like they did the last time I scoured for faerie dust.

I dig my fingers into the nearest pouch and lick the faerie dust off my finger like I might honey I'd just found in a stray piece of comb, fallen from the hive.

It tastes like silence.

IT's dark by the time I come to myself. At first, I don't know where I am. Wood scrapes against my cheek. It takes several blinks for my eyes to adjust in the dark, but when my vision clears, I realize I'm lying atop a rafter, my cheek pressed to its flank. Drool has already hardened at the edge of my lips.

Unease fills my gut. I didn't think about floating being a side effect when I dosed myself. It's a good thing I was in the shed rather than out in the open. The splashing of the waves against the cliffs outside reminds me as much.

Panicked, I scramble down the nearest beam, stuffing my pockets with as many pouches as I can reasonably hide. Once I've locked the storehouse door behind me, I check for the moon's position. It's still over the ocean, meaning there's hope I haven't yet missed dinner.

I'll definitely have missed cooking it, which is unfortunate, since Joel seemed so excited about it this morning. I can't imagine it will do him good if he thinks I forgot about him.

Not to mention, I feel guilty for letting the boys go hungry tonight. So I grab my satchel and begin making my descent, hoping the boys will forgive me, and that no one will smell the honeysuckle on me.

BY THE TIME I reach the reaping tree, I already know something's wrong.

I know it before I hear the voices, high and panicked.

I know it before I hear the pacing footsteps.

I know it before I hear Michael's song.

I know it because the shadows tell me. They don't encroach on my vision like they used to. They don't speak to me aloud. The shadows know better than to get close now that I'm consistently dosing myself with faerie dust, but that doesn't mean the shadows disappear.

They sway in the corners of my vision, keeping their distance, moaning softly as they speckle the ground in the pattern of leaves above, stopping the moonlight. They sway and cry and shift and mourn. If they're screaming, the faerie dust mutes the sound, leaves them shapeless, blurred, harmless.

When I arrive at the reaping tree, the Lost Boys are crowded together in a circle, packed shoulder to shoulder, the ones in the back pushing their way through the cracks between the taller boys, who take up the front.

Only John and Michael stand back, John holding Michael from behind as Michael wriggles and sings, "They found him in his bed, a bottle by his head, the old man is dead, the old man is dead."

My blood runs very, very cold.

When John sees me approaching, he shakes his head ever so slightly, eyes wide and shining.

I snap my neck back over to the Lost Boys.

To the seven Lost Boys.

No.

No.

I count again.

And again.

My counting keeps coming out to seven, but that can't be right, because there are eight.

So instead of counting, I start accounting for them by name.

Simon.

Nettle.

Victor.

Benjamin.

Smalls.

The Twins.

Who's missing?

My breath catches.

No.

My feet carry me over to the boys, uneven as my back begins to ache from my descent. I tripped on a rock on the way here and thought that was a problem worth cursing about.

While the boys shove each other out of the way, I place my hands gently on their shoulders. The touch must be calming, because they part for me. Smalls glimpses me, and a sob bursts from his throat. The same throat that was just yelling to get out of his way.

He opens his mouth like he's going to tell me what's happened, but this time, no noise comes out.

When I place my hand on Simon's shoulder, he says my name, ever so faintly. "Wendy, you shouldn't look…"

But I do.

I look, because it's the only thing one can do in a situation like this. Even though my mind is screaming at me not to. Even though I don't want to know, don't want to remember him this way.

The one boy I couldn't find in the crowd.

Number eight.

He's face-up on the ground, his eyes as wide as ever, except there's no playful light in them. His mouth is slightly ajar, a trickle of blood already crusting in the corner.

"When there was no dinner at the table, we knew something was wrong," says Simon.

"It had to have happened a few hours ago," says Nettle.

"Not possible," says Benjamin. "I asked him when dinner would be ready an hour ago. He said he was going to try to find Wendy because she hadn't shown up for cooking duties and he was worried about her."

My heart stills in my chest.

Simon looks at me and frowns, sympathy welling up in his eyes, but an unspoken question too. A *where were you?*

My jaw works, but no words come out.

Because lying dead on the ground is Joel.

His pinkie is missing.

I DON'T KNOW how long it takes for Peter to find us. He swoops in from above, toppling branches of the canopy as he barrels into the crowd. One shout from Peter, and the Lost Boys part a way for him.

He must have scented the blood.

I stay with Joel, grasping his cold hand in mine.

I don't know why I do it. He's dead. It's not as if he knows I'm here.

Peter's face pales and his whole body stills as he takes in the gruesome sight. Blood stains Joel's shirt, remnants of a knife wound. His flesh is jagged around the stump where his finger used to be. Worse still, blood paints a fox across his cheek.

My stomach turns over, and I pray that he was already dead.

"Tell me everything," Peter says to everyone and no one at once.

Simon's the one who answers. "We found him after Smalls got to the dinner table and noticed it wasn't set. He went to the kitchens and found them empty, then came yelling down the tunnel that something was wrong. That Joel and Wendy were missing." Simon gives me a quick, sidelong glance, one that Peter follows with his gaze.

He doesn't ask me where I was, but that terrifying stillness has overcome him. The blank sheet that seems to wash away all expression of emotion. Or smother it, wrap it up like a crystal ball and tuck it away.

I'm grateful that I don't have to explain to the boys where I was, but I sense the shifting of their feet all the same. The suspicion.

"Benjamin told us that Joel had said an hour ago that he was going to go out looking for Wendy. The group of us set out. A few of us were planning to try to find you, but all it took was stepping out of the Den and..." Simon loses his words.

"You said that man we buried killed Thomas. Killed my brother."

The voice is flat, coming out from the shadows. Victor is staring at Joel, a coldness in his expression that mirrors the corpse.

"Victor—" Peter says, his arms crossed, but Victor cuts him off.

"You said we got him. You said that was the man. That we buried him. That his flesh is rotting in a shallow grave." Victor's voice is warbling on the edge of mania. It's nerve-racking hearing him like this.

"You said—"

My heart hammers in my chest, and before I realize what I'm doing, I grab at it. Peter glances at me, realization striking his face. "Victor, the man on the beach, he had Thomas's bracelet. The one that was missing."

Victor just points to Joel. "So what happened to him?"

"I suppose the most logical explanation is that we have another killer on the island," says John, still holding Michael as he sways back and forth to the tune of the howling wind.

My mind flashes back to what Peter said, about the terrible fates that were woven into the boys' tapestries. The ones this very realm was made to protect them from, to help them escape.

Thomas dead, the first boy who was supposed to meet a treacherous end. Now Freckles and Joel.

Peter and I exchange a knowing look, but he shakes his head, just enough for me to be the only one to notice. I hope.

"Peter, can I talk to you?" I ask.

Victor digs his heel into the earth. "No one's leaving until we find out where everyone was when he died. Wendy, why don't we start with you?"

All eyes turn to me, every one of them wide, keeping them from blinking back tears.

"You heard me. Where were you when you were supposed to be helping in the kitchen?"

My mouth goes dry. I grope for words, but I can't find any. The words should be simple. *I didn't kill Joel. I never would harm any of you.* But the truth of the matter is, I don't remember anything from the time I pressed the faerie dust to my lips to the moment I woke in the rafters.

Instinctively, I check for blood on my clothes. I find none, but my glance betrays my intent, because Victor says, "Checking for incriminating evidence, *Winds?*"

"She was with me," says Peter, crossing his arms. He gives no further explanation, and my cheeks heat. When I cross my arms, the boys' gaze dips to my ring, which I'm absentmindedly twirling around my finger.

"I see," says Victor. "So Wendy gets special treatment. No need to show up to your responsibilities as long as you're having a tryst with Peter."

John coughs audibly, sounding like he's choking. My face goes scarlet with heat, but Peter steps in and puts a hand on Victor's shoulder. "Stand down," he says gently, protectively. "Wendy isn't the murderer."

"Then who is?" asks Victor.

Strangely, the Lost Boys' faces turn, each examining the boy next to them.

It's only then that I realize there's no squeaking coming from my satchel.

When I open the flap, I find Benedict the mouse, belly plump from gorging himself on a pouch of faerie dust I stuffed in my satchel earlier.

He's dead, too.

CHAPTER 40

We bury Joel in the light of the moon, the wind howling a dirge as we do.

We dig him a proper grave. I suppose we tell ourselves that it's to protect his body from the elements, the scavengers Victor wished upon the man who killed Thomas. But that's a lie, just like any of the others we tell ourselves. The maggots and worms and natural decay will get him just the same.

The only difference is we won't have to watch.

So we bury Joel deep, and we tell ourselves it's for his sake, when we know good and well it's for our own.

As we file solemnly back into the Den, our fingernails caked with dirt clots, John pulls me to the side, still clutching onto Michael's hand. He stood back for most of the burial, not out of a lack of desire to help, but because he didn't want Michael getting too close to the body.

I think we all agreed with his decision.

But now John has a crazed look in his eyes. They're darting back and forth, following some course that's invisible to the rest of us.

He waits until the last of the boys files in and says, "It's one of them. It has to be."

I shake my head, like I'm a puppy slogging water out of my ears after taking a plunge. Except there's no clearing the way that everything feels more muffled. Is that from the guilt of losing Joel, when he shouldn't have been looking for me to begin with, or is this just how the world feels now when I come down off of a high from the faerie dust?

"Joel was their friend. He was...different," I say, finding it difficult to air my concerns about Joel now that he's dead. Nausea froths at the base of my throat at the thought of the dead mouse in my satchel, the pet Joel was so proud of himself for tending to. "But I can't think why anyone would want to kill him. And besides, they're just..."

John raises a brow. "Just boys? Wendy, a decade ago, most of them would have been considered grown men in Estelle. You think none of them are capable of wielding a weapon?"

My mind flashes back to Joel, coaxing a mouse to the fire. To Victor, spitting on the corpse of the man who killed his brother. To John, who dreams of forcing Captain Astor to take a blade to his own throat.

My cheeks drain of color.

"Don't tell me they don't have it in them. I think you should know better than anyone that we all do."

The lifeless face of Peter's assailant paints itself on the back of my eyelids when I blink.

"I just don't know why they would do it. Why Joel?"

"To be honest, I would have expected him to do the killing, not the other way around," says John, finding the truth so much easier to say aloud than I ever do.

"After I saw him torturing those rats, I kept my distance for a while. Maybe someone else knew about his...habits. Maybe they were scared of him. People have a tendency to harm the things that frighten them."

John shakes his head, placing the hand that's not holding Michael's onto his chin as he thinks. "Maybe."

"John, do you think..." I squeeze my eyes shut, as if that will help me get the words out.

"That we got the wrong guy before?"

I peek at him from slitted lids, nodding.

"No. The man had Thomas's bracelet. We found Thomas's murderer, that's for sure," John says, each word hauling another coil of iron chain from my shoulders.

"But it's possible that the same person who killed Joel killed Freckles?"

John nods.

I chew on my lip. "That would make some sense as to why Freckles's murderer carved the constellation into his cheek. To make us think the murders were connected."

John's pacing in circles now, Michael following him. "That would explain why the methods of killing were different, too. Maybe whoever killed Freckles didn't intend to do it. If it happened in the heat of the moment, the murderer could have panicked, then tried to make it look like the murders were connected afterward." He halts in place, the abruptness causing Michael to slam into his back. "There's only one problem with that theory."

I gulp. "It would mean marking him with the Reaper's fox wasn't a coincidence. It would mean that whoever killed Freckles knew Thomas. Well enough to think of his favorite constellation, even while panicking."

We stand in silence for a moment. "It could be someone else. In Neverland," I say.

John peers at me from behind his spectacles. They're smudged and scratched after weeks on the island. It's a wonder he can still see out of them. I consider what will happen when they break. Will Peter travel outside of Neverland to fetch him new ones if I ask him to? Will the Sister even allow such an excursion?

"Do you know of anyone else on the island?" he asks.

The captain's swarthy, cruel grin flashes before my eyes, but I quickly stuff it away. It's not possible that he's the murderer. He can barely bring a spoon to his mouth thanks to the drugs I've been force-feeding him. Much less murder a boy and hack off his finger.

"No, but we didn't know Thomas's murderer was here until he attacked Peter, either."

"Which begs the question, how did the murderer end up here?"

John looks at me with that curious gaze I'm so familiar with. This is the point in the conversation when we'd usually brainstorm together, except I already know how the murderer came to be on the island. Through the flaws in Neverland itself. The gaps in the Fabric.

I just can't tell John that. Not without him questioning what else I know about why the Lost Boys are here.

But then another thought strikes me. "There's Tink."

John frowns.

"The faerie who attacked me when she found me in Peter's rooms," I say.

"Ah. The one you called 'suspicious and jealous for no reason,'" says John, referencing a conversation we had after the attack.

I draw back. "Surely you're not defending her."

"I didn't say that. I'm just saying that perhaps she has better intuition than you gave her credit for."

I cross my arms, but it's not as if I have anything to say to that. I am engaged to Peter, after all, which I suppose was exactly what Tink was afraid of.

John just shrugs and continues on, not nearly as bothered by the sentiment he just expressed as I am. "Do you think she has motive?" he asks, wiping his hair from his forehead. It's grown out since we arrived in Neverland. I suppose he no longer has Mother fussing over its length. The thought makes my heart hurt.

"Does a jealous psycho have to have motive?"

In all seriousness, John says, "Jealousy is a motive, Wendy."

"Well, I don't see why she'd hurt one of the Lost Boys," I say. "Not when it's me she's jealous of."

John shrugs. "If she's as obsessed with Peter as he claims, it's possible she envies anyone who has a close relationship with him. Though I still don't think that's the most likely explanation."

"Are you going to share what is, or leave me in suspense?"

"She could be punishing him."

"I'm only doing this because I love you," whispers Michael, staring off into the distance.

My stomach aches, and I reach for my little brother's hand. When he flinches from my touch, a part of me wilts. Things haven't returned to normal between Michael and me since the night I woke up choking him.

I'm not sure if they ever will.

"For what?" I ask, withdrawing my hand to my chest.

John's gaze dips to my finger, where I'm still twisting my cold ring. I try not to think about the possibility that Michael will never trust me again and return to the more urgent matter of the killer loose on the island.

My gut turns over. "You think she killed Joel because Peter proposed to me?"

John, oblivious to the pain this is kindling inside me, says, "How better to punish Peter than to kill one of the people he cares for most in the world?"

My heart pounds, anger flooding my head. "Then why not kill me? Wouldn't that serve more of a purpose? Wouldn't that be more fair?"

John shrugs. "Maybe she went looking for you and instead found the next best thing."

He turns to go, but I grab him by the shoulder, pulling him in for a hug. John tenses, but he wraps his arms around me all the same.

"The murderer cut off Joel's pinkie," I whisper, unable to keep my body from shaking.

John tenses, but his voice remains light. "Maybe the killer thought they could trick the reaping tree into letting them into the Den."

"Freckles's hair was singed at the tips. When I smelled it, it reminded me of the way the rat stank when Joel made it get close to the fire."

We let that settle between us for a moment.

"I know. I'll watch my back. Promise." When John pulls away, he offers me a sad smile. "And Wendy?"

"Yeah?"

"I'm sorry. About snapping at you that night." He clears his throat, unable to bring himself to be more specific, which is fine with me. I'd rather not relive the moment my brother walked in on my and Peter's passionate kiss—or John's assumptions about where that kiss was headed. "I'd been up all night with Michael. It's not an excuse but..." He trails off, and as he rubs the back of his neck, I glimpse the silvery scars from where Michael's scratches have only recently healed and have to look away. "I just...I've watched you hurt for a long time, you know?"

"Peter's not going to hurt me, John," I say, hugging my torso. "He loves me."

Again, John's gaze fixates on the glint of my ring. "Yeah," he says, as if his mind has been transported to another world entirely. "Ma and Pa loved you too."

For a moment, my limbs turn to stone, thinking John has linked our parents' desperation to protect me to what he overheard outside of the parlor. I prepare their defense, all the reasons they thought they were acting in my best interest, misguided as their actions were.

But John only says, "And you still ended up taken, didn't you?"

It shouldn't be as much of a relief as it is.

CHAPTER 41

*T*here's no sleep to be had that night. Not when I have to dose the captain again, lest his rushweed wear off. I don't stick around to feed him, not when the sight of him summons a lump in my throat as I remember how he took my pain and adulterated it, molded it into a justification for murdering my parents.

Not that I would have slept anyway. Joel's murder hangs over the Den, leaving the Lost Boys irritable and sullen. I'd have thought they would suspect each other more than they do, and at first they did, some of them refusing to go off in pairs for chores like usual. But Peter has been meeting with each of them individually, talking them down from their panic.

"Are you certain you're doing the right thing?" I ask Peter one afternoon in the garden as he and I pick the vegetables Joel once tended to.

The feel of fresh soil on my hands is comforting, though it shouldn't be. Not when Joel should be here, nurturing this garden, not me.

"What do you mean?" Peter says, plucking a tomato from the vine and biting into it, somehow managing not to spray juice all over his clothes. He's not wearing his leathers today. I suppose that would be impractical for gardening. Instead, he sports a fitted black shirt that makes no attempt to hide his muscular form and matching pants.

Staring at him when he's not paying attention has been a welcome distraction from my racing thoughts, to say the least.

"Wendy Darling?"

I blink in an attempt to reassemble my thoughts. "By convincing the boys not to be afraid of each other. What if...what if they let their guard down?"

Peter shakes his head. "Fearing one another will only make them vulnerable. They're safer trusting each other than they are letting the killer drive a wedge between them."

When I don't answer, Peter cocks his head to the side. "What's going on in that mysterious mind of yours?"

"I just..." I bite my lip, hugging my torso, my wicker basket nudging my hip as I do. "What if the killer truly is one of the Lost Boys?"

He goes back to picking tomatoes. "It's not."

"But if you're wrong—"

"It's not one of the Lost Boys."

Sensing that's the end of the discussion, I don't push any further. The idea of allowing the boys to continue to wander off in pairs fills me with unease. It's selfish of me, but I'm glad John was clever enough to demand Smalls be his partner in watching Michael at the Den. I don't exactly consider Smalls a suspect, and I feel the three of them are safer together. So far, the killer hasn't dared strike within the Den.

I trace a circle in the soft, damp soil with my big toe. "Can I ask you something?"

"If you're wondering why the onions are kept separate from the rest of the garden," Peter says, gesturing toward the patch of ground across the field, "it's because they're an invasive species."

"Kind of like fae."

Peter offers me a grin. "I was going to say humans are the invasive ones. We fae don't reproduce often enough to be considered invasive."

"I wasn't going to ask about the onions, believe it or not."

Peter runs his hand through his hair. "I don't know, then. I might have to demand something in return."

"And what is it I'm agreeing to?"

"Not sure. I'm sure I'll be struck with a marvelous idea," he says, gaze landing on my mouth.

I blush, tucking my hair behind my ear and rubbing dirt into it in the process. I'm still not over the way he looks at me, but I won't be deterred. "How did you know Captain Astor?"

Peter's smile falters, but he manages to catch it before it slips away. "Why do you ask?"

"I figured if you knew him, you might know something about why he killed my parents."

Peter frowns. "Don't you think I'd tell you if I knew?"

I laugh to hide my frustration. "Of course. But you didn't know my parents. Perhaps if we put our knowledge together..."

Peter appears in front of me, dangling his mouth in front of mine. "Together? Now, that, I like the sound of."

"Peter..." When I turn away, his lips brush my cheek, trailing a path to the fleshy part of my ear, which he bites playfully. Delight ripples through me, competing with my exasperation. "Peter," I manage through giggles, squirming out of his arms. "Be serious. I want to know more about you."

He places his hands on his hips, cocking a brow. "I thought you said this was about your parents. Had I known it was about me..." He winks, flooring me.

No. *No.* I'm not letting him charm his way out of discussing this. "Please."

The playfulness finally drains from Peter's face. "I've already told you everything you need to know about my past. Everything else is irrelevant."

I huff. "The past is always relevant. It shapes who we are, whether we ignore it or not."

"Not here," he says, the twinkle returning to his eyes. He gestures around him toward the tree line of the forest, then toward the beach in the distance, the rolling waves. "Not in Neverland. Our pasts can't find us here."

Oh, how very wrong you are, my love.

"What if they already have?"

Peter's pointed ears twitch. "What are you talking about?"

Realizing I've said too much, that I'm still not ready to hand the captain over to Peter, lest he destroy the vessel holding the secrets of *my* past, I pivot.

"Thomas? Freckles? Joel? Were their pasts irrelevant? Did they manage to escape?"

Peter takes a step back. "You're upset."

"Of course I'm upset!" I cry, tugging the hair at the base of my skull. "We're going to be married, and there's so much about you, about this place, that I don't understand."

Peter's silence threatens to gag me as well, but when he speaks, his voice isn't spiked with anger as I expect, but gentleness. "Do you tell me everything, Wendy Darling?"

My jaw works as I struggle for a response. "Peter, I—"

My fiancé shakes his head, cupping my cheeks in his strong hands. "It's alright, my Darling little thing. You know why? Because I have a lifetime to figure you out. All I'm asking is that you offer me the same patience."

Salt stings at my eyes, and I can't tell if it's the wind or tears, and I nod. "There's only one problem with that."

"Tell me so I can fix it."

I trail my thumb across the back of his hand, still cradling my cheek. "A lifetime with you doesn't seem nearly long enough."

Peter's ears pivot, and I find myself turning to gaze down the path toward which they've rotated.

"Seems like we have company," says Peter, nodding toward John, Michael, and Smalls, approaching us from the tree line. My heart falters, considering what dreadful news they might bring, but Smalls offers me a friendly wave that assuages my panic.

The relief is only momentary, because as they draw closer, I notice how John and Smalls are positioned on either side of Michael, each clutching a hand while Michael wriggles between them.

I race across the field toward them. I'm about to fall on the ground in front of Michael and scoop him into my lap when I remember I can't.

Because my brother is still terrified of me.

I stop short, the balls of my feet scraping against the earth.

Michael lurches, protesting with squeals as he tries to free himself from the others' grips.

"He wouldn't stop scratching himself," explains John. Indeed, streaks of blood line my youngest brother's neck and cheeks. "I know he doesn't like it when we restrain him like this, but I didn't know what else to do. He started clawing at his eyes, and I couldn't..."

"I know," I whisper, aware my reassurance is hardly enough to assuage John's guilt.

"Did something in particular upset him?" asks Peter, lowering himself to a perch. It's a simple gesture, but the way his instinct is to avoid towering over Michael lest he overwhelm him further makes my heart balloon in my chest.

"No, we were just playing with the train set," says Smalls. "Then he started asking for your mother. I tried to tell him she wasn't here right now, but I don't think he could hear me, because he wouldn't stop asking."

John's shoulders slump, his eyes magnified through his thick, smudged lenses. "I don't know what to do."

"Give me a moment," I say, returning to the garden and searching the area for anything Michael can hold to keep his hands busy. There are the vegetables, but I don't want him thinking I'm trying to make him eat anything while he's this worked up. In the end, the best I can do is scoop a handful of wet, cool clay from the earth.

When I offer it to Michael, the whimpers stop as his gaze fixates on the lump of mud in my open palm.

"Here you go," I say, nudging my gift forward.

Michael shrieks, his foot colliding with my nose, and he tries to escape John's and Smalls's grips.

Pain spots my vision, stinging in bursts all over the inside of my skull. I drop the clay, mud staining my face from what's leftover on my palm as I bring my hand over my nose to catch the blood streaming out.

I turn away, a sob swelling in my throat, but I can't weep in front of John. Not when he'll internalize it, think he's only made the situation worse.

"Wendy Darling." Peter appears in front of me, Michael still screaming behind us. "Let me fix it." Gently, he extracts my muddied hand from my nose. I can't imagine what I look like with mingled blood and clay and tears smearing my face. Peter slides his forefinger and thumb down the ridge of my nose. "Well, the bright side is that it's not broken."

"That's...that's good," I manage between sharp inhales.

Peter pulls a roll of bandage cloth from his satchel and uses it to wipe the grime from my face. Thankfully, the bleeding has already subsided by the time he's done.

"I ruined everything for him," I whisper to Peter. "I ruined his life, and now he'll never see his mother again, and I can't even explain to him why. He hates me, and I can't make him understand..."

Peter watches me closely, then flicks his eyes over to the boys. "What if you could give him something familiar? Show him you still love him in a language he understands?"

"I don't know how to do that," I say, soul heavy with resignation.

"He likes games, does he not? Play? Is there a game that's familiar to him? One that might make him feel like he's home?"

My head snaps up so fast I'm shocked it doesn't trigger another nosebleed. "Peter, I'd kiss you if my brothers weren't standing right behind us."

"I could always ask them to leave."

Playfully, I swat him on the shoulder before spinning around to face the boys. Michael is kicking at the ground, but he's not screaming anymore, so that's encouraging.

"Michael," I say, my heart lurching a little when he flinches at the sound of my voice. I summon up the will to continue. "Michael, last one to the top is dead meat."

Michael's foot halts its course in the earth. He doesn't look at me as he whispers, "Last one to the top's dead meat."

He doesn't have to look at me. The iron doors weighing on my chest unfold.

"Smalls, let go," says John, dropping Michael's hand. Smalls frowns but obeys. For a moment, Michael does nothing except stare at the ground, flapping his now-free hands. John is still tensed and at the ready in case Michael tries to scratch himself again.

But then Michael looks me straight in the eye and says, "Last one to the top's dead meat!"

He runs.

John flashes me a dazed grin, but I'm already dashing after Michael, soaking in the lovely feel of moss underneath my feet once I reach the wooded area. I race through the underbrush, not a care in the world for the bruises that are sure to appear on my heels later.

I can't hurt as long as Michael is laughing.

And my brother is laughing, his breathy giggles chiming in with the birds perched above, a melody unlike any a harp or lyre could ever aspire to play.

High above, a dark figure cuts off the rays of light from drifting through the canopy—Peter, watching after Michael from above, ensuring he comes to no harm.

I adore that man.

Smalls zips past me, his fae agility and speed allowing him to maneuver over fallen logs with ease.

Soon enough, I sense John stumbling through the forest behind me, his heavy breathing giving him away before even the pounding of his footsteps.

"I really thought you would be faster than me by now," I huff as we scramble over a mossy boulder, John holding a twig out of my way. "And here you are lagging behind."

John flashes me a grin. "I am faster than you."

A second later, my brother releases the twig, allowing it to flick me in the throat. He chuckles as I yelp, then picks up his speed. He shoots a triumphant glance behind him, glasses askew, then checks the sky, making sure Peter still has an eye on me before he disappears into the brush after Michael.

I'm the last to arrive at the reaping tree, which I suppose Michael chose as his clock tower substitute. Peter's got him in his lap as together they perch on a coiling branch high above us. Smalls races around the base of the tree, wound up by the competition. John is at the base of the tree, hands on his knees, heaving. I assume a similar posture, my heart pounding with exertion.

Peter thuds next to me, setting a humming Michael on the ground next to him.

Breathing becomes easier when Michael waltzes up to me, grabbing my hands and spinning us in circles, singing "First one is dead meat," cheerfully.

I take that to mean that he won.

"You're shaking tonight. More than usual. You were last night, too."

"I'm surprised you care enough to bring it up," I tell the captain, mostly because I'd prefer to avoid discussing the fact that my body is not handling my daily dose of faerie dust well. Not after the quantity I took the day of Joel's murder. I've been jittery ever since racing after Michael today.

"I care inasmuch as it causes you to slosh stew all over my beard. Bits of meat don't simply evaporate, you know, especially in a humid climate like this one. Unless you'd like to help groom it, of course." Captain Astor's eyes glitter as he says it, and I turn away, not wishing to think about my hands on his face. Not wishing to think about how his prickly stubble has grown out into a short black beard that complements his jawline perfectly.

I've been liberal with my rushweed doses lately, meaning I still have to spoon-feed the captain like I'm his nurse. I'd like to think he's humiliated by the experience, but as with everything else, he seems to consider it an opportunity open for exploitation.

My mind is still on Joel. On what John said about the possibility of it being one of the Lost Boys who killed him. Of the possibility that it's Tink stalking me, and picking off the Lost Boys instead.

Or that it's someone else entirely.

Someone on this island we've yet to meet.

Peter's been on the lookout for Tink. He agreed with John that she's the most likely suspect, but Peter has made it clear he will never believe it's one of the Lost Boys who killed their own.

"Wendy Darling, you're off in your own little world again."

I blink, and when my gaze focuses back on the captain's, I find his expression to be curious rather than cruel. "Where do you go," he asks, "when you're not here with me?"

My heart snags on those last two words. The foot of a rabbit, only just too slow to escape a snare. The loose thread of a sweater on a nail someone forgot to hammer all the way into the wooden boards of the countertop.

With me.

"Don't worry about it. It's not somewhere you'd like to follow, I'm sure," I say. "It's rather dark," I add, hastily.

"Being in a dark place with you?" the captain muses. "You're right, I can't think why I might enjoy that."

My tongue might have loosened around the captain in the time I've spent trying to pluck information out of him about my parents, but becoming used to his brazen demeanor has done nothing to keep my cheeks from heating in his presence.

This time, his smirk as he catches my embarrassment incites me rather than silences me. "I can think of a reason," I say brightly.

He cocks his head, though it's a rather sloppy movement given his lack of muscular control at the moment.

"Because you couldn't possibly be interested in a—what was it? —Oh yes, 'a spoiled heiress who looks as if she's hardly been weaned.'"

The captain curdles his lips in concession. "Can't argue with that. I appreciate you for reminding me though. All these days with you being the only woman in sight must have gone to my head."

I shouldn't pocket the fact that he's stopped calling me a girl and started calling me a woman.

I shouldn't, but I do.

"Girl, remember?" I say. "Or was it child?"

"Is that not what I said?"

I bite my lip, fighting the urge to remind him that I'm twenty, well into womanhood by human standards. I figure reminding someone that I'm not a child will only make me sound more like one.

Besides, I'm not sure what I'm hoping to gain by convincing him.

We spend the next few minutes in silence as I pack up the utensils. Without the captain's conversation to drown it out, the spoon rattles against the bowl as I maneuver both into my satchel.

When the captain speaks again, his voice is a low growl. "Tell me why you're shaking, Darling."

I bite my lip and focus on teasing the captain, if only because it keeps my tears from spilling over. "Only if you say please."

"I've only ever said please to one person in my life. You, unfortunately, do not rank as high as her."

We stare at each other a moment, and I fight the urge to glance at his severed Mating Mark. I find myself examining it sometimes, but I only let myself when he's not watching me.

In this staring match, I'm the one who loses, who gives in and averts my gaze.

I'm always the one who breaks first.

"One of the Lost Boys was found dead. Right outside the Den," I whisper, hardly able to get the words out.

I wait for the scathing comment, the cruel words that will prob-ably scrape my insides out, but it doesn't come. Instead, the captain just utters one word. "How?"

I can't look at him, can't look at a living person while I'm discussing such awful acts. "They stabbed him in the gut, then removed his pinkie."

"With what?"

The question startles me. "I don't know. A dagger, I assume." Now that I consider it, I suppose I didn't get close enough to Joel's wound to check. Even if I had, would I have been able to distinguish between the wound of a dagger and a hatchet?

"Hm," says the captain, allowing his head to rest back on the rock now that he's done eating. "So who did it?"

I stare at him slack-jawed. "Don't you think if I knew..." I trail off, realizing I'm not sure what I'd do. Tell Peter so he could have the killer executed for their crimes? Drive the dagger into their heart myself? I don't think I'd mind so much if the killer turned out to be Tink, but if it truly is a Lost Boy, would I want them to meet the same fate?

And does it make me unjust that I would show partiality like that?

"There's a faerie on the island who has a bone to pick with Peter. It's possible she killed the boy to punish him."

"That doesn't seem particularly logical."

I snort. "Does a woman riddled with jealousy have to operate logically?"

The captain's eyes glitter with amusement. "Have you ever met a female murderer?"

"No," I say, because I refuse to count myself among them.

"That's because they don't have a tendency to get caught. They bide their time, and they generally don't leave a mess behind, either."

I stiffen. "My brother thinks she was hoping to find me, then killed Joel when she stumbled across him instead."

The captain's brows lift. "And do you believe that?"

I say nothing.

"You said you've never met a female murderer, but don't I remember you telling me you've killed before?"

My heart stutters, my mouth dry. "That was in self-defense."

The captain waits patiently until I give in to those piercing eyes of his and relay the account of Thomas's murderer's death.

"You said it was self-defense," he says once I finish.

I bristle, my pitch soaring. "It was."

"No, it wasn't. You were defending Peter, were you not? Was the man coming after you?"

"Peter's my..." I swallow my words, training my hands at my sides to keep them from stroking my Mating Mark. That doesn't stop Captain Astor's eyes from fixing upon the smattering of golden flecks. "He's my fiancé. Murdering him would have been no different from ripping my heart out."

The captain stares at me for a long time. Long enough that I have no choice but to avert my attention to the foggy night beyond the cave. "I guarantee you it wouldn't. If Peter had died, you'd still be right here, heart beating whether you wanted it to or not."

"That man deserved to die." I sound like I'm convincing myself more than the captain, so I turn toward him and add, "He killed two more of the Lost Boys."

At this, the captain's fae ears perk. "How do you know?"

"We found a bracelet belonging to one of the boys on the man," I say while I give him tonight's dose of rushweed.

The captain winces at the taste. "Forgive me; I'm not aware of the rules. Is possessing a piece of jewelry enough to charge and execute a man for murder in this realm?"

I fist my fingers into the charcoal sand. "He did it. I know he did."

"Whatever you say, Darling," says the captain. He closes his eyes, looking much too peaceful for a man being held captive. "Say, how well do you know that fiancé of yours?"

My heart thuds. "Better than you."

The captain's grin is painted on. "Oh, I highly doubt that."

"You keep saying that, but you refuse to offer any evidence."

"Well," he says, lolling his head to the side lazily. "I don't have a bracelet to hand over, now do I?"

Anger slices through my veins, but I rein it in. "Why don't you just tell me what you know?"

"Would you believe me, Darling, if I did?"

CHAPTER 42

*I*t's dark on the way back to the Den. Darker than usual, given the moon is a bare sliver in the sky, and the streaks of vibrant light haven't come out to dance, obscured by wistful clouds.

Maybe that's why I don't see her coming until it's too late to scream.

As if I would scream, anyway. As if my body would grant me the privilege of fighting back.

Vibrant blue eyes blink at me through long golden eyelashes, appearing just in front of my face, just as a hand clamps over my mouth. Long, jagged fingernails dig into my neck, already drawing blood, sending me back to the night she scratched my Mating Mark up with her claws.

The scars have healed over since then, but I'm not sure she'll let that happen this time.

Scars don't heal on a corpse.

I at least possess the presence of mind to struggle and thrash, which is more than I can say for the last time I was attacked. Perhaps stabbing that man to death changed me in more ways than one. Even so, Tink's grip is firm, and before I can grab at my dagger, she plucks it from my belt and uses it to slit three gashes between the knuckles of my right hand.

This time, I do scream, though there's no one to hear it. Not through her clamped fingers. Not over the roaring waves and the mournful wind.

Pain rips through me, and Tink knots her fingers through my hair as she gags me and drags my body across the wet sand. Loose pebbles jab at me as I struggle, but it's no use. Even if my scream could alert anyone, it would only be the captain, who can't help me in his drugged state.

Who wouldn't help me anyway, I realize.

A few moments later, Tink uses the knot she's made in my hair to thrust my face into the waves. When I try to flip over, the back of my head hits stone. The stars that pepper my vision are nothing compared to those that fill the murky void when my gasp, reflexive as the freezing water submerges my body, causes me to inhale a mouthful of water.

The salt burns on its way down, stinging my throat, corroding my lungs. I can no longer feel the rest of my body, but I trust that it's thrashing. Making pitiful splashes in an already tumultuous sea that won't even notice.

I'm dying, and it's happening too quickly and too slowly all at once. Death is so painful, I want nothing more than for it to be over, but as the blackness encroaches, my body fights back.

Wanting so desperately to live.

Part of me reaches for the last bits of faerie dust left in my system from today's dose, but the panic of my body is flushing it out, metabolizing it.

I'm going to drown sober.

I'm going to drown feeling every bit of it.

But then fingers jerk at my collar, dragging me from the water. I expect to find Peter, come to rescue me, but it's still Tink, her short golden hair darkened from being soaked. Saltwater peppers her face, sticking to her eyelashes.

She stares down at me with lips curved in the shape of malice, eyes the color of ice.

"Why are you doing this? I've done nothing to you," I whisper, though my voice comes out more like a croak as my body expels the saltwater. I spit some of it in her face, and Tink actually smiles. She cranes her head at me, silent as ever.

"You're not going to answer me?" I ask. "That's the least you could do."

I'm shocked by my forwardness. The captain's right. I'm not brave. Not one to speak my mind or have the right words pop into my head at the perfect moment. But something about my comment seems to land with the faerie. I glimpse it in the way her sternum caves in, ever so slightly, easy to glimpse on her thin frame.

For a moment, I think she's going to shove me back under, but then the shadows creep up behind her. Panic swells in my chest as they stumble over her thin shoulders and slide down her collarbone until they're dripping from her hands and all over me.

I can't breathe, because now they're slipping into my mouth, drowning me in a crueler fashion than the water, because at least the water couldn't taunt me as I died.

Tink's blue eyes shine through the shadows. As she examines them swarming her body on the way to get to mine, a sick pleasure overtakes her pale features.

For a moment, the shadows relent. Just long enough for me to ask, "You can see them too?"

I can't tell if I'm desperate for them to be real, desperate for them not to be.

Tink's grin is cruel, vengeful, but she nods ever so slightly.

With one hand still gripping my shirt, she takes the other and allows the shadows to coalesce on her palm. She brings the orb to her mouth, and with envy still glinting in her eyes, forms a circle with her chapped lips, then blows the orb into my face.

It crawls over me like a spider, and I can feel Tink's shoulders shaking in laughter, though I can't hear the sound over the splash of the waves. I claw at my face, digging my fingers into my flesh.

Tink drops me, leaving the waves and the shadows to fight over me like hyenas for a corpse.

Water splashes around me, rocks digging into my spine as shadow and water take turns plunging into my nose, washing my throat in scalding fire.

I scream, but they swallow the sound and wait hungrily for more.

Now that the shadows are inside me, they take shape, growing limbs and heads.

No.

In the darkness, I feel for the pebbles beneath my hands, grounding me, mercifully warning me which way is down. I push myself up. As soon as I'm upright, relief swells through me, making room in the haze of the shadows. In the distance, I spot the trees.

And I run.

FEET AGAINST PEBBLES, formed under the weight of waves. Sand spiking through my toes, then pebbles again, this time rounder, more bulbous.

I welcome grass at my heels like water to a parched throat. Like air to drowning lungs.

Groping for my way back to the Den through the shadows, my fingers slam against bark. It's not much to go off of, but it's enough.

I run like that, hurtling myself from tree to tree. The shadows are wrapping their fingers over my eyelids like a lover from behind, whispering, "Guess who" into my ears. My stomach is queasy with dread and sloshing brine, the remnants of what didn't make it into my lungs.

I stumble forward, tree by tree, praying I'm heading in the direction of the Den. But the further I run from the beach, the more the shadows begin to dissipate. Eventually, the last one of their tendrils slips away, leaving me alone in the dark woods.

My entire body shivers with mingled relief and cold. I'm not sure why the shadows stopped following me. Perhaps they're like the shadows at the shed, which seem to like to congregate in a single place. Perhaps they're bound to a specific area.

The relief doesn't last long. I'm soaked and shivering, and my thin clothes are clinging to my body, sucking away any heat I have left.

That, and I'm lost.

The shadows might have fled, but with the moonlight barely lighting my path, there's nothing to indicate where I am. Just the tall trees of the forest, all looking the same with their red-tinted bark.

There's no landmark in sight. Until, that is, my bare foot steps on something cold, and moist, and pliable.

The instant urge to retch spikes my stomach, especially when the spongy substance beneath my feet makes a popping sound, a horrible stench filling my nostrils.

I know what it is before I even look down. Fighting back a disgusted sob, I pull my foot from a purposefully shallow grave.

Dizziness overwhelms me when I make the mistake of looking down. Thomas's killer has met the fate Victor wished for him. His eyes are plucked out, probably by a murder of crows. Judging by the way something white and opaque still glows within their sockets in the moonlight, I'd venture to guess larvae have taken up residence. The man's cheeks are sunken in. There's barely any flesh left on him.

It's shameful and awful, and I want to vomit, because I did this to this man with my dagger. If Peter or the captain or Victor or John were here, they'd tell me I shouldn't feel guilty. That the man murdered a child and deserved what he got.

But I'm so tired of being told how I feel.

I have a hard enough time determining that for myself without everyone in the world inserting their opinion, confusing me and muddling my mind.

It's half shame and half anger that propels me as I thrust my fingers into the soft dirt and begin throwing clumps of it on the body. Victor's had his time to mourn. His time to stew in anger. It's not healthy for him to sit and watch this man's body rot every day; I don't care what anyone else says. It's not good. Not natural.

Not natural. That's what my mother's alienist had said about me. When he showed me those vile sketches and I didn't shed a tear.

I cover the man's face first, the face where Victor spat. I don't want to have to look at it anymore, don't want to have to know it's out here.

When I move on to the chest, I discover a bulge in the man's front coat pocket. I didn't notice it before, not when the man was alive and his body filled out his clothes. Now that he's decomposed, every bulge in his clothing seems more noticeable.

I slip my hand into the pocket. My fingers brush against parchment. My memory goes back to the closet, to finding the sketch of Thomas and the other boys. Wind ruffles the tattered parchment's edges as I pull it out.

Unfolding it proves to be a task, my fingers trembling, but as I open it, the moon shifts into a window in the canopy, illuminating its contents.

My heart trembles. It's another sketch of Thomas's, except this one's just of him and Victor. It's not nearly as advanced as the one I found in the pantry. This sketch is done with less precise hands, the shading overdone, leaving both his and Victor's faces looking warped. It shouldn't surprise me that the murderer picked this, too, off of Thomas's body after he killed him. I used to read stories about serial murderers who kept trophies from their victims. Why take just the bracelet when you could take this, as well?

Still, I find it odd that Thomas would have kept this one on his person, when it's clearly not his best work. Maybe it was the first he ever felt proud of. Or maybe he just liked to keep it with him because it's of him and his only family.

Either way, I stuff the parchment into my pocket. If Victor's pain is at all like mine, I think he might appreciate keeping this. Especially if it was special to Thomas.

I finish burying the man, then, my limbs worn with exhaustion, stumble back home, no longer lost now that I have the starting point of the shallow grave.

On the way, I find myself tapping my fingers against the parchment, the beginnings of a dreadful idea tugging at the back of my mind.

CHAPTER 43

I'm staring at the parchment the next morning when Peter slips into my room.

Immediately, I pull my coat collar up to hide the bruises on my neck from where Tink held me down last night. The wounds between my knuckles I tuck underneath my sleeves.

"There's my utterly traditional fiancée," Peter says, sliding on the bed next to me, then saying "Oops" as he scoots further from me.

My stomach twists in me. I don't particularly find the joke funny, so why does my laugh come out so genuine?

He's been teasing me incessantly about choosing not to move into his room quite yet. I can't quite explain why I'm not ready for that. Not when I already made the mistake of telling Captain Astor. Not when I can still feel the sting of his taunts scraping at my throat.

You shouldn't have told me that.

Besides, I find comfort in the fact that Peter doesn't expect me to open those wounds for him until I'm ready.

Peter leans in, sweeping me into his arms and pressing a kiss to my lips, drowning away any of the gnawing in my stomach I feel at his jesting. I melt into his arms, though I swat him away when he starts to play with the buttons of my dress.

"You know, you could have already been my wife," he says, "considering that matters to you so much."

"It wouldn't have counted," I say. "You wanted to marry me in the sky."

Peter presses soft kisses against my jawline. "I would have thought you'd have found that romantic."

"There wouldn't have been any witnesses," I laugh.

"Wendy, Wendy. Always so beholden to everyone else's rules."

I bite my lip and try to focus on how nice it feels to have him close, on the way I'm utterly astounded every time Peter kisses me, every time he tells me he wants me.

"We could have had the Lost Boys be witnesses, you know."

"They will," I say. "Just not yet."

Peter pulls away, though he's gentle. "Why wait?"

"Because," I say, searching for the words. When I find them, I discover they're not something I want to admit to myself, so instead I appeal to Peter's nature. "Don't you think anticipation is half the fun? The dreaming and planning and hoping? I just need a little time."

Peter cocks his head to the side. "To convince yourself you're excited?"

"No." My heart turns over, and I grasp at his hand. "No, I don't have to convince myself. I'm already plenty convinced. I'd just like some time to savor our engagement, that's all."

Peter's eyes betray him, glancing over to the shimmering freckles on my left jawline.

My breath catches, guilt plaguing me, though I can't seem to pinpoint why. "Peter." And because I don't know that I'll have the strength to deny him if he keeps looking at me like that, I ask, "Would you tell me more about Tink?"

The desire in Peter's eyes runs cold, his shoulders tensing. "What would you like to know about her?"

I shrug, running my hand over the sheets. I can't exactly tell

Peter about the attack last night, not without him asking questions about why I was out so late to begin with. "We're betrothed," I settle on, twisting my emerald ring around my finger like it's a costume ring and I'm a leading lady putting on my best performance. "It's natural for me to be curious about your history. And it's okay. I know you have parts of your past you don't want to talk about. If this is one of them, I'll drop it. But I figure if this is a topic you're more indifferent to than the others..."

The tension in his shoulders releases. "You're *jealous*." He says the word like it's honey on his tongue.

"I am sharing an island with my fiancé's previous lover."

He scratches behind his ear. "I'm just not sure what there is to tell you other than what we've already discussed. We came here together. It didn't work out. Now, she won't leave."

I crinkle my brow. "Oh, I don't know. There's the question of how you met. Was it at the orphanage? Was she from your hometown? I'm also curious as to why it didn't work out between the two of you. Or why you let her stay here terrorizing your guests."

A sly grin quirks on his mouth. "When you put it like that, Wendy Darling, it's like you're trying to make me sound suspicious."

I flick him on the shoulder and he laughs. "Tink and I didn't meet at the orphanage, but I was employed there when I met her. I was out on an errand. She was traveling with a merchant's caravan. We did what foolish youths tend to do and fancied we were in love. When the merchant's caravan went ahead, she stayed behind, working as a tavern maid in town. After I met the Sister, I asked Tink to accompany us to Neverland. She said yes."

"And the Sister allowed that?"

"The Sister thought a female touch would do the Lost Boys good."

I frown. "But the Lost Boys acted like they'd never met a woman until me."

A shadow overcomes Peter's face. "When Tink awoke in Neverland—well, it was too much for her. The boys were ill for a time when they first arrived. By the time they came to, Tink's mind had already fled her."

The blood drains from my cheeks. "Because she's a shadow-soother? Because the shadows drove her mad?"

"I tried to help her," says Peter. "She wouldn't let me. It was clear she couldn't be trusted around the boys. Not without lashing out."

My mind flashes back to attacking Michael in the night, and my spirit wilts.

Peter must notice my reaction, because he interlocks his fingers with mine. "You're not like her, Wendy Darling. You let me help you."

The illusory taste of faerie dust buds on my tongue, cloyingly sweet. I think of the entire day I lost to the dust, floating in the rafters of the storehouse while Joel was being stalked and brutally murdered.

Tink's choice isn't the one I would have made, but I'd be lying to myself if I said I didn't understand it. Still, I'd take the daily doses of faerie dust over Tink's crazed violence any day.

"What's that? A love letter for your fiancé?" asks Peter, the cheerful disposition returning to his face as he snatches the parchment out of my hand. Lost in thoughts of Tink, I'd forgotten I was holding it. Immediately, his eyes widen, then his face softens. "I haven't seen one of his sketches like this since—" He flicks his blue eyes up at me. "Where did you get this?"

His tone is about as casual as my laugh just now. All effort. Each note meticulously placed.

"Just found it stuffed in a dresser. He sure did leave his artwork all over the place, didn't he?" I say.

What a Darling little liar, I hear the captain's voice taunt.

Peter stares at me for half a moment, then breaks out into a gentle smile. The kind that melts my heart and pinches it with guilt for lying to him. I don't particularly want to tell him about the events of last night. If I explain how I was attacked by Tink and ended up at the dead man's grave, I'll have to explain why I snuck out at night, and I still haven't gotten the information I need out of the captain.

Or you don't want *him dead,* a voice—a very stupid, foolish voice — whispers in my ear.

As Peter rises to go, I ask him, "What were you going to say earlier?"

Peter's ears flick as he spins back around. "When I was going to say what?"

"When…" I let out a laugh. "You trailed off earlier. You said you haven't seen one like this since…?" I circle my hands around each other in question.

Peter scratches at the back of his head. "I was going to say since before…" He peeks out into the hallway to check none of the Lost Boys are around. "Before Neverland. That looks like one of the sketches Thomas drew in his early days at the orphanage."

My blood runs cold. "That wouldn't make any sense, though."

Peter shrugs. "He probably had it in his pocket when the Sister brought him to Neverland."

"Right. I suppose that's a reasonable explanation."

Peter just smiles, and it's the type that would typically melt me. "Can you think of a more reasonable explanation? Actually," he laughs, "can you think of another explanation at all?"

I shake my head, and it's the grandest lie I've ever told.

AT BREAKFAST, I can't keep my eyes off Victor.

Off the structure of his cheekbones, the slight curve of his nose. My morbid mind takes his face and flashes it upon the skull of the dead man's corpse, trying to make any of the features match, begging them not to.

The more I stare, the more my mind plays tricks on me, lures me into the worst possibility imaginable. But I can't think of a more rational explanation for why the man I killed had a sketch in his pocket that predates Neverland.

I tell myself Peter's right, that Thomas just happened to have it in his pocket when he came to Neverland. It's easier to believe he kept it with him at all times—his only memory of a life before. The life that was snatched from him.

That's the simplest explanation.

But it's not the one my mind grasps onto.

It takes a morsel of evidence, and instead of drawing logical conclusions, it crafts a story. One where it wasn't Thomas who brought this sketch of his into Neverland. One where it traveled to Neverland in the same pocket from which I plucked it last night.

Meaning the man came here looking for Thomas and Victor. Meaning he knew them before, and was motivated enough to traverse realms to find them.

Even down that path of logic, there's a place the signs lead. One where I could put all this to rest and remain somewhat innocent.

Peter's made comments about the warden of the orphanage that make me question the type of relationship he had with the children. Perhaps the warden was obsessed with the boys he lost, and his own wicked inclination drove him to seek them out.

Perhaps he killed Thomas and Freckles, angry that they'd escaped his control. If he already had Thomas's sketch, he could have hired a seer to use it to track him to Neverland, much like Captain Astor had done with my pocket watch.

In this version of the story, I get to be the hero.

I get to be the one who saved not only Peter's life, but Victor's and Simon's and Nettle's and Benjamin's and Smalls's and the Twins'.

But the man wasn't going after Victor when I killed him.

He was going after Peter.

Perhaps that's why my mind fixates on a single moment. Victor, in sheer hatred, spitting upon the corpse of the man, who now that my mind has run off with me, shared Victor's forehead, his cheekbones, his nose.

My mind weaves a story that doesn't leave much room for me to be the hero.

CHAPTER 44

*T*hat night, when Peter is out making his rounds around the island, searching for the killer, I sneak into his room.

It's just like I remember it from both the night Tink attacked me and the night he pressed the faerie dust to my lips and lifted me to the heavens in a swirl of color. My mouth salivates with the memory.

I swallow my spit and remind myself that the dose Peter's given me is enough. My parched throat disagrees.

I'm not sure what exactly I'm looking for. Evidence of the boys' histories, maybe. It's not that I don't trust Peter, I just can't tell him what's spurred my curiosity without betraying that I've been hiding the captain from him. All I want are records of some sort. Surely he's kept something from the orphanage—it was his home too, wasn't it?

I'm not sure what I'm hoping to find in the records. Perhaps evidence that the orphanage warden took an unwholesome interest in the boys. Evidence that he was the man I killed on the beach. It doesn't make complete sense, given Peter would have recognized him. Then again, I wouldn't put it past Peter to keep a matter hidden with the intention of protecting the happiness of those he loves.

There's nothing of note in the drawer to the bedside table. Nothing underneath the bed, either. I could go through the piles of trinkets—pocket watches and such—but something tells me that would be a waste of time.

It's then I consider exactly where Peter would hide something he didn't want the Lost Boys finding.

The book on etiquette sitting on Peter's bedside table. Of course.

When I crack it open, my heart flutters as my fingers brush along the ridges of paper, into which has been cut a rectangle. Inside of it is a leather book. It looks to be a journal of some sort, but it could very well be a book of transactions for all I know.

Slowly, holding my breath, I unbind the shoestring strip holding the journal together.

The pages fall open, shooting dust into the air, but I swallow my cough lest I make enough noise to alert any of the boys who might be wandering the halls for a snack in the middle of the night.

Ridges of ink press against my fingertips as I run them over the pages. I realize this is the first time I've ever seen Peter's handwriting. It's slanted and seems to bounce right off the page.

The first entry is a continuation of a thought about how to construct a decent kitchen in the Den, and I get the impression this journal isn't the first Peter has filled. I suppose I just have to hope that the information I need is here.

I sit cross-legged on the bed, take a breath, and begin to read.

When the Sister first wished to bargain with me to save the boys, I remember thinking it was a treacherous sort of deal. The type humans tell their offspring not to strike with the fae.

I should have listened to those instincts. Shouldn't have let my youthful optimism blind me to what exactly the Sister was placing on my shoulders should anything go wrong.

But I'd told myself nothing would go wrong. All would go to plan, and we'd remain safe in a world, if not of my own design, then at least born of my own imagination.

I thought I could keep them from growing up.

I keep thinking about the blessing she bestowed on me. The gift she presented me so that I would be up to my task if the day ever came. It felt like a blessing then. One I would never have to use for terror, but could drink the benefits of ever after.

But something is changing in the boys.

Thomas keeps asking me about what happened before Neverland. If he and Victor have any living family back home.

At first, I dismissed his questions as natural curiosity.

But then he asked me if there was a warden where he came from.

I avoided the question best I could, but there was no mistaking Thomas's agitation when I refused to answer. The Sister won't like it if she knows he's asking questions.

We thought that wiping their memories would solve the problem, but it seems the effects of the spell are wearing off.

I tell myself I can fix it before it goes too far.

Telling myself that is working less and less.

If Thomas remembers, it's only a matter of time before the other boys discover the truth.

When the Sister bestowed on me my gift, it was so that I would not falter if it came time to end them. She'll see Thomas's knowledge as a disease, ready to infect the others.

It's all I can think about anymore.

THE REST of the journal is empty.

There's a whipping sound as the pages slap together when I slam the book shut.

Letters, written in Peter's script, coil and swirl in my vision.

End them.

It's only a matter of time before the other boys discover the truth.

She'll see Thomas's knowledge as a disease.

End them.

End them.
End them.

My heart races and pounds, confusion rippling through me. It doesn't make sense. I crack the journal back open, skimming over the passage, thinking I've understood it wrong, but the more my eyes scan over the lines, the more condemning they read.

I don't understand.

Peter brought the boys here to save them. To keep them sheltered from their fates. Why would he ever think to end them, and what does that even mean?

And what did Thomas remember? What memory was dreadful enough to get him killed?

My mind rewrites the story Peter originally told me. He claimed the boys were brought to Neverland to keep from infecting their region with a terrible plague, to keep them from meeting their horrible fates.

But what if he lied?

No. That doesn't make sense. Victor told me that all the boys were ill when they first awoke in Neverland, which supports Peter's story.

Maybe it wasn't so much that he lied, but that he omitted part of the truth. Perhaps the Lost Boys witnessed something they were never supposed to see, something the Sister wished to keep hidden. What if that's why she was truly there that night—to silence witnesses, then excuse her actions under the guise of preventing the spread of a plague?

Conflicting thoughts muddle my mind, attacking me from all directions.

Even if Peter killed Thomas at the Sister's command, it doesn't explain the murders of Freckles and Joel.

Unless...

Freckles didn't care for Thomas. Did his disdain have something to do with Thomas's returning memory? What if Thomas told

Freckles what he remembered? If it reflected negatively on Peter, I could see Freckles not wanting to believe it. Could see him thinking that Thomas was trouble—spreading harmful rumors for attention.

That still doesn't explain Joel's death, though.

Besides, there's something else Peter said in his journal that bothers me.

I thought I could keep them from growing up.

In Estelle, you aren't considered of age until you turn twenty, but like John said the other night, that's only been the case for a few decades. Most of the surrounding kingdoms still consider adulthood to commence at sixteen.

I think back to Peter, to the way he spoke of coming of age as if it were a death sentence.

I've never asked how old the boys are. I've been assuming that most of them are around fifteen or sixteen, except for Smalls. All I know is that Thomas was the oldest.

But something is changing in the boys.

My whole body goes numb. Was there more to that than I thought at the time? Some innate belief that life ends at that age, or at least innocence does? Would Peter, if he truly believed that, take up the dagger just like the Sister and plunge it into the Lost Boys' chests, just to keep them from what he perceived to be a worse fate —growing up?

My head spins. Is it even real, the story he told me about the Sister? Or is it just a figment of his imagination? According to the journals, she was the one who tasked Peter with killing the boys if it became necessary.

But what if he's simply given himself an excuse? A mission for ending them when they start to grow up?

Panic strikes me as I consider the time. How much of it has passed since we arrived in Neverland? John is years past his sixteenth birthday.

Will Peter kill him too?

Panic overcomes me, squeezing down in my chest, as I think of the hands I let touch me all over. Had Freckles's blood still been underneath Peter's fingertips the night I let him dig them into my back as he catapulted us into the air? Had the same mouth that drowned me in kisses also lured Joel out of the Den, away from the other boys, offering to go help him look for me?

I search for a third explanation, but I keep coming back to the same two: Either Peter is killing the boys to keep the Sister's secret, or he's a madman.

And the crazed man I killed on the beach—I know now, in my very gut, who he is. The story paints itself in my mind. A man discovers his boys have been taken. How they ended up in the orphanage, I can't reckon, but that's hardly relevant. He sets off on a journey to find them, guided only by his anguish. An anguish of soul that, of course, leads him straight to Neverland.

Where he hunts down the man who had taken his sons.

The man who had killed Thomas, his little boy.

My hand finds my mouth, grasping onto my silent screams as I imagine it all unfold. A father finding the discarded carcass of his oldest boy on the sand. A broken-hearted man sobbing and taking the boy's bracelet, wearing it around his own wrist to carry a piece of his lost boy with him. Just like he carried a sketch of both boys in his pocket. The same sketch that had led him all the way to Neverland.

And then he'd found him—the Shadow Keeper who had taken everything from him. The being who had squeezed the breath from his son. Ended him in the name of saving him from a worse fate. A fate he didn't get the chance to choose.

He'd been about to enact justice.

Instead, he'd found himself on the wrong end of my blade.

CHAPTER 45

$\mathcal{I}$ tell myself there has to be an explanation.

Peter saved my life. Peter set me free. I owe him the conversation, at least. A chance to explain what was written in the journals.

As I'm pacing his floor, wading through my swirling thoughts, a voice calls out from beyond the shadows of the tunnels.

It's calling my name.

Wendy Darling, it whispers.

Did I take my dose of faerie dust today? I can't seem to remember.

My bare feet halt in place as a chill snakes up my spine. Slowly, I tread to Peter's door and peek into the hall. At the end of Peter's hall, there's a tangle of roots that make up the structure of the wall.

The voice whispers my name on the wind, and the roots unfurl. Behind them gapes the mouth of a dark tunnel. Tears sting at my eyes as dread strums at my heart. The voice is wrapped in silky tendrils, like Peter when he used to speak to me from his shadow form. I bite my lip, unsure, but the shadows call again.

And I've always listened.

· · ·

THE TUNNEL IS SMALLER than the hall, so I have to crouch to enter. Thorns tug at my hair as the top of my head scrapes the ceiling. The further into the tunnel I go, the more the walls constrict around me, pressing in on my shoulders.

It's almost as if only shadows are supposed to be able to crawl through here.

Voices echo through the tunnel, but they're different from the voice that led me here. The voice that called my name was multi-layered, as if comprised of several voices. These are more distinct— one sultry, one familiar.

Eventually, the tunnel curves, and I peek around it.

Beyond, in an alcove where the tunnel opens into a cave, is Peter. Except it's not the Peter I've come to know, but the Peter who came to take me away from the clock tower. His body is encased in shadows, his wings ethereal plumes that bat erratically, writhing in the darkness.

He's on the ground, kneeling.

That's the most terrifying part of all.

Because he's kneeling before the source of the other voice.

It's coming from a woman.

Shadows form into sensual curves, hugging the woman's body tightly. At once, I'm struck by her beauty, though faintly, in the back of my mind, I recognize the error in this, given I'm unable to make out the features that would make her so. She stands above Peter on a dais, looking down upon him.

I don't know how I know this, but I get the impression there's a sense of derision on her face, underneath all those swirling shadows.

There's an alluring beauty there, and I'm a child who can't seem to help but stand on her tiptoes and touch her fingers to the burner.

I steel myself, used to Peter's glamour more than I was when I first arrived. I bite down on my lip until I draw blood, but at least the pain keeps me tethered to reality. The reality that this shadow is dangerous and doesn't care for my well-being.

"Tell me, Peter, why is it that you appear so displeased to see me?" pouts the woman, tracing a shadowed finger in a trail along Peter's shoulder blade. Even underneath the shadows, I can sense him tense at her touch. Bile coils at my throat when she takes her sharp fingernail, protruding in inky rivulets from the shadows, and traces it up his neck, resting it at his chin to force him to look at her.

"You once sought me out. Do you not remember those days? How eager you were to find me when all the others claimed I didn't exist?"

"I didn't revere you then as I should have," says Peter, the same emptiness in his voice as the night I chased him up the cliff and found him mourning the dead Lost Boys in his own peculiar way.

The shadow woman tsks. "You act as if you revere me now."

"I fear you," says Peter.

"Hmm. If only it were as impossible for fae to lie in this realm as in another I'm privy to. Perhaps I should find a way to set the same curse upon you, my love."

"Is that what you want? For me to speak the truth?" asks Peter.

"Why would I wish for you to lie to me?"

"You always ask if I find you beautiful. If you wished to know the truth, you would not ask such foolish questions."

I expect the woman to rear back with a shriek, but she doesn't. Her shadows curl around her like the edges of a smile. "I always did like you, you know. Uninhibited by what shackles the rest of us."

"You're partly to blame for that," Peter says.

The female laughs again. "I've only ever given you the gifts you requested. Have I ever gifted you with anything you did not beg from me with your very own lips?"

Something about the way she says *beg* has a pang of envy roiling through me. The sensuality of her tone. I sense that if I could see her eyes, they'd be ravenous with desire.

"Do not act as if I've denied anything you've ever asked," she says. "Speaking of which, tell me, Peter, why have you yet to take advantage of my most recent gift?"

When Peter remains silent, she slices his chin with her fingernail.

He doesn't even flinch.

"You've yet to take her, but why?" she says. "When you've craved the Darling girl for so long?"

Shock barrels through me, and hurt too, the shadow woman's words directly contradicting what Peter told me the night we first danced in the sky, that he never desired me until I came to the island. That he barely remembers visiting me as a child.

I wait for him to contradict her. To explain to her exactly what he explained to me, but again he keeps silent.

I linger, telling my feet they should go. That anything else I might garner from this conversation will only harm me. That if the shadow woman realizes I've been eavesdropping, she'll be vengeful indeed. But my feet are plastered to the floor, stuck in the quicksand of my own curiosity. The kind that wishes to wound me, it seems.

Besides. I have to know about Thomas. About Freckles and Joel and the man whose life I took. I have to know if I've fallen asleep in the arms of a murderer.

If that morning on the beach, I soaked my hands in the wrong man's blood.

"It couldn't be that you're holding out for someone else, could it?" asks the shadow woman, and I catch it—her desperation. It's in the way her voice hikes a bit. It's not love or adoration for Peter, but a desire for conquest. The longing to be longed for.

When I first arrived, Peter told me the Sister has no friends. Only lovers and slaves. I can't help but wonder if some hold both titles.

I think I might be ill. What all has Peter been required to do while within the servitude of this woman?

But then I remember the bargain that Peter could use against me at any moment. What might I be required to do in the service of his pleasures?

You've craved her, is what the shadow woman said. *For how long*, my mind wonders, and I'm scrambling to make it mean anything other than what I think. That he lied to me in the trees, that he's wanted me since childhood.

That Peter is sick, and that his craving for me is not the same way I crave him.

If that's the case, then with the bargain he holds over me, not only could he force himself upon me, he could keep me from fighting back. Could trick me into thinking I'm enjoying it.

A horrible thought crosses my mind.

What if Peter has already taken his side of the bargain? What if he's already taken me up on it and commanded me to forget? If he's commanded me to obey whatever he asks, he could technically wipe my memories. He could whisper in my ear that I was developing feelings for him. He could be the one controlling my attraction to him, my trust.

But no.

The Sister doesn't seem to think he's taken me. Surely she'd know if he had.

But he still lied about hardly noticing me all those years when he was in his shadow form. I can't quite wrap my mind around the logic of it all. Why lie when, through the bargain, he could make me believe anything he wanted me to? It doesn't make sense. Or perhaps it does, and the anxiety of the moment is making it difficult to fit the pieces together.

"I would have taken her many times," Peter says, his wings rippling, "but my other half refuses to allow it on anyone else's terms but hers. He wishes to woo her, it seems."

My heart stops in my chest, my breathing too, chills snaking up my arm.

He's not himself when he's like this, I remind myself. No matter how many times I repeat it, I'm not confident it will be enough. Not when his journal is tucked into my inner coat pocket, the words inside as heavy as iron, as incriminating as a signed confession.

"Is there anything else?" Peter asks, returning to his previous state, on one knee in front of the shadow woman. She paces around him, stalking him like a cat would its prey. As she does, she traces her fingers lovingly, tenderly up his back.

Peter's shadows lurch with every curve of his spine that her fingers travel. My stomach lurches with him as my pity for his slavery grapples with my anxiety over what Peter might have done on her behalf.

"You've grown displeased with me," she says. "Increasingly so, since administering the boys' unfortunate fates."

The way the shadows leaching from the hem of her gown curve toward Peter has my stomach reeling. I hold my breath and wait for him to deny his part in it.

That moment never comes.

Instead, Peter just says, "You know I don't like messes."

It's like I'm being stabbed through the ribs. I have to clamp my hand over my mouth to keep from crying out in pain.

"I'm surprised their deaths matter to you, of all people," the Sister responds as I bite back silent sobs.

"I don't like losing what belongs to me. Any more than I'd like losing the pair to my sock," says Peter.

The apathy with which he says it infiltrates my chest as the boys' faces flash across my mind. Thomas. Freckles. Joel.

I remind myself Peter's different in this form.

As if that will ever be enough.

"Don't act as if I didn't warn you that this might happen. Your kind might have ascribed the term Fates to my sisters and I, but make no mistake, Fate itself is a different force entirely. My sisters and I can only coax it in a certain direction. We cannot force its hand."

Peter's cruel laugh echoes through the cave. "You wouldn't call strangling one boy and stabbing two forcing Fate's hand?"

"Those boys were ill. You knew from the beginning you might not save all of them. All we can do is try to cut off the disease before it continues to spread. I'll be honest; I'd hoped it would have ended with Thomas, but you should have killed him long before you did. You had better be careful, Peter. Or I'll start to wonder whether you're up to the task, or if I should consider Neverland a failed trial altogether."

My cheeks drain of color at her implications. At the images

racing through my mind—Neverland dissolving into shadows, the realm unraveling with the boys still trapped within it.

This time, Peter cranes his neck up to look at her as she steps in front of him. "And you should know better than anyone else why I am capable."

Again, I get the sense the awful creature is smiling. "Of course. You're right. How could I doubt you?"

She takes her hand off his back, then turns as if to go. She must think better of it, because she says, "And Peter?"

"Yes, my lady?"

"I want the last of the ill ones dead before morning."

In a whirl of shadows and smoke, she disappears.

Immediately, Peter collapses.

His shadows waft off of him like smoke being driven away in the wind, until all that's left is his pale flesh, chafed by the whirl of shadows. He clutches his fists to the ground, back still facing me, the darkness of the cavern obscuring any part of him I would feel guilty about witnessing, especially since he doesn't know I'm here.

His breathing is labored, but I get the impression it's more out of relief that she's gone than pain from the transition. Some shadows remain, clinging to his spine around where his wings fuse, but when he moves, the light shifts and casts a glow upon his bare shoulder.

Rather, it reveals a glow glimmering on his back.

What I thought were shadows appear more like a tattoo.

Except it's not a tattoo at all.

It's a Mating Mark.

CHAPTER 46

*I*t's a tree painted in gold, its trunk breaking through a stone, its canopy reaching toward the heavens.

I mean *reaching* quite literally.

The branches curve across Peter's shoulder blade into the shape of an extended hand. Above the tree are golden freckles, like mine. Except they aren't freckles at all.

They're stars.

I find my fingers tracing the path of my Mark—the way the crisp golden dots curve from my left cheek down my jaw.

A sickle.

I feel the way they scatter at the bottom. At least, I'd always assumed they were scattering. But now that I see Peter's Mark, I'm sure their placement is intentional.

My stars make the hood.

Peter's make the robe.

Together, we form the Reaper.

The Reaper and the Oak.

There's even a fox, clawing at the base of the tree, despite the fact that there are no roots to find underneath, no woman's soul left behind to fetch for his master.

The sight of the Mating Mark scalds the backs of my eyes, over-lapping with the vision of a corpse on a beach.

I'd stabbed a grieving father in the back. Then told his only living son a lie that had led him to spit on his father's corpse. To dump it in a shallow grave and obsessively watch the earth pick the flesh from his father's bones.

I had done that.

I'd done it to save Peter.

I'd done it before I even trusted him, really. Before I even loved him. It was like someone else had taken control of my hands, sent me into a frenzy. I'd realized then and there that I would sacrifice everything to keep what I'd wanted most from this life.

I'd driven a knife into an innocent man's heart, and I hadn't even given him a chance to speak.

Slowly, I find my fingers tracing my Mark, feeling its ridges.

You're mine, Peter had said.

I hadn't known how absolute of a statement that had been. How, of everything in the world I'd cowered from, that should have been the one thing I feared the most.

My Darling little thing, he'd called me when he brought me to Neverland, and I'd let him mold me into just that. A possession. His. Until I slaughtered his avengers for him. Silenced the evidence against him.

Peter never needed to call in his bargain. Because he's my Mate, and that was always going to be enough to influence my decisions. Especially when I didn't know to guard against them. He'd told me once that his glamour could influence me only because I let it, only because I was drawn to him.

He'd simply neglected to mention *why* I was drawn to him.

You've been craving her for so long.

My mind keeps replaying the Sister's words, like it can't quite process them until it's heard them thousands of times.

But it's not her words I can't process.

It's that Peter's my Mate.

It hits me like a shard of shrapnel to the chest, lodging there. The harder I try to dig it out with my fingernails, the more infected the wound becomes.

I can't.

I can't be Peter's Mate.

Not after what I just witnessed.

He killed those boys, ended their lives so they wouldn't come of age. Or so they wouldn't spread the plague to the others. I can't quite fit the two together in my mind as I scramble to make sense of it all.

Peter. My Peter, I might believe. But Peter isn't just the male who took me flying in the sky, who taught me not only to fall but to like falling. Peter is the creature who just writhed before me, callous and cruel and thirsty for death. Peter is the voice who said he would have taken me long ago, if not for his gentler side restraining him.

Peter is the one killing the Lost Boys.

And my Mate plans to kill more of them tonight.

As I RACE to slip from the tunnels, I trip over a root. A root I'm fairly certain wasn't there before.

When I go down, I land with a yelp, then immediately cover my mouth.

Inside the cavern, a hunter shifts to attention. I can practically see his beautiful face, his glinting blue eyes narrow, his lithe shoulders roll, his ears flatten back as he senses me.

"Wendy Darling," he says. Footsteps pad in my direction as he follows me into the tunnels, and I'm cursing the root that came up to grab me. I attempt to wrestle my ankle from its clutches, but it's no use. No use at all.

The vine only curls tighter around my ankle, confirming that this land is loyal to one person and one person alone. It helped me when it believed me to be in Peter's good graces.

I sense that is no longer the case.

Peter rounds the corner, having pulled on a pair of trousers and looking massive with how he has to hunch to fit through the tunnel. Something tells me he entered as a billow of shadows.

"Wendy?" he asks. "How long have you been standing down here?"

There's no use in forcing my shaking voice to calm. I'll have to work with my fear if I want to sound at all convincing. "I had another nightmare," I say, blinking back genuine tears. "I didn't want to wake my brothers, so I came looking for you."

Peter's eyes narrow. "How long were you standing there?"

I bite my tongue to keep from gagging as I recall the vile words Peter spoke about me just now. The sick, pitiful girl inside whose entire purpose was to convince a man to care for her aches to believe that her Mate is good at heart. That he's simply haunted by the wicked creature within.

But Peter's usually pale eyes are black as soot, even over the whites.

Even if there is a version of Peter I'm safe with, it's not this one. The version that's half-fae, half-shadow. I'm not sure which of them has been killing the Lost Boys, but I have my guesses.

"Wendy," he says, and this time it's a command.

"I saw the Sister," I say, hating how even now, knowing what I know, I still feel compelled to answer, an urge to please him. "I was so terrified, I ran as soon as my legs would move."

The lie feels too convenient. Too rehearsed. Peter doesn't appear convinced, and he doesn't kneel to help with the root that's now scaling up my ankle, pin-pricking thorns into my flesh.

I wince as a thorn lodges itself in, but Peter doesn't so much as bat his eyelashes. Granted, I don't know why he would. Not when it's clear that whatever shadow creature dwells inside him still has at least some semblance of control.

"She won't be happy if she discovers you saw her," he says, glancing down at my leg.

"Won't she know as soon as she looks at the tapestry of Neverland?"

Peter's shadows curl inward. It's amazing he's able to tolerate being so constricted in this tunnel; the muscles of his back have to be aching. "She's not omniscient. The tapestry displays a handful of crucial events, but if it included all the details, it would be never-ending."

A terrifying smile overcomes his face, all glinting teeth. "Perhaps I should leave you here for her. For next time. She's been increasingly displeased with my offerings as of late." Peter cocks his head, then squats, spreading his legs apart as he props his elbows on his knees and examines me. His wings expand, like a feline stretching its limbs. "But that would be a waste of your pretty flesh, wouldn't it? When I could keep you for myself?"

I cringe underneath my shackles, remembering Peter's apology when he first brought me to Neverland.

I apologize for my lack of manners. It's more difficult to control myself in that form.

I close my eyes, wishing to drown out the sight of this Peter, the version I only recognize from my nightmares. This isn't him, I remind myself. This is the monster. This is whatever the Shadow Sister has cursed him to bear.

"Peter," I say, hoping his name on my lips will draw him out to me. It's a foolish, stupid hope, because the Peter kneeling before me lets out a dry, hungry cackle.

"You're such a pretty little girl," he says, running his fingers over the curve of my hip. I swat him away, digging my nails into the back of his hand, hard enough to produce blood, though he shows no reaction other than flicking his head toward my face.

"Tell me, Wendy Darling, why did you follow the shadows if you didn't crave a little darkness?"

Fear crawls up my throat, and I consider screaming. But what good would that do? The only ones around to alert are the Lost Boys, who adore Peter to a fault and would do nothing to contradict him. John would come for me, I have no doubt, but the only thing that would accomplish would be getting him killed.

But then I remember. If I'm Peter's Mate, then he's just as much mine.

So I slip my fingers to the nape of his neck and pull him in.

He groans at the kiss, his lips devouring mine, a violence to the passion I'm unaccustomed to. Even now, I hate myself for the desire it ignites within me as my Mating Mark silences my good sense. Pain lances my back as Peter digs his talons into my skin, my blood screaming at me to fight back as it hits the cold, dank air. My heart beats wildly in my chest, tears stinging at my eyes, but then Peter's grip on me loosens, his body melting into me.

He pulls back, blinking, and the inky glaze over his eyes washes away.

"How badly did I behave?" is his first question.

"Not exactly like a gentleman," I breathe sharply.

"I wouldn't anticipate so," says Peter, all frivolity sucked out of his features, even if he is back to himself. He withdraws his hands from my back; the talons are gone, but there's blood caking his fingernails. He stares at his hands in numb shock. "Wendy, I didn't mean to..."

"I know," I blurt quickly, still wincing. I don't know if my resolve can handle an apology from Peter at the moment. My throat goes dry as Peter rips the roots from my ankles. I contemplate running now that I'm free, but I'm not sure what that would accomplish given Peter's fae speed and agility. "I saw you," I say instead, then I push myself up, wrapping my arms around him and trailing my fingers over the divots in his right shoulder blade.

The Mark that makes me his.

Peter goes still, like he's contemplating whether what I'll say will allow him to let me go.

"You didn't tell me you were my Mate," I whisper, considering all the moments of weakness surrounding Peter that I in my naivete attributed to fae glamour.

"You didn't ask."

"Why?"

"Because I'm not the kind of Mate you've always dreamt of, Wendy Darling."

My throat hurts. "You lied," I say. "All the times you said you didn't want me."

Peter turns to me, and he attempts to regain his playful demeanor, but fumbles it as he replies, "What is a lie, Wendy Darling, but a story we tell ourselves? And are stories lies if they make the world a more bearable place?"

"Is that what you do to the Lost Boys, too?" I say, realizing how carefully I need to tread around this topic. Peter still doesn't know I heard enough to convince me he's the murderer. "Is that how you have to earn their love and loyalty? By lying to them about what a monster you are? Because you know what they'd do as soon as they learned the truth?"

Peter actually snorts. "Tell me, Wendy Darling, what is the truth?"

I open my mouth, but I fall short for words.

So instead, I wipe the grime on my pants and go to walk away.

A hand grabs my wrist, but it's gentle—the type of grasp I could wriggle out of if I tried.

"What? Readying to call in your bargain?" I ask, my tone all acid.

"Would you like me to?" Peter asks, that wicked grin revealing a set of dimples. Even now, the sight of him takes the breath out of me, and I hate myself for it.

I'm not especially brave, nor am I exceedingly clever, but there's something I've always excelled at. Leaving a conversation making others feel as if I've been convinced. Even better, as if I agreed with them the entire time.

So I let the wicked smile of Peter's slip onto my face, mirroring it in my expression.

"No need," I say, dipping my voice low and seductive. "Because as much as I'm yours, you're mine. And I intend to keep you, my shadowed little thing."

Peter's face flashes feral, and he grabs my hand, leading me out of the tunnels and into his rooms. My heart slams against my chest as he closes the door behind him, then picks me up and lays me on his bed.

If I allowed it, I think I could let him kiss away the pain.

I'll at least let him believe he has.

CHAPTER 47

When Peter first laid me on his bed, I'd been resolved to do whatever it took to keep him distracted from killing the next boy on the Sister's list. But then his hands trailing my body had sent me back to my parents' parlor, to the feel of velvet underneath my fingernails as I dug them into the chair upholstery, trying to focus on any sensation other than what the men did to me. I'd been on the edge of panic, seeing shadows in the corners of my vision.

So I'd slipped my hand into the pocket of my trousers, then pressed my powder-dusted fingertips to Peter's mouth.

"I'm sorry," I'd whispered as his eyes went wide, his body still with the rapid effects of the rushweed. Even now, for the life of me, I can't fathom why I apologized, except that the betrayal in his blue eyes had rent my Mated soul in two.

Part of me wonders if I should have killed him then. But as of now, he's sprawled across his bed, body immobilized for the time being.

I give myself three breaths when I get back to my room.

Three breaths to trace the Mating Mark on my face. To feel its dips and rivulets in my skin. I used to think of them as freckles, but now their shape reminds me of tears.

Three breaths to hold onto that dream I've had since I was just a child.

When my lungs rattle on the fourth breath, I tuck my hands by my sides.

And let the dream shatter.

"John." I shake my brother awake. He rolls over, saliva glistening on his cheek as he rubs his eyes.

He looks so young like this.

Not young enough.

"Mmm?"

"Pack yours and Michael's stuff, then meet me by the storehouse. You'll have to climb, but it's less steep on the western side of the bluff," I say.

This seems to get John's attention. His eyes shoot open, and he props himself up on his elbow in the cot. "What's wrong?"

"Nothing," I lie. "But I need you to trust me."

"How am I supposed to trust you when you wake me up in a panic and tell me we're leaving in the middle of the night, but nothing's wrong?"

"Fine." I bite my lip. "Something's very wrong, but I don't have time to tell you. I'll tell you on the way, all right?"

John stares me down, but he doesn't argue. He just hops out of the bed and starts packing, much too loudly for my preference.

"I HAVE AN OFFER TO MAKE YOU."

"Are you going to say please?"

I grit my teeth and stare down the man who ruined my life. Captain Astor is still drowsy from yesterday's dose and can barely move his toes. Still, he stares at me with such arrogance. Like he's the one with the upper hand. Like he's the one who has me in invisible shackles.

"You came searching for me," I say. "You need me for something;

I know you do. Well, you found me, found a way into Neverland. I need you to take my brothers and me to the spot in Neverland that got you from our realm to this one."

It's a gamble, especially because Peter claimed the gaps only work in one direction—entering Neverland. But Peter's a liar, and I'd be willing to bet this is just one of the falsehoods he's told to keep the Lost Boys from escaping Neverland.

The captain flashes his teeth at me. "Darling, you found me half-dead, washed up on the beach. Do you want me to take you and your brothers on my back and swim you out to the middle of the ocean? Something tells me if you had your arms wrapped around me, one of us would enjoy it significantly more than the other."

I don't give him the opportunity to expound on which one of us he thinks that is. "No. There's no way you weaseled your way into Neverland without having an escape plan. If I hadn't found you and drugged you, I'd be tied up and stuffed in a barrel on a ship somewhere in the middle of the sea."

The captain pouts. "Come now, Darling. You really think I'd stuff you in a barrel? Really, tying you up is where I draw the line. I do possess some morals, you know."

I jut out my hand, but he just stares at it as it dangles midair.

"You seem to be forgetting that my arms don't work," he says. "Besides, the annoying thing about bargains is that they have to be beneficial to both parties."

"The part that's beneficial to you is that I don't let you starve. Slowly."

The captain's eyes flicker. "I wasn't aware humans could grow spines this late in their development. Even so, I don't believe you."

"I'd do it without batting an eye."

"Tell me, did you ever come up with more incriminating evidence for that poor deranged man you gutted, or was he not wearing any more jewelry?"

My face pales, and even in the moonlight, the captain's fae eyes sense it. Home in on the blood draining from my face. "Ah. So there is more to that story, after all."

"Just get us out of here. Anything you want."

"This sounds familiar. You should be careful with how many people you give your anythings to. Soon enough, you'll have people shouting conflicting orders at you. It might just tear you limb from limb."

Tears stream down my cheeks. "Please. Please, I'm begging you. Just get my brothers out."

He stares at my outstretched hand, then without feeling says, "I don't strike fae bargains anymore. Too messy. Too many unintended consequences."

"Then I give you my word," I say, infusing my voice with as much fervor as I can. "Just tell me what you want from me, and I'll do it."

The captain considers me for a moment. Opens his lips, then shuts them again. Then he grins. "You, my dear, are a Darling little liar."

I gasp, like I've been struck across the face. "I'm not lying."

The captain rolls his eyes. "You say you'll free me, give me anything I wish in return, but you're only saying that because you've discovered something unsettling about that boy with wings. Something you think is new, but has always been there, lurking under the surface."

"I'm done with him," I say, hugging my torso. I know better than that, know it will only signal weakness to the vile captain, but I can't help myself.

"If only," he says, considering me. "Then perhaps you and I could make a good team. But we've already established I know him better than you do, and I'm aware of his devices—the type of weak minds he preys upon. And you, Wendy Darling, are weak-minded. I've known it since the moment I laid eyes on you, saw you dolled up in that horrific wedding garb, decked out like a porcelain doll up for auction. As empty-headed as one, too."

"I'm not stupid," I say, clenching my torso as I bite back tears.

The captain's face almost softens. "No. No, you're not. And isn't that the tragic bit of this story?"

I'm sobbing now, and I hate myself for it. Hate myself for baring my weakness in front of this awful man, for reinforcing every unflattering word he says about me.

"Don't fret, Darling. I'll see you when the winged boy has his claws in you again, when he's convinced you that your mind is playing tricks on you. Of all the ways you were wrong to doubt him. Then the two of us can go back to our typical banter. It's much more pleasant that way, don't you think?"

"I hate you," I seethe.

"I hate you back, Darling." He smiles.

I throw a rock at him on my way out.

CHAPTER 48

*a*ngry tears sluice down my face, rinsed away in the rain of an oncoming storm as I hurtle myself down the beach and toward the cliffside.

Stupid, stupid man. I could have helped you. I could have saved you, I think to myself, though that's the opposite of what I should be concerned about in the moment. Still, I can't help but wonder what will happen to the captain when the tide comes in. I'd left him close to the mouth of the cave out of spite. I'd only wanted to frighten him, make him wonder whether the waves would get close enough to carry him away, swallow him in their greedy depths.

I'm unsure that I judged the distance correctly.

I imagine his corpse rotting away like Victor's father's, except instead of worms laying their young in his eye sockets, it'll be the fish and the bottom-feeders.

My heart aches, and it's stupid for doing so.

I push the captain from my mind, cursing him and leaving him to rot in my past. I have my brothers to save.

Sand scratches against my bare feet as I run, and I can't help but regret that the captain didn't decide to assist us. It was a risk, offering myself in exchange for him helping get John and Michael to safety. But leaving Neverland through a gap in the Fabric seemed like a more sure way of getting my brothers out of here than my current plan.

But I suppose faerie dust is how we entered, so faerie dust is how we must go.

I'm hesitant to dose my brothers again. When I think of it, I remember my mother tipping the faerie wine to my lips. The way I scorned it at first, but then, after exposure, began requesting it. John and Michael didn't seem to have trouble after that first dose that had carried them here, but neither had I when Peter gave me the tiniest bit at the storehouse or when he'd offered me just enough to dance with him in the stars.

It was the third dose that had done me in. This will be their second. No, I realize with dread. Peter gave Michael another dose when he panicked outside the reaping tree. Still, better addicted to faerie dust than dead. That's what I tell myself, anyway. A gnawing voice in the back of my head can't help but wonder if that's what my mother told herself, too.

I'm so lost in thought, I don't notice the figure until I smack into him.

He's all lean muscle, and at first I think it's Peter. Fear shoots through me, but then I realize the pull of the Mating Mark is absent, and I breathe a sigh of relief.

"Going for a nighttime run? You are insane," says Simon, his dark eyes glittering with friendly teasing. "Better back away from me before Peter sees and gets the wrong idea," he says.

I do just that, stepping back quickly. "Peter's here?"

Simon wrinkles his brow. "No. It was just a joke."

"Oh." I force my mouth into a smile. "Right."

Simon's cheerful disposition dips into concern. "You all right, Winds?"

"Of course. Just couldn't sleep, that's all." I'm breathing too heavily. "Thought I'd wear myself out pretty good before trying to go back to bed."

Simon wrinkles his nose. "You think you're gonna sleep better when you stink like that?"

I'm not in the mood for it, but I punch him in the chest playfully, trying to keep up my ruse.

That seems to appease Simon's worries a bit. Part of me wonders if I should ask him what he's doing out here so late, but I feel like time is slipping through my fingertips like grains of sand. I've no idea how long it will be until Peter can move and realizes I've left.

"Well, I'm not quite worn out yet," I say, and Simon grins sheepishly.

"Right, I won't keep you then. See you in the morning, Winds."

He walks away, but I'm frozen in place. Dread keeps me sutured there, on the beach between the Den and the cliffs. The space between the Lost Boys and my brothers.

You can't save them all, I remind myself. But I know deep down that's not entirely true. It would be possible to get all the Lost Boys out of here, the same way I intend to get my brothers out. The problem is getting them to believe me. The Lost Boys practically worship Peter. What are the chances that they'll believe he's the one picking them off?

Still, a vision glances through my mind. Yellowed bruises on a lifeless neck, singed hair, a missing pinkie, Simon's eye sockets the ones eaten out by worms. My stomach twists, and I twist with it.

"Simon," I say weakly. Almost in a whisper. Almost hoping he won't turn around, that I'll be able to go off with my brothers in peace and tell myself for the rest of my life that I tried.

He turns around, hands in his pockets. "Yeah, Winds?"

My heart thumps wildly. This is stupid. There's no way I'll be able to get all of them out of here. At least one of them will go running off and find Peter out of blind loyalty.

But Simon is my friend. How can I live with myself if I let him die?

"You're not safe here." I make myself rush the words out, before I become too much of a coward to speak them.

He flashes me a confused smile. "Of course I'm not. Have you seen the size of the nightstalkers on this island?"

Grief punctures my heart. I glance at the moon. It might as well be a shooting star for how it's moving through the sky. "No. Simon, I mean, you're not safe with Peter. None of the Lost Boys are."

A shadow ripples from out of nowhere, overtaking Simon's face. "What? Don't tell me the two of you had a lovers' spat?"

I shake my head emphatically. "No, you have to listen to me. Peter. This place. It's not what you think it is."

"I've never known what Neverland is."

Tears sting at my eyes. "If you stay here, if any of you stay here, you're going to die."

"We're all going to die eventually, Winds. It's just part of the fae curse."

A lump forms in my throat. Simon adores Peter so much, and it kills me to rip that brotherly facade out from under him. But I don't know how else to make him understand. Parchment crinkles against my fingertips as I slip Peter's journal out of my pocket and hand it to Simon.

He glances at me warily before opening it, eyes tilting down and darting across the open page, lit by the bare moonlight.

I can tell when he gets to the end by the way his muscles tense around his jaw.

"Where did you get this?"

"It's one of Peter's journals."

"I don't understand."

"I know," I say, then quickly explain what Peter told me about ransoming the boys' lives from their Fates. About the fact that Neverland was made specifically to protect them.

"I don't understand…" he says, jerking his head up toward me. "End them?" he says, his voice pleading. Like he's begging me to enlighten him with a reasonable explanation of what those words mean.

It's then I know I've got him. It's written in understanding that dawns on his face, followed by the grief, the anger.

"Thomas," he whispers, his voice sounding as if his throat is clenched up.

I nod. "Freckles and Joel, too. My brothers and I are leaving. We're taking faerie dust and getting out of here. I want you and the Lost Boys to come with us."

Simon shuffles in the sand. "The others won't believe this."

I wince. "You did."

Simon winces too, then presses his fingers to his forehead. "I've known something was wrong for a while now."

"Tell them Peter had to go away. That he left me instructions to get the lot of you out of Neverland. That strangers are coming in the same way as..." My throat closes up at the betrayal of the lie. "Thomas's and Freckles's and Joel's killer. It's not safe here anymore. I'm to get the lot of you out and meet him on the other side."

Simon blinks. "That might work."

I nod. "It'll have to."

Simon turns to go, then spins back around. "You won't leave without me? You'll wait there, at the shed, until I get back?"

A lump rises in my throat. "I promise."

The moonlight glances off the moisture in Simon's eyes as he turns and runs.

SCALING the cliffside takes less time than it should. Perhaps I'm propelled by fear this time. Perhaps I'm so distracted by my thoughts that it only seems faster.

Either way, John and Michael are already waiting for me by the time I arrive.

Michael is pacing, trying to get to the edge of the cliff to lean over. John's hand is interlocked with his, letting him just close enough to look, but with a wide enough gap between him and the edge where he won't fall.

"I've already broken into the shed," John says, tugging at a sack of faerie dust at his waist. He goes to untie the clasp with one hand, but I shake my head.

"Get just enough for the two of you," I say. "I won't be far behind."

John stills. "What do you mean, you won't be far behind?"

I sigh. "The other Lost Boys are meeting us here. I'm getting them out too."

"Wendy. What's going on?"

I bite my lip. "Just take Michael and go. I'll explain on the other side. Meet me back at the clock tower, okay?"

John lets out a gust of air. "I'm not leaving without you."

"John," I plead. "You have to get Michael out of here."

"No. I have to get both of you out of here."

"I'm not your responsibility, John."

"Yes, Wendy. You are." John's heaving now, and I recognize the desperation in his voice, his expression. "I've always looked after you."

My heart wilts as I remember John sleeping outside my room, ready to jump out and slay the shadows before they took me. Before I let them take me. John's always been there to grab my hand before I go teetering off the edge, always been there to keep me tethered to the earth.

I remember soaring with Peter, two forces pulling me in opposite directions.

"John, you have to let go," I say. "I have to learn to take care of myself."

John swallows. "Well, let me know when you do. I'll happily give up looking after you then, but as of now, I'm yet to be convinced."

His words sting, but he's not being unfair. I'm the one who fell for a monster, after all. I'm the one who led my brothers into an adder's den, then tried to convince them they were safe there. I'm the one who gave up on trying to get them out, and instead settled for my own blissful nothingness, rather than fighting for them to have a real life.

"Michael can't stay here," I say.

"First sign of danger, I'll get him out," says John.

I nod, recognizing my brother won't be dissuaded.

So we wait, the shadows pooling around us. I remember the first time I came here, the shadows swarming me until I couldn't breathe. There's still today's lower dose of faerie dust in me, warding them away.

It makes me sick thinking I have Peter to thank for that.

An hour passes according to the placement of the moon, when a shadow appears from the tree line.

John tenses behind me, and I do too. But there are no wings to the shadow. It's just Simon, looking forlorn.

Simon, alone.

"They wouldn't come," he says, shaking his head. "It's just us."

I let out a choking sound. "None of them?"

Simon bites the inside of his cheek and shakes his head.

Pain lances through my heart, a grief I wasn't expecting. In my mind, I glimpse the boys' faces, each one of them. Benjamin, Victor, Nettle, Smalls, the Twins. Except none of them are smiling.

They're as dead as driftwood, eyes wide open to the canopy above, mouths slack in horror.

I swallow and use it to steel myself. "All right, then. John, get a dose for Simon and let's go."

Michael sings back to me. "Time to go!"

John doesn't answer.

"John?" I whirl around. John is there, but his body's gone slack, limp against a figure behind him, obscured by the shadows of the warehouse.

Michael teeters precariously toward the edge of the ridge, looking downward.

My stomach spoils.

"Michael, come here," I whisper.

He doesn't pay me any attention, just keeps picking at dandelions near the edge.

"Michael," I beg, then when he doesn't listen, I say, "Simon, please go get my brother."

Simon shifts behind me. When he comes into my vision, he offers me an apologetic glance. I'm going to be sick. Despite that,

Simon grabs Michael's hand, leading him slightly away from the edge. "I'm sorry, Winds," he says. "There are just some things you don't understand."

"We really are sorry," says the figure in the shadows. Shimmering eyes glint in the darkness. John is limp in his arms, poised with a wet cloth dipped over his mouth.

Out steps Nettle, blond hair ghostly in the moonlight.

His lips twist into a sad smile as he places a blade to John's throat. "I told you, Winds. I remember. I remember everything."

CHAPTER 49

"Simon?" I ask, my feet begging me to step away, my soul tethered to the life of my brothers. "What's going on?" It's not Simon who answers.

"We didn't want to have to hurt you. Everyone likes you, Winds," says Nettle, and his voice is all innocence, no cruelty. "We like John and Michael too."

"I didn't tell John anything," I say in a rush. "He knows I wanted to get us out, but I didn't tell him anything more than that."

Nettle blinks back tears. "He was getting close anyway. He would have figured it out, eventually. I followed him at night, when you were gone. Did you really think he didn't notice? You didn't wonder why he said nothing?"

Realization dawns on me. While I was out visiting the captain, John was doing his own investigating.

"I don't understand why you're protecting Peter. If the two of you know what he plans to do to you."

Nettle shakes his head. "That's where you're wrong, Wendy. Peter's the best of us, but it means that he was never going to be strong enough to do what had to be done."

My heart stops in my chest. "Peter didn't kill Thomas?"

Slowly, Nettle shakes his head.

"How do you know?"

Simon lifts his face, his fingers still twined in Michael's hand. "Because I did."

My breath leaves me, panic overtaking my bones. My mind tries to picture it—innocent, kind Simon killing Thomas in cold blood. Strangling the air from his lungs, but I can't picture it. Can't imagine it. Simon, who was the first to befriend me. Simon, who talked and joked with me for long hours as we went on hunts.

"No. No, Simon, you couldn't. You couldn't have..."

"Winds, please," he says, his face distressed and pleading. "Please don't make this worse. I didn't mean to. I didn't mean..." His eyes go out of focus, like they're trying to roll back in his head, but he's willing them to stay put. "We were just roughhousing, like we always did. It was nothing. I got him in a headlock, then I..." His breathing goes ragged. "I didn't know. Didn't realize what I was doing. I guess I held on too long. We were just having fun, I swear. I didn't mean to..."

The picture swarms in my head, making me dizzy. A pair of boys laughing as they wrestle, like they always do. Simon getting a hold of Thomas's neck. Squeezing too hard. Thomas beating at his shoulders, trying to tell him something is wrong. Simon thinking it's just part of their game. Thomas's lips turning blue. Simon not being able to tell from behind.

Simon blanches, and I watch as he tugs Michael further away from the edge.

"It wasn't your fault," I tell Simon. "It couldn't have been your fault."

Simon stares at me blankly. "Tell Victor that."

"Does he know?" I ask.

"None of them can know," says Nettle.

"Simon," I say, breathlessly. I hate to feel relieved at this news. In fact, I feel sick, but it's not as if this misunderstanding can't be resolved. "I know you didn't mean to. I know you. I promise I won't tell the other boys. Not unless you ask me to. You don't deserve for them to hate you."

He just stares at me blankly, like he's not processing what I'm saying.

"The rest of Peter's journal," I say. "Remember what I told you on the beach? Each of you were destined to meet terrible fates, too early. Too young. Before you came to Neverland, you were supposed to die of the plague. Peter worried that, even though you escaped death once, fate might still find you here. It wasn't you, Simon. It was an accident. Thomas's fate, come to get him. There's nothing you could have done."

I expect a reaction from Simon. Signs that he's struggling with relief and guilt, something. But he just keeps staring at me with mournful eyes, and says, "Oh, Winds."

I glance back and forth between him and Nettle. "You don't understand," I say. "Simon's not a killer. Neither of you are."

Nettle shakes his head. "That, Wendy, is where you're wrong. I'm afraid you're the one who doesn't understand."

I shake my head. "No, Simon. You've just gone through something traumatic. And Nettle, you lost your friend. But there's help, I promise. The two of you are good kids." Except they lost more than one friend, my mind reminds me. But I'm scared to ask what happened to Freckles and Joel.

Simon sobs. Nettle doesn't. He just lets out a wry laugh.

"Come on, Winds. Who told you that Neverland was created to keep the Lost Boys from suffering untimely deaths?"

"Peter," I say, who I now realize wasn't behind the death of Thomas at all. Meaning he was lying to the Sister about killing him. Who's to say he didn't lie about killing Freckles and Joel, too?

"Think, Wendy. Is that really what Peter said?"

I frown, crinkling my brow. "Of course. He told me the Sister came to take your lives early to keep you from suffering. To keep you from dying of the plague."

"Think. Did Peter ever say that? Did he ever say that we were going to die of *the* plague?"

I run back through my memories, siphoning through them.

She told me there was a plague within the walls of the orphanage, one that had already infected the boy. A disease that he'd already spread to some of the others.

"He said it was a plague. I assumed..." But that couldn't be right. "He had to have been talking about the plague. Neverland—it was made to keep you safe. It was made to protect you. All of you, from dying of the illness."

Simon squints, squeezing tears from his eyes as he rests his forehead in his hand. "No, Winds. No, it wasn't."

I turn slowly to Nettle, to Nettle, who remembers everything. He cranes his head at me, sympathy dousing his expression. "Think, Wendy. Did he tell you what the symptoms of this plague were?"

My mind goes wild, frantic, sure Peter told me of rotting limbs and rattling lungs and slow death. But there's nowhere for my flitting mind to perch. Victor said he'd woken in Neverland deathly ill, that all of them had.

I'm about to mention as much when Nettle interrupts my racing thoughts. "Neverland wasn't made for keeping our fates out, Wendy. It was made to keep us in. Neverland isn't a haven. It's a prison."

MY MIND GOES BLANK, whirring.

"A prison. You're just..." Children is what I mean to say, though they're not much younger than I am. And when I look at Simon, I don't see a child. I see a young man carrying a secret heavy enough to crush him.

But then it hits me—the story of the three Sisters. The Middle Sister's job had been to dispose of evildoers before they could reap great harm in their realms. "The Sister who came to kill you...it wasn't the Youngest Sister, taking pity on you. It was the Middle Sister," I say, my words croaking in my throat. "She didn't come to spare you from an awful death. She came to stop you before..." I whip my head to Simon. "But she made a mistake. She was only supposed to take the worst of murderers. You didn't mean to kill Thomas."

"I didn't," says Simon. "But afterward." He won't look at me. Instead, he just stares at Michael. "I liked it. I was horrified, yes. But after it happened, I kept reliving how it felt when that last breath escaped his lungs. Kept wishing I'd known what was happening then, so I could have known to relish that moment."

My heart goes cold.

"I hate myself for it. I promise I do, Winds."

"Simon. Simon, you need help. There's help…" I want to tell him of the doctors back home who assisted the ill with things like this. "You're sick. You didn't mean to."

But even as the words come out, they sound less and less convincing.

"The shadows will tell you, you know. If you listen. If you don't block them out," says Nettle.

"You're a shadow-soother, too?" I ask.

"Must not be as good of a one as you," he says. "Peter never dosed me half as much as he did you. Never dosed any of us like he did you."

My heart goes cold in my chest. "The shadows were torturing me."

"Yeah, the truth has a tendency of doing that sometimes," he says, then looks casually out into the distance. "I couldn't sleep that night —the night the Sister visited us. I heard the whole thing, you know. Didn't remember, of course, once I got to Neverland. The Sister wiped our memories once we got here—the spell made us sick for weeks." I think back to the illness Victor recounted upon his arrival. Nettle continues, "But one day I stopped eating the onions. You know, I never did like onions. Not even before. Too bitter. Started giving my portion to Simon when Peter wasn't looking. I adored Peter as much as the next Lost Boy, but the texture made me gag. That's when the shadows started whispering to me. That's why Peter gave us the onions—there's something wrong with them, something that makes it so that we can't hear the shadows when they're in our system."

I rifle through memories, trying to reconcile Nettle's claim about the onions with my encounters with the shadows. I've been eating the onions throughout my time in Neverland, yet they've still been able to reach me, except for when I've taken the faerie dust. And the second time Tink attacked me.

Peter made it seem like my ability to see the shadows was unique, but if Nettle can see them too...

I don't get the chance to finish that thought, because Nettle's not done. "But even though my mind didn't remember what happened before Neverland, my shadow did. I was so upset the night the Fate came to visit the orphanage, so terrified, my shadow drank the memory, drank up my pain. It remembered it so that I didn't have to. Then it told me the truth."

I blink back tears. "What's the truth, Nettle?"

"She was going to kill all of us that night. You see, that orphanage was the special sort. The kind for boys who demonstrated abnormal behaviors, according to the alienists. There were doctors there who were supposed to help us, but most of the time they either beat us when the lights were on or crawled into our beds when the lights were off. The warden was the worst of them. Always said the human touch had healing properties. That it was medicine all in itself.

"We went into that orphanage as freaks, every last one of us, but by the time they were done with us, we were killers. Not technically. None of us had any blood on our hands, but it was in our hearts. One night, I told Thomas what the warden did to me after the lights were off. After everyone else went to sleep. He said the warden did the same to him. So we decided just how we'd kill him. How we'd chop off his privates first, while he was awake, then we'd hack off the rest of him bit by bit, just like he'd done to our souls over the years.

"Except the night the Fate came, I realized that wasn't all Thomas had planned. He was angry, you see, that none of the other staff had come to save him in the night. I understood, of course. I hated the staff as much as him, but there were those who I don't think had a clue what was going on. But he wasn't just angry with them. He was angry with the other boys, too. For not waking up in the night and hearing what was being done to him. For waking up, and being too scared to do anything. Thomas was angry at the world, angry at our parents for letting the shrinks convince them to take us away. He hated everyone, everyone except Victor. And his father, who hadn't consented to the boys' being committed to the orphanage. You see, Thomas didn't just want the warden. He wanted everyone. Everyone who had ever made a decision that led us into danger, whether they knew what they were doing or not. Whether they'd been tricked and lied to or not."

My heart shivers. I remember asking Peter if Thomas had been the first boy the Sister intended to kill.

"Do you know what would have happened, Wendy, had the Sister not intervened that night?"

I open my mouth; the only sound I can manage is hardly audible over the howling wind that pierces the night.

"*Do you know what would have happened?*" Nettle is yelling now, his voice breaking over the wind.

"No. I don't—" I don't want to know, but I stop myself, seeing the desperation in Simon's eyes. I'm afraid if I shield myself from anything at this point, he'll see it as a sign that I'm shielding myself from him. "I don't know."

"It was written in the tapestry, no matter how many times the Middle Sister tried to undo it. I was going to help Thomas butcher the warden. But it wasn't going to stop there. Thomas had our files, each and every one of them, underneath his bed. Thomas had the names of our parents, their addresses, our siblings even. Every person who knew they were sending us away. Every person who could have raised their voice to stop it. He was going to have us butcher them all.

"He'd already started recruiting them. I didn't even know it at the time," says Nettle. "I thought our plan to take down the warden was the only one, but he'd already planted seeds in the minds of the other boys. All but Peter, who was on staff at that point. He wanted to kill Peter too, for knowing what they did to us at that orphanage, and choosing to come back and work there. The things he was going to convince us to do, Wendy…"

"Peter brought you here, convinced the Sister to extract you from your realm to keep you from becoming killers? To give you a chance at a life where you could remain innocent?" I ask.

"*Innocent* is rather subjective," scoffs Nettle. "Hard to be innocent when someone's held you to your bed in the middle of the night while your friends are trying to pretend they're asleep."

"You were innocent, though. Even if you didn't feel it. You didn't do anything wrong," I insist.

Nettle's shaking now. "I hate that Sister. She came for us too late. If she really wanted us to stay innocent, she would have slit our throats in the middle of the night before we ever set foot in that wretched place."

My words of comfort get hung up in my throat. For some reason, they don't feel appropriate. Instead, I say, "I thought Peter was supposed to end you when you came of age, but that wasn't it at all. He was supposed to kill you if you showed signs of becoming murderers."

Nettle nods, then swallows. "He was never going to be able to do it, though."

My mind goes to Joel. Of him coaxing a rat into the fire.

A stone forms in my belly.

"You didn't tell me it was all Thomas's idea," whispers Simon to Nettle. "You said we were all going to grow up to slaughter our parents. But all this time, he was the one who was going to put our hands to the hilt."

"He was hardly going to have to," Nettle insists. "Thomas, Benjamin, and Smalls were going to die the week of the massacre, after the guard rounded them up and caught them. Joel was going to hang a week later. Simon here was going to run off to Estelle and stalk whores in the night, never to be caught. I—" Nettle stops, steeling himself.

My heart thuds as I watch realization click into place behind Simon's eyes. "Ironic that Thomas was the one to die first."

No. "Your memories were wiped in the hopes that none of you would remember the atrocities you suffered before," I say. "So none of you would remember what had driven you to plot against your family, your town. Peter was trying to cure you."

Nettle's eyes are glowing with rage now. I can't help but notice the way his grip tightens on my brother, John's head slumped to the side. "You can wipe someone's mind, but you can't wipe someone's soul. It's like trying to yank a fishing hook out of your flesh once it's already wrapped around a tendon. You can't rip that out without losing something else in the process."

"You knew, somehow," says Simon, his gaze blank as he stares at Nettle. "You knew it was me who killed Thomas. I thought it was because you could see it in my eyes, see through my grief. I thought it was because you remembered something about me, something from before. Something that made me a killer through and through. You came to me afterward and told me you could help me. That you could protect me. Keep me from hurting anyone else. I was so sure I was a monster, I never stopped to question how you knew."

My heart stops in my chest. "Thomas's death wasn't an accident, was it?"

Nettle's rage is visceral now, reddening his features. "Peter and the Sister might have wiped Thomas's memories, but they couldn't wipe what was in his heart. You can't just fix someone like that, someone like him."

My mind goes back to the picture, the happy-go-lucky smiling boy on the parchment. Is it true that a darkness lurked beneath the surface, unable to be expunged?

"Clearly he and Victor were close," I say. "It's not as if he wasn't capable of loving."

"He wasn't healed. Like I said, it's not possible to fix someone like Thomas. He came out of the womb with some part of his soul missing. One day, he was going to snap, and then he was going to kill us all."

"You told Thomas what you remembered," I say.

Nettle rolls his eyes. "I gave Thomas the chance to repent. A chance to convince me he'd changed. He denied having those inclinations."

"That's because he didn't *remember*," I say, exasperation slipping into my tone. "That's why he started asking Peter questions. You frightened him, and he wanted to know if you were telling the truth."

"Whether he remembered or not is of no consequence. The point is that he was hiding his inclinations, refusing to admit to them. He knew he was a monster, yet he wouldn't let me help him. Besides, he kept telling everyone that I was lying about remembering our pasts. Trying to undermine me in case I ever thought it prudent to tell them about the freak living in their midst. He did such a swell job of making me look like a sniveling idiot grasping for attention, even Peter didn't take it seriously. Of course, then when you got here and started asking about what I remembered, I had to think fast. I'd heard Michael singing that nursery rhyme, so I knew if I referenced it, you'd recognize the details and think I was confused."

"How did you do it?" Simon asks, eyes glassed over. "How did you kill Thomas?"

"Rushweed," I answer for Nettle, realization washing over me. "He dosed Thomas with rushweed before you and he wrestled. Made it look like an accident. Knew you'd choke him from watching you wrestle all the other times." Victor's warning when he gifted me the pouch of rushweed after Tink's first attack returns to my mind. "If you steep it, the effect is delayed, but it's dangerous because it can cause breathing difficulty with exertion. Nettle slipped it into Thomas's tea. The exertion of wrestling must have activated the rushweed. His muscles would have gone limp. He wasn't able to tap on your arm and tell you he couldn't breathe."

Simon gags. "You. You made me kill my friend. You made me like it."

"Better he ruin one of us than all of us," says Nettle. "We all have it in us, somewhere—that craving for blood. The inclination to take our pain out on something living. It's tattooed on our souls. You're the purest of us, Simon. It had to be you. I knew you'd be the only one who could handle it. Who could learn to get the cravings under control."

Simon's shaking now.

"Simon, please," I say. "Please bring Michael over here to me."

Simon doesn't appear to hear me. "You made me a killer."

"But I didn't make you like it. That was all you, Simon. Can't you see, Wendy, why someone needed to step in?"

I feel as if I'm going to be sick. "You knew Joel tortured animals sometimes. You told me in the kitchen that night that Peter had relocated him to the garden."

"You have to know it's a sign of an imbalanced mind," says Nettle, then he stares sadly down at John. "As is the ability to chop off one's own finger."

My heart stops. "What? No, John did that to get into the reaping tree."

"You really think that's the case?" Nettle says. "It's not natural, Wendy, to harm oneself. You shouldn't be able to make your mind do it. None of us who end up in this place are natural. Besides, I overheard what he said in the bathroom about wanting to take vengeance out on the man who killed your parents. He's going to trigger that vile part of himself someday, if he hasn't already."

"Nettle," I say, trying to keep my voice steady. I reach my palms out in an appeasing gesture, but Nettle shakes his head, and I bring them back to my sides, fisted. "John came here because of me. No Fate came to get him. I made a bargain with Peter to bring him and Michael along. They're here because of me, not because of some Fate. Not because of anything to do with them."

"No one just comes here, Wendy. Not even you. Did you think we wouldn't notice you wandering off? Did you think we couldn't see it in your eyes? Your pupils—they were pits by the time you came back from your little excursion the night Joel died. We see the effect the faerie dust has on you. It's only a matter of time."

My breath fogs the dark, moonlit air in front of me. "Only a matter of time until what?"

"Until John's a killer like the rest of us. You. Me. Simon. You think the way you stabbed that man was normal? I saw the wound. That wasn't the kind of blow you administer in self-defense. There's a rage inside of you, Wendy. One that you don't often let out, but when you do..." Nettle whistles.

"No," I say, shaking my head. "I didn't know. I didn't know he was innocent. He was coming after Peter. There's so much I didn't know."

"Did it stop you from liking it?" asks Simon, his voice dry. "When you let him fall to the ground, did you like it?"

"Simon." I blink back tears. I open my mouth to say of course not. That killing that man has been haunting me since the moment I took his life. It's all true, but Simon's eyes are begging me to be like him. Like he sees some purity in me, and he's thinking if perhaps I could struggle with the same brand of darkness, he could glimpse a light in himself as well. And then I hear John's voice, echoing the same sentiment. Wondering if it felt good, cathartic.

I swallow any words of reassurance, and something like a shadow overcomes Simon's face.

"You know we're right," says Nettle. "You know there's evil in your brother, just like the rest of us."

"There's evil in all of us," I say. "There's evil in the people back home." I think of my suitors in the parlor. Of my mother, who left me in there with them. Of the creature who dwells within Peter. Of Captain Astor, who for all his cruelty, cherished his wife so dearly. "That doesn't make us special."

"No," says Nettle. "No, it doesn't. But it does make us dangerous."

"What are you going to do?" I ask, dreading the fact that I think I already know.

Nettle glances at Simon, like he thinks he'll be able to console me better. Simon barely looks at me. "Peter was supposed to take us out if we started showing signs of going down that path. So far, he hasn't. We worry he's grown too attached."

"So the two of you have taken it upon yourselves?" I ask. "That's why you killed Joel."

"You saw him with those innocent animals, Wendy."

Salty tears sting at my eyes. "Joel needed help. He hadn't killed anyone yet."

"It was only a matter of time."

"Of course it was only a matter of time," I snap. "He was tortured, abused. Broken as a child. And then he had even the memory of that taken away from him. You said yourself that the memories couldn't take away the damage that had been done. The body remembers that sort of thing, even if the mind doesn't. Joel needed help, and the two of you stalked him down in the night and killed him."

Simon shakes his head. "I didn't hurt Joel." I can't help but notice he says nothing about Freckles. I consider how sick Simon was the day he came to tell Peter about Freckles's death. How he kept having to take breaks to vomit in the woods.

Nettle offers him a withering look. "As if you didn't know I did it. You're as complicit as I am. So is Wendy. You sure did make it easy, luring him out into the open while you were high as the rafters in this storehouse."

The words stab at my chest, but all it does is make me crave more, more, more. Behind Nettle and John is the shed, and within it, I can hear the faerie dust whispering to me, promising me.

I can take away your pain.

I should have trusted Peter. Should have come to him about the journal and had him explain. Should have trusted my Mate.

Darling, oh so trusting. For some reason, I hear the sentiment in Captain Astor's voice. *Trusting, except for the one time it actually counts.*

"And Freckles?" My voice warbles. I imagine them luring him out to the cove, far enough away that no one would hear his screams. Was it Nettle who drove the dagger into his belly, ruthless and vindictive, or Simon, apologizing to Freckles for what had to be done?

Nettle's blade quavers. "Freckles's response to Thomas's death was unnatural. He didn't care like the rest of the Lost Boys. It was almost like he was glad Thomas was gone."

"*You* were glad to be rid of Thomas!" I practically scream.

Nettle shakes his head slowly. Like he feels sorry for me. "I did what was necessary. I bore that burden for everyone else. For Freckles to be pleased about his friend's murder just because he was jealous of the attention everyone gave Thomas… You can't tell me that wasn't a sign of something sinister."

I can hardly breathe, hardly address Nettle's way of thinking. Instead I ask, "What if we can keep the other boys out of trouble? What if we can keep them from showing signs of murder? I'm sure there's something to be done."

Nettle shrugs. "It's our fate, Wendy. Did you escape yours?"

Panic floods me. There's no reasoning with Nettle, and the knife in his hand flashes at John's throat. Still, he could have killed John immediately, but he didn't. He wanted to explain himself to me. Needed to explain himself to me.

Wendy Darling, an expert at making others feel heard. Just a mirror, showing people the parts of themselves they'd like to see. Never my own person.

I've always hated that quality of mine, but now that I'm face to face with John's potential murderer, I realize something.

Mirrors can be sharp, too, when they're already broken.

I nod, gulping, and then I do what I do best. "It was cruel of the Sister to trap you here. Cruel of her to give Peter hope for you, when she knew all along this was inevitable."

Nettle blinks, surprise overtaking his face. "I don't blame Peter," is all he says.

I shake my head. "I know you don't. How could you? How could any of us? He's only been trying to protect us from ourselves."

"He likes to pretend that everything is happy. That everything is okay. He's wrong, but it was nice getting to pretend for a while, wasn't it?" says Nettle. "But now that I know the truth, I can't go back to pretending."

"I know. I know you can't."

And then I let my voice shake. Let it rattle in anger. "The Sister should have let Peter take the rest of you. Should have killed Thomas in his bed. He was the one that was the true threat. None of this would have happened if it weren't for him."

"It was his idea the whole time. He was the one who planted it," says Nettle. "And once that seed took hold, got its roots in me, I couldn't yank it out, no matter how hard I tried. I never wanted to thirst for blood. I never wanted any of this. I never..." The muscles in his neck flex as he wrestles with the words. "I never wanted to have to hurt my friends. They're my friends. You know that, Winds."

"I know," I whisper.

I'm halfway across the cliff now, my hand outstretched slightly, hoping Nettle will welcome my embrace. He's just a boy, after all. A boy who never had anyone hold him just for the sake of keeping him safe. Even now, with all he's done, though the dread of him makes my skin crawl, pity wells up within my stomach.

And for a moment, I think it's going to work. But then Nettle squints, locking his eyes onto mine. Pleading.

It's a look begging for forgiveness. Forgiveness I'm not going to be willing to offer.

"I won't hurt Michael," he promises. "He's innocent. And Peter will take care of him. You and I both know that. He'll be safe, and none of us will ever corrupt him."

"Nettle, please. No one has to be corrupted."

"Maybe that was true once," he says. "But not anymore."

His hands tremble, and I lunge.

There's a moment when everything slows down, though not to a halt as it should. I watch as blood beads on John's skin as Nettle presses the blade to his throat. Self-loathing warps Nettle's face, but it does nothing to curb his impulses.

He felt the urge to kill, so he found a way to justify it. A way to make it righteous.

The scream is on the cusp of my throat as Nettle's hand flexes, as he begins to slide the blade across John's throat. My hand is outstretched, but I'm not going to reach him in time.

But then the knife falls, clattering against the rock beneath. John's limp but unharmed body is next, the grass softening the impact of his head against the ground.

Nettle is shaking, a gargling sound scraping from his throat. He stares down at his ribs. At the dagger hilt protruding from his side.

"Oh, thank the Sisters," he says, and the desperate relief in Nettle's voice rattles me to my core.

Behind him stands Simon, his hands red with Nettle's blood. His face is blank as he drives the hilt in further, sending Nettle to his knees.

When Nettle falls face-first onto the grass, Simon takes a sharp inhale, then slowly looks up at me. "He made me believe I killed Thomas," he says, as if the blood on his hands needs explaining. As if I walked in on the blood-spattered aftermath of a crime, rather than witnessing the whole thing.

"I know," is all I say.

"Careful, Michael, or you're sure to fall." Our necks snap to the side, Michael's voice summoning us out of the moment.

My legs break into a run, a mad dash for my little brother, whose voice has heightened in pitch after watching Nettle bleed out. He's at the edge of the cliff, kicking stones and watching the crumble of dirt and debris fall into the crashing sea below.

But the cliffs aren't prepared for my brother's weight. Or maybe they are, and the sea is simply hungry, the cliffs executing the sea's bidding. Because the edge of the cliff collapses underneath my brother's feet.

I hurtle myself across the grass, flinging my hand at his ankle. My fingers brush the heel of his boot.

And then Michael slips away.

I'm sure I scream. At least, my mouth opens and air whooshes through my throat, but it's caught up in the wind, which carries away my scream like I don't deserve the catharsis of agony.

Because I let my brother fall.

I did this, in alerting Simon. In trying to rescue all of them, I failed my brother, who it was my job to protect.

No. No, no, no.

I'd distracted Nettle long enough for Simon to sneak up on him, and I'd traded one brother for the other.

Soft dirt scrapes underneath my fingernails, causing a shooting pain as I drag myself to the edge of the cliffside. The idea of looking makes me want to vomit, but I have to. Can't bear the idea of not honoring Michael by sheltering myself from the evidence of my failure.

I hope he passed out on the way down.

I hope he flew higher than the faerie dust ever took me.

Foaming, angry waves lash up against the cliffside, obscuring the surface of the water in a foggy haze. I try not to imagine the waves beating my brother's body against the shore, but refusing to imagine it feels like refusing to be there with him in his pain. But then, a dark form appears from the mist, a shadow from my memories.

A shadow with wings.

My hands somehow find my mouth as I choke out a sob, throat burning. I watch in trepidation and hope and agonizing fear as the shadow takes form below, as it soars upward out of the fog, shooting past the edge of the cliff and into the sky.

Peter lets his wings relax, and floats ever so gently in front of me, his blue eyes flickering with a fierceness I've yet to see.

In his arms is Michael.

My brother is whispering, "Do you want to do it again?"

CHAPTER 50

*I*n the end, we bury Nettle in a grave that's deep enough for the worms not to get him.

Or, at least deep enough so that we don't have to acknowledge them.

Tears stream down Simon's face as he does it, and I can't help but stare at him. As I watch him take clods of dirt and earth and cover the boy he murdered, the boy who turned him into a murderer, I marvel at how Simon has changed so much in such a short time.

When I first arrived, Simon was all smiles and laughter. Would do anything to cheer me up when I thought my worst nightmare had come true by being brought to Neverland.

Now there's none of that person left. Only agony and grief, and a potent self-loathing I can almost smell.

Except...that's not right. This is the same Simon I met my first day here. That Simon had already strangled his friend. The boy who had nudged me and flirted with me and teased me had already gotten a taste for murder, already wrestled with his craving for taking lives.

I wonder then how often the people whose smiles wash away

our pain are only masking their own, overexerting themselves to make sure everyone else is okay, when inside, they're withering away while no one else notices, too caught up in their own problems.

"I'm sorry, Simon," I say, placing my hand on his shoulder as Peter watches over John and Michael.

"For what." Not a question as much as a resignation.

"For not seeing. For not noticing."

Simon doesn't look at me. He just pauses for a moment, as if he too has a blade lodged in his ribcage. "Don't worry about it, Winds," he says.

Then he goes back to digging.

My heart aches for my friend, anxiety welling in my stomach. I'm still not sure what Peter will do with him now that we know he was complicit in the murders. Part of me wishes to keep that to myself, but hiding the truth seems like the worst thing possible for Simon right now.

Seems like it's been the worst thing for all of us.

When the grave is done, I meander back to Peter's side. He's leaning over John, whom we've spread across the grass.

"He hasn't quite woken up yet," says Peter. "He was dosed pretty heavily with somnium oil. Might be a few days before he comes to."

Anxiety stirs in my chest. "But he will wake up, won't he?"

Peter turns to me and nods. "He'll wake up. I'll make sure of it."

Anxiety still prickles at my insides, but there's something about Peter's words that makes them seem even more trustworthy than they did before. Despite not telling me that Neverland was a prison, I know he only kept it to himself to protect the boys. To keep any of them from turning out like Nettle.

"What happened tonight, Wendy?" Peter asks, landing his sparkling blue eyes on me.

I glance up at Michael.

"Do you think he'd understand if he overheard?" Peter asks.

"I'm never sure what he understands," I say. "Sometimes I think it's quite a bit more than we give him credit for."

Peter nods, then reaches into his satchel. At first I think he's going for faerie dust, and my heart gives a little lurch. But then he pulls out a set of earmuffs and puts them on Michael's head. At first I think Michael will shake them off, but his face goes slack with peace as the muffs block out the wind. He actually lies on his back, still for a while, staring up at the stars.

"He never does that," I say. "Stays still like that."

"Maybe he's chasing something the rest of us can't hear," says Peter, softly. His words tug on the knots in my belly. There's no way Peter just happened to have earmuffs on hand.

"You made them especially for him?" I say.

Peter scratches his head. "I might have borrowed them from a wealthy family from another realm. I assure you they had plenty to spare."

We sit in silence for a while as Simon continues digging Nettle's grave.

"You're not going to ask me why I poisoned you?" I ask.

"I'm considering whether I want to know."

I bite my lip. "You mean you already know, and you'd rather me not confirm it."

Peter sighs, running his hand through his hair.

So I tell him. I tell him of the horrors I found in his journal. Of the assumptions I'd made about him murdering the boys. How those assumptions had been confirmed by Peter's conversation with the Sister. I tell him of Nettle's aversion to the onions, of how the shadows whispered to him, of his plot to kill Thomas and make Simon believe it was his fault. When I get to the part about Freckles's death, I pause.

"Which one of them did it?" Peter asks.

I bite my lip. "They never said. But I have my suspicions." I consider the pieces of the puzzle that never quite fit—the carving of the fox into Freckles's cheek, the singeing of his hair. The way someone removed Joel's pinkie.

Clearly, someone was trying, not only to tell us the murders were connected, but to warn us of the next victim. Freckles's hair was singed, the scent reminiscent of Joel's from how he used to coax rats into the fire. And Joel's pinkie—that was clearly meant to indicate John as the next victim.

Like one of the killers wanted to be caught.

It would explain why there was nothing on Thomas's body predicting Freckles's death if Simon didn't know about Nettle's schemes until after Thomas's corpse was discovered. But did he participate in the murders, or did he leave his clues on the victims' bodies afterward?

We both stare at Simon for a while, contemplating.

"What are you going to do to him?" I ask, softly, walking my fingers through the grass and interlacing them with Peter's. It's a plea, really. One on Simon's behalf.

Peter doesn't answer me. He just stares straight ahead, a blankness on his face.

"Peter." It's not as much of a question as it is a plea.

"None of this would have happened if I hadn't insisted the Sister let us bring Thomas with us," he says. "Originally, she offered to let me take the other boys, but she wanted Thomas for herself. Said he was destined to cause bloodshed, no matter where he ended up."

I squeeze Peter's hand. "She was wrong. You see that, right?"

Peter turns and looks at me, face blank. "All I see is a pool of blood. An abundance of death, following these boys wherever they go."

I shake my head. "But none of it by Thomas's hands. You gave that back to Thomas. His innocence. You took him out of that wretched place, and he became something different. You set him free."

"And now he's dead. And so are Freckles and Joel and Nettle. And Simon—"

"You don't have to hurt him, Peter," I say. "He was manipulated. Nettle tricked him into believing he was a murderer, until he was. I know you meant well, but it's not good for them—not remembering. You only wanted to shield them from pain, but they still feel it, every last one of them. I've seen the shadows beneath their eyes, the way some of them cry without knowing why. Their past is affecting them, whether they remember it or not. The Lost Boys need the truth, difficult as it is to bear."

Peter turns to me. "And the truth about Simon? That he killed some of them? How do you think they're going to handle that? You didn't see them, Wendy. You didn't see the murder in their eyes back at the orphanage. You think you see the shadows now, but the hate that festered in their souls... If you want to tell them the truth, it won't protect Simon."

"So what are you going to do, then?" I ask.

Peter doesn't answer.

"What are you going to do with him?"

"I don't know yet."

Panic whirls in me. "I know you're supposed to dispose of them. I know..." I sigh, slipping my hand into my pocket and removing the journal. I've already told him that I read it, but there's something about showing it to him that feels even more invasive. Peter stares down at it, and where I expect to see anger, I find nothing.

"How much of it did you read?"

"Enough to know that the Sister will expect you to kill Simon for what he did. Enough to know that's why she gifted you with your shadow magic. So you could do what needs to be done."

Peter glances down at the ground and fiddles with a blade of grass.

"You don't have to obey her, you know," I say.

"She's my master. You know that as well as anyone. You've seen what she can do to me. How she can make me kneel."

"But you defied her already."

His brow raises. "Did I?"

"You didn't kill Thomas."

Peter sighs. "Thomas wasn't showing signs of murder when he died. He died because of what Nettle remembered from his past. I wasn't required to end Thomas."

I bite my lip. "Joel—surely you knew what he was capable of. You'd seen him torturing the animals. You didn't kill him, though."

"Didn't have to. Nettle did that for me."

"Exactly. Nettle, not Simon."

Peter cocks his head to the side. "Wendy."

"But there's got to be something you can do. You even went as far as making the Sister believe you killed them." I fidget my toes in the earth, thinking. "Because you were afraid if she knew one of the Lost Boys was on a killing spree, she'd kill all of them. You've already defied her and won. Can't you see that? Didn't you say that she can't see everything in those tapestries of hers?"

Peter's smile doesn't reach his eyes. "I'll try to think of something."

"Promise?" I ask.

He squeezes my hand. "I promise I'll try."

I nod, holding onto that promise with all my heart. "Why didn't you tell me this was a prison?"

"Because I didn't want you to be afraid of them. I didn't want you to see them any other way than how I see them."

I frown, brushing the hair from Peter's face. "And what if the way you choose to see things is flawed? What if refusing to acknowledge the flaws of others hurts them worse in the end?"

Peter actually smiles at that. "Then I suppose it's a good thing I have you to help me see."

"Your secrets don't protect us..." I say, tears stinging at my eyes. "You were dosing the onions with faerie dust, weren't you? To keep the boys from seeing the shadows?"

Peter blinks. "Yes. Well, no. Not exactly. But I mixed faerie dust into the soil."

"Why not do that with all the vegetables?"

Peter grimaces. "Onions are best for obscuring the taste."

"You said I was a shadow-soother, but that's not all that special, is it? Otherwise you wouldn't have worried about dosing the Lost Boys."

"The Lost Boys are...well, let's just say the fact that they can shadow-soothe and also be accepted by the reaping tree...it's not a coincidence."

My chest goes numb. "Because there's something missing in us."

Peter avoids addressing that inference. Instead he says, "I still can't quite understand why the shadows' affinity for you is so strong. Few fae can communicate with them. With humans, it's almost unheard of. Like I said, you likely have fae blood in your heritage, but that shouldn't be enough."

"Or explain why the onions didn't work on me."

Peter shakes his head. "No, it doesn't. For some reason, you needed something stronger."

"Do you think John and Michael are shadow-soothers?"

Peter stares at the ground in front of him. "I don't know."

I bite my lip. I don't think I'm ready to consider what this might mean for my brothers anyway. So I change the subject. "How did you know where to find us tonight?"

He cranes his chin down, giving me a knowing look. "After you poisoned me, it wasn't too far of a stretch to assume you'd be trying to escape. That you'd need faerie dust to do it, more than you already had, assuming you'd try to take all the boys with you. Once the poison worked its way through my system, I came straight here."

I frown, wondering why Peter's body was able to flush the poison so much faster than Captain Astor's. Perhaps it has to do with his shadow magic. "So you came to steal us back?"

"I came to beg you to stay."

His dark lashes falter a bit as his eyes droop, taking in my face, scanning my Mating Mark. "I can't do this without you, Wendy. Tonight made that plenty evident. I can't see what you see. Feel what you feel. There's something in me that's missing, and it leaves these boys vulnerable."

I hesitate. "Your shadow form?"

Peter blanches. "It amplifies the worst parts of me, yes."

"So you could kill the boys if it came down to that."

Peter's gaze goes glassy, and he stares off into the distance. We're going to have to discuss this at some point. As much as I care for Peter, the way he acted toward me in the tunnels chills my bones.

Knowing that darkness dwells inside him...it doesn't change the way I feel about him, but I'd be a fool not to be wary.

Still, he's lost one of his own tonight, and I'm too empty to confront him about it at the moment. Instead, I venture a different direction. "That's why you came for me? Because you need my help?"

"I came because I need you. You asked me before why I didn't tell you about the Mating Mark." He runs his hand through my hair, tucking it behind my ear. "Remember what it was like the first time you flew in my arms? That terror, that exhilaration that seeps down your legs, making them so weak you feel as if they'll no longer function once you're back on the ground? I could get drunk on that feeling, Wendy Darling. But I'm not like you. I don't like to fall. Ever since your hand brushed mine in that clock tower, I've known you were going to be the highest high I'd ever reach. That once I got a taste of you..." He trails off, peering down the cliffs into the raging sea below. "Well. We always have to come back down eventually, don't we? I didn't tell you because I didn't want to acknowledge it myself. Didn't want anyone else to have that kind of power over me. But I can't ignore it anymore. I'm afraid I don't possess that sort of self-control."

His gaze dips, lingering on my mouth. "Legend has it that when the Fates weave Mates," Peter says, trailing his finger down the mark on my face, feeling its every ripple and fold, "they wind the two from the same thread, splitting it down the middle. That neither are whole until they find one another."

"But they don't always find each other," I say. "I thought it was rare."

Peter's eyes glint with mischief. "That, Wendy Darling, is where your history books told you wrong. Mates always find one another." My heart races underneath his touch as he cups my chin with his knuckle. "They can't help themselves," he whispers. "The draw is too intense. They belong to each other the same way a heart belongs to the ribcage, a root belongs to the tree. One cannot function without the other."

"If we can't help ourselves, you'd think you wouldn't have been able to keep it in that we're Mates," I say, that single doubt robbing me from the thrill of sinking into the moment with him.

"I already told you; I didn't want to frighten you."

My heart is hammering. "Why did you think that would frighten me?"

A mischievous smile curves on Peter's lips. "Because, Wendy Darling, you don't think it would have terrified you to know that you belong to me?"

"And if I still want to leave?" I ask. "If I don't want to keep my brothers somewhere they'll always be in danger?"

Peter lets out a breath. "Then I guess I'll just have to pretend the part of my soul you take with you never existed."

I swallow. "But you'd let me go."

"Only if you wanted me to."

I trace my memories back to Victor's father, the man whose name I don't even know, can't even honor. "I killed an innocent man because of this." Absentmindedly, I trace my fingers over my Mating Mark. "Because of us."

Peter lets out a slow breath. "Thomas and Victor's father was imprisoned—debtor's prison, if you can believe it. Sentenced to ten years after he couldn't repay the debt he'd taken out to keep his family fed. When the doctors came to take Thomas and Victor away, he was the only one to protest, but he had no rights to them considering his sentence." Guilt pierces my gut, then snaps the hilt, leaving the blade in my flesh for good measure. This poor man's family had been ripped away from him, and I'd sentenced him to death without trial for trying to reunite them.

Peter continues, "Thomas used to send his father drawings. I think he was the only person in the world other than Victor that Thomas truly forgave."

"Before Neverland," I say. "Before he forgot."

Peter nods. "I didn't realize who he was until I saw Thomas's old drawing in your hand. Even then, I couldn't see what good it would do to tell you. Seemed the type of thing best left to ignorance."

Tears well up in my eyes, a question lingering there. How can I stay with Peter, knowing what my love for him does to me? What it does to others. But then my mind calls back to the night at the clock tower. "You said yourself in the clock tower I've always belonged to you. I think I've always known that."

And how can I be afraid of something that's always been true, something I've carried around with me in the pockets of my soul, knitted up inside me? We humans, we only fear the unknown. It's not in us to fear the present.

"The only thing I ever truly feared was not finding the broken piece of my soul," I say, blinking the tears away. "I don't ever want you to let me go."

In answer, he presses a claiming kiss to my lips. "Then I won't. I want you, Wendy Darling. More than I want to take my next breath."

His words send a shudder of delight through my bones, bringing tears to my eyes.

"If you'll stay with them for a while, I need to tend to Simon," says Peter softly as he pulls away.

"What are you going to do to him?" I ask, regretting the question as soon as I ask it.

Peter takes my cheek into his palm and presses a kiss on my forehead. "I'm going to fight for him."

CHAPTER 51

*I*t's half past the full moon the next evening when I'm finally able to slip out of bed and sneak to the cave by the shoreline. My limbs feel beaten down by the events of the night—the empty, weighted feeling of having watched both of my brothers fall into harm's way.

John slept the day away, his body still working through the somnium oil. I stayed by his side for hours. Occasionally, he flitted into consciousness, but only long enough to tell me he was sorry, though I can't imagine what for. Probably for not protecting me like he thinks is his responsibility.

Peter stayed busy today, warding off the Lost Boys' questions. He plans to tell them the truth once the shock of Nettle's death wears off. I'd feared this would only cause paranoia, but when Peter explained that the boys' heightened emotions might cause them to ostracize Simon, I'd had to agree that waiting was the best solution.

The events of last night wrestle with my weary muscles as I make my way to the cave. It's like my feet are sutured to the sand and my muscles themselves have withered away into nothing. Not only that, but something occurs to me when I reach the shoreline, when the foam of the tide sloshes against my feet.

Tink submerged me underneath these waves. But why halfway drown me, then let me go? I'd figured she'd just been bored. That watching the shadows chase me across the island had been a sort of sport.

But as the saltwater air stings my nostrils, a different narrative forms.

Tink had chosen to keep the shadows close. She'd denied Peter's help, refused to use his faerie dust to keep the shadows at bay.

The shadows had been quiet until Tink shoved me under the waves. Until the panic of drowning had brought them back. Maybe it was adrenaline flushing the faerie dust from my system; maybe the shadows simply grow louder when one comes close to death, but they'd swarmed me and then chased me straight to the grave of Victor's father, where I'd found Thomas's original sketch.

Had Tink wanted me to examine his body? Something about that idea fills me with unease, but I tell myself she probably just wanted me, Peter's fiancée, to know I murdered an innocent man.

By the time I reach the mouth of the cave, my heart is already pounding.

My mind soon flits to my anxious anticipation of seeing the captain. I've had to ward myself against his accusations in advance. *Told you the winged boy would get his hooks back into you,* he'll say.

I've mostly decided on short, careless retorts.

There's no use arguing with the captain. I don't have to explain myself to him, of all people. I'd made a mistake in refusing to trust Peter. That's all. And I certainly don't have the energy to tell him of Nettle's murderous heart, of Simon's pain.

I'm exhausted and weary and want nothing but to curl up in bed and let my body melt effortlessly into the sheets.

But the captain needs his dose, so here I am.

When I enter the mouth of the cave, I can't help but notice the way the water laps up, blocking my path slightly. Strange, the tide never comes in this far. As I wade up to my knees in the sloshing water, my heart stops.

Lantern light trembles against the back walls of the cave as I lift my arm, trying to get a good view of the inside.

The cave is covered in water.

Enough to douse my boots, my knees.

No.

Panic surges through me and I lunge, hardly keeping my wits about me. It's a stupid, foolish move, because the lantern goes sputtering out as soon as the flame touches the water, submerging me in darkness.

Still, I claw at the bottom of the cave, searching the water in panic.

No, no, no.

Salt sprays into my eyes as my fingers find no purchase other than the pebbles and grime that coat the bottom of the cave. I'm not sure what I'm hoping to find. For my fingers to brush against a familiar white tunic, the stubble of a beard that desperately needs to be shaved.

I tell myself I don't want him dead because he's the last chance I have of discovering the truth behind the deaths of my parents.

I tell myself Captain Astor deserved to drown.

So why do I dread my fingertips grazing bloated flesh? Why does a sob linger at the ready in my throat for the man responsible for the brutal murder of my parents?

No, no, no.

The wind howls outside, the storm reminding me who's to blame for taking the captain away from me. I'm about to give up when my flailing hand clasps against something behind me, underneath the water.

My stomach lurches at the feel of a hand, the brush of a ripple of skin I know so intimately because of how often I've touched the Mating Mark on my face.

No.

My stomach twists over, but then the hand contracts, gripping me tightly and pulling me backward. I go to scream, but the sound gets caught in my throat.

There's a moment when my body betrays me—when it interprets the feel of his arms clasped around me as finally being safe.

Then his hand clamps over my mouth, and the illusion bursts.

"I knew you were a Darling little liar," he whispers, the prickle of his beard scraping against my ear. "Worried I was dead? Worried you'd forgotten about me and let me drown? You are a forgetful little thing. I suppose I should count myself lucky that it slipped your mind to dose me last night."

A pit forms in my stomach. The captain's prediction still stings against my ear. *I'll see you when the winged boy has his claws in you again.* I'd left in a rage, which is exactly what he'd wanted, what he'd been trying to accomplish every time he provoked me—to rile me until I lost my wits, until I forgot to feed him his dose of rushweed.

"It's a good thing you did, too. Water was up to my mouth by the time I got enough strength back to claw myself up the side of that boulder you propped me against." His lips brush my ear, and my entire body shivers, but he only clutches me tighter, pulling me flush against his chest, my back turned to him.

I summon the courage to scream, but it's no good. Not with his fingers curved over my lips. Not with the wind howling. Not with the Den too far away for anyone to hear.

"Now's when you're supposed to fight back, Darling." The captain's voice is so silky that in any other context, I might have assumed he was speaking to a lover.

I kick and flail at him, but his grip holds steady, my human strength no match for him.

"I told you to fight back," he says, slipping his hand from my mouth, stroking my cheek like a dare.

Dread lances through me at the malice in his voice. "We both know it's not any use," I say, choking back tears.

"That does seem to be your anthem, doesn't it?" says the captain, but there's no amusement in his voice. "I've been waiting, you know. For you to slip up."

"I offered you a way out. I would have freed you," I say.

"Why make a bargain when I knew I could win my freedom

394

myself? Besides, Darling. Tell me, what were you coming back for? I thought you were going to get yourself and your brothers off this island."

My breath catches in my throat. "I don't have to explain myself to you."

"No, you certainly do not. Not when I already know you, your type. You're weak, always have been. How close did you get to your escape before he reeled you back in with pretty words? Tell me, Darling, could you taste the freedom on your lips, feel the sun of the real world painting your skin? Were you soaring when he shot you down? Or did you even make it that far?"

"Please. Please let me go," I say, my voice warbling, tears stinging at my eyes. I hate myself for crying, for melting in his arms, my limbs going as weak as his accusations suggest.

But I'm just so very tired.

"*Please?*" He spews the word like it disgusts him.

Then he throws me over his shoulder and carries me away.

CHAPTER 52

*W*ater sloshes against the captain's boots as he carries me out of the cave and across the beach. I bounce against his back, watching where his boots leave prints in the black sand.

Not that it matters. Once we slip through whatever gap in the Fabric Captain Astor entered through, it's not as if his footprints will do Peter much good. I struggle and wriggle against the captain's grip, his fae body hardly affected by the time I spent subtly starving him. Even beating against his firm back ends up being more humiliating than helpful. I'm like an infant, balling my fists in a struggle for power I'm years away from attaining.

So I stop.

I suppose that makes me weak, like the captain often accuses me of, but if these are to be my last moments in Neverland, I'd like to take the time to appreciate my home.

So I steady my labored, panicked breaths with the salty tang of the ocean air. Close my eyes and fill my lungs with its scent, make myself memorize the way it tingles in my nostrils and fills my exhausted body with life.

Then I open my eyes and start counting the pebbles, focusing in on their glossy sheen. My toes long to feel the weight of them pushing up against the soles of my feet, and I mourn the fact that I didn't linger to teeter on their unsteady surface before. Even the disgusting kelp with their glossy bulbs and monstrous tendrils catch my attention, beg me to mourn them.

Last of all, I crane my neck and glance toward the center of the island, where high above the canopy, one massive tree grows taller than the rest. I know I'm only fooling myself, but I try to imagine John and Michael racing to the top of it, waving to me from its branches, Michael chanting, "Last one to the top's dead meat."

I close my eyes again and imagine the earth beneath my racing feet. Let Michael's laughter echo through my skull. Soak in John's competitive grin, taunting me as we race through the woods. Just one last time.

And then I let myself think of Peter. Let myself wonder how long it will take him to find me, if there will be any of me left.

My mind conjures a shadowed pair of wings in the distance, just above the treetops. The figure curves, leaning in toward me.

Once we've traversed farther down the beach than I've ever been brave enough to venture, we reach a bay with sparkling blue water. The kind of cove that looks as if it belongs on a tropical beach, not a frigid place like Neverland.

The water glistens turquoise, drawing on the early morning light. Even the reflection from this stunning cove, ringed by a set of dark, sleek boulders, can't make the white fog dissipate.

But there's something that can.

Shadows cut through the fog, poisoning the white clouds with ink. At first, it looks as if I'm gazing upon an oil landscape onto which a child has taken a pen. But then the shadows begin to take shape, and something sharp pokes through the haze.

It's a woman, or rather, the shape of one. Except she has a tail instead of legs, and shadows for a braid. She's soaring through the air, too slowly to be natural, her body too still.

But then more shadows follow, and my eyes adjust to what they're seeing.

The massive hull of a ship breaks through the fog, a mermaid its figurehead. Though only the bow of the vessel is visible, it's enough for me to gape in awe at the size of it.

The wind blows, and the fog cuts away. The shadows remain.

The ship is impressive. Shadows swarm it, most of them condensing to form its solid shape, from its long, lithe hull to its mast that charges into the heavens. Darkness billows in the breeze, forming the shape of a black, unmarked sail.

"This is yours," I whisper, hardly able to contain the awe in my voice as I gape at the beautiful structure.

"Darling, meet the—" The captain halts, his shoulders trembling a bit. Maybe it's the exertion of carrying me all this way after being partially starved for so many days. Perhaps he feels for his ship the same way I feel for Peter, a massive hole in my chest at the idea of being separated.

From the deck of the ship, someone yells, waving both hands. My human ears can't detect what they're saying over the waves and wind, but soon other forms appear on the deck, peering over at their captain.

The captain lets out an audible sigh, and I realize the relief isn't for his ship as much as it is for his crew. "Entry to Neverland was a tad rocky," he explains. "We arrived in the midst of a storm. I stayed at the helm trying to man the ship and ended up getting thrown overboard."

"And your crew didn't bother to look for you?" I ask.

He grunts, amusement tingeing his voice. "I'm not fond of being rescued. They know that. They also knew my orders were to remain hidden in the fog offshore."

"And if you had died? Would they have waited for you forever?"

"They would have known if I was dead," is all he says.

I have little time to ponder his unsatisfactory answer, as something barrels into the captain's side.

The impact sends me careening toward the ocean. Sand smacks against my face, saltwater burning my nostrils as I inhale a mouthful. I come up from the water sputtering, but at least there are no shadows around keeping me from knowing which way is up.

Salt burns at my eyes, but I fight through the dizziness. Dizziness? I place my hand on my skull. When I pull it away, my palm is slick with blood. The sight makes me queasy, but I force myself to watch the scene unfolding ahead.

The captain is upright, but he's fighting off his attacker with bare hands, weaponless.

The attacker has wings.

Wings made of shadows.

Relief mingled with fear ripples through me. He came; Peter came for me. I watch as he wrestles with the captain. As Peter pulls his dagger from his belt.

I'm not sure why I do it, but my mouth betrays me, and I let out a scream of fright. It's not a signal, but it's enough to catch the captain's attention. Enough for him to glance at the dagger in Peter's hands and feint just in time to keep the blade from finding a home in his chest.

Panic engulfs me. I don't know why I did that. It's going to cost Peter the fight.

Down the side of the ship's hull, ropes dangle as the crew climbs down the sides of the ship and into the frothy water. I recognize a few of them. The large bald man who tried to steal Michael. Evans, his deep brown skin and beautiful smile, now fused with bloodlust and the thrill of a fight rather than that of a dance. As each of the crew climbs down, my mind doesn't just see them, but the faces of the innocent suitors, necks bloodied, that fell at each of their feet.

The cove fights against me, weighing down my legs, but I slog toward Peter and the captain with all my might. I don't know what I intend to do. Halfway there, I realize I should be running toward the Lost Boys. Running toward the Den, toward my brothers, warning John to take Michael and leave Neverland before the pirates can ransack the island.

My mind knows the direction I should be headed, but there's

something digging into my chest, an anchor that ties me to Peter, pulling me in.

So I, weak little coward that I am, rush into the fray.

PETER IS SURROUNDED, pirates flanking him on all sides. While he keeps partially to his fleshly form, shadows whip from Peter's hands, strangling the pirates as they advance, but there are too many of them.

Too many of them for Peter to focus on the captain. Whose dagger is reared back, ready to soar.

I'm not sure what my plan is; I don't even have Peter's dagger at my side. But I know my one bargaining chip.

The captain wants me.

I have no idea what for, but nothing else matters at this moment except making sure the captain's glinting knife gets nowhere near Peter.

"*Stop*," I scream.

As if my words are infused with magic, Captain Astor complies, his fingers closing around the hilt of the blade just before it leaves his fingertips. For a moment, I'm stunned he obeyed, but quick as a flame to a dry wick, the captain pivots, lunging for me.

The world around me shifts, and again the sharp blade finds my throat.

Peter stops in his tracks. It's like watching smoke freeze. "Don't touch her."

"Oh, it's a little too late for that," says the captain, brushing the place on my neck where my Mating Mark ripples, the same patch of skin he stroked the night of the masquerade ball, causing my breath to hitch. "Should have come for her a tad earlier, if that's what was important to you."

Peter glances at the crew, though none of them advance. They won't until their captain wills it.

"The rest stay in that monstrosity of a tree," Captain Astor says, nodding toward the Den. "From what Darling here tells me, none of you should have any issues getting in."

My stomach plummets. I don't even remember telling the captain where the Lost Boys stay. What the reaping tree requires of each of us. How much information did he siphon out of me when I thought I was the one interrogating him?

"Please, just let them go," I whisper. "I'll come with you. Just don't hurt any of them."

"I'm getting a little weary of you saying that, Darling," says the captain, whispering in my ear. "Come now, come up with something a bit more clever. Or at least with a little more fight in you."

Peter holds out a hand, warily. "What do you want?"

"Drop the dagger and we'll talk."

Peter glances toward me, swiftly, then slowly kneels, placing his dagger in the sand.

It should fill me with panic, seeing Peter in a state of surrender, but the part of me that watched my parents slay themselves by their own hands is filled with relief.

"And put those hideous tendrils away while you're at it."

Annoyance flashes across Peter's face, but he does as he's told, his shadows slinking back into his wings.

"Now then," says the captain. "I want you to give her to me."

Peter cranes his neck to the side, then opens his mouth carefully. "From over here, it looks like you already have her."

"Only because I took her from you," says the captain. "But I'm afraid that's not going to be enough."

Peter breathes out sharply. "You know I won't do that." Then, as if regaining his composure, putting up that wall of casual charm, Peter flashes the captain a practiced grin. "I'm selfish with my things, Captain. I suppose it's an only child thing."

At that, the blade in the captain's hand jerks, nicking my neck. I let out a gasp as pain ripples through me, but the captain draws the knife away from my throat quickly, before it can do any more damage.

"Careful with the jokes, Peter," the captain says, voice warbling. "I'm not in the mood."

Fear glances off of Peter's form, and I wonder then if he'll give himself over to the shadows. If that would make him fast enough to break through the captain's grip before he can slit my throat. If he would be able to control himself around me after it was done.

I wait for the carnage.

Peter sighs, then a cruel smile overtakes his face. "What's in it for me?"

CHAPTER 53

*M*y heart stops. It's less about Peter's words than it is the casualness with which he says them. Like I'm a piece of valued property he's been hanging onto for when the right customer comes along. I know it's only part of the game—Peter has to stall the captain while he comes up with a plan—but it's unsettling how convincing he is in this role.

"I asked what's in it for me," Peter repeats.

Captain Astor chuckles, sliding the blunt edge of the knife against my throat. "What's in it for you is that I don't spill your girl's blood and force you to drink it."

Peter's wings flick with the delight of a challenge. A game. "You plan to spill it either way, don't you? If you're going to do it, I'd rather it be done with."

My heart stops in my chest. "Peter."

"Ah, so it seems the little martyr didn't mean all her selfless words, did she?" says the captain with a tsk. "So eager to sacrifice yourself for others, as long as you know the others will never let that happen. This is what happens when children are made to feel as if they're the most important thing in the world."

Fear barrels through me, and I search Peter's face for some sign he's bluffing. Buying time, that's what he's doing.

My Mate crosses his arms. "Again, I'm going to need more persuasive terms if I'm going to let you run off with my Darling little possession."

Bluffing. He's bluffing.

"Why do I get the feeling you already have something in mind?"

Peter's smile has my faith faltering. Greed flickers in his stunning blue eyes. For a moment, I wonder if he'll ask the captain for an unconditional favor.

When he doesn't, it hits me that it's because he doesn't think the captain is stupid enough to take it. The realization is like a needle to my lungs.

Peter considers the captain for a moment, then says, "Never cause any harm to me or the Lost Boys again, and you can have her."

Something aches in my chest. It's exactly what I wanted, exactly what I asked for. So why does it hurt so to hear it from Peter's lips?

The captain's bristle scrapes against my cheek as he cocks his head to the side. "I'm afraid that's a bit too absolute for my tastes."

Peter waits, the muscles in his crossed arms still tensed.

"How about this?" says the captain, his voice sultry. Calculating. "I'll never harm you or the Lost Boys again, so long as you stay within the confines of Neverland."

Peter's eyes flash with an emotion I don't recognize. "If you're putting limitations on my end, I'll ask the same of you."

I wait for Peter to make sure the captain doesn't touch me, doesn't harm me, but he doesn't. Instead, he says, "You get her for a month."

The captain laughs, and it's dry with the salt air that breezes past my ear. "Five years."

My heart stops in my chest.

Peter just grins. "Are we really going to waste time like this?" My heart starts back up as Peter offers his hand. "Six months with Wendy."

The captain pauses. "A year."

A year. So much could happen in a year. My mind whirls back to my first season out in society. The last year I maintained my innocence, unaware that I should have been savoring it. There had been an entire year of balls and courtships before the parlor became a place of incense-ridden nightmares.

Peter just shakes his head. "You'll grow tired of her before then," he says. As if he knows from experience. As if the length of time I've been in Neverland has felt never-ending. "Trust me. Six is a mercy."

His words are barbs in my ribcage, ones I'll be trying to reason away for the next six months. Reminding myself he's only saying these things to barter down my imprisonment.

But barbs hurt, whether Peter meant for them to sting or not.

Keeping his dagger to my throat, the captain extends his left hand, his Mating Mark as lifeless as ever as it slithers to converge at his wrist, breaking off into gray fringes at the beginning of his forearm.

"I thought you said you don't make fae bargains anymore," I hiss.

"Here's something about me you should know, Darling," the captain says. "Sometimes, I lie."

Their hands meet, and something silky, the silver lace of a fae bargain, snakes up both of their forearms.

My chest aches.

"Always a pleasure doing business with you, Nolan," says Peter.

The captain bristles, but so subtly I imagine I'm the only one to notice.

Peter turns.

And flies away.

I watch him for a long while, even as the captain wrestles me to the ship. This time, he doesn't bother carrying me over his back.

I don't struggle.

I'm too busy watching my Mate fly away, his shadows for wings disappearing into the distance.

I'm too busy expecting for him to turn around, awaiting the crafty side of Peter to have figured out a way around the bargain.

My eyes are fixed heavenward until the two wings turn to spots in the white sky.

I'm still staring when Captain Astor passes me off to the bald man, who heaves me onto the deck of the ship. My feet feel as if they should fall through, as if the shadows, solid as they might feel, shouldn't support me.

But I don't fall.

I just sway with the rhythm of the current beneath us.

Chains rattle as the crew brings the anchor on board, and I'm left stunned—an abandoned isle in the middle of the sea, watching the world shift around me. Vaguely, I hear the claps as the crew embrace the captain and slap him on the back. Vaguely, I feel their gazes drag across my body, examining their captain's prize.

And still, I gaze up at the sky.

No one comes.

A shape appears next to me. I expect the captain to grab hold of me, to drag me to his rooms beneath the ship and humiliate me completely. Instead, he stands with me on deck as the winds pick up the sails and carry the ship away.

We watch as Neverland grows smaller.

I teeter toward the edge, tingling filling my fingertips as the waves grow treacherous below us.

"Try to jump, and you won't like what happens after I drag you out of the water."

"Seems fair," I say, my voice a thousand miles away.

"And why's that?"

"Because you didn't very much like what I did to you when I dragged you out of the water."

The captain grunts at that, but out of the corner of my eye, I catch him glancing at me.

"What are you going to do to me?" I ask.

"You won't like that much either."

I turn to him. "Is it better not knowing?"

The captain examines me, and for once, he doesn't seem cruel.

Just tired. But he says nothing. I suppose even cruel pirates feel shame.

He opens his mouth to say something, but the ship gives a tremendous shake, throwing me into the captain's chest. He catches me in his arms, holding me tight as my heart pounds. I struggle out of his grip, and he actually lets me go as the ship reels and shakes.

"I knew it," I whisper, flashing the captain a quick grin.

The one he offers back is one of pity.

I spin around, gaze toward the heavens. Waiting for the shadowed wings to appear. For evidence of what rocked the ship to come barreling out of the sky. But the heavens only grow closer, glimmers of golden smoke painting them above us. When I turn toward the ocean again, I watch as the hull breaks from the grip of the waves, floating above the surface. Twin pipes stand tall in the center of the deck. That's where the golden plumes are coming from.

"It's the faerie dust," says the captain. "We use it to power the ship when the wind proves obstinate."

My heart feels as if it's being plucked from my ribcage like meat off the bone.

We're flying, but it's nothing like flying with Peter. Nothing like falling, hurtling through the heavens. There's the gentle sway of the boat in the wind, but it makes me feel unsteady, not free.

"I thought…"

But what do I even say? That I thought, even if it turned out Peter's love wasn't enough, at least our Mating Mark would compel Peter to fight for me? The same Mating Mark that compelled me to dig into the chest cavity of the man who tried to lay a finger on Peter. The Mark made me a murderer for him, so why isn't it forcing him to fight for me?

The words escape me, melding in on each other, and I have to wrangle the last of them in.

"He's not coming for you, Darling. Best get used to that idea."

I stand and watch at the hull, hope wavering, until it becomes as small as the dot that is the Lost Boy's island below us. We sail through the clouds, the heavens, until even the island isn't visible through the fog. Until everything I have left to love is gone, my brothers just a faint memory.

Suddenly, the captain's grip closes around my wrist. I realize then I've been stroking my Mating Mark absentmindedly. Slowly, he pries my fingers away from it.

"I thought..."

"You've believed plenty that's not true."

As we fly, the morning moon sets, bidding us farewell. I have a feeling about where we're going. The second star to the right. Though I suppose it's to the left from this angle. It's not as if my human vision can locate the stars now that it's morning anyway.

I feel it when we hit the distortion, because that's when the pain hits me, strong and swift. Like being punched in the gut or having your fingernails plucked from your flesh one by one.

I fall to the deck, writhing in agony, my Mark searing hot against my flesh as I leave the world that is Peter's.

"It hurts," I say, cracking beneath the weight of the pain.

"Get up," says the captain.

I don't.

Instead, I let the pain take me, let it sear the edges of my mind. And for a moment, I hope it connects me to Peter. Hope he felt that same ripping as my body left Neverland. Hope that pain tethers us to each other like the Mating Mark didn't.

Like his love for me didn't.

That's probably a silly thought.

But I've always had an abnormally high pain tolerance.

I laugh, and it's the maniacal sort. Because as the pain hooks into me, twisting through my sternum, I know exactly what Peter will do.

He'll tuck it away. Pretend it doesn't exist.

He'll go and visit our favorite places and remember me for the happy times we spent together, and he won't give a second thought to my pain.

Pain.

The memory floods back to me of stitching Peter's wound, while all the while, he didn't tremble or shake. Not once did he cry out, not even when my hands quivered as they pierced his skin with a makeshift needle.

I have an abnormally high pain tolerance.

Even when the Sister drew blood from his cheek with a scratch, he didn't flinch.

The Sister had offered him a gift. To do what's necessary. That's what she'd said. What his journals had said.

At the time, I'd thought it was Peter's shadow powers she was referring to. Lethal weapons that would make killing easier.

Except that was never going to make killing easier for Peter. For Peter, who loved the Lost Boys like his own. Peter, who bargained his own life away to protect them.

I'm not the kind of Mate you want.

There's something in me that's missing.

When I asked him if he was referring to his shadow form, he'd said it amplified his worst qualities. I hadn't realized the nuance in his words at the time, but what if he was saying that the Sister's curse remained with him all the time? That his shadow form only made it worse?

"Get up," says the captain, but I'm laughing now, laughing so hard it hurts my ribs.

"Great," he says. "You're as crazy as you are weak-minded."

"He can't feel pain," I gasp.

The captain stills, staring down at me.

"He can't feel pain. That's the gift she granted him. She wanted him to be able to kill the Lost Boys if he needed to, even though he loves them. I can...I can take away your pain..." I cry, tears pouring out. "She took away his pain. That's why he didn't tell me I was his Mate. Because he can't feel it like I can. He can only feel the high bits, not the agony. He knew I'd end up hurt."

"I fail to comprehend why you find this funny."

I just smile at the captain, the stabbing feeling in my chest finally numbing. Above us, the wistful clouds reflect the vibrant hues of a new day in a realm that might as well go back to sleep for all I care.

For a moment, I think the captain will kick me, but in the end, he just walks away, leaving me wallowing on the deck in a cold sweat.

Peter's not gifted; he's cursed. It's not that he chooses not to love me, it's that he can't. Because when the Sister took away his pain, she inadvertently took part of what it is to love.

But that's the thing about curses.

It's in their nature to be broken.

BONUS PROLOGUE

TALAWRENCEBOOKS.COM

To read the bonus prologue of *Losing Wendy* from the perspective of Peter's shadow form, sign up to my newsletter on my website! You'll also receive a map of Neverland (drawn by Thomas) and updates on upcoming books in the series.

ACKNOWLEDGMENTS

For the ability to find enjoyment in the work my hands have found to do, I thank God, who has granted me abundantly more than I could ever think to ask for.

Jacob, I'm convinced your thoughts go directly to my happiness before you even consider your own. If that's not the case, your actions indicate nothing less than a firm dedication to my well-being. Thanks for looking after me.

Dad, thanks for convincing me to make the murders in this book more heart-wrenching. I'm sure my readers aren't thanking you, but I am.

Mom, thanks for tolerating my three o'clock wanderings as a child. You'll be proud to know that they're now a part of my daily work routine.

Rachel Bobo, I'm not sure where else I would find a friend who would actually come up with a scale for my emotional patterns during my writing process. Thanks for helping me, anticipating my "this book is the worst piece of fiction ever written" phase so that I could implement strategies to bypass it this time around.

Morgan, Alyssa, and Bethany, your insights continue to be invaluable to me. Thanks for gushing over the rough product so that everyone else can enjoy the prettier version.

Christine, thank you so much for your keen eye and for always having something kind to say about my stories when I'm feeling the most nervous about them.

Karri, I'm pretty sure your covers are the reason my books sell. They're all gorgeous.

ALSO BY T.A. LAWRENCE

The Severed Realms

A Word So Fitly Spoken

A Tune to Make Them Follow

A Bond of Broken Glass

A Throne of Blood and Ice

A Realm of Shattered Lies

A Swoony Solstice

Of Tangles and Tinsel

The Astoria Chronicles

The Keeper of the Threshold

The Secret of Atalo

Printed in Great Britain
by Amazon